GIANT DAYS

VOLUME TWO

BOOM! BOX

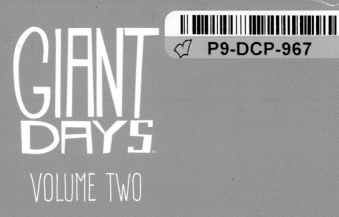

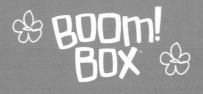

Ross Richie CEO & FOUNDER
Matt Gagnon EDITOR-IN-CHIEF
Filip Sablik PRESIDENT OF PUBLISHING & MARKETING
Stephen Christy PRESIDENT OF DEVELOPMENT
Lance Kreiter VP OF LICENSING & MERCHANDISING
Phil Barbaro VP OF FINANCE
Bryce Carlson MANAGING EDITOR
Mel Caylo MARKETING MANAGER
Scott Newman PRODUCTION DESIGN MANAGER
Irene Bradish OPERATIONS MANAGER
Christine Dinh BRAND COMMUNICATIONS MANAGER
Sierra Hahn SENIOR EDITOR
Dafna Pleban EDITOR
Shannon Watters EDITOR
Eric Harburn EDITOR
Whitney Leopard ASSOCIATE EDITOR
Jasmine Amiri ASSOCIATE EDITOR

Chris Rosa ASSOCIATE EDITOR
Alex Galer ASSISTANT EDITOR
Cameron Chittock ASSISTANT EDITOR
Mary Gumport ASSISTANT EDITOR
Kelsey Dieterich PRODUCTION DESIGNER
Jillian Crab PRODUCTION DESIGNER
Kara Leopard PRODUCTION DESIGNER
Michelle Ankley PRODUCTION DESIGN ASSISTANT
Aaron Ferrara OPERATIONS COORDINATOR
Elizabeth Loughridge ACCOUNTING COORDINATOR
José Meza SALES ASSISTANT
James Arriola MAILROOM ASSISTANT
Stephanie Hocutt MARKETING ASSISTANT
Sam Kusek DIRECT MARKET REPRESENTATIVE
Hillary Levi EXECUTIVE ASSISTANT
Kate Albin ADMINISTRATIVE ASSISTANT

BOOM! BOX™

GIANT DAYS Volume 2, April 2016. Published by BOOM! Box, a division of Boom Entertainment, Inc. Giant Days is ™ &
© 2016 John Allison. Originally published in single magazine form as GIANT DAYS No. 5-8. ™ & © 2015 John Allison. All
rights reserved. BOOM! Box™ and the BOOM! Box logo are trademarks of Boom Entertainment, Inc., registered in various
countries and categories. All characters, events, and institutions depicted herein are fictional. Any similarity between any of the
names, characters, persons, events, and/or institutions in this publication to actual names, characters, and persons, whether
living or dead, events, and/or institutions is unintended and purely coincidental. BOOM! Box does not read or accept unsolicited
submissions of ideas, stories, or artwork.

A catalog record of this book is available from OCLC and from the BOOM! Studios website, www.boom-studios.com, on the
Librarians page.

BOOM! Studios, 5670 Wilshire Boulevard, Suite 450, Los Angeles, CA 90036-5679. Printed in China. First Printing.

ISBN: 978-1-60886-804-9, eISBN: 978-1-61398-475-8

GIANT DAYS

CREATED & WRITTEN BY
JOHN ALLISON

ILLUSTRATED BY
LISSA TREIMAN (CHAPTERS 5-6)
AND ## MAX SARIN (CHAPTERS 7-8)

COLORS BY
WHITNEY COGAR

LETTERS BY
JIM CAMPBELL

COVER BY
LISSA TREIMAN

DESIGNER
KARA LEOPARD

ASSOCIATE EDITOR
JASMINE AMIRI

EDITOR
SHANNON WATTERS

CHAPTER FIVE

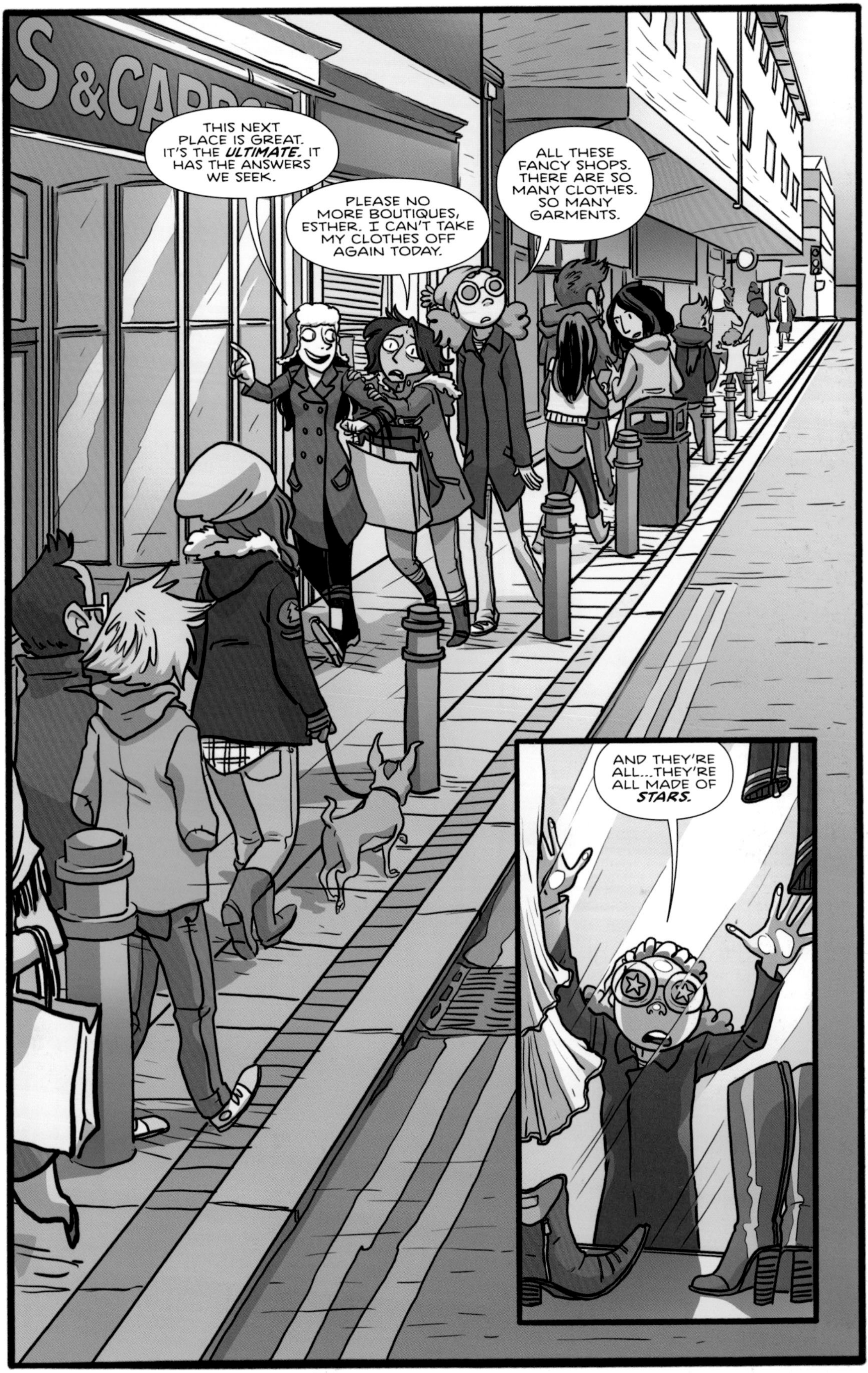
S &CARP
THIS NEXT PLACE IS GREAT. IT'S THE *ULTIMATE.* IT HAS THE ANSWERS WE SEEK.
PLEASE NO MORE BOUTIQUES, ESTHER. I CAN'T TAKE MY CLOTHES OFF AGAIN TODAY.
ALL THESE FANCY SHOPS. THERE ARE SO MANY CLOTHES. SO MANY GARMENTS.
AND THEY'RE ALL...THEY'RE ALL MADE OF *STARS.*

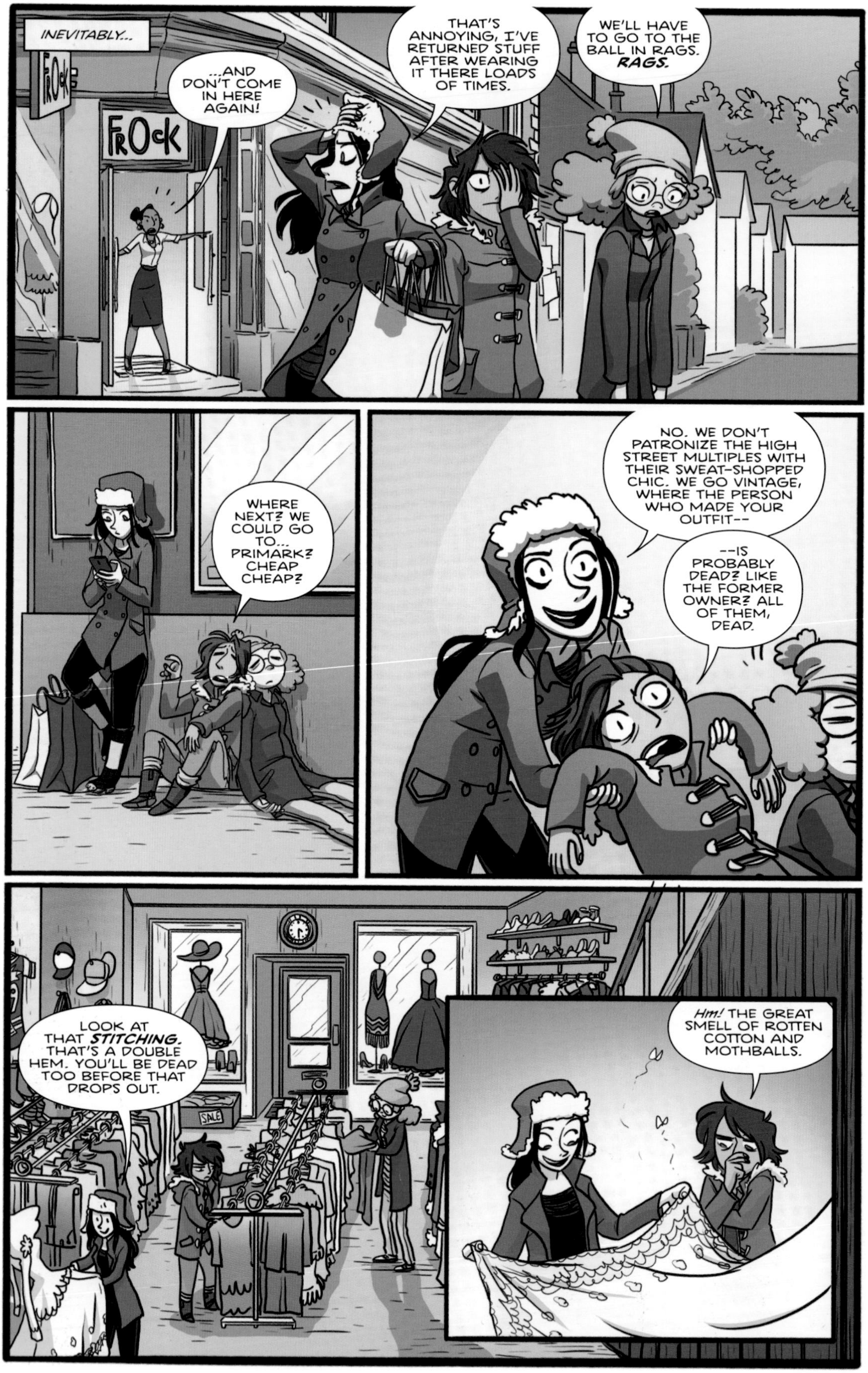
INEVITABLY...
FROCK
FROCK
...AND DON'T COME IN HERE AGAIN!
THAT'S ANNOYING, I'VE RETURNED STUFF AFTER WEARING IT THERE LOADS OF TIMES.
WE'LL HAVE TO GO TO THE BALL IN RAGS. *RAGS.*
WHERE NEXT? WE COULD GO TO... PRIMARK? CHEAP CHEAP?
NO. WE DON'T PATRONIZE THE HIGH STREET MULTIPLES WITH THEIR SWEAT-SHOPPED CHIC. WE GO VINTAGE, WHERE THE PERSON WHO MADE YOUR OUTFIT--
--IS PROBABLY DEAD? LIKE THE FORMER OWNER? ALL OF THEM, DEAD.
SALE
LOOK AT THAT **STITCHING.** THAT'S A DOUBLE HEM. YOU'LL BE DEAD TOO BEFORE THAT DROPS OUT.
HM! THE GREAT SMELL OF ROTTEN COTTON AND MOTHBALLS.

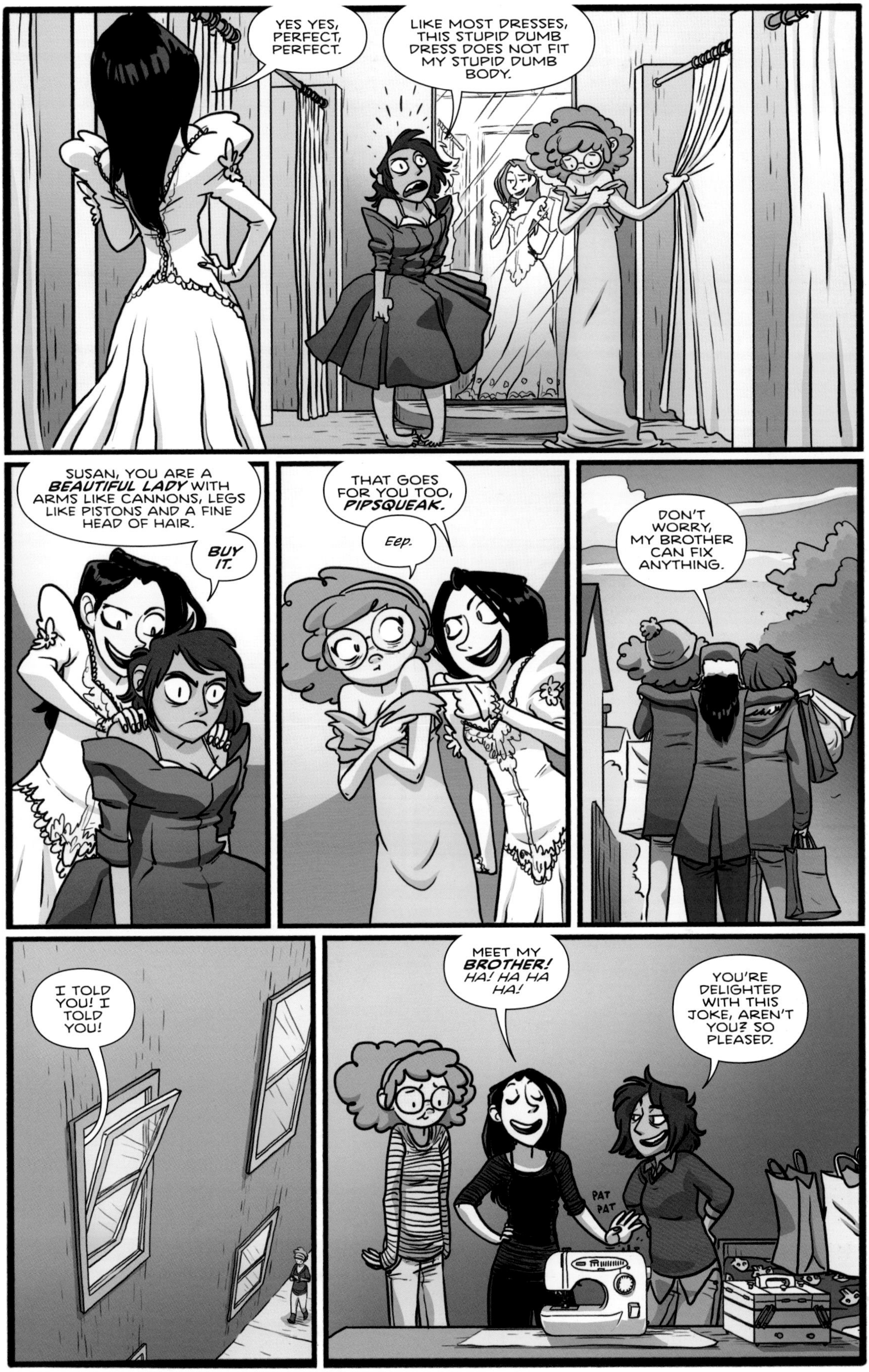
YES YES, PERFECT, PERFECT.
LIKE MOST DRESSES, THIS STUPID DUMB DRESS DOES NOT FIT MY STUPID DUMB BODY.
SUSAN, YOU ARE A BEAUTIFUL LADY WITH ARMS LIKE CANNONS, LEGS LIKE PISTONS AND A FINE HEAD OF HAIR.
BUY IT.
THAT GOES FOR YOU TOO, PIPSQUEAK.
Eep.
DON'T WORRY, MY BROTHER CAN FIX ANYTHING.
I TOLD YOU! I TOLD YOU!
MEET MY BROTHER! HA! HA HA HA!
YOU'RE DELIGHTED WITH THIS JOKE, AREN'T YOU? SO PLEASED.
PAT PAT

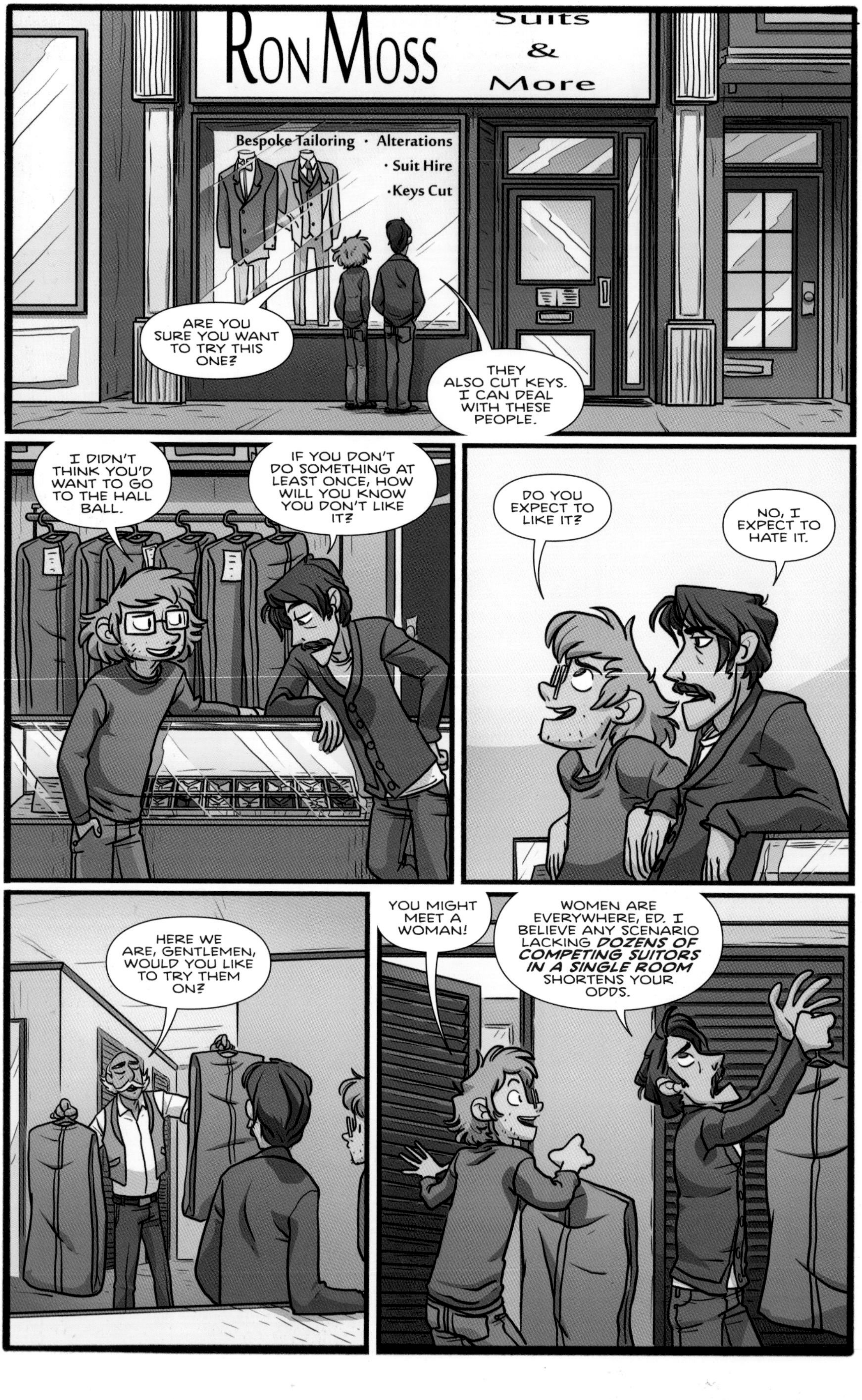
RON MOSS
Suits & More
Bespoke Tailoring • Alterations
• Suit Hire
•Keys Cut
ARE YOU SURE YOU WANT TO TRY THIS ONE?
THEY ALSO CUT KEYS. I CAN DEAL WITH THESE PEOPLE.
I DIDN'T THINK YOU'D WANT TO GO TO THE HALL BALL.
IF YOU DON'T DO SOMETHING AT LEAST ONCE, HOW WILL YOU KNOW YOU DON'T LIKE IT?
DO YOU EXPECT TO LIKE IT?
NO, I EXPECT TO HATE IT.
HERE WE ARE, GENTLEMEN, WOULD YOU LIKE TO TRY THEM ON?
YOU MIGHT MEET A WOMAN!
WOMEN ARE EVERYWHERE, ED. I BELIEVE ANY SCENARIO LACKING ***DOZENS OF COMPETING SUITORS IN A SINGLE ROOM*** SHORTENS YOUR ODDS.

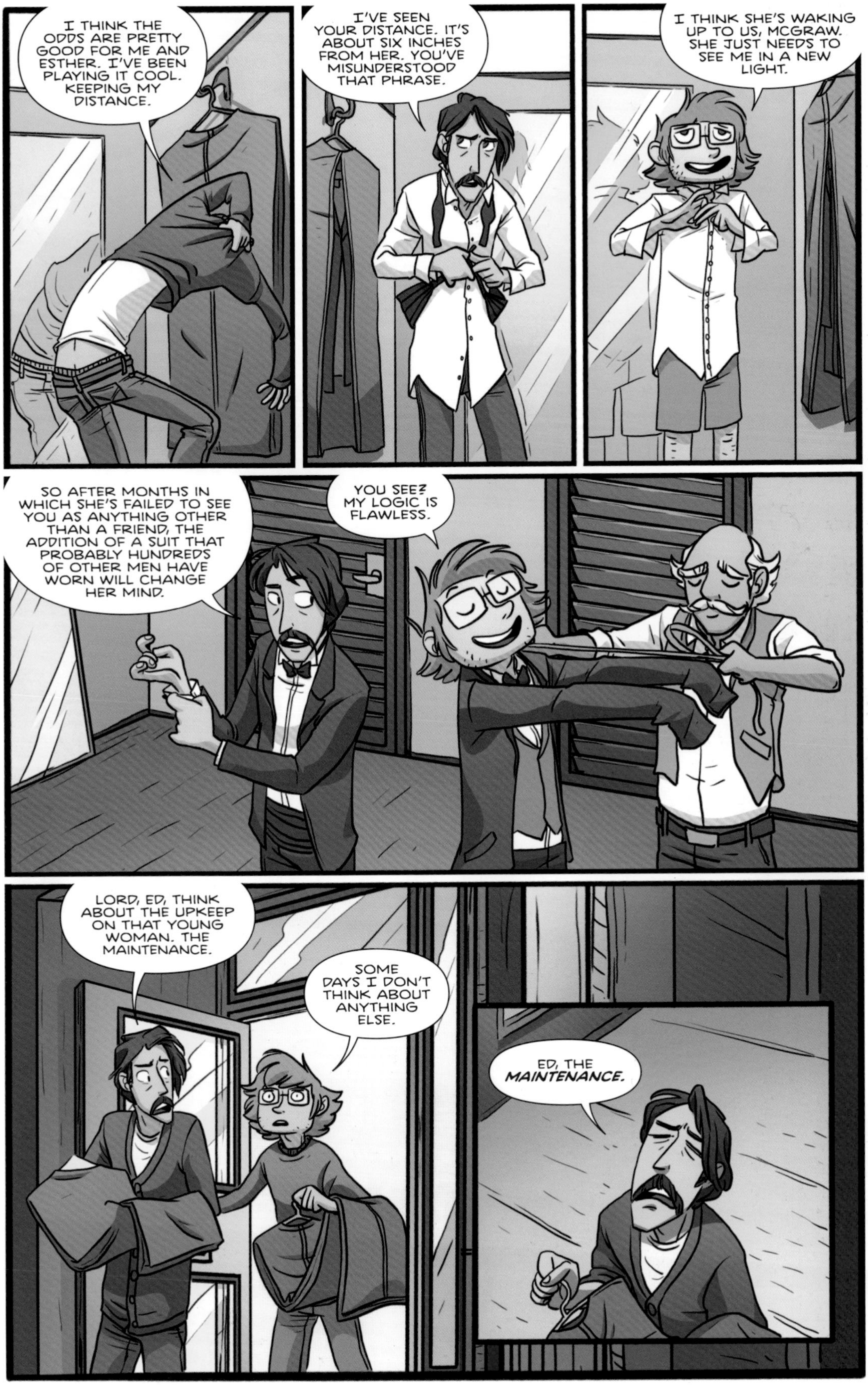
I THINK THE ODDS ARE PRETTY GOOD FOR ME AND ESTHER. I'VE BEEN PLAYING IT COOL. KEEPING MY DISTANCE.
I'VE SEEN YOUR DISTANCE. IT'S ABOUT SIX INCHES FROM HER. YOU'VE MISUNDERSTOOD THAT PHRASE.
I THINK SHE'S WAKING UP TO US, MCGRAW. SHE JUST NEEDS TO SEE ME IN A NEW LIGHT.
SO AFTER MONTHS IN WHICH SHE'S FAILED TO SEE YOU AS ANYTHING OTHER THAN A FRIEND, THE ADDITION OF A SUIT THAT PROBABLY HUNDREDS OF OTHER MEN HAVE WORN WILL CHANGE HER MIND.
YOU SEE? MY LOGIC IS FLAWLESS.
LORD, ED, THINK ABOUT THE UPKEEP ON THAT YOUNG WOMAN. THE MAINTENANCE.
SOME DAYS I DON'T THINK ABOUT ANYTHING ELSE.
ED, THE *MAINTENANCE.*

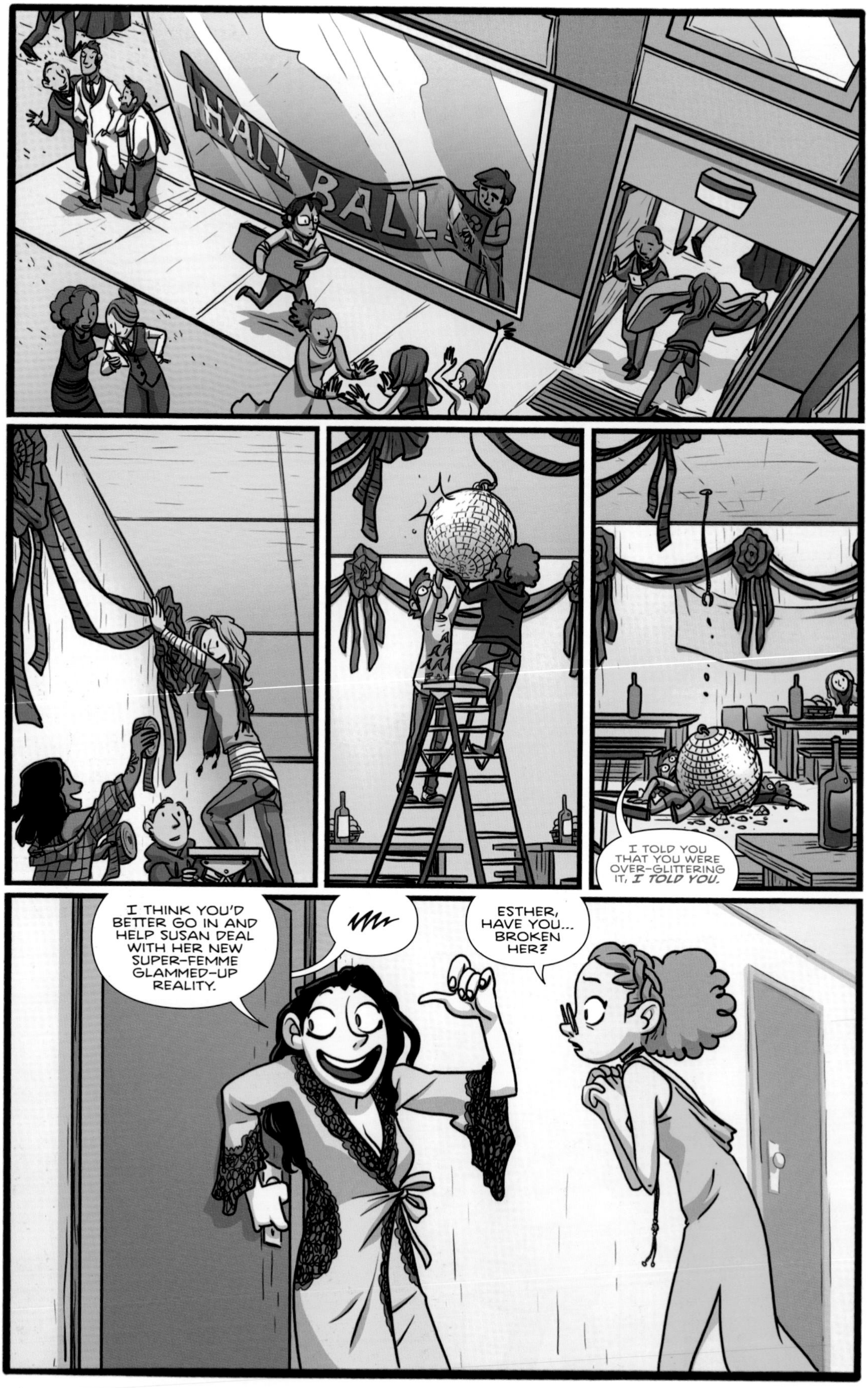
HALL BALL
I TOLD YOU THAT YOU WERE OVER-GLITTERING IT, I TOLD YOU.
I THINK YOU'D BETTER GO IN AND HELP SUSAN DEAL WITH HER NEW SUPER-FEMME GLAMMED-UP REALITY.
ESTHER, HAVE YOU... BROKEN HER?

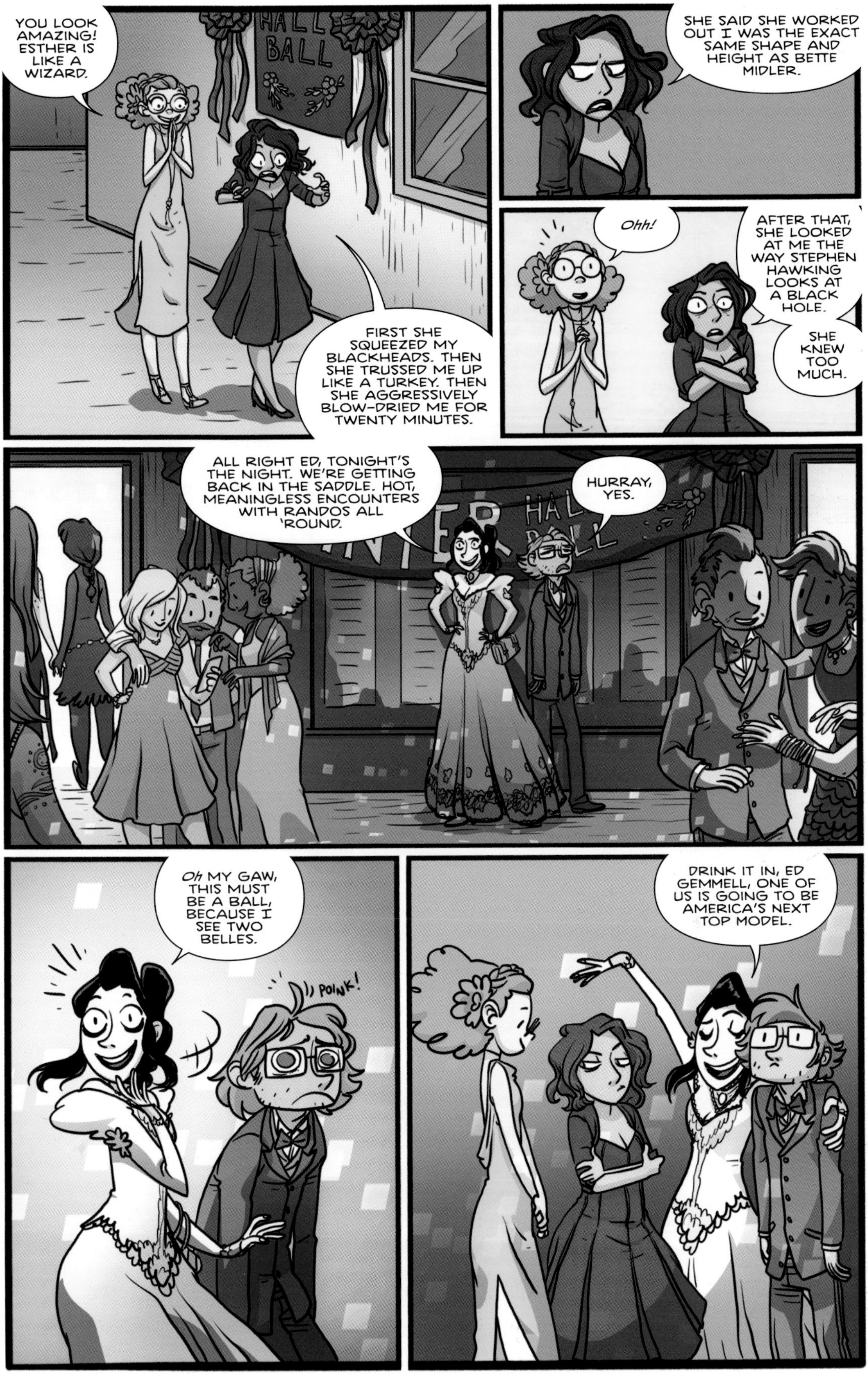
HALL BALL
YOU LOOK AMAZING! ESTHER IS LIKE A WIZARD.
FIRST SHE SQUEEZED MY BLACKHEADS. THEN SHE TRUSSED ME UP LIKE A TURKEY. THEN SHE AGGRESSIVELY BLOW-DRIED ME FOR TWENTY MINUTES.
SHE SAID SHE WORKED OUT I WAS THE EXACT SAME SHAPE AND HEIGHT AS BETTE MIDLER.
Ohh!
AFTER THAT, SHE LOOKED AT ME THE WAY STEPHEN HAWKING LOOKS AT A BLACK HOLE.
SHE KNEW TOO MUCH.
ALL RIGHT ED, TONIGHT'S THE NIGHT. WE'RE GETTING BACK IN THE SADDLE. HOT, MEANINGLESS ENCOUNTERS WITH RANDOS ALL 'ROUND.
HURRAY, YES.
Oh MY GAW, THIS MUST BE A BALL, BECAUSE I SEE TWO BELLES.
POINK!
DRINK IT IN, ED GEMMELL, ONE OF US IS GOING TO BE AMERICA'S NEXT TOP MODEL.

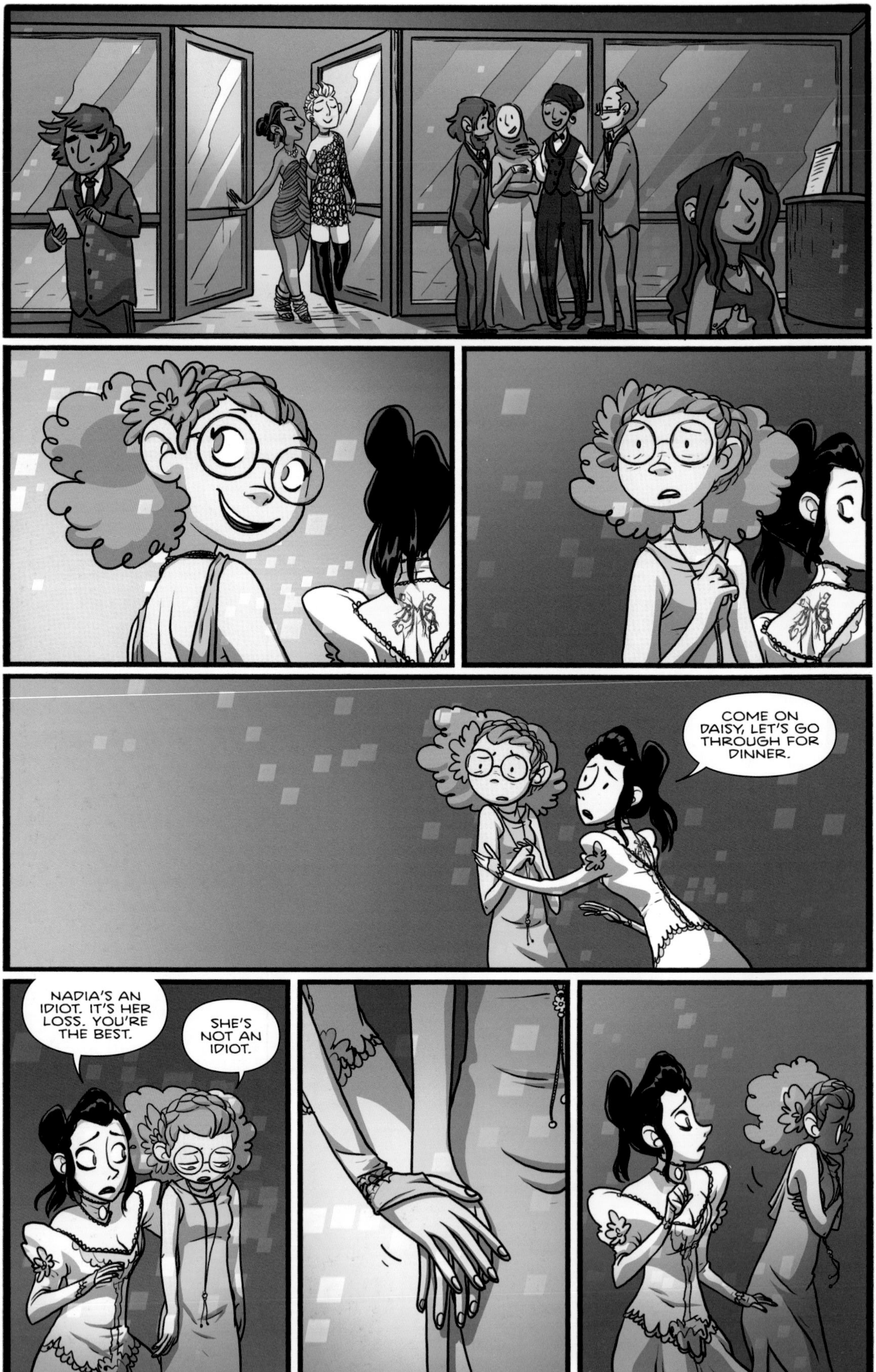
COME ON DAISY, LET'S GO THROUGH FOR DINNER.
NADIA'S AN IDIOT. IT'S HER LOSS. YOU'RE THE BEST.
SHE'S NOT AN IDIOT.

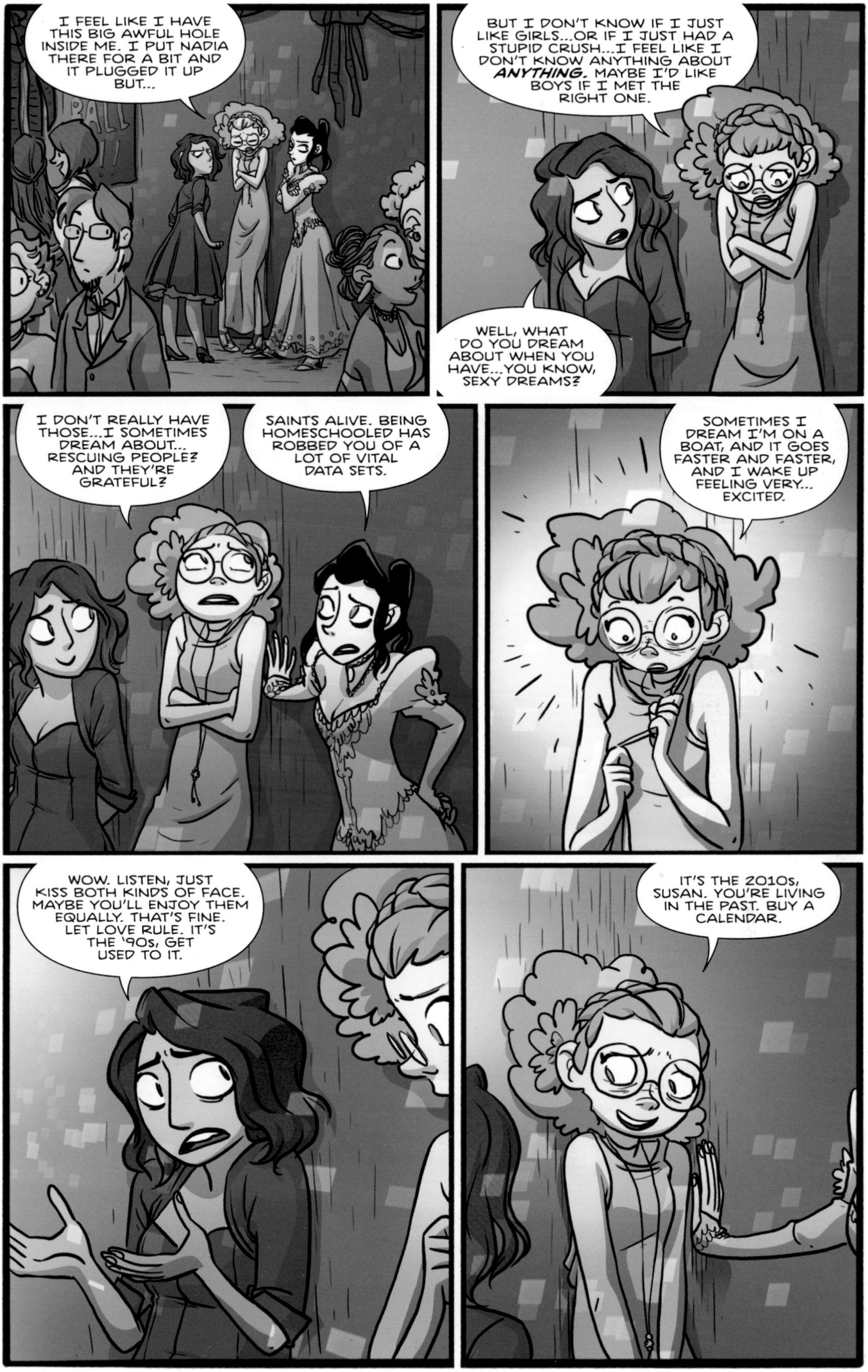
I FEEL LIKE I HAVE THIS BIG AWFUL HOLE INSIDE ME. I PUT NADIA THERE FOR A BIT AND IT PLUGGED IT UP BUT...
BUT I DON'T KNOW IF I JUST LIKE GIRLS...OR IF I JUST HAD A STUPID CRUSH...I FEEL LIKE I DON'T KNOW ANYTHING ABOUT ***ANYTHING.*** MAYBE I'D LIKE BOYS IF I MET THE RIGHT ONE.
WELL, WHAT DO YOU DREAM ABOUT WHEN YOU HAVE...YOU KNOW, SEXY DREAMS?
I DON'T REALLY HAVE THOSE...I SOMETIMES DREAM ABOUT... RESCUING PEOPLE? AND THEY'RE GRATEFUL?
SAINTS ALIVE. BEING HOMESCHOOLED HAS ROBBED YOU OF A LOT OF VITAL DATA SETS.
SOMETIMES I DREAM I'M ON A BOAT, AND IT GOES FASTER AND FASTER, AND I WAKE UP FEELING VERY... EXCITED.
WOW. LISTEN, JUST KISS BOTH KINDS OF FACE. MAYBE YOU'LL ENJOY THEM EQUALLY. THAT'S FINE. LET LOVE RULE. IT'S THE '90s, GET USED TO IT.
IT'S THE 2010s, SUSAN. YOU'RE LIVING IN THE PAST. BUY A CALENDAR.

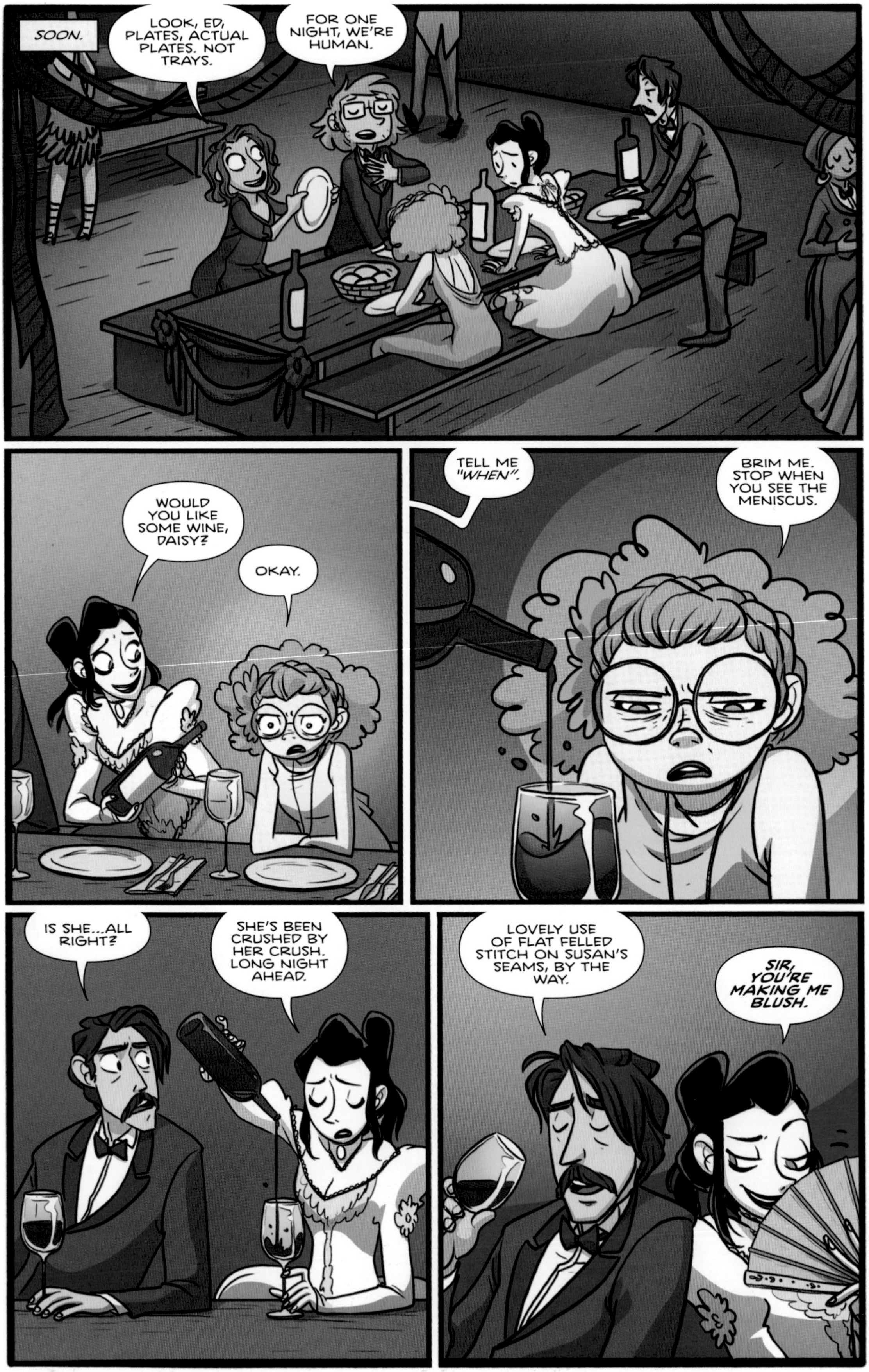
SOON.
LOOK, ED, PLATES, ACTUAL PLATES. NOT TRAYS.
FOR ONE NIGHT, WE'RE HUMAN.
WOULD YOU LIKE SOME WINE, DAISY?
OKAY.
TELL ME "WHEN".
BRIM ME. STOP WHEN YOU SEE THE MENISCUS.
IS SHE...ALL RIGHT?
SHE'S BEEN CRUSHED BY HER CRUSH. LONG NIGHT AHEAD.
LOVELY USE OF FLAT FELLED STITCH ON SUSAN'S SEAMS, BY THE WAY.
SIR, YOU'RE MAKING ME BLUSH.

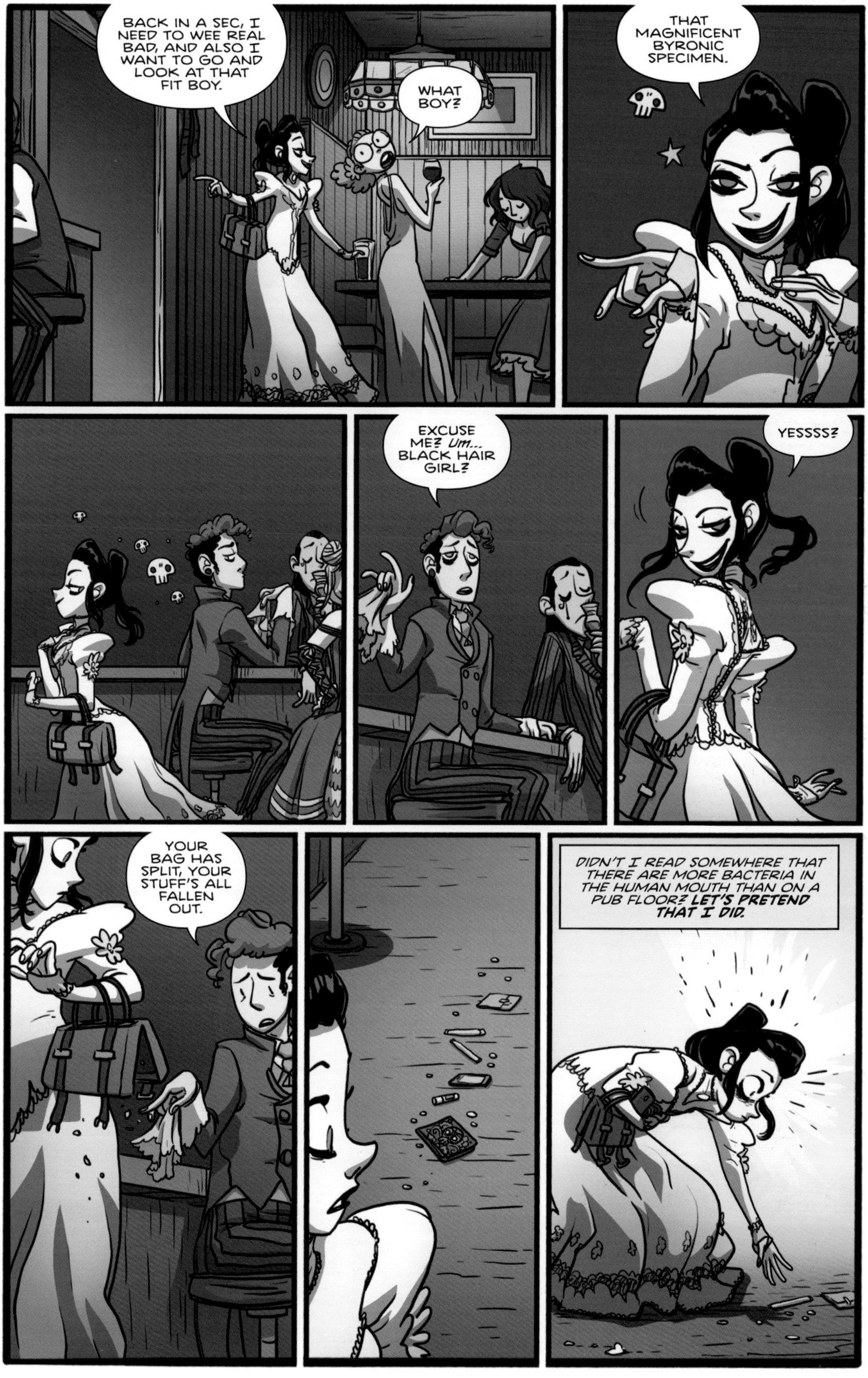
BACK IN A SEC, I NEED TO WEE REAL BAD, AND ALSO I WANT TO GO AND LOOK AT THAT FIT BOY.
WHAT BOY?
THAT MAGNIFICENT BYRONIC SPECIMEN.
EXCUSE ME? UM... BLACK HAIR GIRL?
YESSSS?
YOUR BAG HAS SPLIT, YOUR STUFF'S ALL FALLEN OUT.
DIDN'T I READ SOMEWHERE THAT THERE ARE MORE BACTERIA IN THE HUMAN MOUTH THAN ON A PUB FLOOR? LET'S PRETEND THAT I DID.

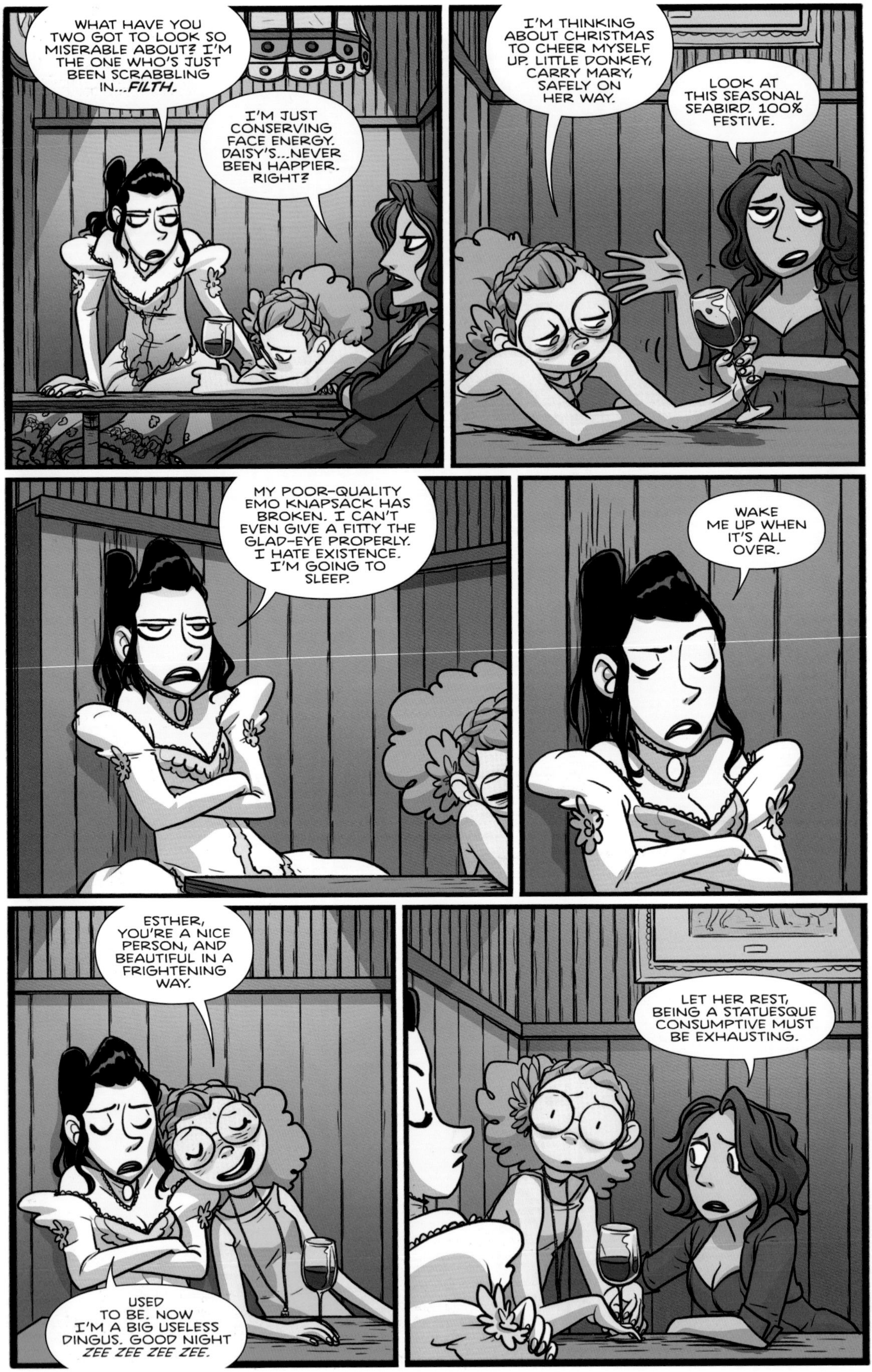
WHAT HAVE YOU TWO GOT TO LOOK SO MISERABLE ABOUT? I'M THE ONE WHO'S JUST BEEN SCRABBLING IN... *FILTH.*
I'M JUST CONSERVING FACE ENERGY. DAISY'S... NEVER BEEN HAPPIER. RIGHT?
I'M THINKING ABOUT CHRISTMAS TO CHEER MYSELF UP. LITTLE DONKEY, CARRY MARY, SAFELY ON HER WAY.
LOOK AT THIS SEASONAL SEABIRD. 100% FESTIVE.
MY POOR-QUALITY EMO KNAPSACK HAS BROKEN. I CAN'T EVEN GIVE A FITTY THE GLAD-EYE PROPERLY. I HATE EXISTENCE. I'M GOING TO SLEEP.
WAKE ME UP WHEN IT'S ALL OVER.
ESTHER, YOU'RE A NICE PERSON, AND BEAUTIFUL IN A FRIGHTENING WAY.
USED TO BE. NOW I'M A BIG USELESS DINGUS. GOOD NIGHT *ZEE ZEE ZEE ZEE.*
LET HER REST, BEING A STATUESQUE CONSUMPTIVE MUST BE EXHAUSTING.

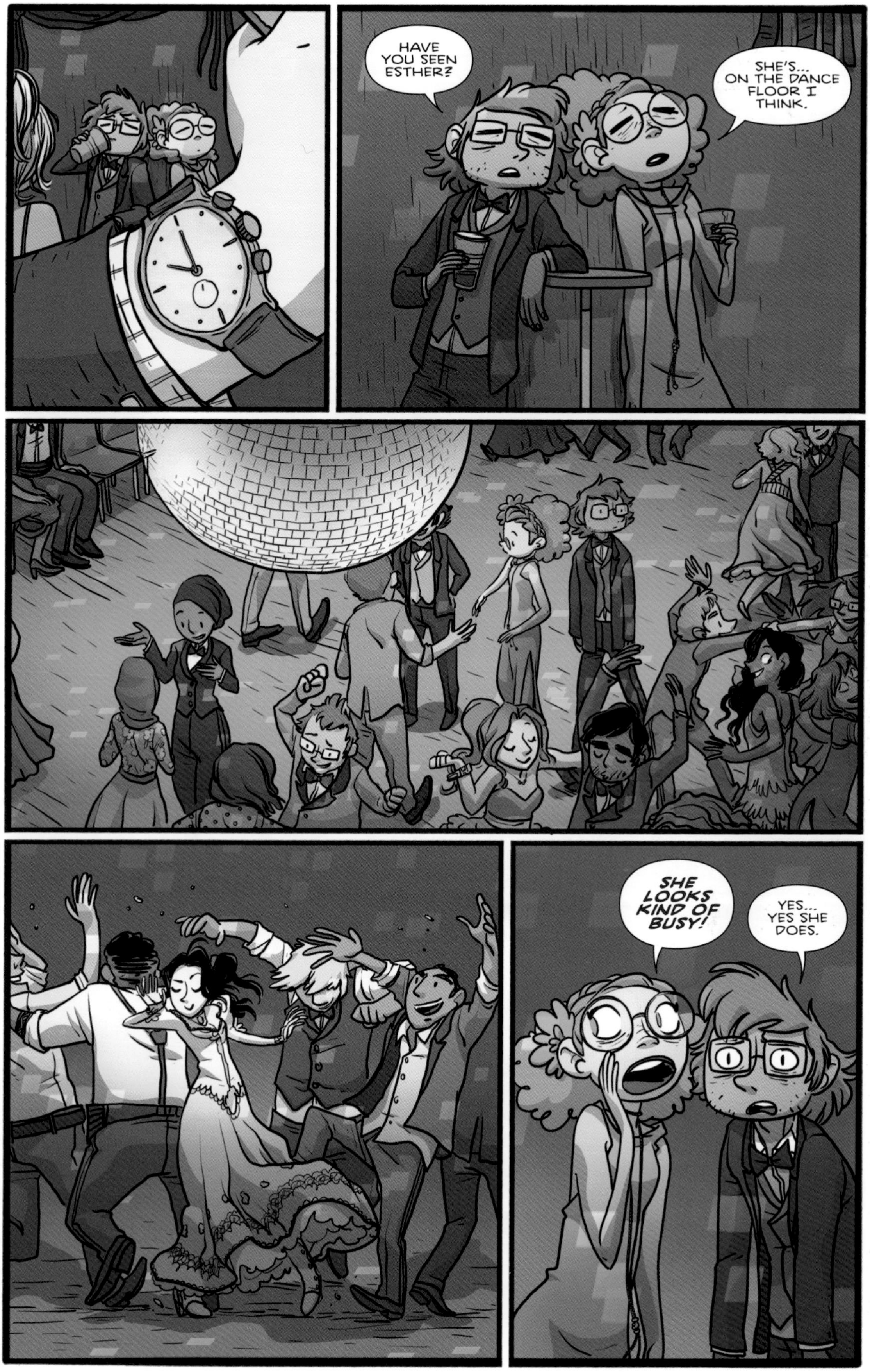
HAVE YOU SEEN ESTHER?
SHE'S... ON THE DANCE FLOOR I THINK.
SHE LOOKS KIND OF BUSY!
YES... YES SHE DOES.

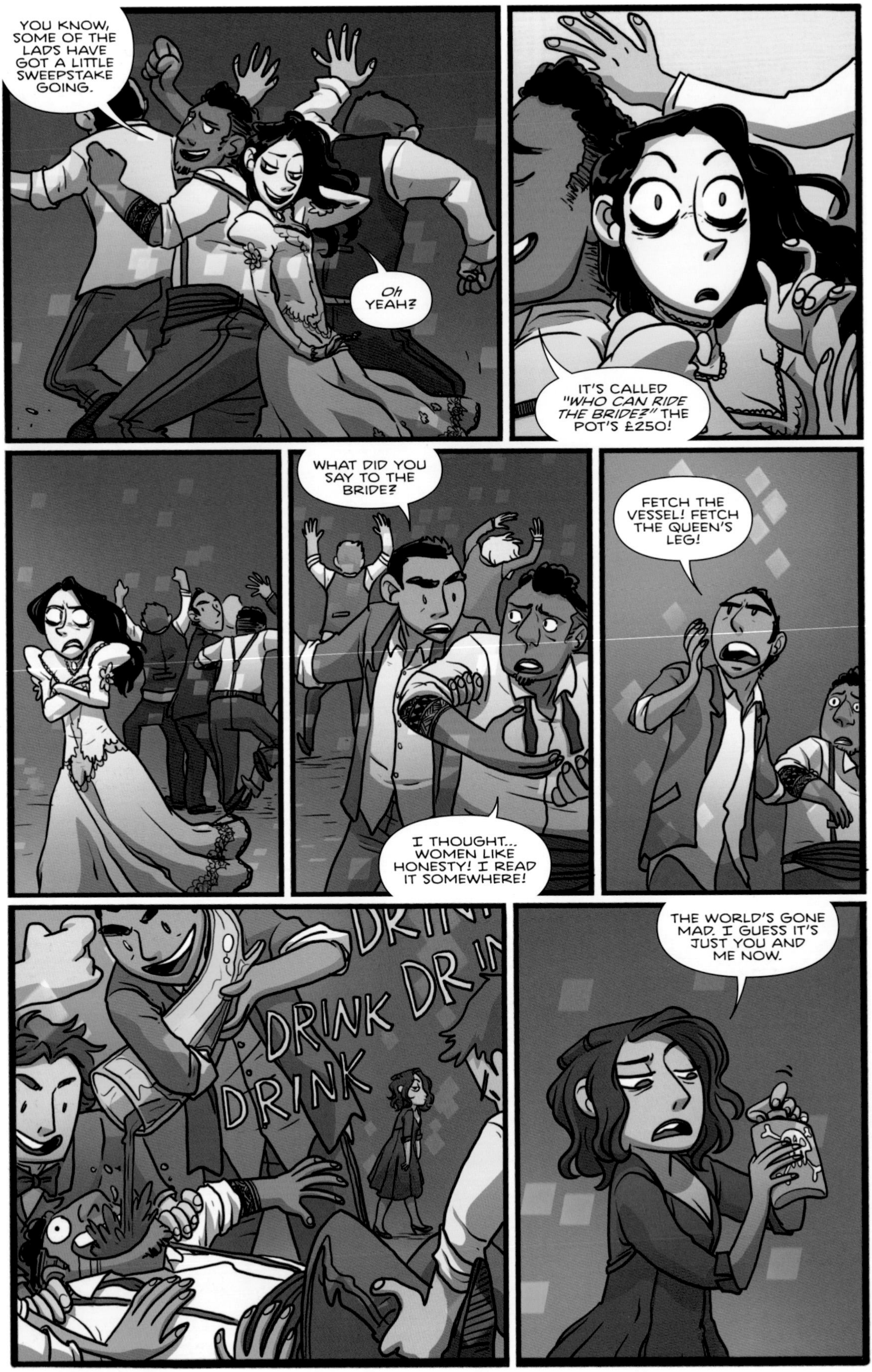
YOU KNOW, SOME OF THE LADS HAVE GOT A LITTLE SWEEPSTAKE GOING.
Oh YEAH?
IT'S CALLED "WHO CAN RIDE THE BRIDE?" THE POT'S £250!
WHAT DID YOU SAY TO THE BRIDE?
I THOUGHT... WOMEN LIKE HONESTY! I READ IT SOMEWHERE!
FETCH THE VESSEL! FETCH THE QUEEN'S LEG!
DRINK DRINK DRINK
THE WORLD'S GONE MAD. I GUESS IT'S JUST YOU AND ME NOW.

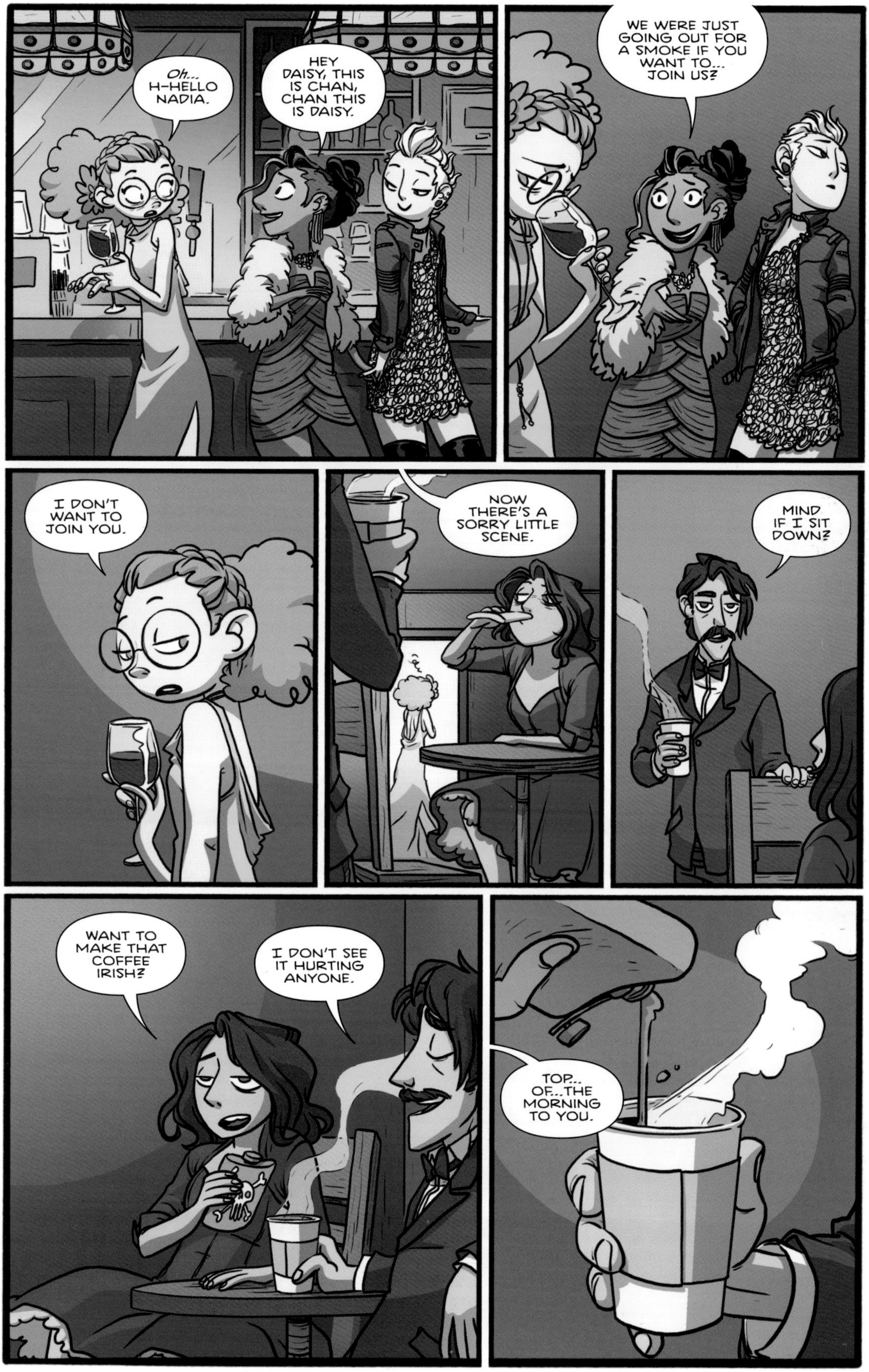
Oh... H-HELLO NADIA.
HEY DAISY, THIS IS CHAN, CHAN THIS IS DAISY.
WE WERE JUST GOING OUT FOR A SMOKE IF YOU WANT TO... JOIN US?
I DON'T WANT TO JOIN YOU.
NOW THERE'S A SORRY LITTLE SCENE.
MIND IF I SIT DOWN?
WANT TO MAKE THAT COFFEE IRISH?
I DON'T SEE IT HURTING ANYONE.
TOP... OF... THE MORNING TO YOU.

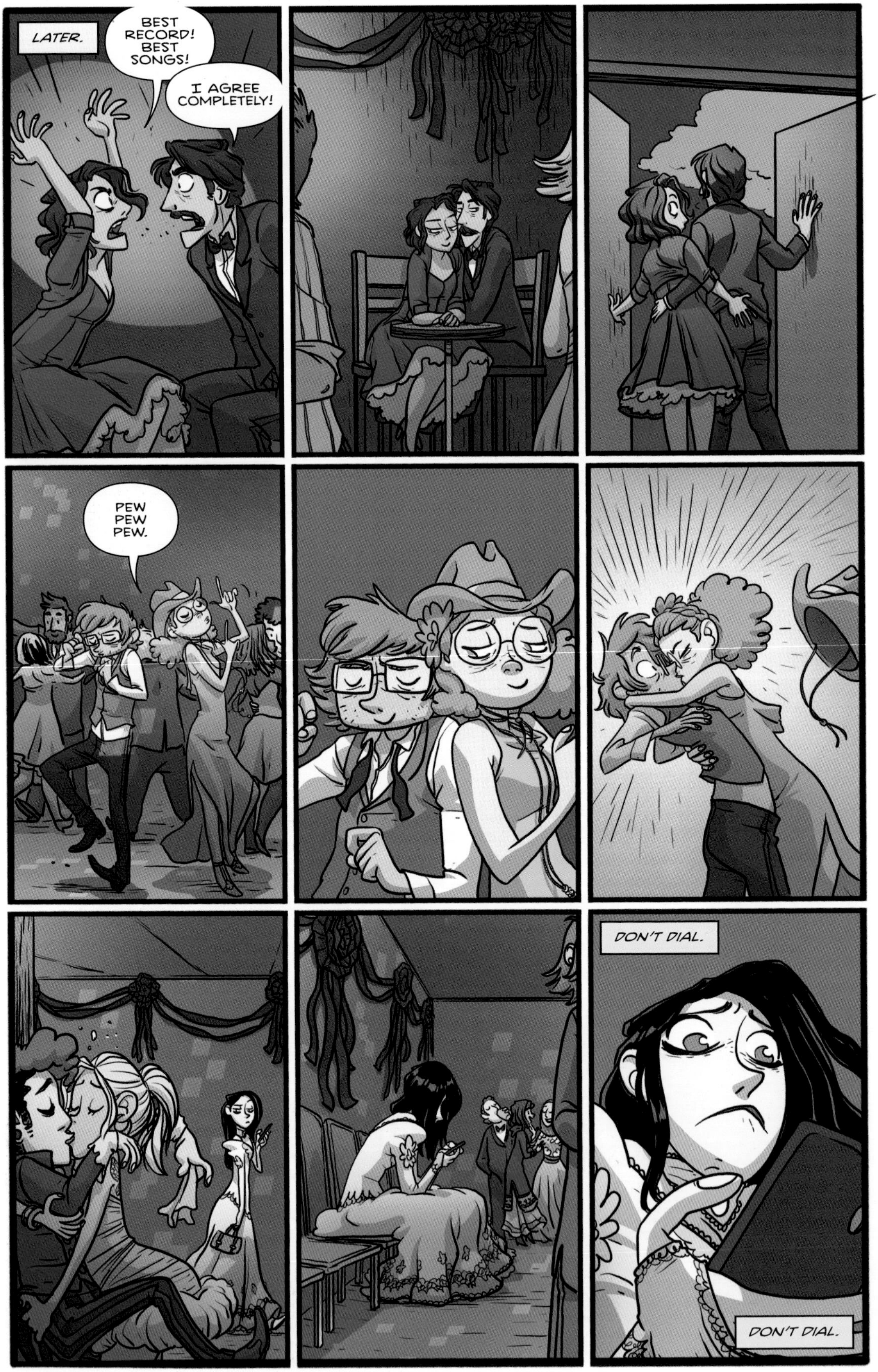
LATER.
BEST RECORD! BEST SONGS!
I AGREE COMPLETELY!
PEW PEW PEW.
DON'T DIAL.
DON'T DIAL.

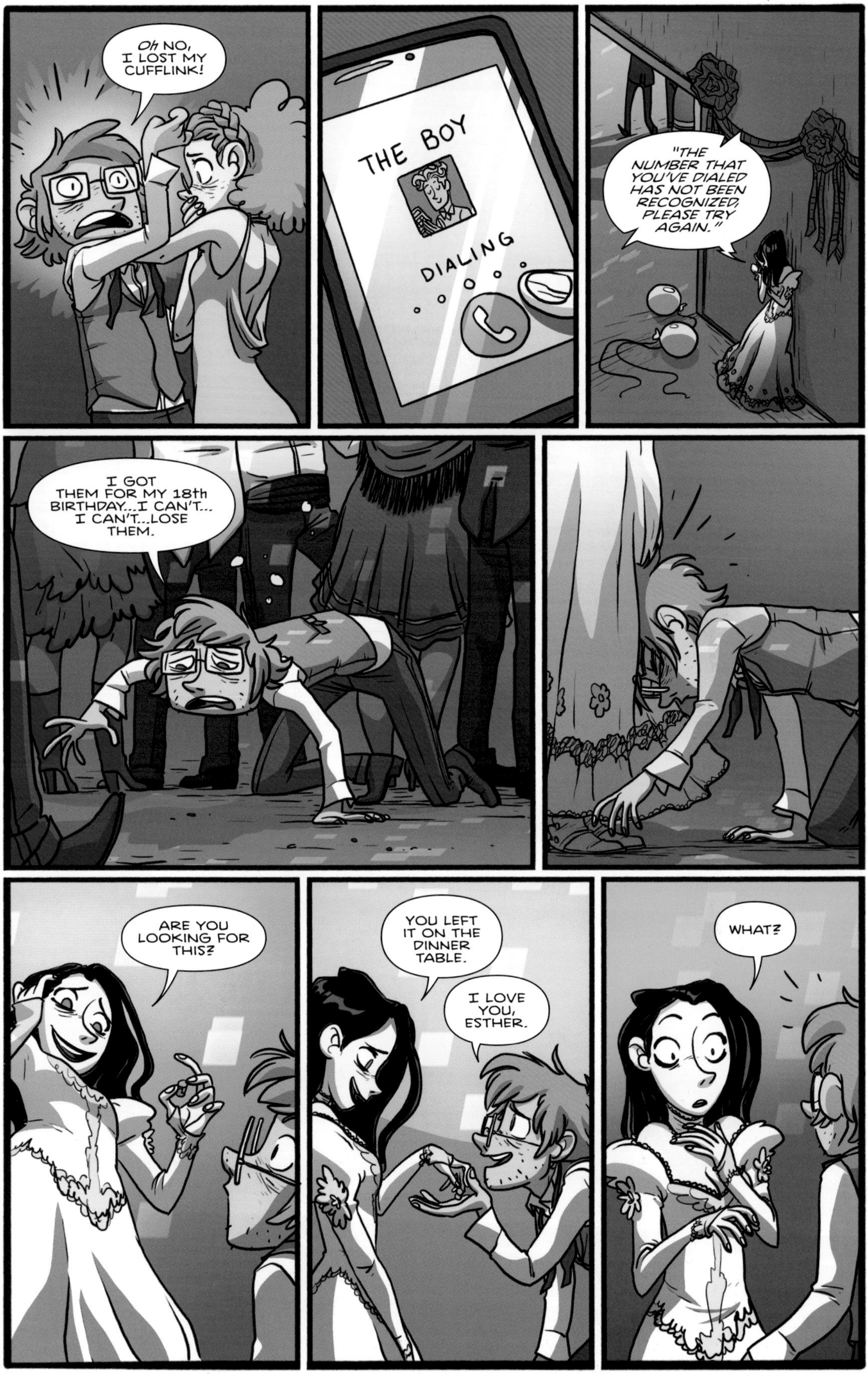
Oh NO, I LOST MY CUFFLINK!
THE BOY
DIALING
"THE NUMBER THAT YOU'VE DIALED HAS NOT BEEN RECOGNIZED, PLEASE TRY AGAIN."
I GOT THEM FOR MY 18th BIRTHDAY...I CAN'T... I CAN'T...LOSE THEM.
ARE YOU LOOKING FOR THIS?
YOU LEFT IT ON THE DINNER TABLE.
I LOVE YOU, ESTHER.
WHAT?

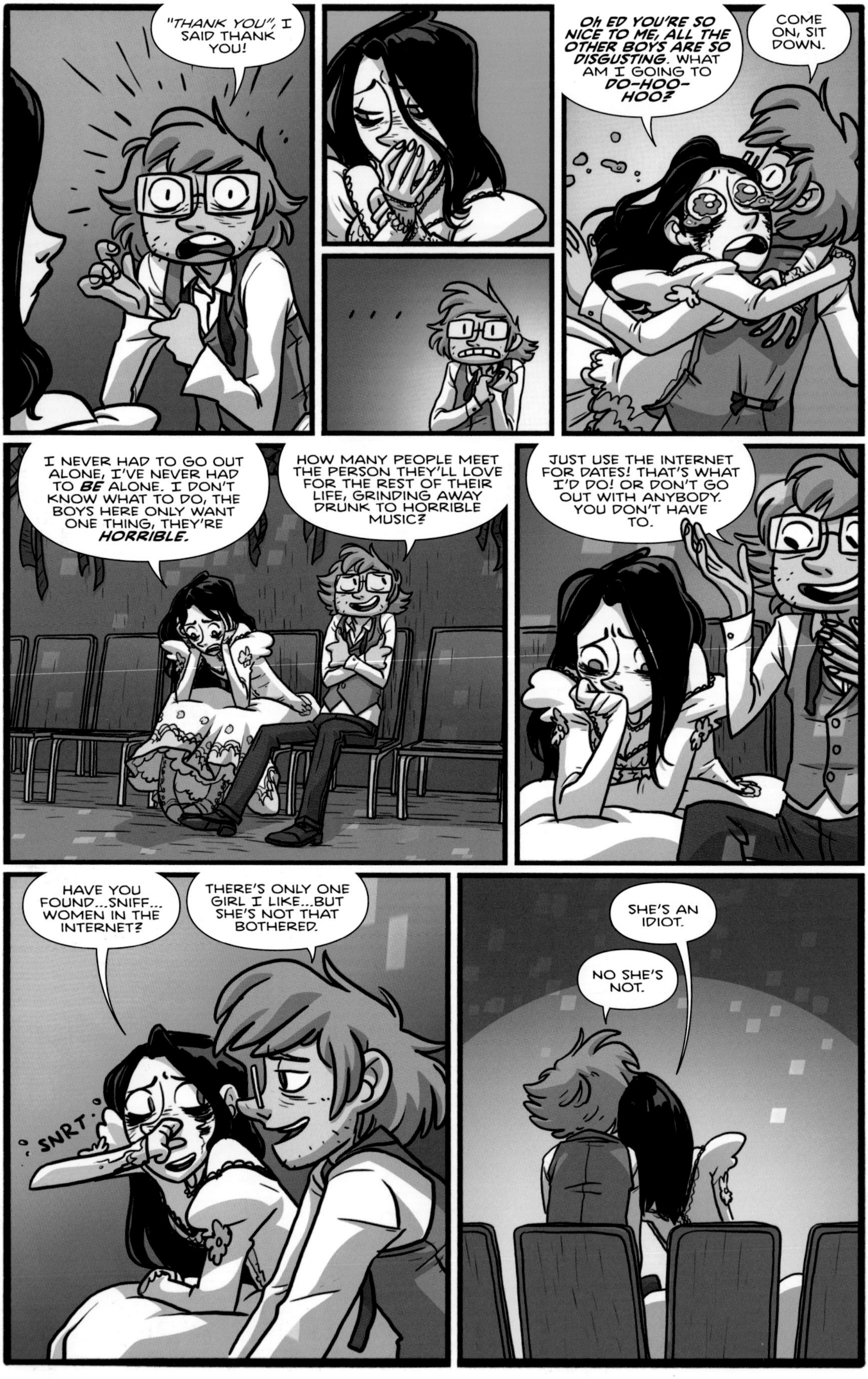
"THANK YOU", I SAID THANK YOU!
Oh ED YOU'RE SO NICE TO ME, ALL THE OTHER BOYS ARE SO DISGUSTING. WHAT AM I GOING TO DO-HOO-HOO?
COME ON, SIT DOWN.
I NEVER HAD TO GO OUT ALONE, I'VE NEVER HAD TO BE ALONE. I DON'T KNOW WHAT TO DO, THE BOYS HERE ONLY WANT ONE THING, THEY'RE HORRIBLE.
HOW MANY PEOPLE MEET THE PERSON THEY'LL LOVE FOR THE REST OF THEIR LIFE, GRINDING AWAY DRUNK TO HORRIBLE MUSIC?
JUST USE THE INTERNET FOR DATES! THAT'S WHAT I'D DO! OR DON'T GO OUT WITH ANYBODY. YOU DON'T HAVE TO.
HAVE YOU FOUND...SNIFF... WOMEN IN THE INTERNET?
THERE'S ONLY ONE GIRL I LIKE...BUT SHE'S NOT THAT BOTHERED.
SNRT
SHE'S AN IDIOT.
NO SHE'S NOT.

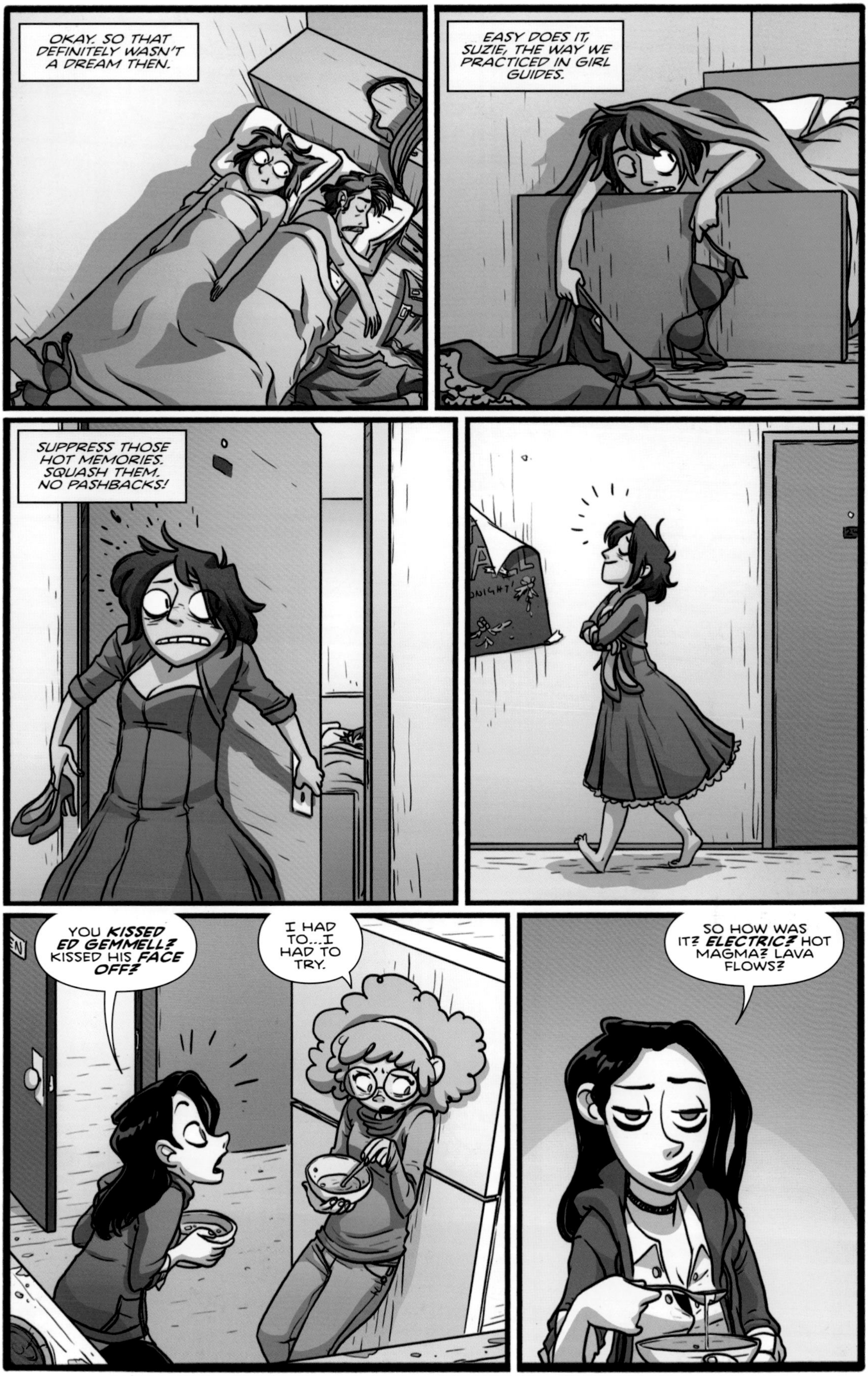
OKAY. SO THAT DEFINITELY WASN'T A DREAM THEN.
EASY DOES IT, SUZIE, THE WAY WE PRACTICED IN GIRL GUIDES.
SUPPRESS THOSE HOT MEMORIES. SQUASH THEM. NO PASHBACKS!
YOU KISSED ED GEMMELL? KISSED HIS FACE OFF?
I HAD TO... I HAD TO TRY.
SO HOW WAS IT? ELECTRIC? HOT MAGMA? LAVA FLOWS?

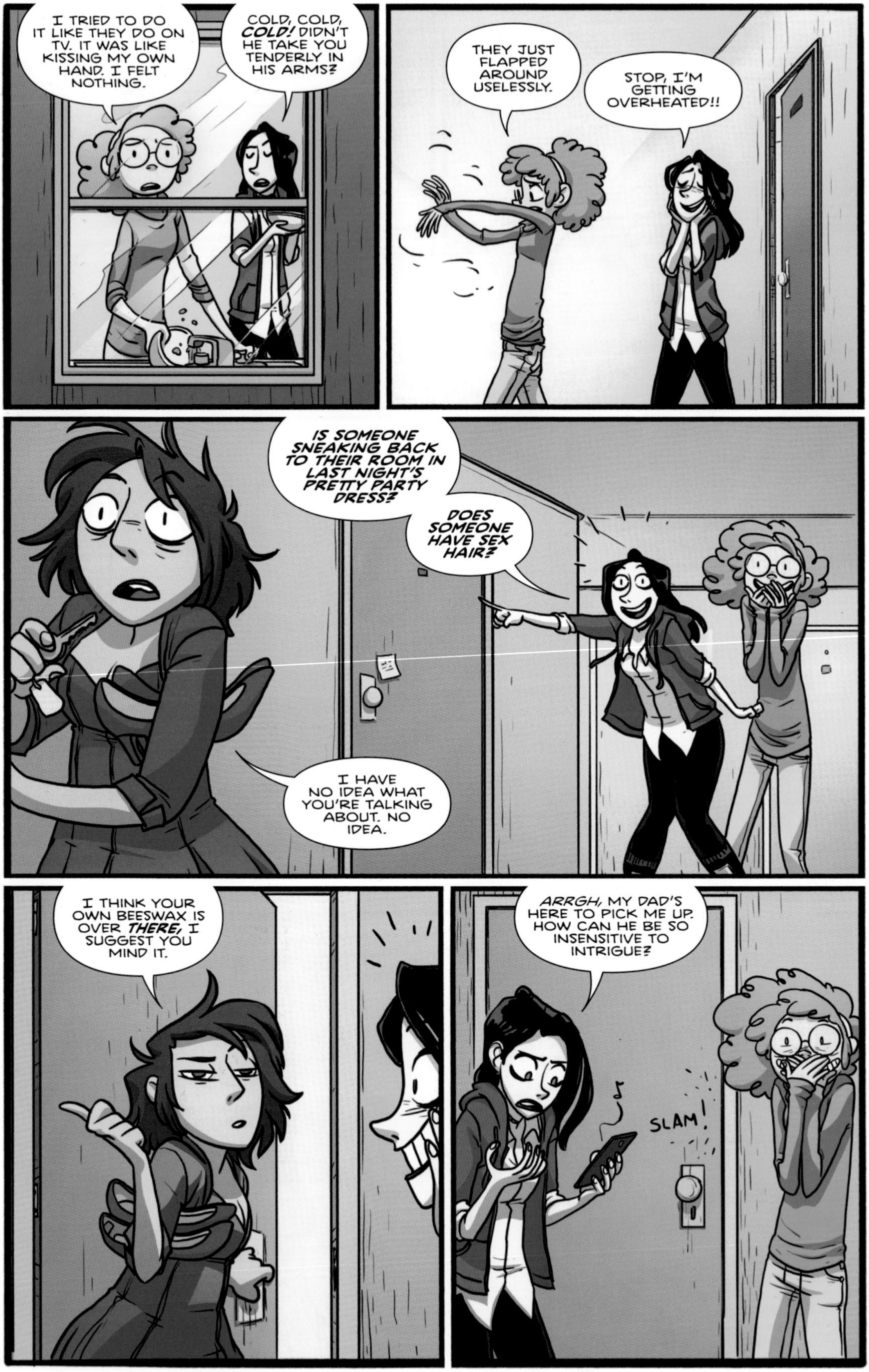
I TRIED TO DO IT LIKE THEY DO ON TV. IT WAS LIKE KISSING MY OWN HAND. I FELT NOTHING.
COLD, COLD, COLD! DIDN'T HE TAKE YOU TENDERLY IN HIS ARMS?
THEY JUST FLAPPED AROUND USELESSLY.
STOP, I'M GETTING OVERHEATED!!
IS SOMEONE SNEAKING BACK TO THEIR ROOM IN LAST NIGHT'S PRETTY PARTY DRESS?
DOES SOMEONE HAVE SEX HAIR?
I HAVE NO IDEA WHAT YOU'RE TALKING ABOUT. NO IDEA.
I THINK YOUR OWN BEESWAX IS OVER THERE, I SUGGEST YOU MIND IT.
ARRGH, MY DAD'S HERE TO PICK ME UP. HOW CAN HE BE SO INSENSITIVE TO INTRIGUE?
SLAM!

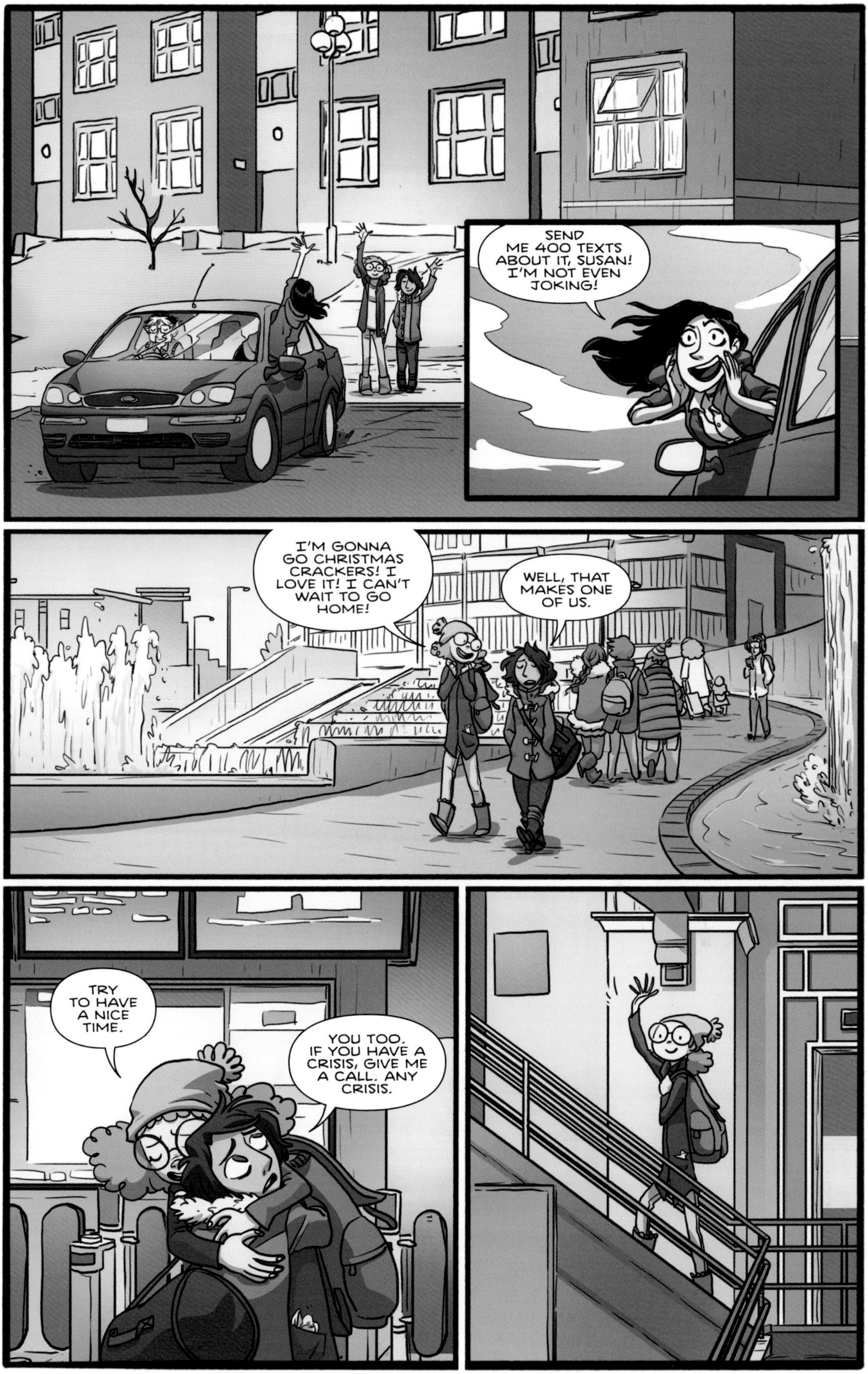
SEND ME 400 TEXTS ABOUT IT, SUSAN! I'M NOT EVEN JOKING!
I'M GONNA GO CHRISTMAS CRACKERS! I LOVE IT! I CAN'T WAIT TO GO HOME!
WELL, THAT MAKES ONE OF US.
TRY TO HAVE A NICE TIME.
YOU TOO. IF YOU HAVE A CRISIS, GIVE ME A CALL. ANY CRISIS.

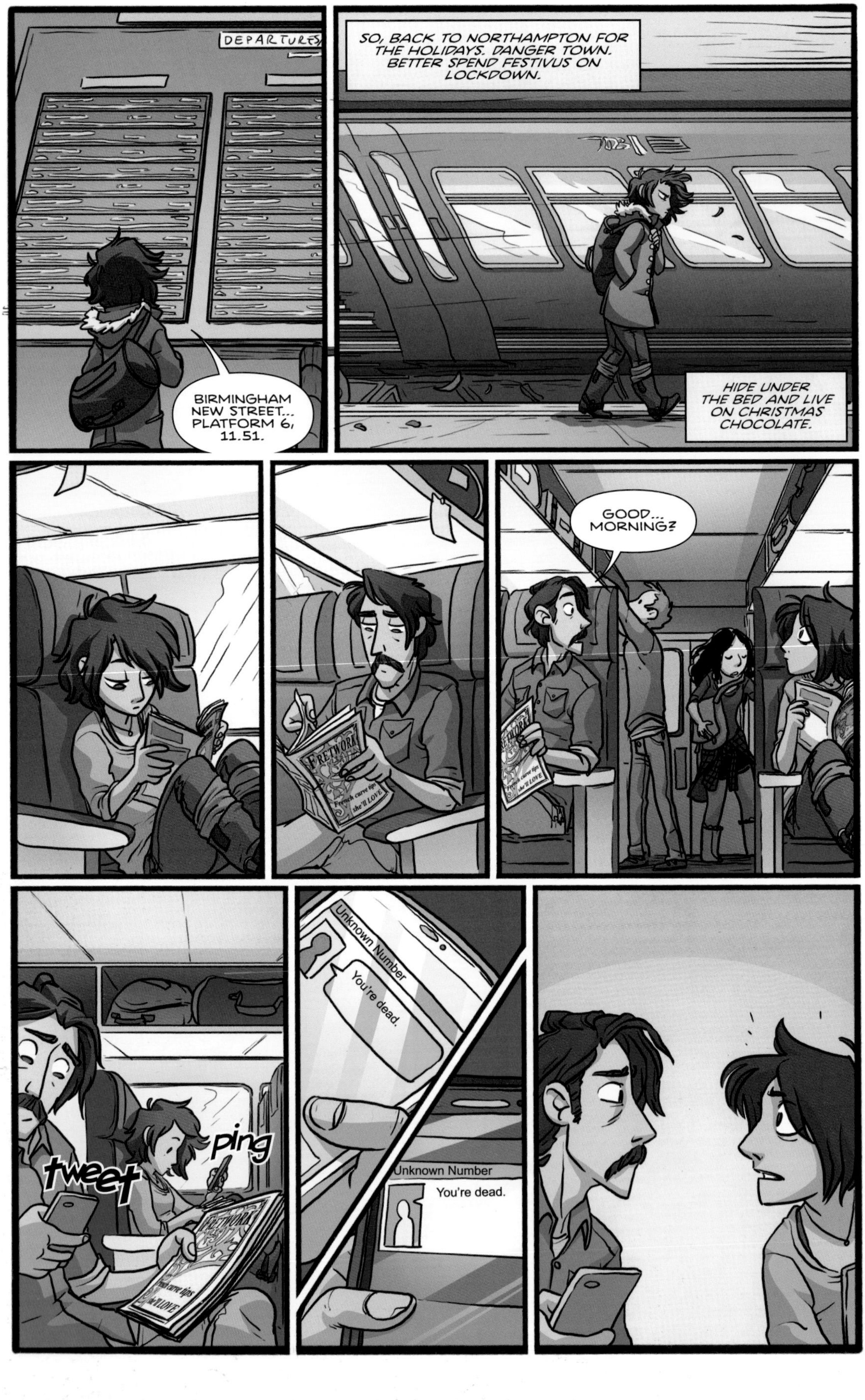
DEPARTURES
BIRMINGHAM NEW STREET... PLATFORM 6, 11.51.
SO, BACK TO NORTHAMPTON FOR THE HOLIDAYS. DANGER TOWN. BETTER SPEND FESTIVUS ON LOCKDOWN.
HIDE UNDER THE BED AND LIVE ON CHRISTMAS CHOCOLATE.
FRETWORK
French curve tips she'll LOVE
GOOD... MORNING?
tweet
ping
Unknown Number
You're dead.
Unknown Number
You're dead.

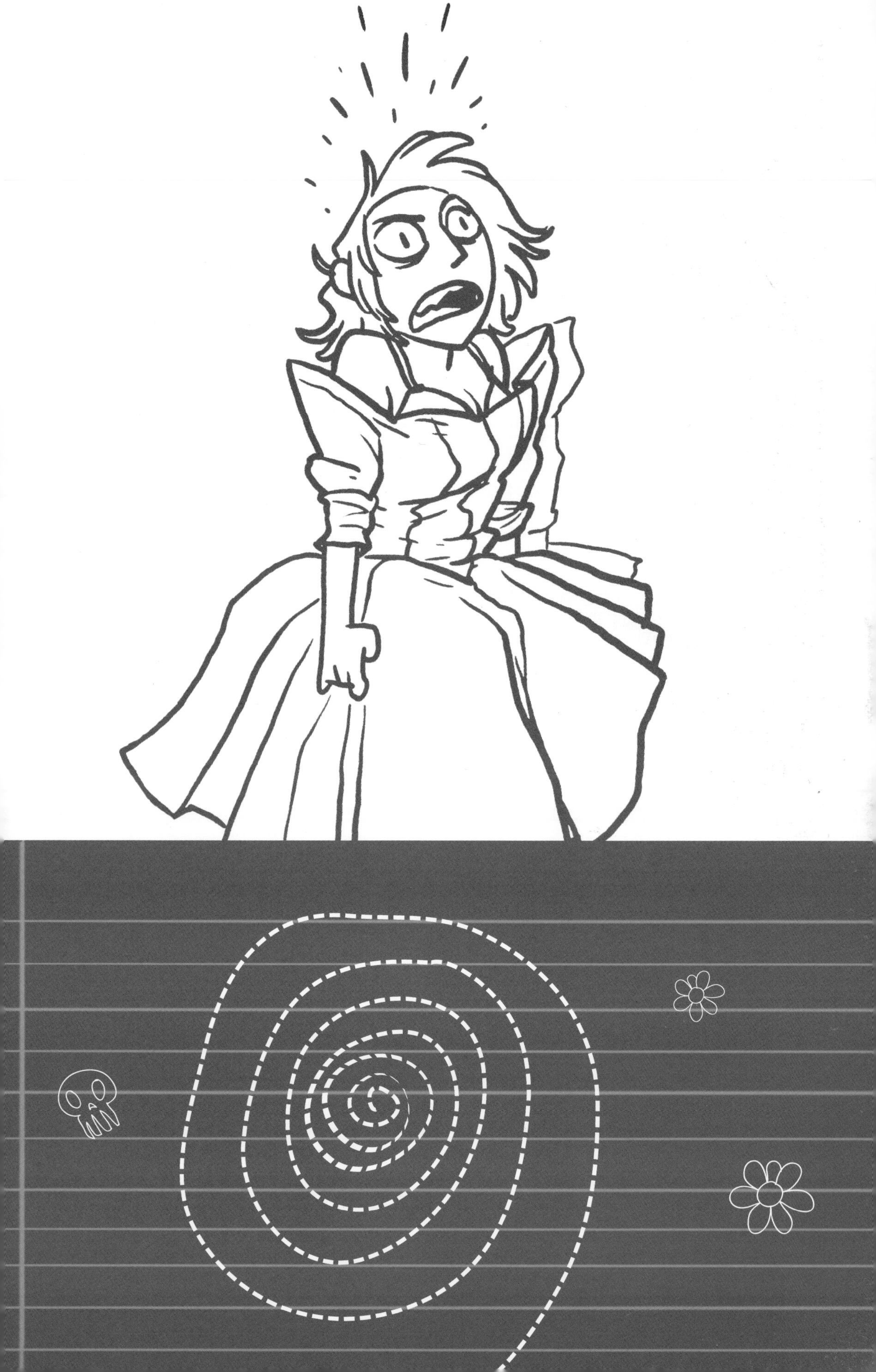

CHAPTER SIX

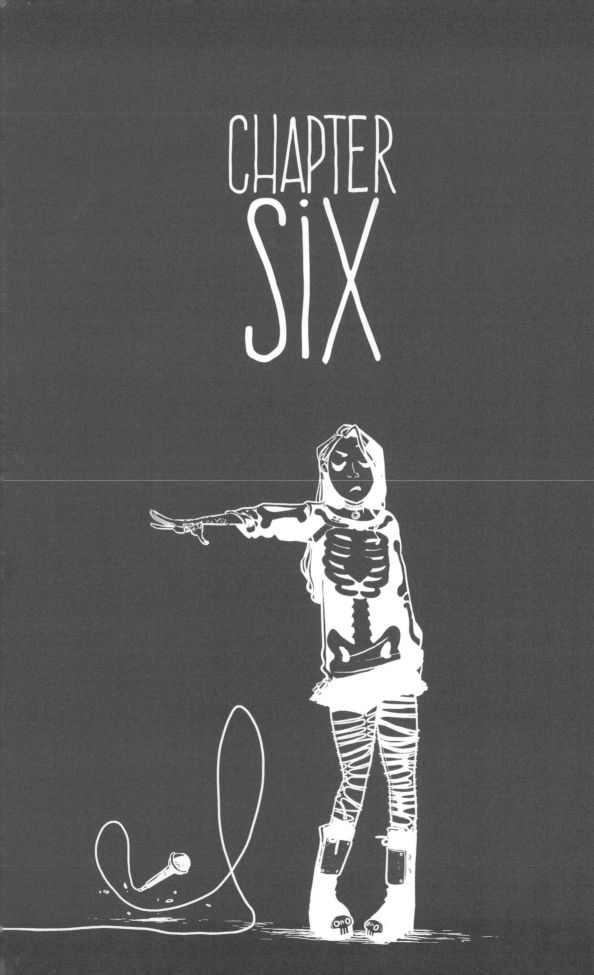

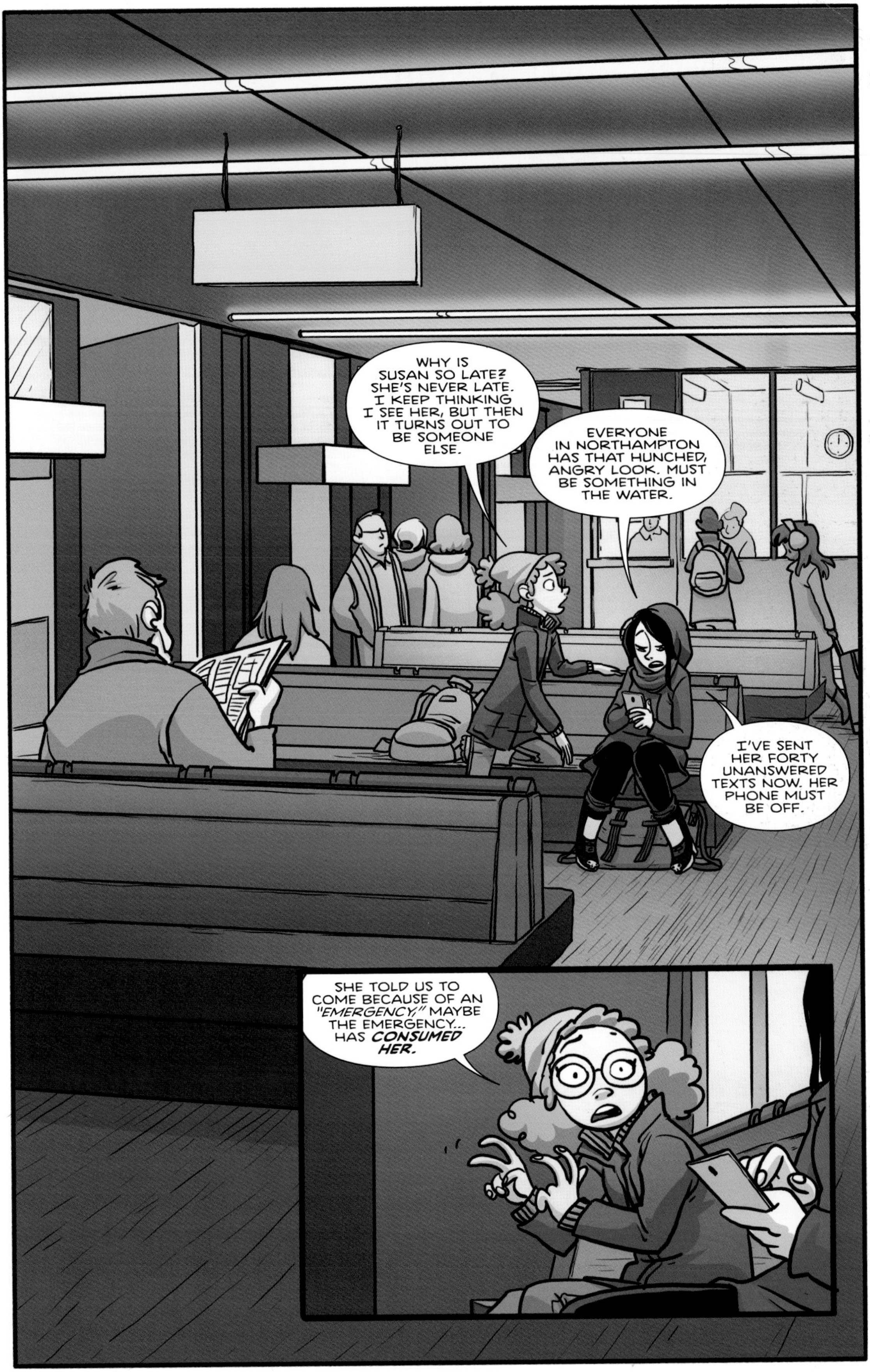
WHY IS SUSAN SO LATE? SHE'S NEVER LATE. I KEEP THINKING I SEE HER, BUT THEN IT TURNS OUT TO BE SOMEONE ELSE.
EVERYONE IN NORTHAMPTON HAS THAT HUNCHED, ANGRY LOOK. MUST BE SOMETHING IN THE WATER.
I'VE SENT HER FORTY UNANSWERED TEXTS NOW. HER PHONE MUST BE OFF.
SHE TOLD US TO COME BECAUSE OF AN *"EMERGENCY,"* MAYBE THE EMERGENCY... HAS ***CONSUMED HER.***

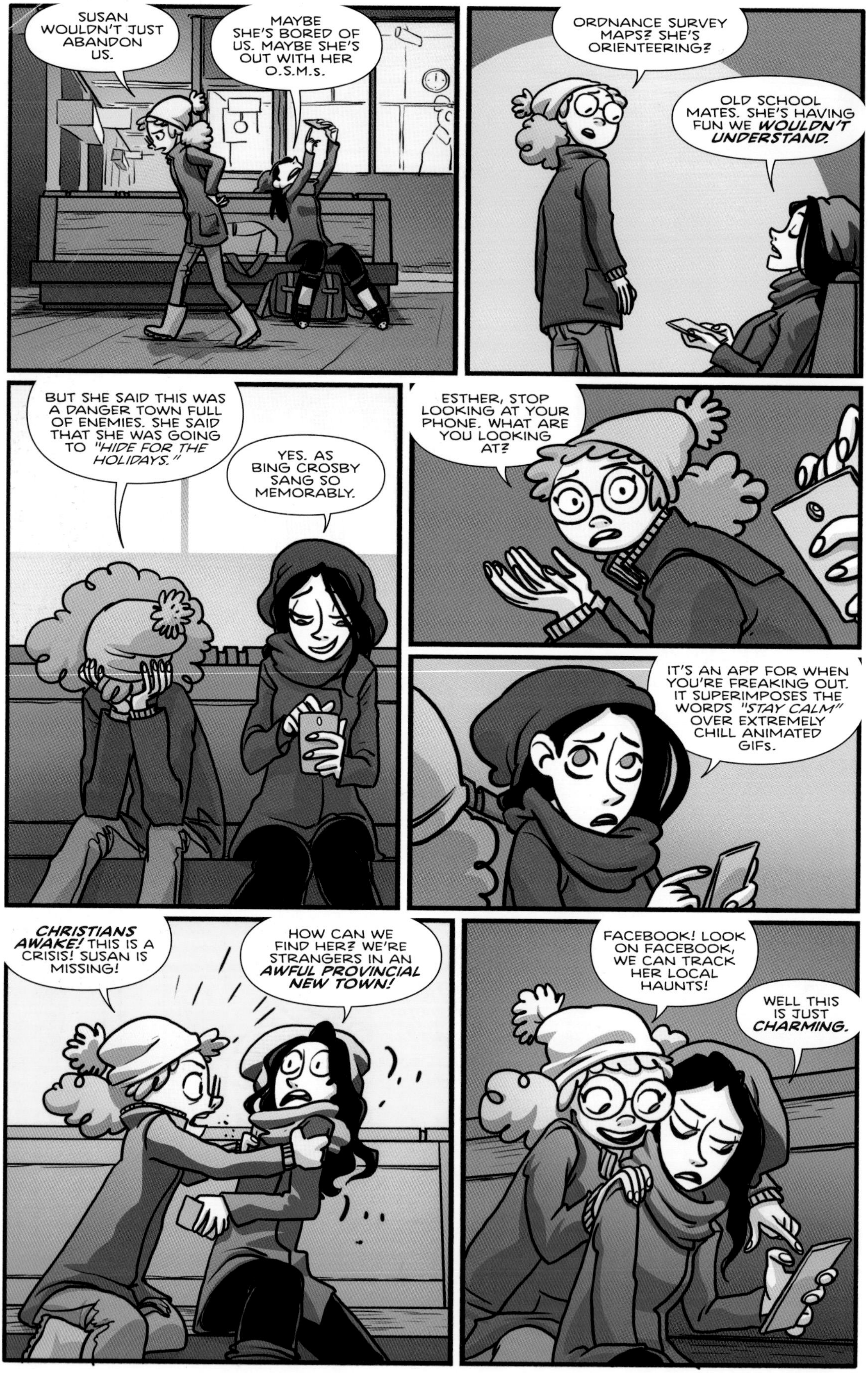
SUSAN WOULDN'T JUST ABANDON US.
MAYBE SHE'S BORED OF US. MAYBE SHE'S OUT WITH HER O.S.M.s.
ORDNANCE SURVEY MAPS? SHE'S ORIENTEERING?
OLD SCHOOL MATES. SHE'S HAVING FUN WE ***WOULDN'T UNDERSTAND.***
BUT SHE SAID THIS WAS A DANGER TOWN FULL OF ENEMIES. SHE SAID THAT SHE WAS GOING TO *"HIDE FOR THE HOLIDAYS."*
YES. AS BING CROSBY SANG SO MEMORABLY.
ESTHER, STOP LOOKING AT YOUR PHONE. WHAT ARE YOU LOOKING AT?
IT'S AN APP FOR WHEN YOU'RE FREAKING OUT. IT SUPERIMPOSES THE WORDS *"STAY CALM"* OVER EXTREMELY CHILL ANIMATED GIFs.
CHRISTIANS AWAKE! THIS IS A CRISIS! SUSAN IS MISSING!
HOW CAN WE FIND HER? WE'RE STRANGERS IN AN ***AWFUL PROVINCIAL NEW TOWN!***
FACEBOOK! LOOK ON FACEBOOK, WE CAN TRACK HER LOCAL HAUNTS!
WELL THIS IS JUST ***CHARMING.***

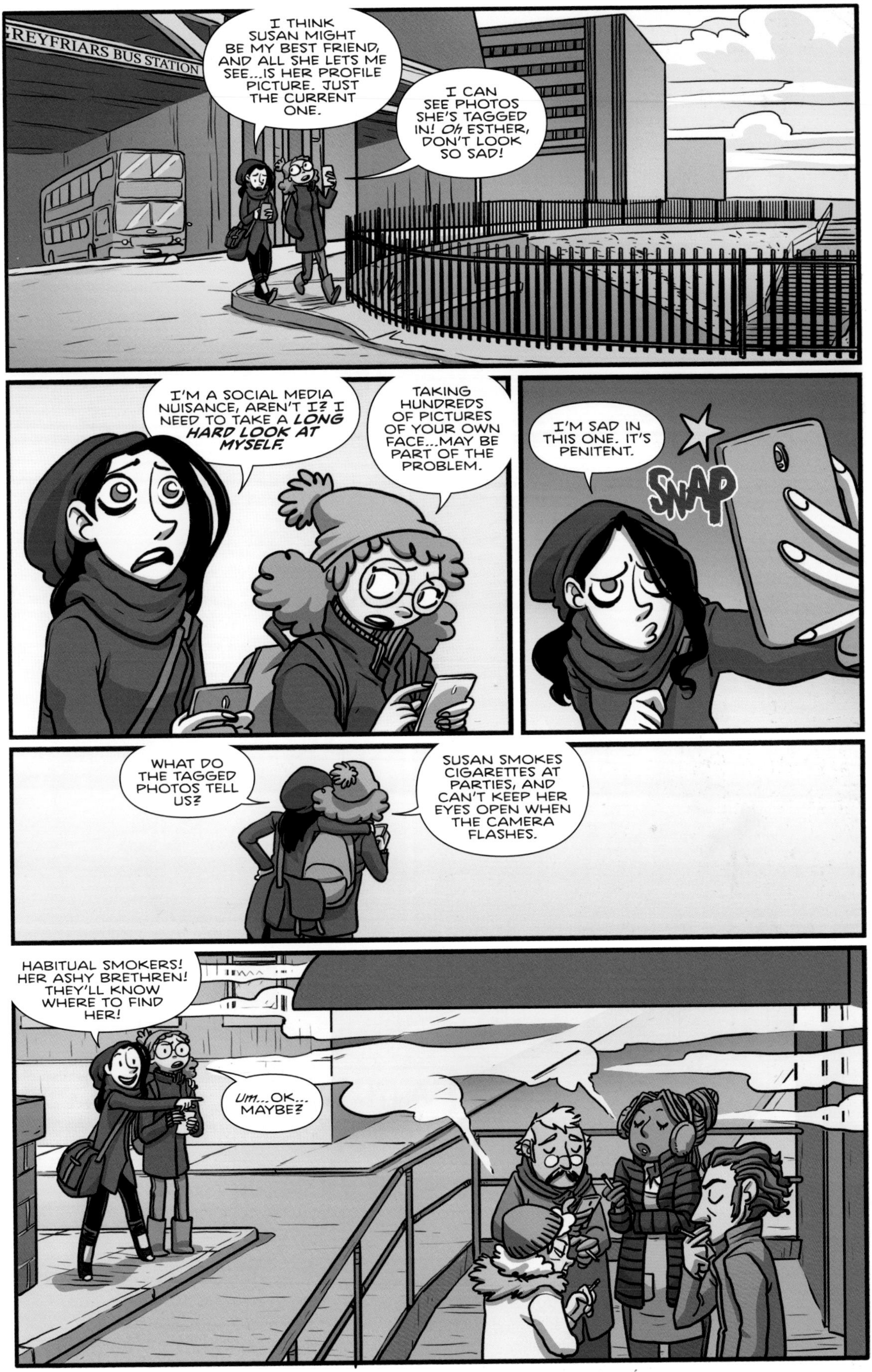
GREYFRIARS BUS STATION
I THINK SUSAN MIGHT BE MY BEST FRIEND, AND ALL SHE LETS ME SEE...IS HER PROFILE PICTURE. JUST THE CURRENT ONE.
I CAN SEE PHOTOS SHE'S TAGGED IN! *OH* ESTHER, DON'T LOOK SO SAD!
I'M A SOCIAL MEDIA NUISANCE, AREN'T I? I NEED TO TAKE A ***LONG HARD LOOK AT MYSELF.***
TAKING HUNDREDS OF PICTURES OF YOUR OWN FACE...MAY BE PART OF THE PROBLEM.
I'M SAD IN THIS ONE. IT'S PENITENT.
SNAP
WHAT DO THE TAGGED PHOTOS TELL US?
SUSAN SMOKES CIGARETTES AT PARTIES, AND CAN'T KEEP HER EYES OPEN WHEN THE CAMERA FLASHES.
HABITUAL SMOKERS! HER ASHY BRETHREN! THEY'LL KNOW WHERE TO FIND HER!
UM...OK... MAYBE?

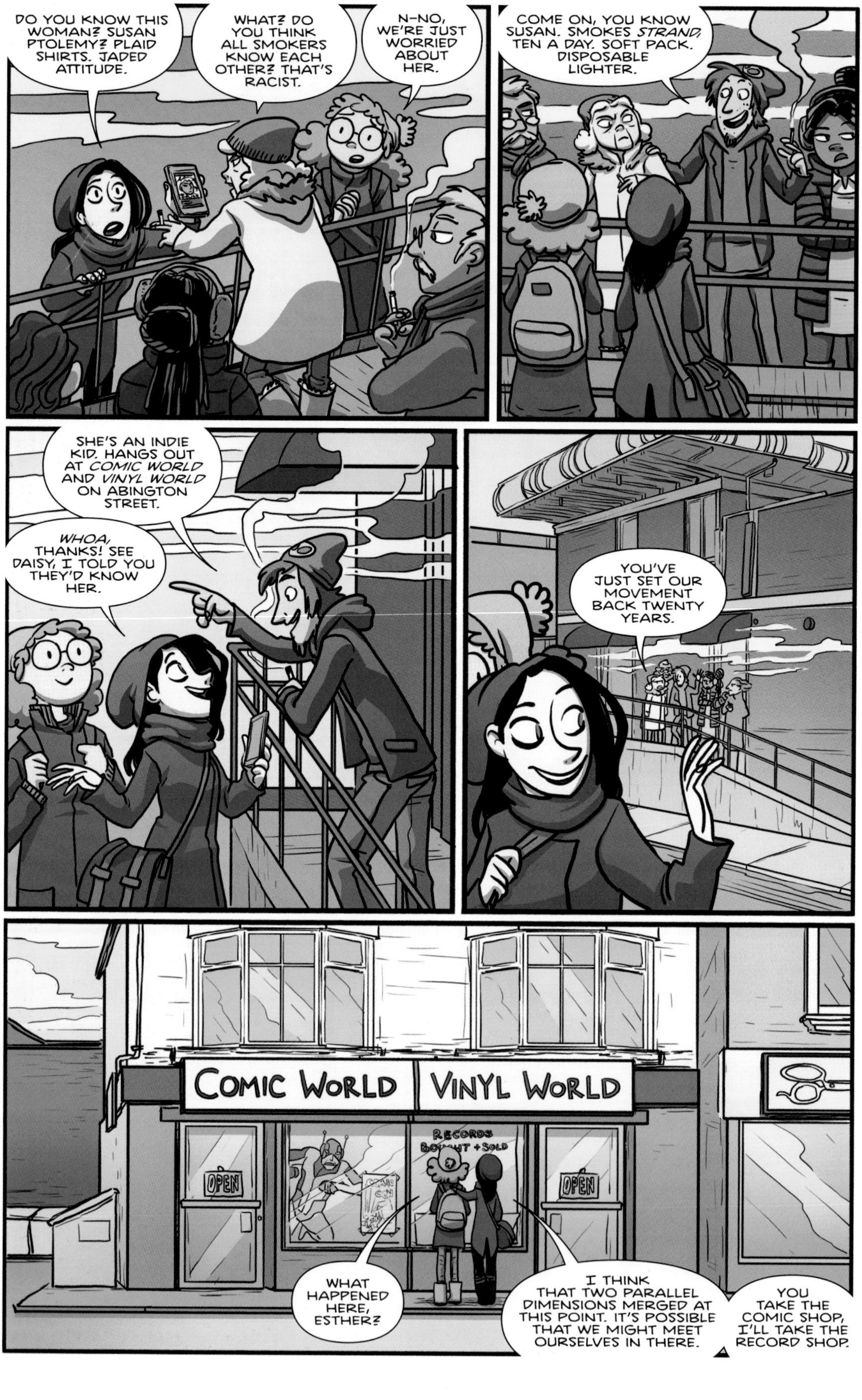
DO YOU KNOW THIS WOMAN? SUSAN PTOLEMY? PLAID SHIRTS. JADED ATTITUDE.
WHAT? DO YOU THINK ALL SMOKERS KNOW EACH OTHER? THAT'S RACIST.
N-NO, WE'RE JUST WORRIED ABOUT HER.
COME ON, YOU KNOW SUSAN. SMOKES *STRAND,* TEN A DAY. SOFT PACK. DISPOSABLE LIGHTER.
SHE'S AN INDIE KID. HANGS OUT AT *COMIC WORLD* AND *VINYL WORLD* ON ABINGTON STREET.
WHOA, THANKS! SEE DAISY, I TOLD YOU THEY'D KNOW HER.
YOU'VE JUST SET OUR MOVEMENT BACK TWENTY YEARS.
COMIC WORLD
VINYL WORLD
OPEN
OPEN
WHAT HAPPENED HERE, ESTHER?
I THINK THAT TWO PARALLEL DIMENSIONS MERGED AT THIS POINT. IT'S POSSIBLE THAT WE MIGHT MEET OURSELVES IN THERE.
YOU TAKE THE COMIC SHOP, I'LL TAKE THE RECORD SHOP.

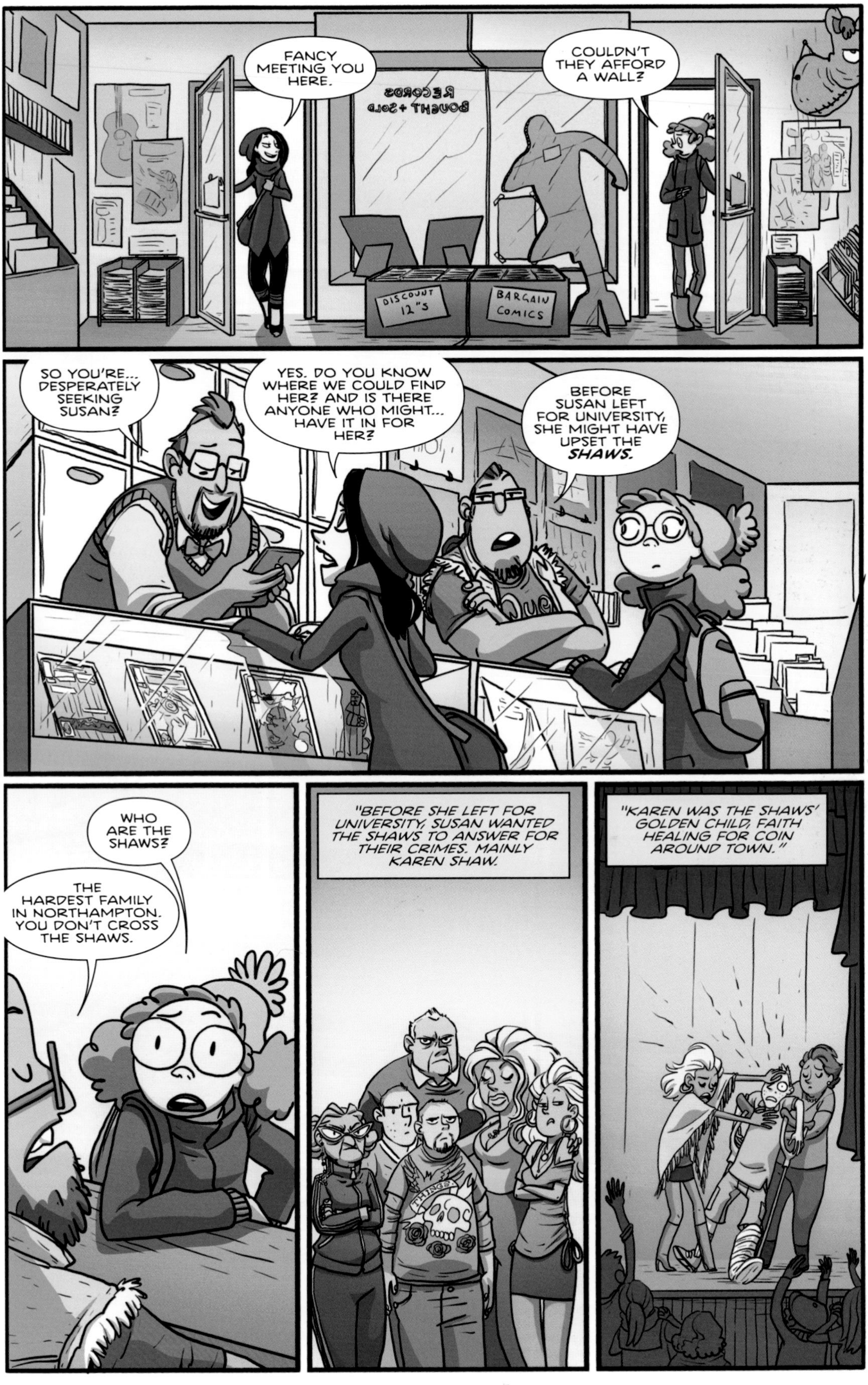
FANCY MEETING YOU HERE.
COULDN'T THEY AFFORD A WALL?
RECORDS BOUGHT + SOLD
DISCOUNT 12"S
BARGAIN COMICS
SO YOU'RE... DESPERATELY SEEKING SUSAN?
YES. DO YOU KNOW WHERE WE COULD FIND HER? AND IS THERE ANYONE WHO MIGHT... HAVE IT IN FOR HER?
BEFORE SUSAN LEFT FOR UNIVERSITY, SHE MIGHT HAVE UPSET THE SHAWS.
WHO ARE THE SHAWS?
THE HARDEST FAMILY IN NORTHAMPTON. YOU DON'T CROSS THE SHAWS.
"BEFORE SHE LEFT FOR UNIVERSITY, SUSAN WANTED THE SHAWS TO ANSWER FOR THEIR CRIMES. MAINLY KAREN SHAW.
"KAREN WAS THE SHAWS' GOLDEN CHILD, FAITH HEALING FOR COIN AROUND TOWN."

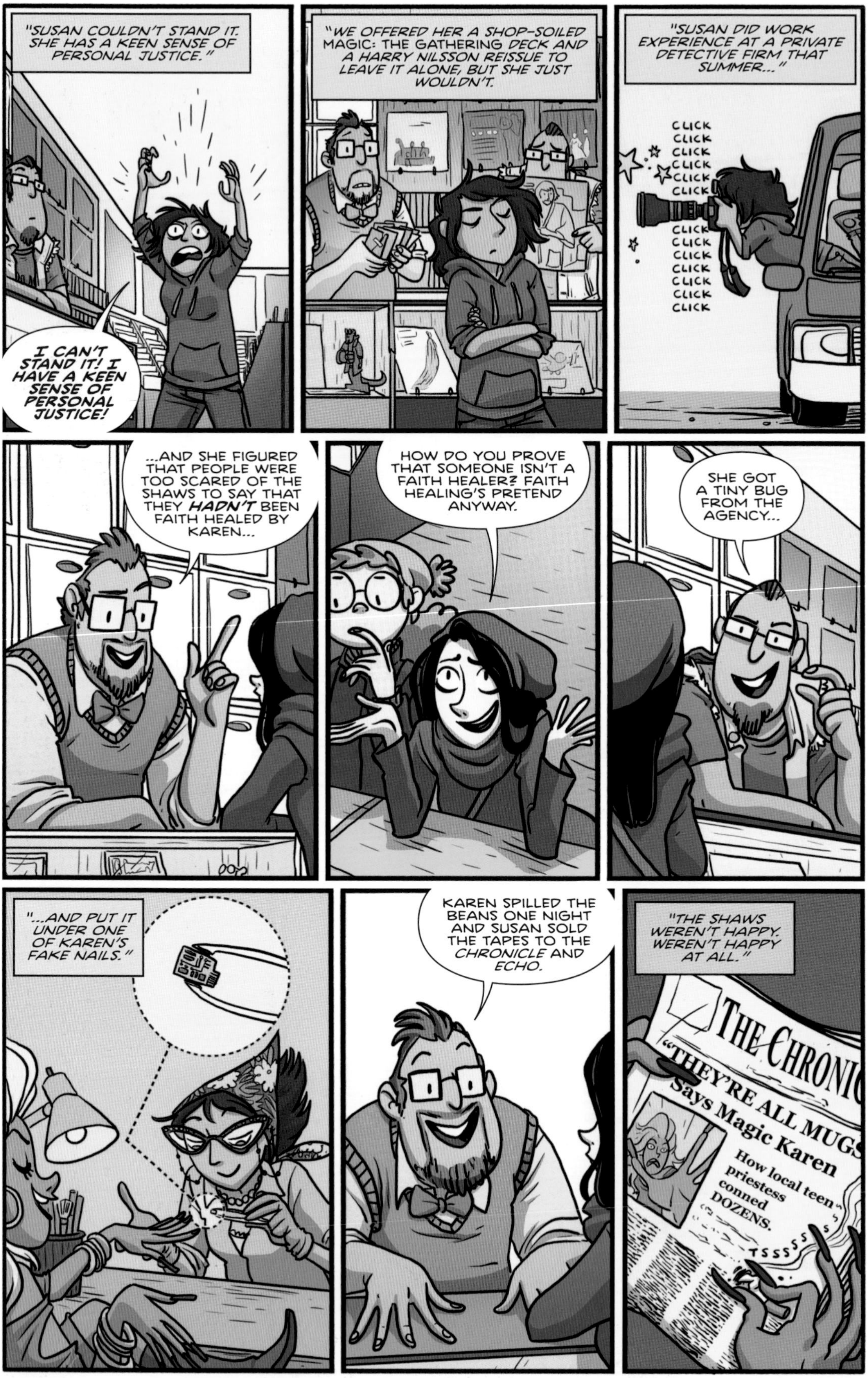
"SUSAN COULDN'T STAND IT. SHE HAS A KEEN SENSE OF PERSONAL JUSTICE."
I CAN'T STAND IT! I HAVE A KEEN SENSE OF PERSONAL JUSTICE!
"WE OFFERED HER A SHOP-SOILED MAGIC: THE GATHERING DECK AND A HARRY NILSSON REISSUE TO LEAVE IT ALONE, BUT SHE JUST WOULDN'T.
"SUSAN DID WORK EXPERIENCE AT A PRIVATE DETECTIVE FIRM THAT SUMMER..."
CLICK CLICK CLICK CLICK CLICK CLICK
CLICK CLICK CLICK CLICK CLICK CLICK CLICK
...AND SHE FIGURED THAT PEOPLE WERE TOO SCARED OF THE SHAWS TO SAY THAT THEY HADN'T BEEN FAITH HEALED BY KAREN...
HOW DO YOU PROVE THAT SOMEONE ISN'T A FAITH HEALER? FAITH HEALING'S PRETEND ANYWAY.
SHE GOT A TINY BUG FROM THE AGENCY...
"...AND PUT IT UNDER ONE OF KAREN'S FAKE NAILS."
KAREN SPILLED THE BEANS ONE NIGHT AND SUSAN SOLD THE TAPES TO THE CHRONICLE AND ECHO.
"THE SHAWS WEREN'T HAPPY. WEREN'T HAPPY AT ALL."
THE CHRONIC
"THEY'RE ALL MUGS"
Says Magic Karen
How local teen priestess conned DOZENS.
TSSSSSSS

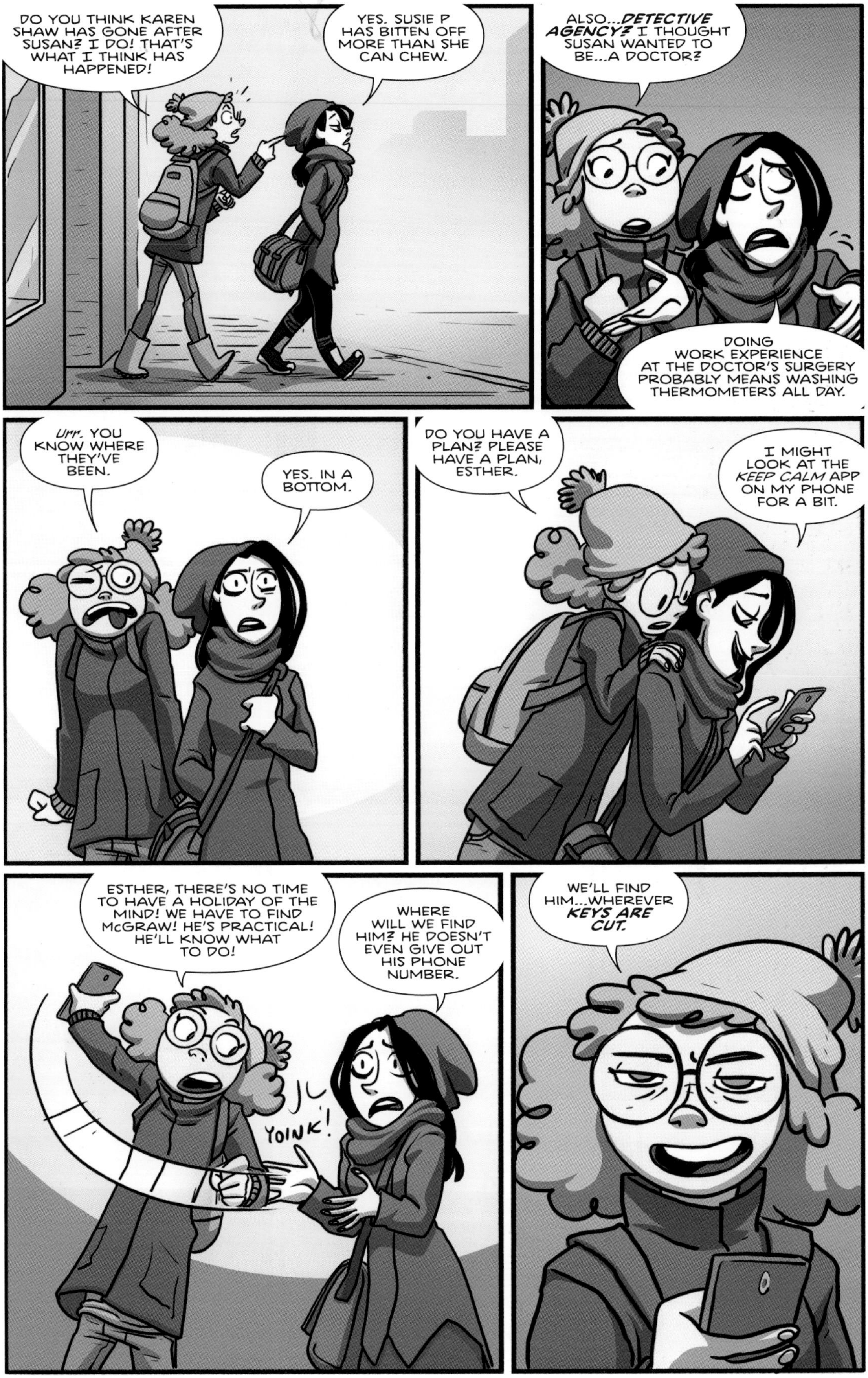
DO YOU THINK KAREN SHAW HAS GONE AFTER SUSAN? I DO! THAT'S WHAT I THINK HAS HAPPENED!
YES. SUSIE P HAS BITTEN OFF MORE THAN SHE CAN CHEW.
ALSO...*DETECTIVE AGENCY?* I THOUGHT SUSAN WANTED TO BE...A DOCTOR?
DOING WORK EXPERIENCE AT THE DOCTOR'S SURGERY PROBABLY MEANS WASHING THERMOMETERS ALL DAY.
Urr. YOU KNOW WHERE THEY'VE BEEN.
YES. IN A BOTTOM.
DO YOU HAVE A PLAN? PLEASE HAVE A PLAN, ESTHER.
I MIGHT LOOK AT THE *KEEP CALM* APP ON MY PHONE FOR A BIT.
ESTHER, THERE'S NO TIME TO HAVE A HOLIDAY OF THE MIND! WE HAVE TO FIND McGRAW! HE'S PRACTICAL! HE'LL KNOW WHAT TO DO!
WHERE WILL WE FIND HIM? HE DOESN'T EVEN GIVE OUT HIS PHONE NUMBER.
YOINK!
WE'LL FIND HIM...WHEREVER ***KEYS ARE CUT.***

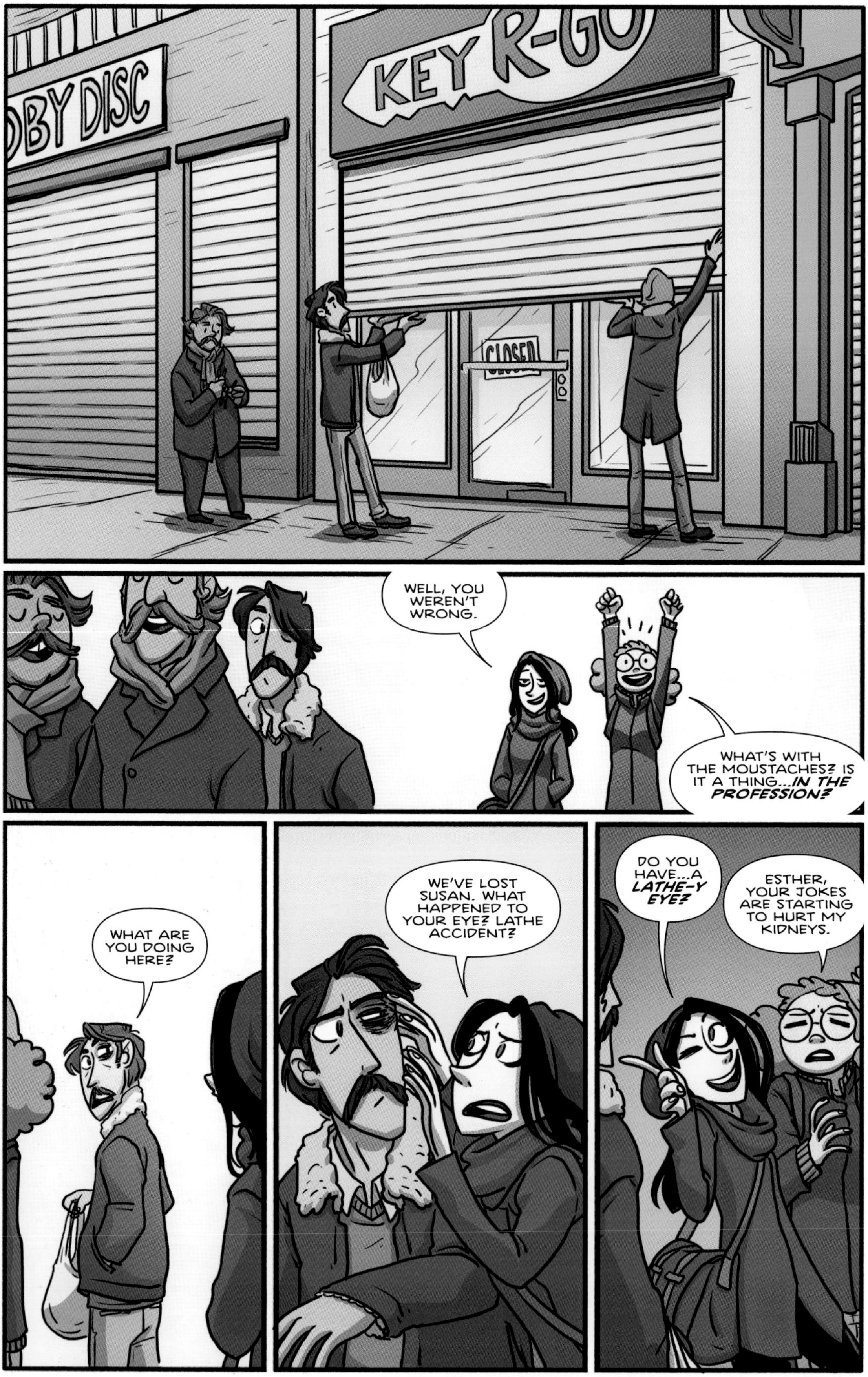

DBY DISC
KEY R-GO
CLOSED
WELL, YOU WEREN'T WRONG.
WHAT'S WITH THE MOUSTACHES? IS IT A THING...*IN THE PROFESSION?*
WHAT ARE YOU DOING HERE?
WE'VE LOST SUSAN. WHAT HAPPENED TO YOUR EYE? LATHE ACCIDENT?
DO YOU HAVE...A *LATHE-Y EYE?*
ESTHER, YOUR JOKES ARE STARTING TO HURT MY KIDNEYS.

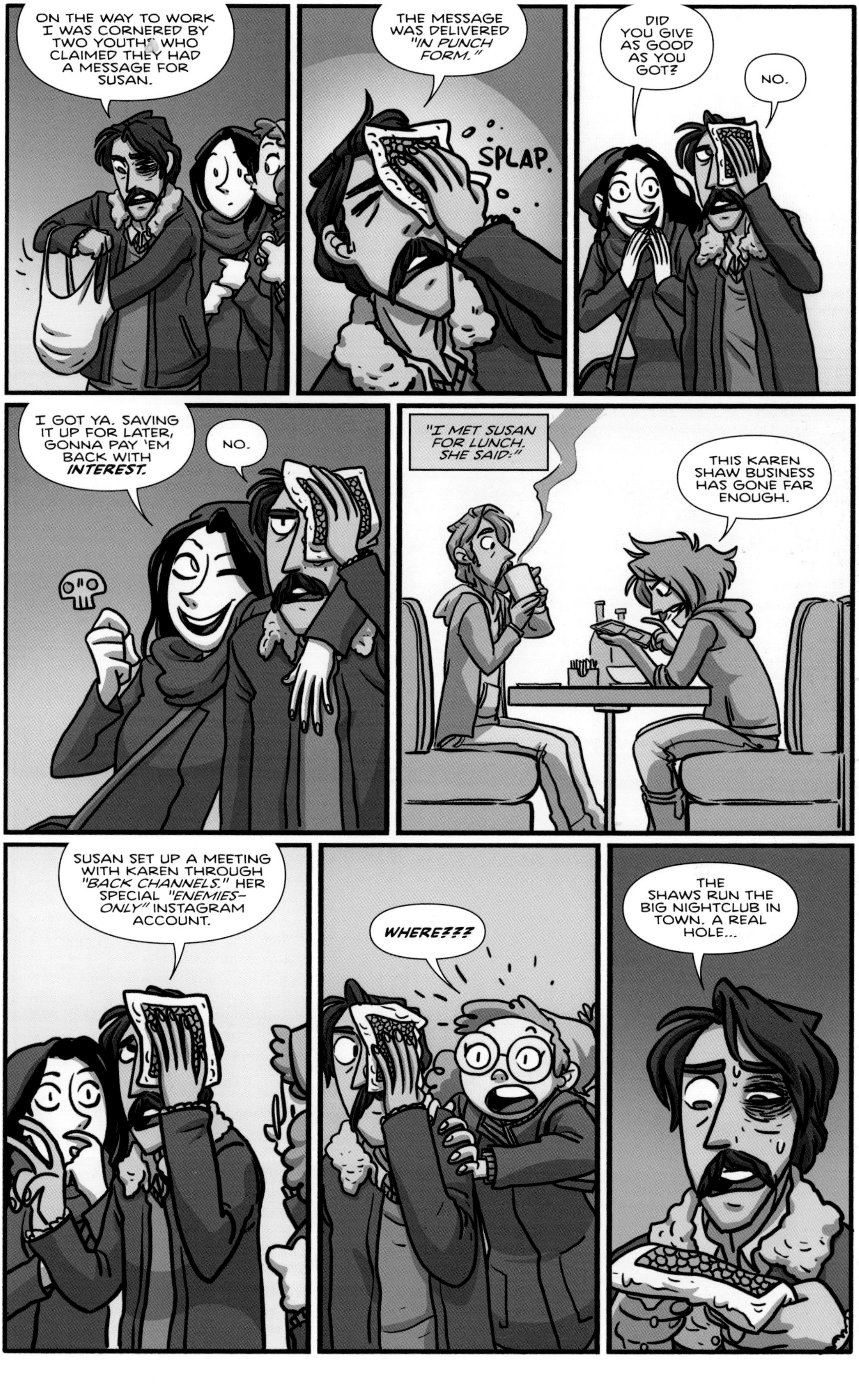
ON THE WAY TO WORK I WAS CORNERED BY TWO YOUTHS WHO CLAIMED THEY HAD A MESSAGE FOR SUSAN.
THE MESSAGE WAS DELIVERED *"IN PUNCH FORM."*
SPLAP.
DID YOU GIVE AS GOOD AS YOU GOT?
NO.
I GOT YA. SAVING IT UP FOR LATER, GONNA PAY 'EM BACK WITH ***INTEREST.***
NO.
"I MET SUSAN FOR LUNCH. SHE SAID:"
THIS KAREN SHAW BUSINESS HAS GONE FAR ENOUGH.
SUSAN SET UP A MEETING WITH KAREN THROUGH *"BACK CHANNELS."* HER SPECIAL *"ENEMIES-ONLY"* INSTAGRAM ACCOUNT.
WHERE???
THE SHAWS RUN THE BIG NIGHTCLUB IN TOWN. A REAL HOLE...

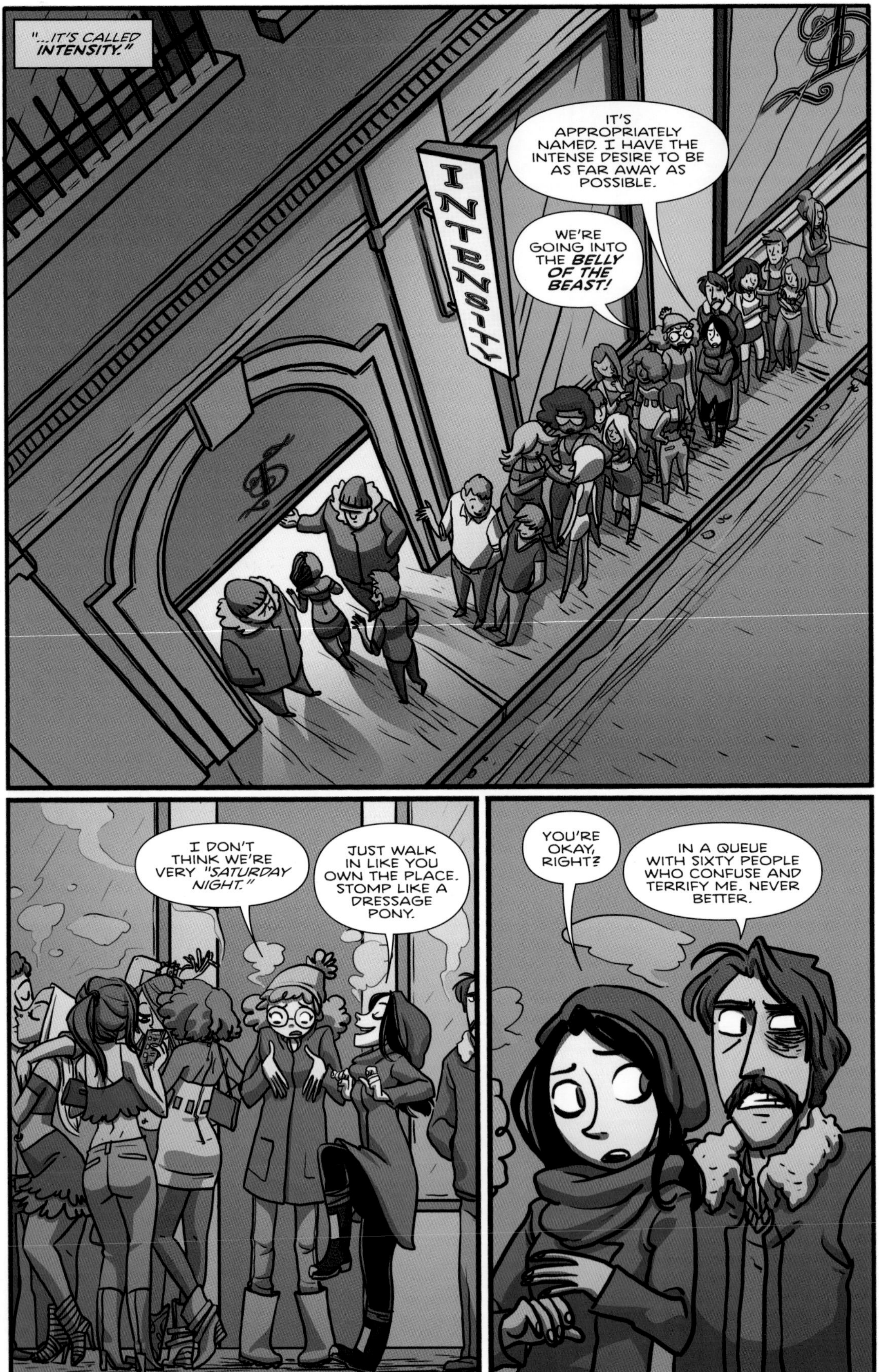
"...IT'S CALLED INTENSITY."
INTENSITY
IT'S APPROPRIATELY NAMED. I HAVE THE INTENSE DESIRE TO BE AS FAR AWAY AS POSSIBLE.
WE'RE GOING INTO THE BELLY OF THE BEAST!
I DON'T THINK WE'RE VERY "SATURDAY NIGHT."
JUST WALK IN LIKE YOU OWN THE PLACE. STOMP LIKE A DRESSAGE PONY.
YOU'RE OKAY, RIGHT?
IN A QUEUE WITH SIXTY PEOPLE WHO CONFUSE AND TERRIFY ME. NEVER BETTER.

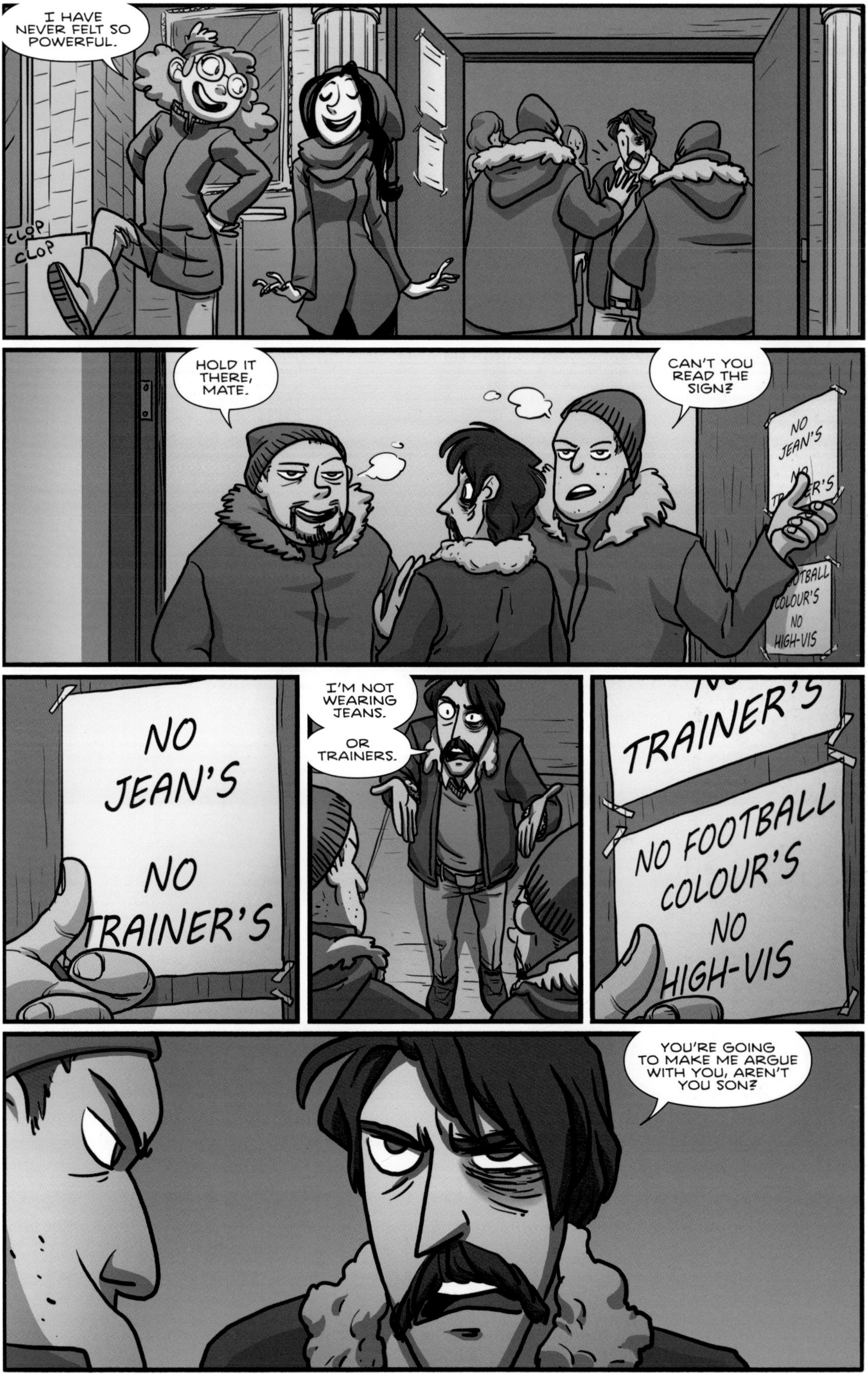
I HAVE NEVER FELT SO POWERFUL.
CLOP
CLOP
HOLD IT THERE, MATE.
CAN'T YOU READ THE SIGN?
NO JEAN'S NO TRAINER'S
NO FOOTBALL COLOUR'S NO HIGH-VIS
I'M NOT WEARING JEANS.
OR TRAINERS.
TRAINER'S
NO FOOTBALL COLOUR'S NO HIGH-VIS
YOU'RE GOING TO MAKE ME ARGUE WITH YOU, AREN'T YOU SON?

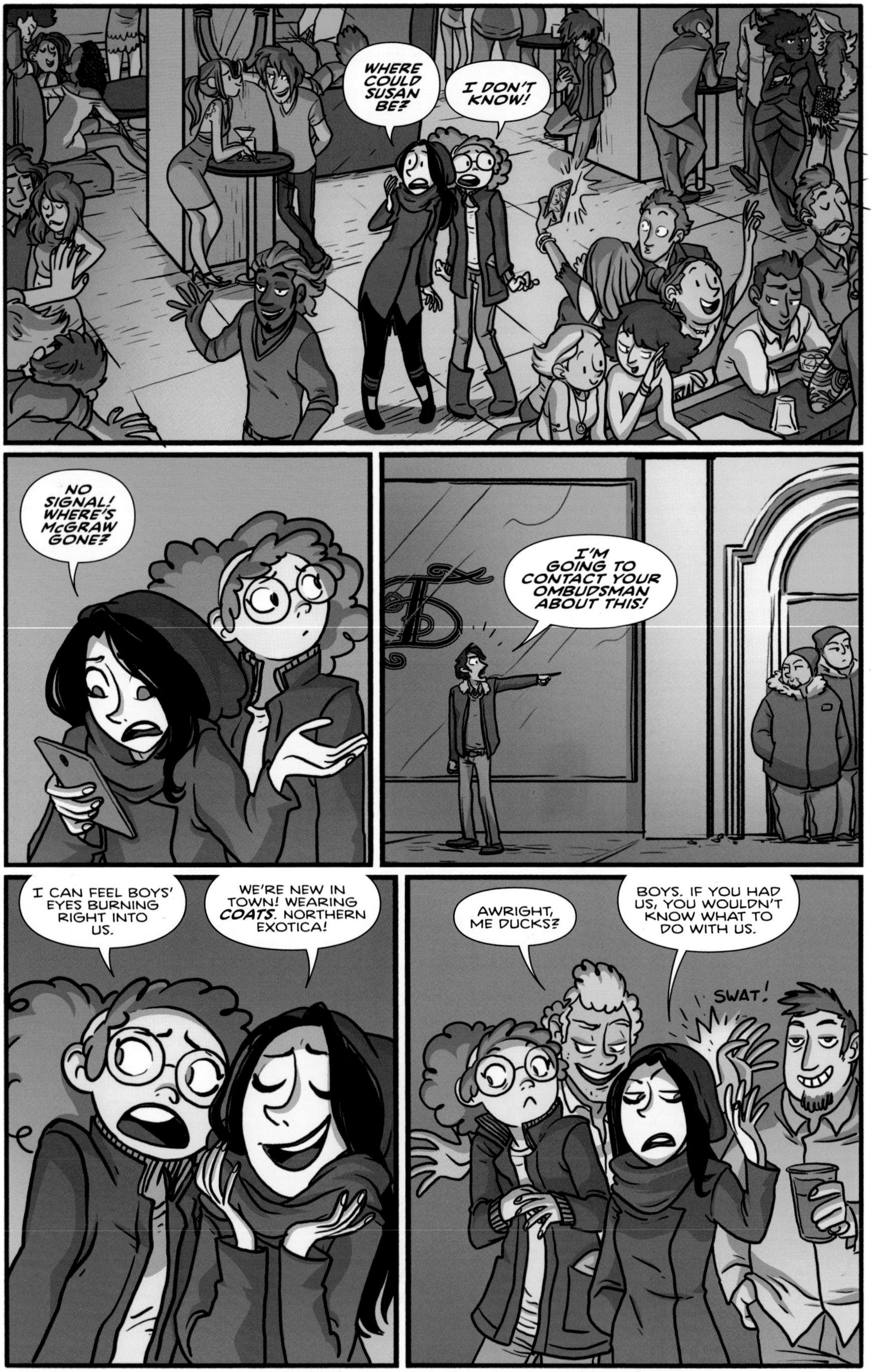
WHERE COULD SUSAN BE?
I DON'T KNOW!
NO SIGNAL! WHERE'S McGRAW GONE?
I'M GOING TO CONTACT YOUR OMBUDSMAN ABOUT THIS!
I CAN FEEL BOYS' EYES BURNING RIGHT INTO US.
WE'RE NEW IN TOWN! WEARING COATS. NORTHERN EXOTICA!
AWRIGHT, ME DUCKS?
BOYS. IF YOU HAD US, YOU WOULDN'T KNOW WHAT TO DO WITH US.
SWAT!

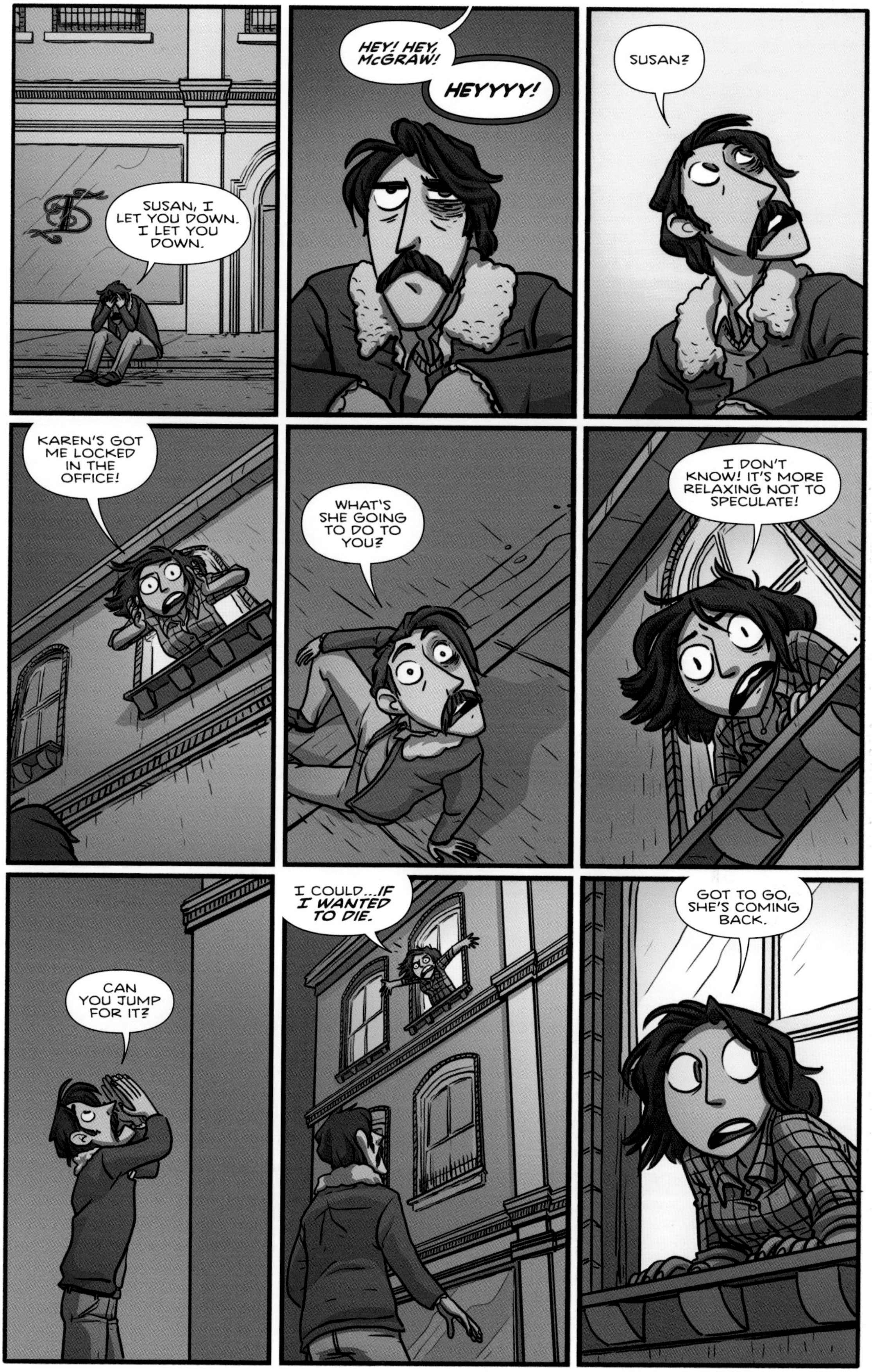
SUSAN, I LET YOU DOWN. I LET YOU DOWN.
HEY! HEY, McGRAW!
HEYYYY!
SUSAN?
KAREN'S GOT ME LOCKED IN THE OFFICE!
WHAT'S SHE GOING TO DO TO YOU?
I DON'T KNOW! IT'S MORE RELAXING NOT TO SPECULATE!
CAN YOU JUMP FOR IT?
I COULD...IF I WANTED TO DIE.
GOT TO GO, SHE'S COMING BACK.

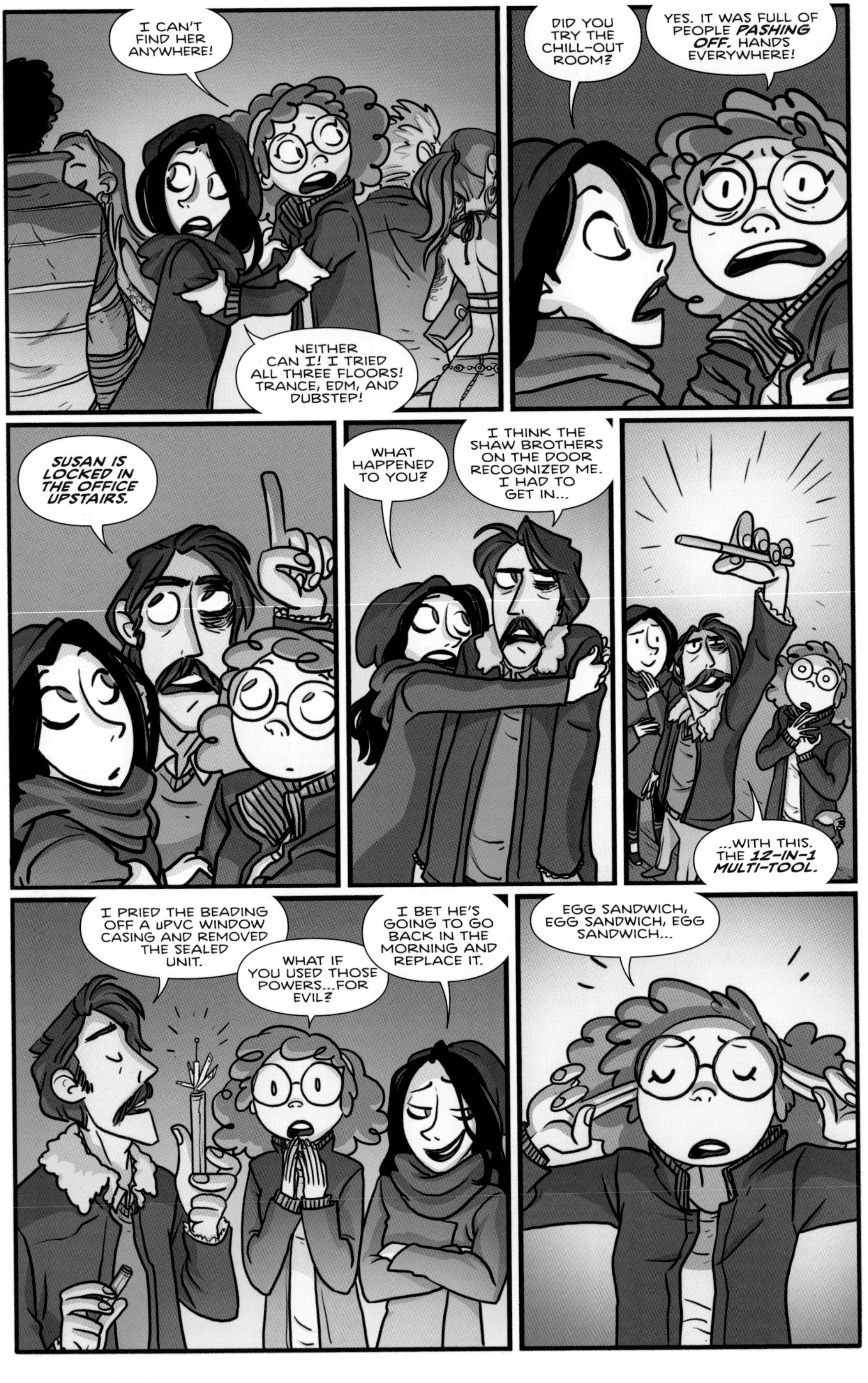
I CAN'T FIND HER ANYWHERE!
NEITHER CAN I! I TRIED ALL THREE FLOORS! TRANCE, EDM, AND DUBSTEP!
DID YOU TRY THE CHILL-OUT ROOM?
YES. IT WAS FULL OF PEOPLE PASHING OFF. HANDS EVERYWHERE!
SUSAN IS LOCKED IN THE OFFICE UPSTAIRS.
WHAT HAPPENED TO YOU?
I THINK THE SHAW BROTHERS ON THE DOOR RECOGNIZED ME. I HAD TO GET IN...
...WITH THIS. THE 12-IN-1 MULTI-TOOL.
I PRIED THE BEADING OFF A uPVC WINDOW CASING AND REMOVED THE SEALED UNIT.
WHAT IF YOU USED THOSE POWERS...FOR EVIL?
I BET HE'S GOING TO GO BACK IN THE MORNING AND REPLACE IT.
EGG SANDWICH, EGG SANDWICH, EGG SANDWICH...

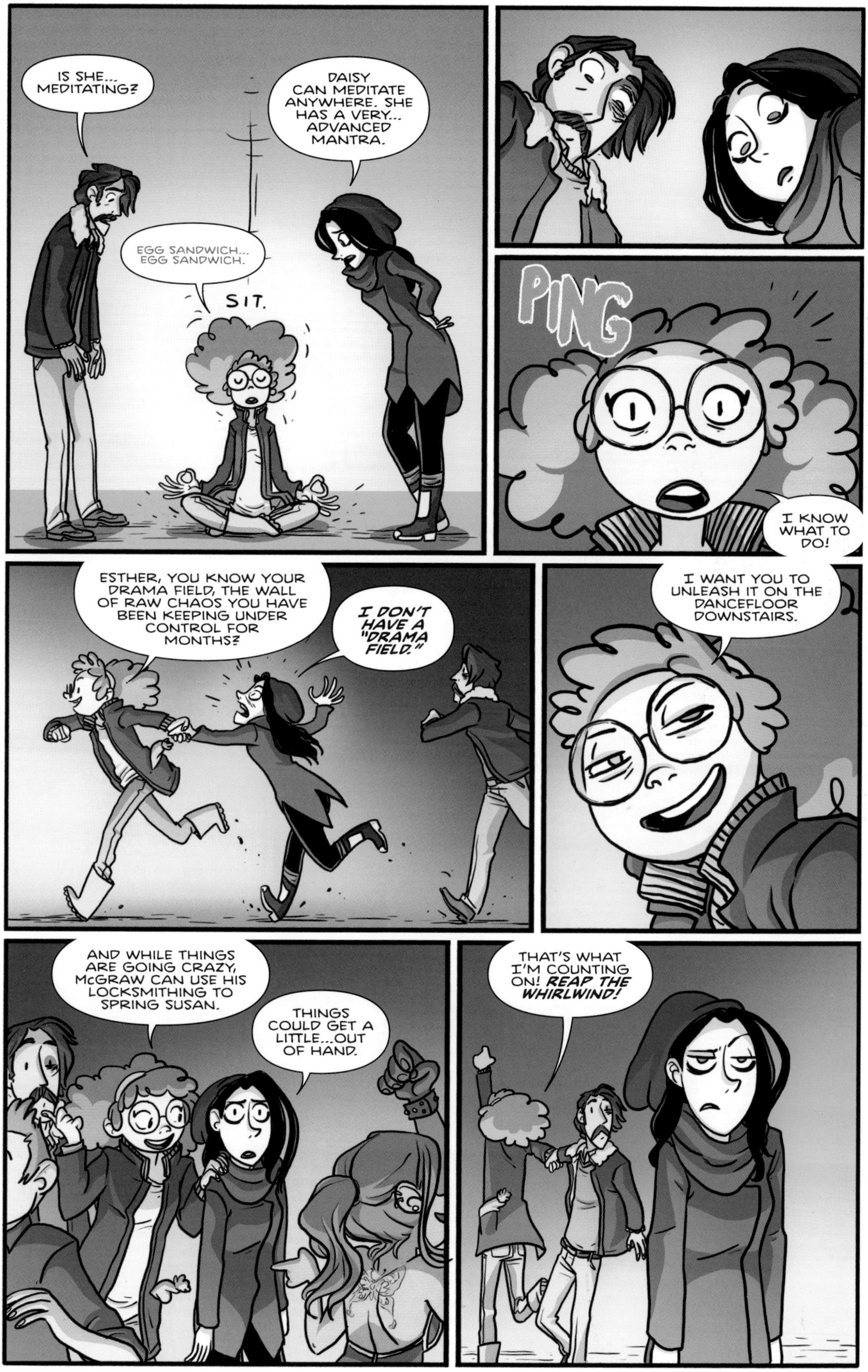
IS SHE... MEDITATING?
DAISY CAN MEDITATE ANYWHERE. SHE HAS A VERY... ADVANCED MANTRA.
EGG SANDWICH... EGG SANDWICH.
SIT.
PING
I KNOW WHAT TO DO!
ESTHER, YOU KNOW YOUR DRAMA FIELD, THE WALL OF RAW CHAOS YOU HAVE BEEN KEEPING UNDER CONTROL FOR MONTHS?
I DON'T HAVE A "DRAMA FIELD."
I WANT YOU TO UNLEASH IT ON THE DANCEFLOOR DOWNSTAIRS.
AND WHILE THINGS ARE GOING CRAZY, McGRAW CAN USE HIS LOCKSMITHING TO SPRING SUSAN.
THINGS COULD GET A LITTLE...OUT OF HAND.
THAT'S WHAT I'M COUNTING ON! REAP THE WHIRLWIND!

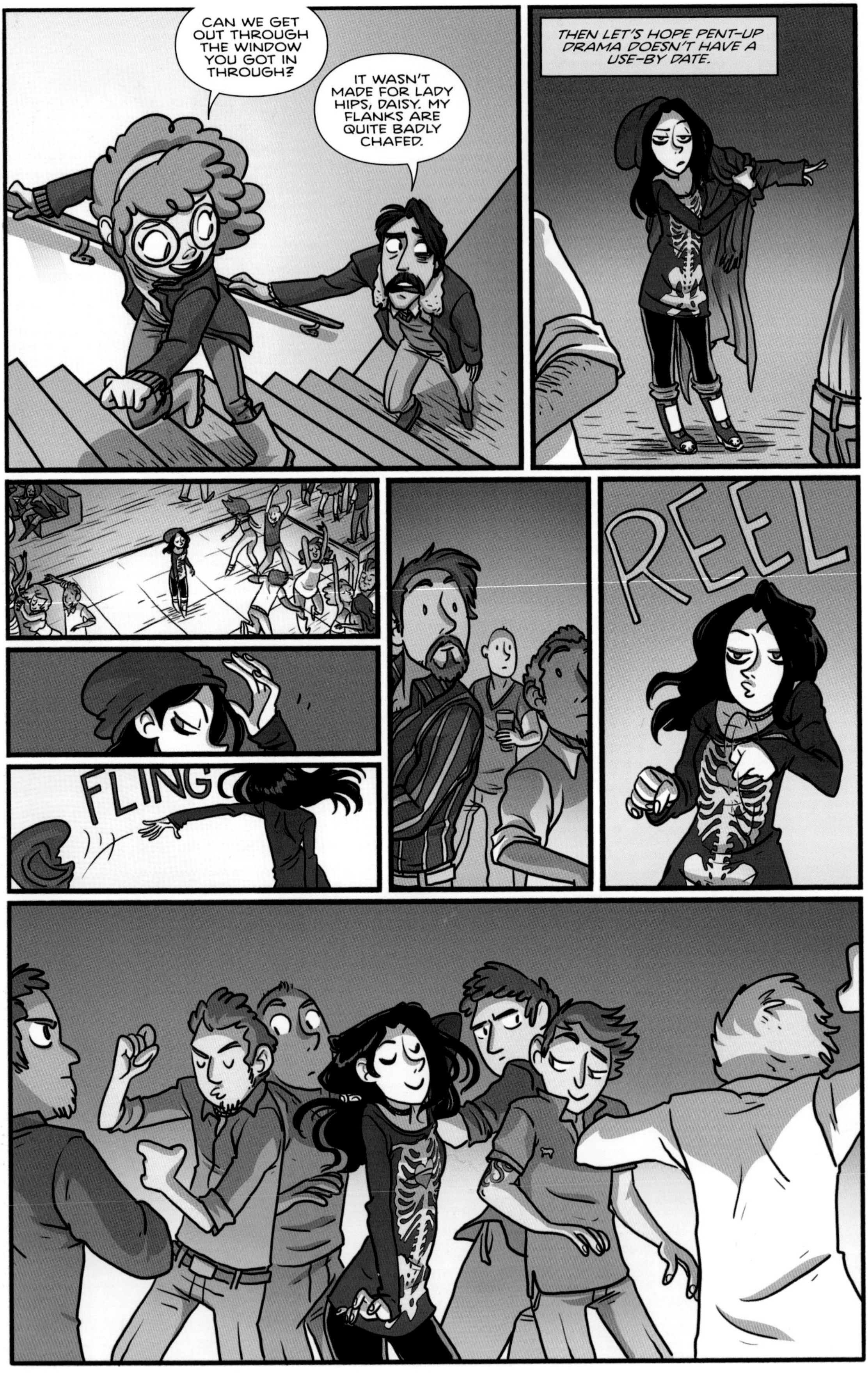
CAN WE GET OUT THROUGH THE WINDOW YOU GOT IN THROUGH?
IT WASN'T MADE FOR LADY HIPS, DAISY. MY FLANKS ARE QUITE BADLY CHAFED.
THEN LET'S HOPE PENT-UP DRAMA DOESN'T HAVE A USE-BY DATE.
FLING
REEL

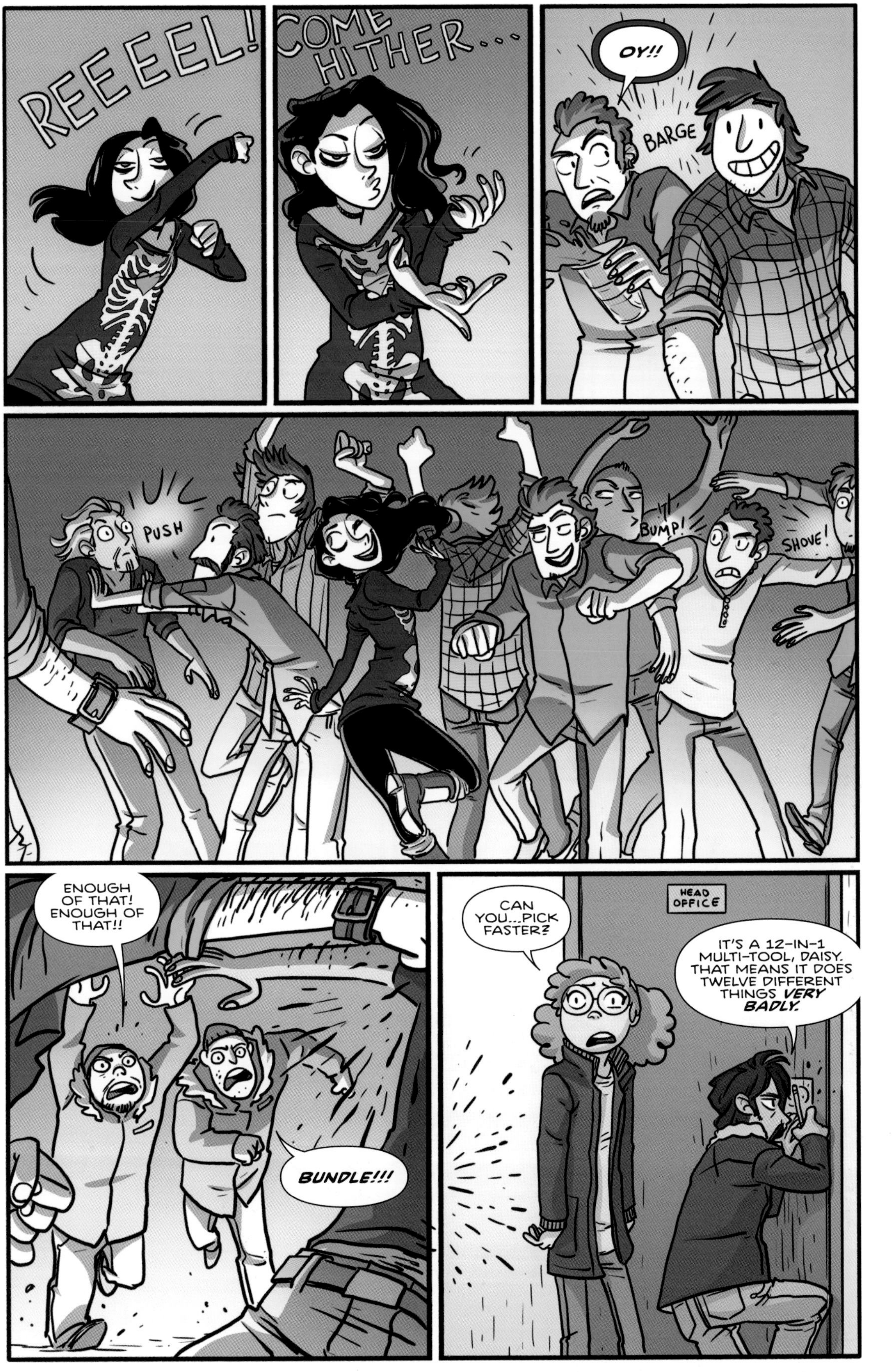
REEEEL!
COME HITHER...
OY!!
BARGE
PUSH
BUMP!
SHOVE!
ENOUGH OF THAT! ENOUGH OF THAT!!
BUNDLE!!!
HEAD OFFICE
CAN YOU...PICK FASTER?
IT'S A 12-IN-1 MULTI-TOOL, DAISY. THAT MEANS IT DOES TWELVE DIFFERENT THINGS *VERY BADLY.*

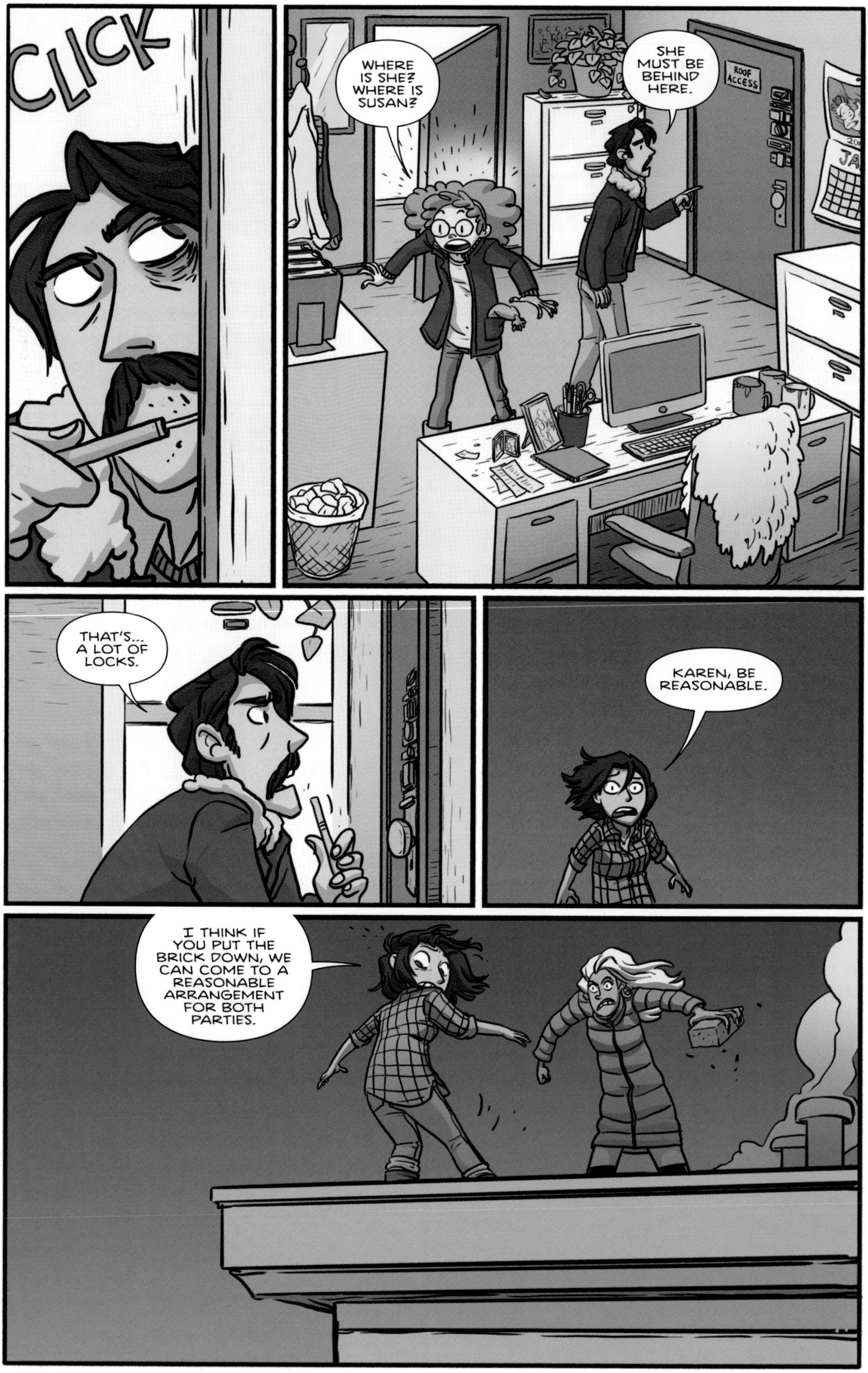
CLICK
WHERE IS SHE? WHERE IS SUSAN?
SHE MUST BE BEHIND HERE.
ROOF ACCESS
THAT'S... A LOT OF LOCKS.
KAREN, BE REASONABLE.
I THINK IF YOU PUT THE BRICK DOWN, WE CAN COME TO A REASONABLE ARRANGEMENT FOR BOTH PARTIES.

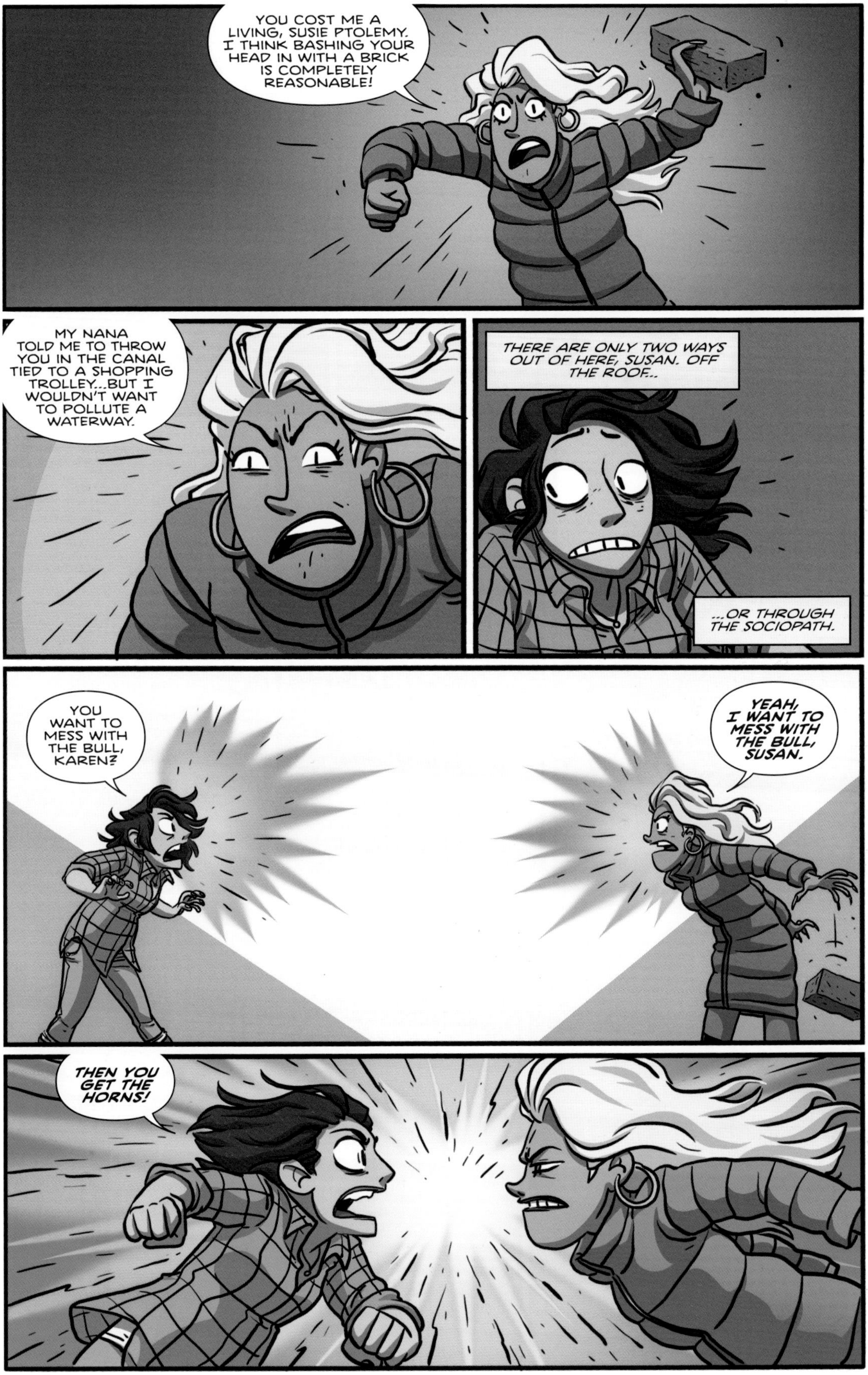
YOU COST ME A LIVING, SUSIE PTOLEMY. I THINK BASHING YOUR HEAD IN WITH A BRICK IS COMPLETELY REASONABLE!
MY NANA TOLD ME TO THROW YOU IN THE CANAL TIED TO A SHOPPING TROLLEY...BUT I WOULDN'T WANT TO POLLUTE A WATERWAY.
THERE ARE ONLY TWO WAYS OUT OF HERE, SUSAN. OFF THE ROOF...
...OR THROUGH THE SOCIOPATH.
YOU WANT TO MESS WITH THE BULL, KAREN?
YEAH, I WANT TO MESS WITH THE BULL, SUSAN.
THEN YOU GET THE HORNS!

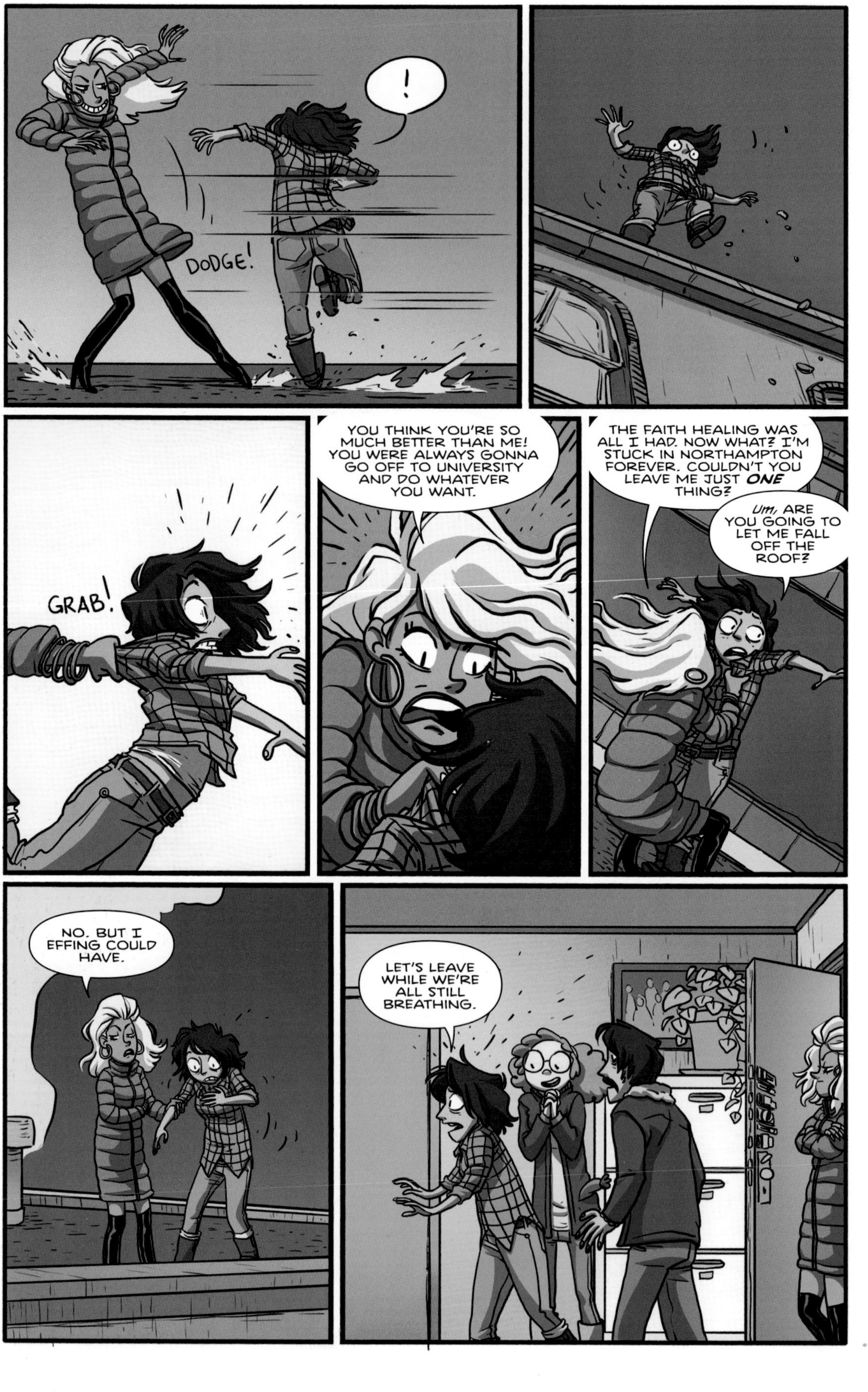
!
DODGE!
GRAB!
YOU THINK YOU'RE SO MUCH BETTER THAN ME! YOU WERE ALWAYS GONNA GO OFF TO UNIVERSITY AND DO WHATEVER YOU WANT.
THE FAITH HEALING WAS ALL I HAD. NOW WHAT? I'M STUCK IN NORTHAMPTON FOREVER. COULDN'T YOU LEAVE ME JUST ONE THING?
Um, ARE YOU GOING TO LET ME FALL OFF THE ROOF?
NO. BUT I EFFING COULD HAVE.
LET'S LEAVE WHILE WE'RE ALL STILL BREATHING.

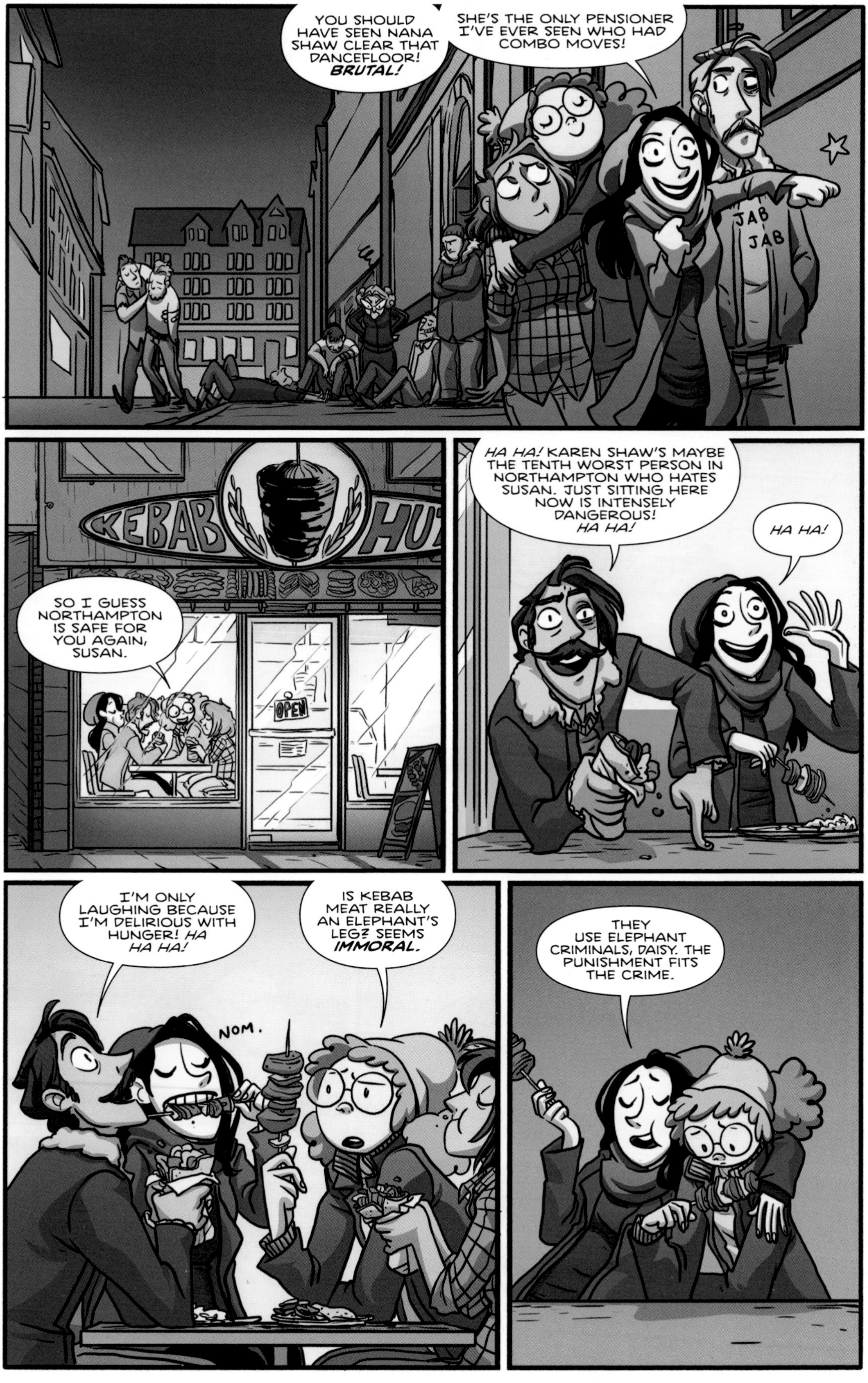
YOU SHOULD HAVE SEEN NANA SHAW CLEAR THAT DANCEFLOOR! ***BRUTAL!***
SHE'S THE ONLY PENSIONER I'VE EVER SEEN WHO HAD COMBO MOVES!
JAB JAB
KEBAB HUT
SO I GUESS NORTHAMPTON IS SAFE FOR YOU AGAIN, SUSAN.
OPEN
HA HA! KAREN SHAW'S MAYBE THE TENTH WORST PERSON IN NORTHAMPTON WHO HATES SUSAN. JUST SITTING HERE NOW IS INTENSELY DANGEROUS! *HA HA!*
HA HA!
I'M ONLY LAUGHING BECAUSE I'M DELIRIOUS WITH HUNGER! *HA HA HA!*
NOM.
IS KEBAB MEAT REALLY AN ELEPHANT'S LEG? SEEMS ***IMMORAL.***
THEY USE ELEPHANT CRIMINALS, DAISY. THE PUNISHMENT FITS THE CRIME.

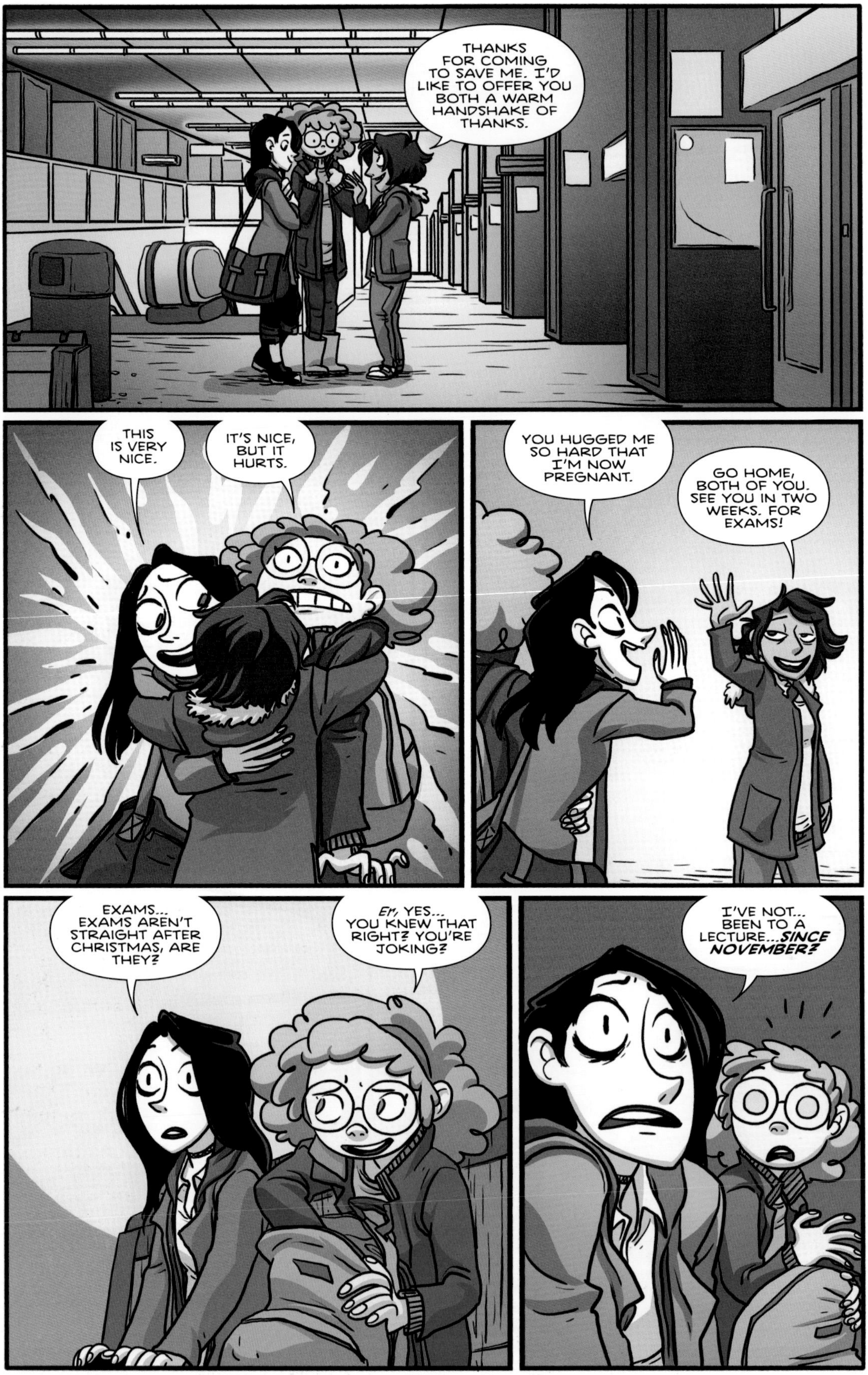
THANKS FOR COMING TO SAVE ME. I'D LIKE TO OFFER YOU BOTH A WARM HANDSHAKE OF THANKS.
THIS IS VERY NICE.
IT'S NICE, BUT IT HURTS.
YOU HUGGED ME SO HARD THAT I'M NOW PREGNANT.
GO HOME, BOTH OF YOU. SEE YOU IN TWO WEEKS. FOR EXAMS!
EXAMS... EXAMS AREN'T STRAIGHT AFTER CHRISTMAS, ARE THEY?
Er, YES... YOU KNEW THAT RIGHT? YOU'RE JOKING?
I'VE NOT... BEEN TO A LECTURE... ***SINCE NOVEMBER?***

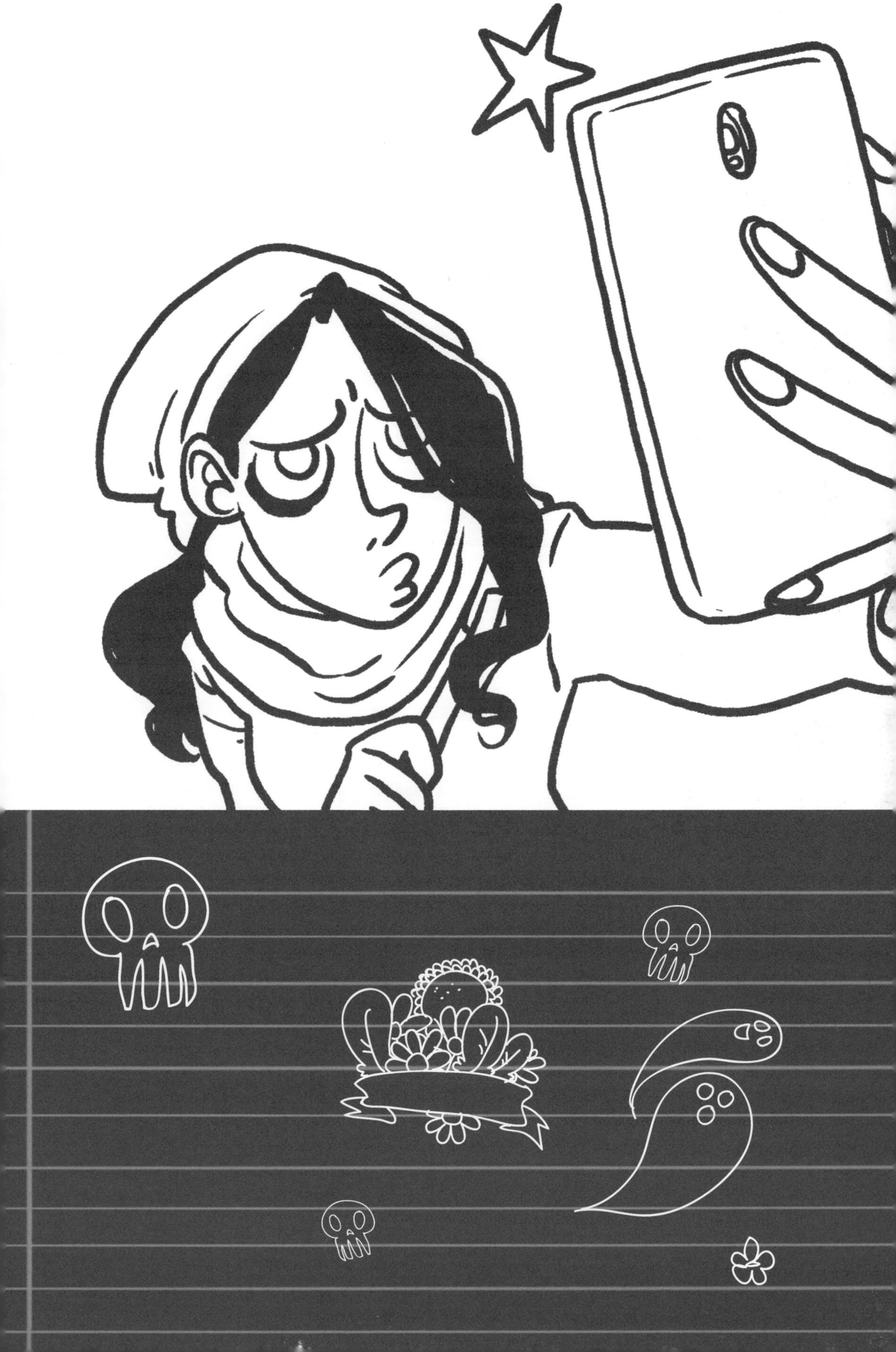

CHAPTER
SEVEN

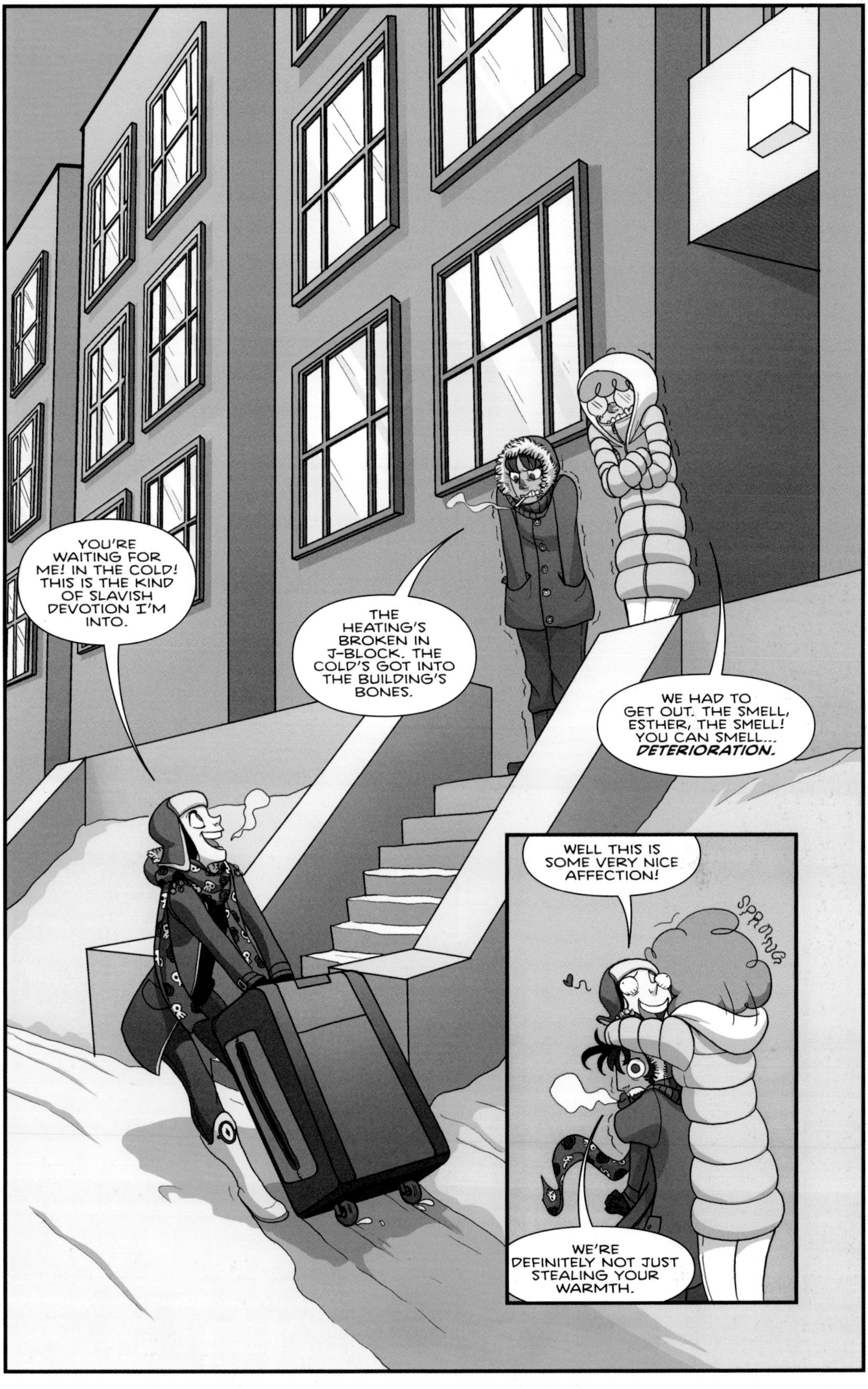
YOU'RE WAITING FOR ME! IN THE COLD! THIS IS THE KIND OF SLAVISH DEVOTION I'M INTO.
THE HEATING'S BROKEN IN J-BLOCK. THE COLD'S GOT INTO THE BUILDING'S BONES.
WE HAD TO GET OUT. THE SMELL, ESTHER, THE SMELL! YOU CAN SMELL... ***DETERIORATION.***
WELL THIS IS SOME VERY NICE AFFECTION!
SPRONG
WE'RE DEFINITELY NOT JUST STEALING YOUR WARMTH.

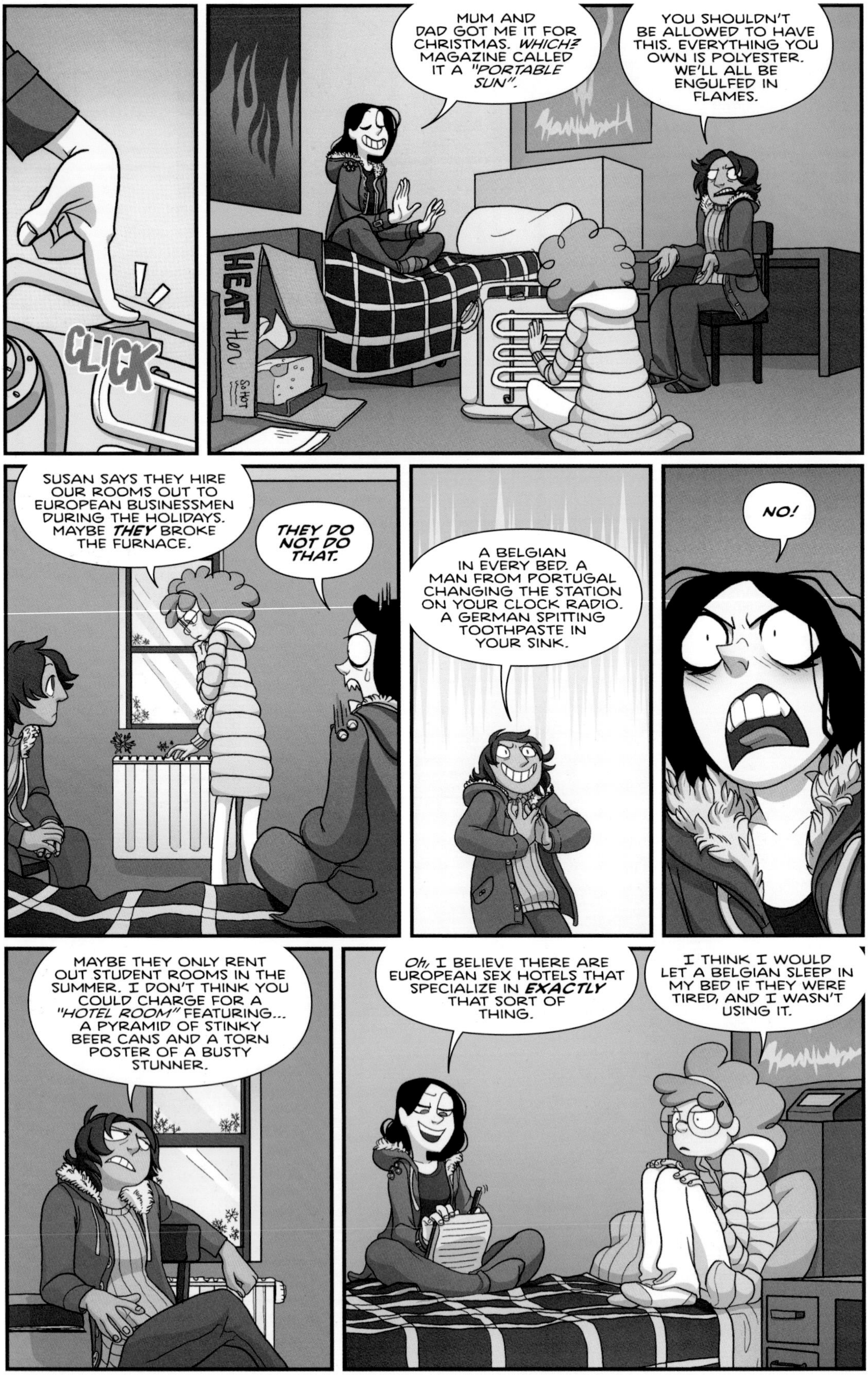
CLICK
MUM AND DAD GOT ME IT FOR CHRISTMAS. *WHICH?* MAGAZINE CALLED IT A *"PORTABLE SUN"*.
YOU SHOULDN'T BE ALLOWED TO HAVE THIS. EVERYTHING YOU OWN IS POLYESTER. WE'LL ALL BE ENGULFED IN FLAMES.
HEAT
SUSAN SAYS THEY HIRE OUR ROOMS OUT TO EUROPEAN BUSINESSMEN DURING THE HOLIDAYS. MAYBE ***THEY*** BROKE THE FURNACE.
THEY DO NOT DO THAT.
A BELGIAN IN EVERY BED. A MAN FROM PORTUGAL CHANGING THE STATION ON YOUR CLOCK RADIO. A GERMAN SPITTING TOOTHPASTE IN YOUR SINK.
NO!
MAYBE THEY ONLY RENT OUT STUDENT ROOMS IN THE SUMMER. I DON'T THINK YOU COULD CHARGE FOR A *"HOTEL ROOM"* FEATURING... A PYRAMID OF STINKY BEER CANS AND A TORN POSTER OF A BUSTY STUNNER.
Oh, I BELIEVE THERE ARE EUROPEAN SEX HOTELS THAT SPECIALIZE IN ***EXACTLY*** THAT SORT OF THING.
I THINK I WOULD LET A BELGIAN SLEEP IN MY BED IF THEY WERE TIRED, AND I WASN'T USING IT.

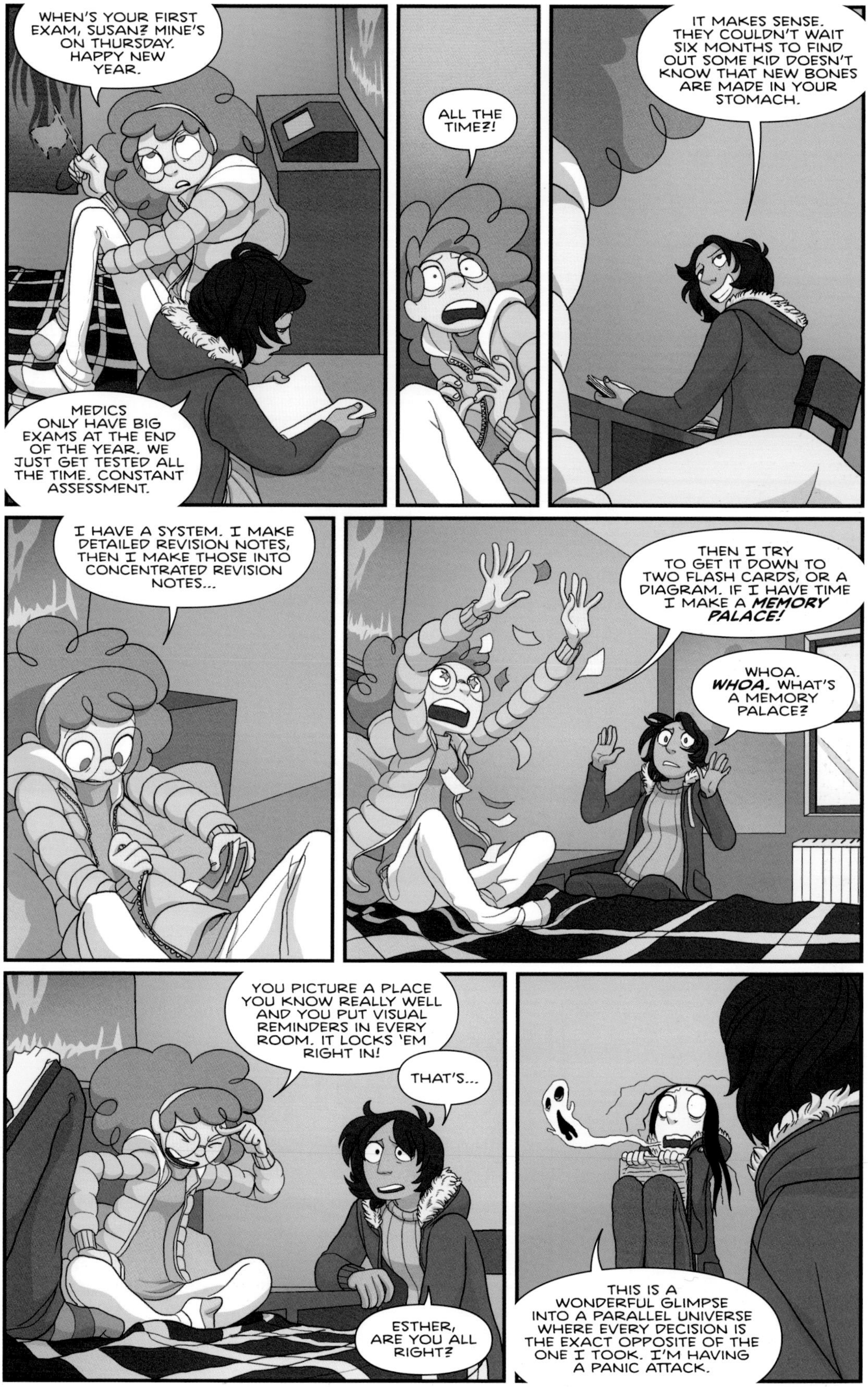
WHEN'S YOUR FIRST EXAM, SUSAN? MINE'S ON THURSDAY. HAPPY NEW YEAR.
MEDICS ONLY HAVE BIG EXAMS AT THE END OF THE YEAR. WE JUST GET TESTED ALL THE TIME. CONSTANT ASSESSMENT.
ALL THE TIME?!
IT MAKES SENSE. THEY COULDN'T WAIT SIX MONTHS TO FIND OUT SOME KID DOESN'T KNOW THAT NEW BONES ARE MADE IN YOUR STOMACH.
I HAVE A SYSTEM. I MAKE DETAILED REVISION NOTES, THEN I MAKE THOSE INTO CONCENTRATED REVISION NOTES...
THEN I TRY TO GET IT DOWN TO TWO FLASH CARDS, OR A DIAGRAM. IF I HAVE TIME I MAKE A ***MEMORY PALACE!***
WHOA. ***WHOA.*** WHAT'S A MEMORY PALACE?
YOU PICTURE A PLACE YOU KNOW REALLY WELL AND YOU PUT VISUAL REMINDERS IN EVERY ROOM. IT LOCKS 'EM RIGHT IN!
THAT'S...
ESTHER, ARE YOU ALL RIGHT?
THIS IS A WONDERFUL GLIMPSE INTO A PARALLEL UNIVERSE WHERE EVERY DECISION IS THE EXACT OPPOSITE OF THE ONE I TOOK. I'M HAVING A PANIC ATTACK.

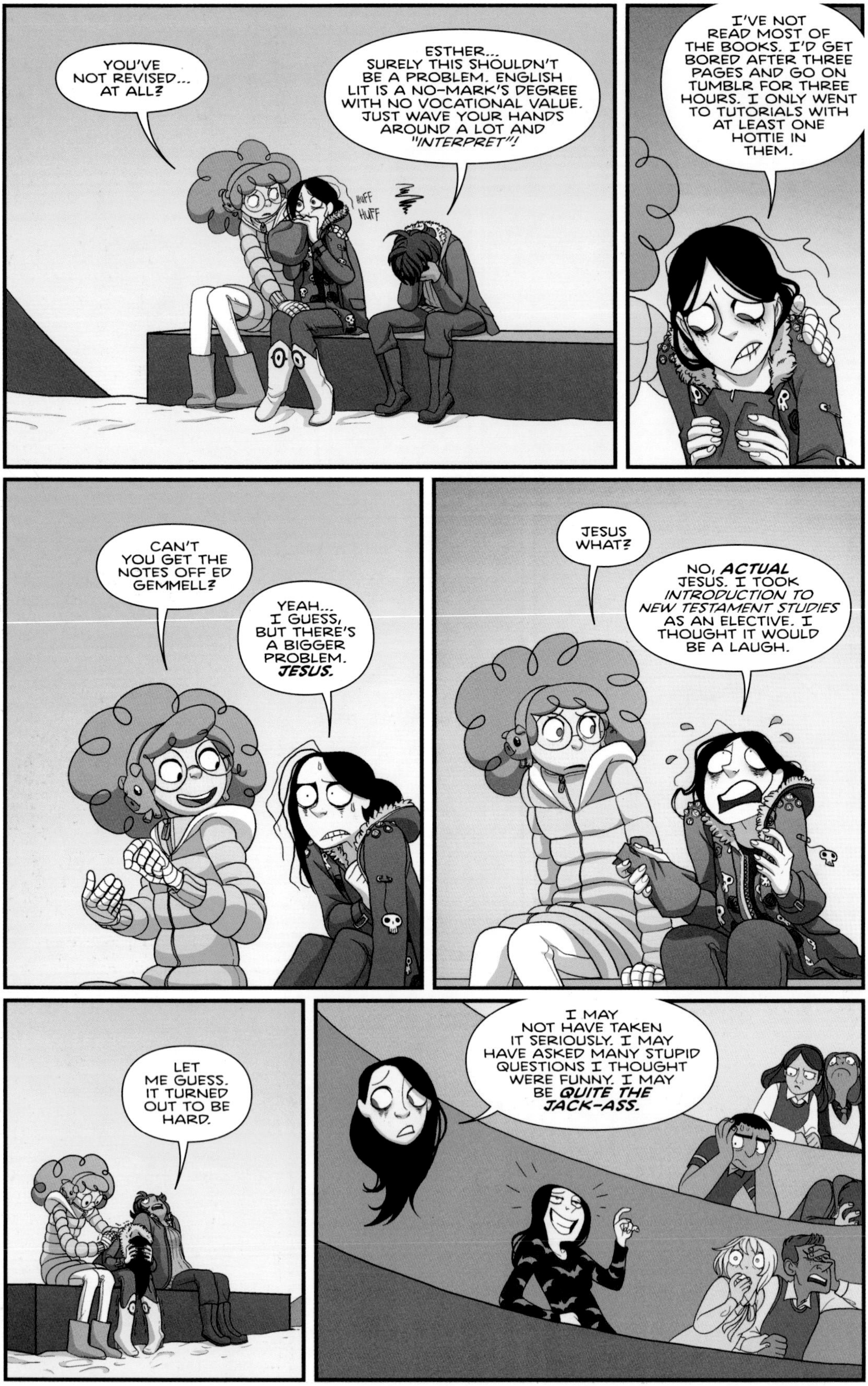

YOU'VE NOT REVISED... AT ALL?
ESTHER... SURELY THIS SHOULDN'T BE A PROBLEM. ENGLISH LIT IS A NO-MARK'S DEGREE WITH NO VOCATIONAL VALUE. JUST WAVE YOUR HANDS AROUND A LOT AND *"INTERPRET"!*
HUFF HUFF
I'VE NOT READ MOST OF THE BOOKS. I'D GET BORED AFTER THREE PAGES AND GO ON TUMBLR FOR THREE HOURS. I ONLY WENT TO TUTORIALS WITH AT LEAST ONE HOTTIE IN THEM.
CAN'T YOU GET THE NOTES OFF ED GEMMELL?
YEAH... I GUESS, BUT THERE'S A BIGGER PROBLEM. ***JESUS.***
JESUS WHAT?
NO, ***ACTUAL*** JESUS. I TOOK *INTRODUCTION TO NEW TESTAMENT STUDIES* AS AN ELECTIVE. I THOUGHT IT WOULD BE A LAUGH.
LET ME GUESS. IT TURNED OUT TO BE HARD.
I MAY NOT HAVE TAKEN IT SERIOUSLY. I MAY HAVE ASKED MANY STUPID QUESTIONS I THOUGHT WERE FUNNY. I MAY BE ***QUITE THE JACK-ASS.***

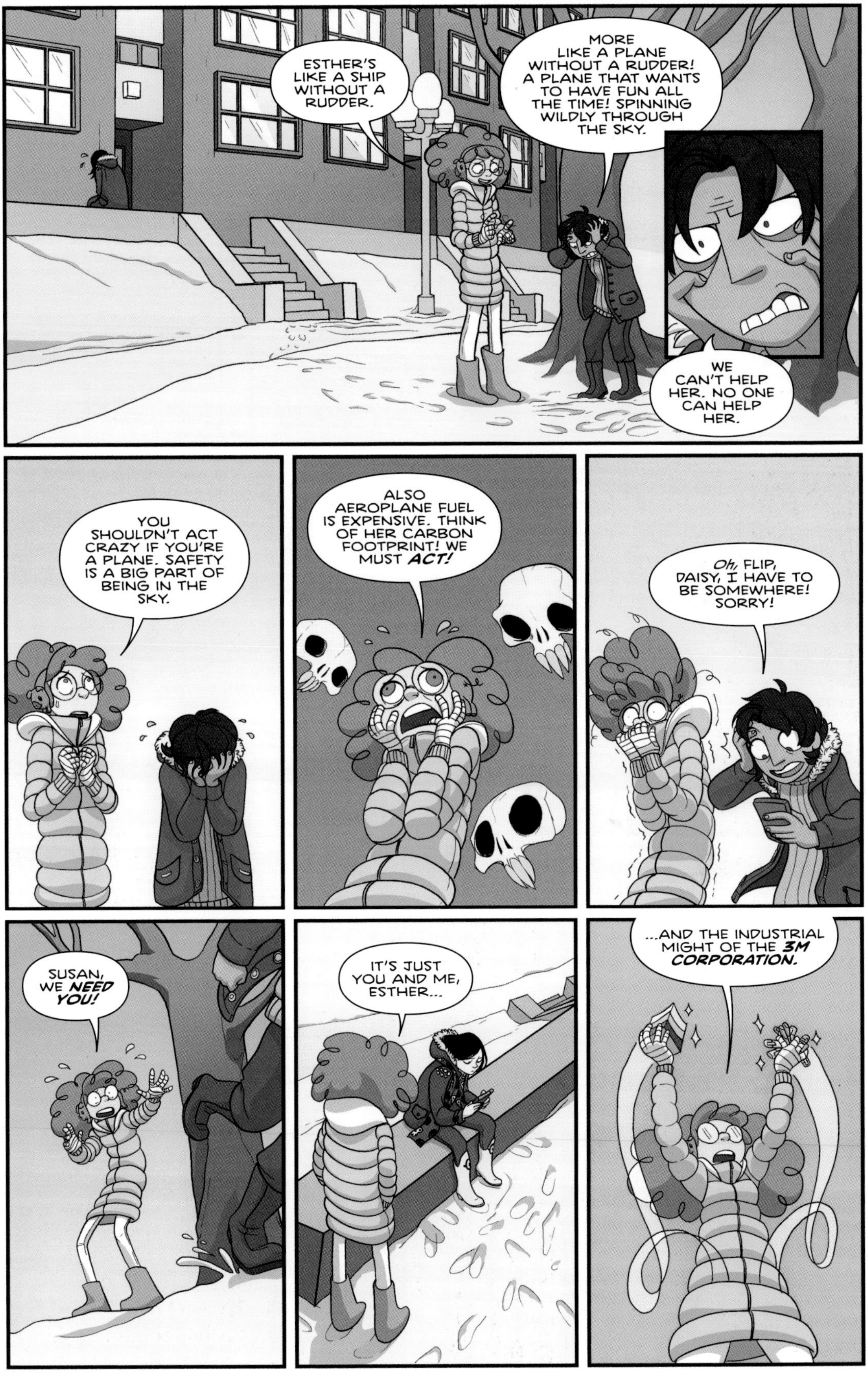

ESTHER'S LIKE A SHIP WITHOUT A RUDDER.
MORE LIKE A PLANE WITHOUT A RUDDER! A PLANE THAT WANTS TO HAVE FUN ALL THE TIME! SPINNING WILDLY THROUGH THE SKY.
WE CAN'T HELP HER. NO ONE CAN HELP HER.
YOU SHOULDN'T ACT CRAZY IF YOU'RE A PLANE. SAFETY IS A BIG PART OF BEING IN THE SKY.
ALSO AEROPLANE FUEL IS EXPENSIVE. THINK OF HER CARBON FOOTPRINT! WE MUST ACT!
Oh, FLIP, DAISY, I HAVE TO BE SOMEWHERE! SORRY!
SUSAN, WE NEED YOU!
IT'S JUST YOU AND ME, ESTHER...
...AND THE INDUSTRIAL MIGHT OF THE 3M CORPORATION.

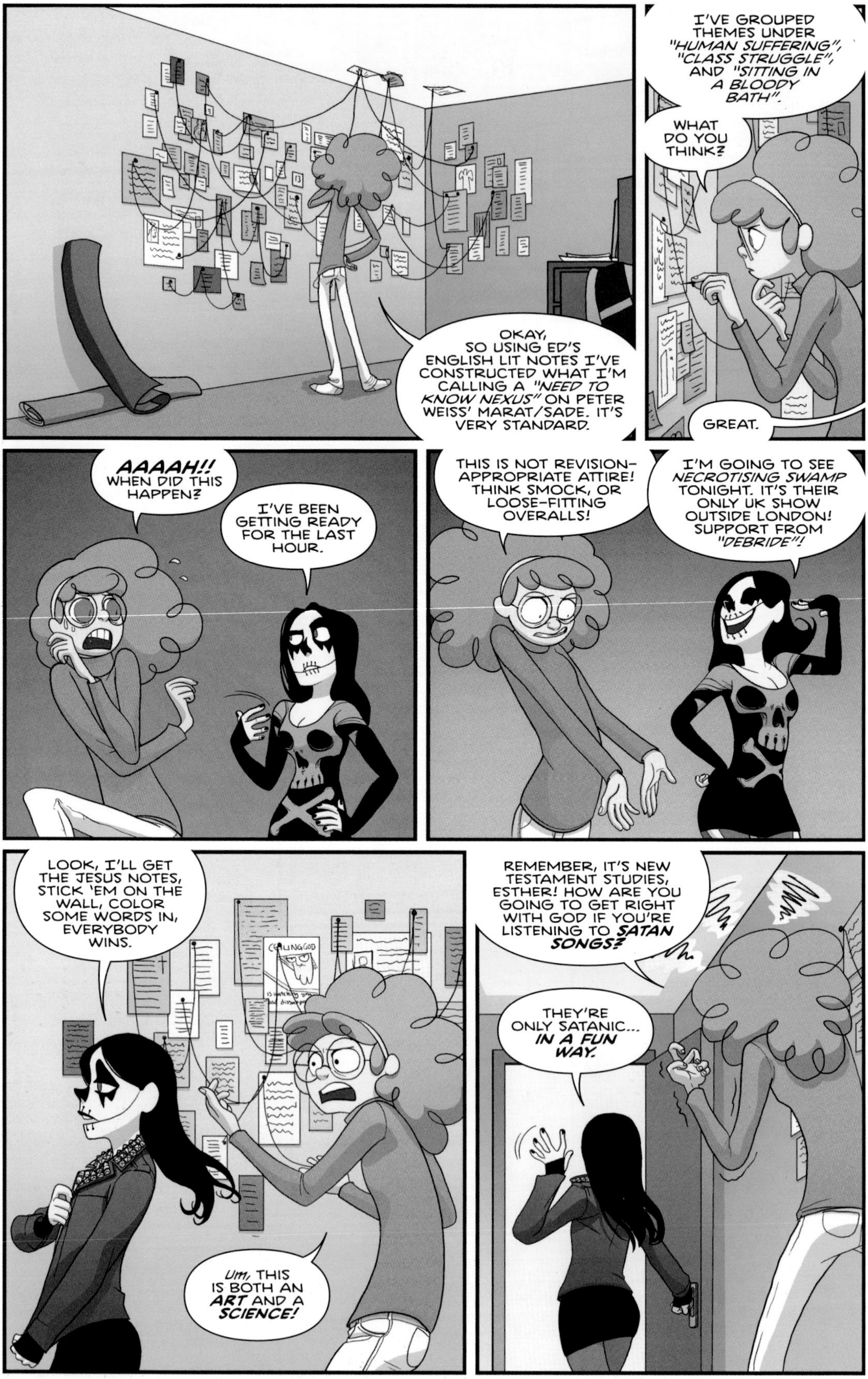
OKAY, SO USING ED'S ENGLISH LIT NOTES I'VE CONSTRUCTED WHAT I'M CALLING A "NEED TO KNOW NEXUS" ON PETER WEISS' MARAT/SADE. IT'S VERY STANDARD.
I'VE GROUPED THEMES UNDER "HUMAN SUFFERING", "CLASS STRUGGLE", AND "SITTING IN A BLOODY BATH".
WHAT DO YOU THINK?
GREAT.
AAAAH!! WHEN DID THIS HAPPEN?
I'VE BEEN GETTING READY FOR THE LAST HOUR.
THIS IS NOT REVISION-APPROPRIATE ATTIRE! THINK SMOCK, OR LOOSE-FITTING OVERALLS!
I'M GOING TO SEE NECROTISING SWAMP TONIGHT. IT'S THEIR ONLY UK SHOW OUTSIDE LONDON! SUPPORT FROM "DEBRIDE"!
LOOK, I'LL GET THE JESUS NOTES, STICK 'EM ON THE WALL, COLOR SOME WORDS IN, EVERYBODY WINS.
UM, THIS IS BOTH AN ART AND A SCIENCE!
REMEMBER, IT'S NEW TESTAMENT STUDIES, ESTHER! HOW ARE YOU GOING TO GET RIGHT WITH GOD IF YOU'RE LISTENING TO SATAN SONGS?
THEY'RE ONLY SATANIC... IN A FUN WAY.

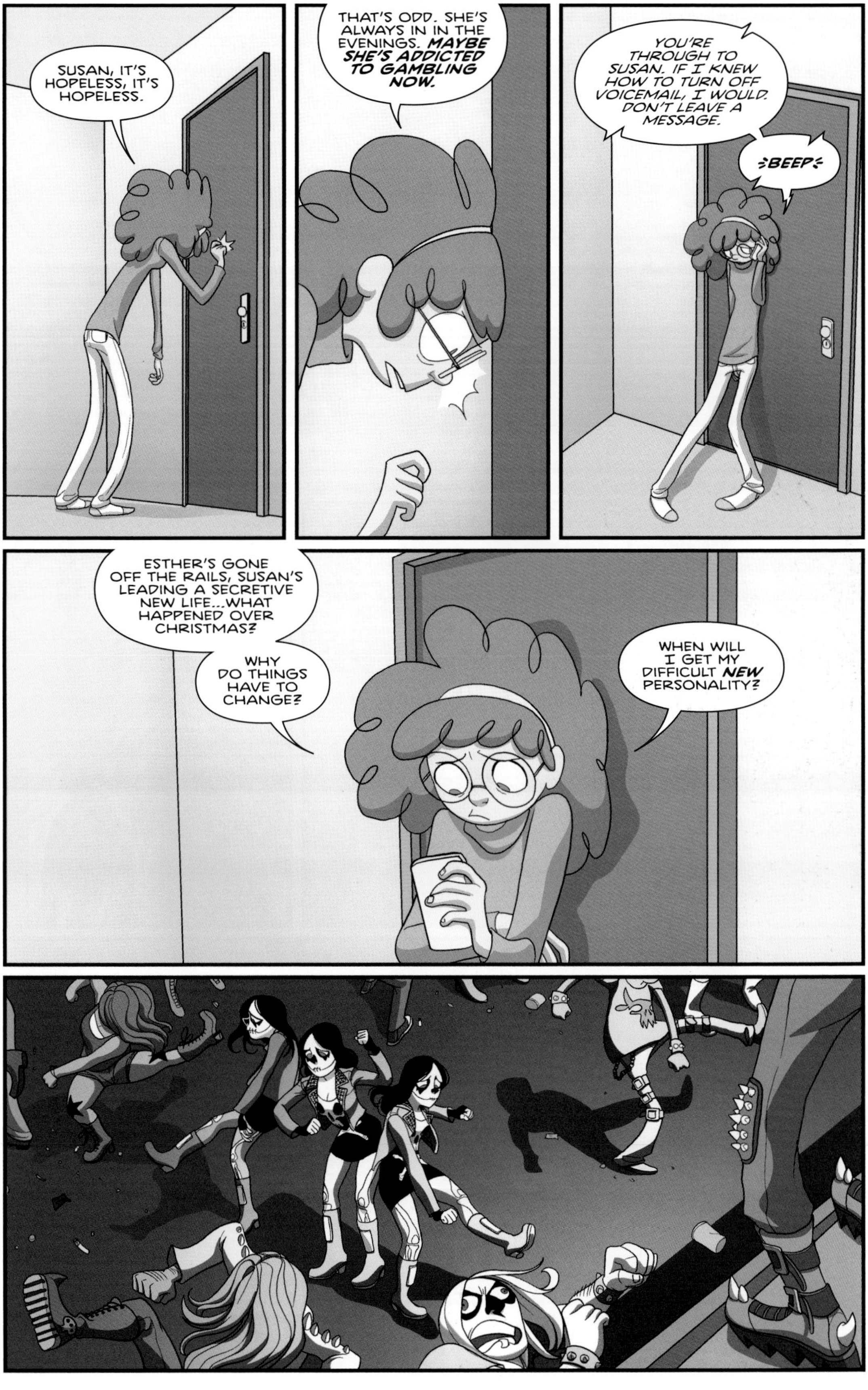
SUSAN, IT'S HOPELESS, IT'S HOPELESS.
THAT'S ODD. SHE'S ALWAYS IN IN THE EVENINGS. MAYBE SHE'S ADDICTED TO GAMBLING NOW.
YOU'RE THROUGH TO SUSAN. IF I KNEW HOW TO TURN OFF VOICEMAIL, I WOULD. DON'T LEAVE A MESSAGE.
BEEP
ESTHER'S GONE OFF THE RAILS, SUSAN'S LEADING A SECRETIVE NEW LIFE...WHAT HAPPENED OVER CHRISTMAS?
WHY DO THINGS HAVE TO CHANGE?
WHEN WILL I GET MY DIFFICULT NEW PERSONALITY?

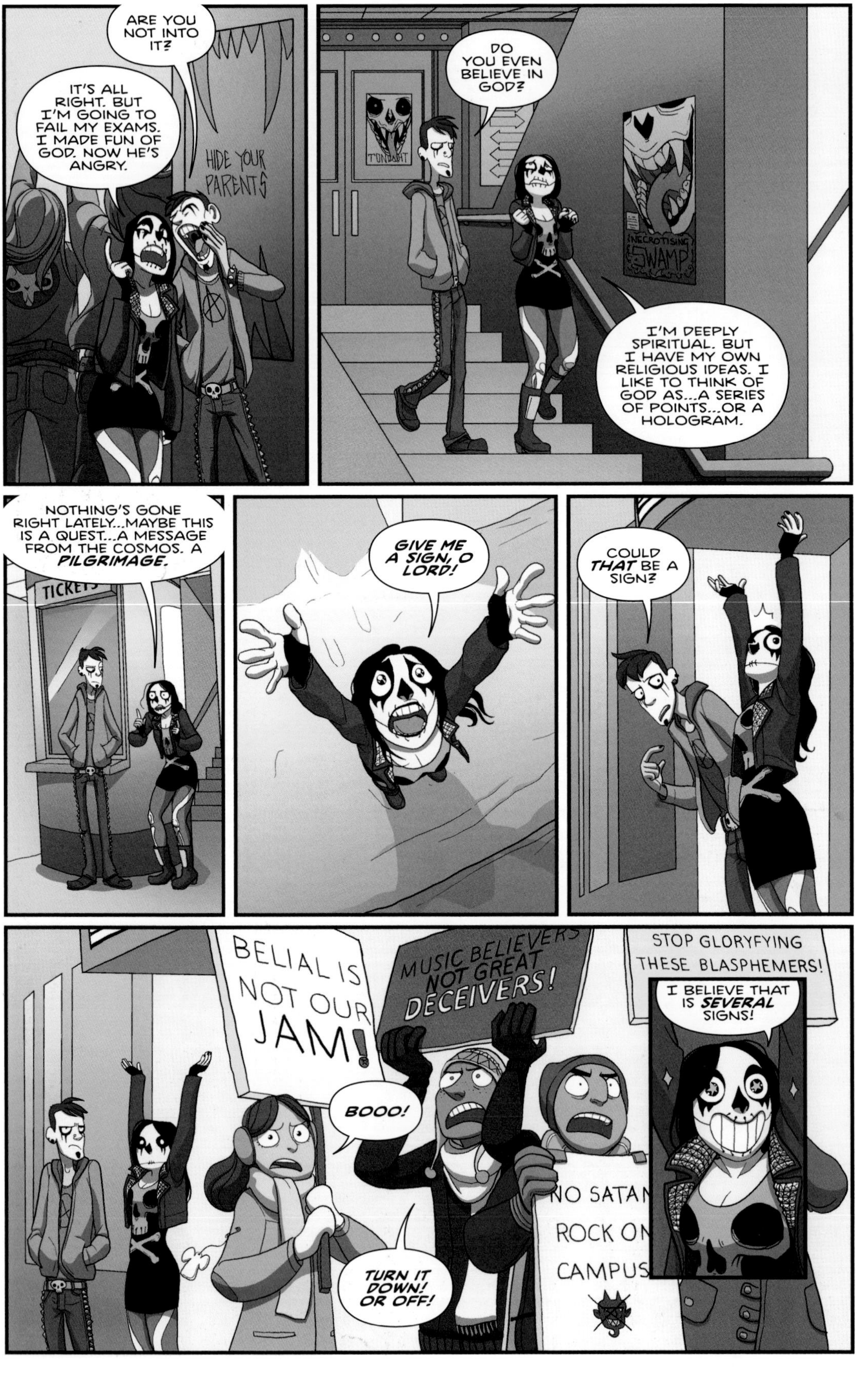
ARE YOU NOT INTO IT?
IT'S ALL RIGHT. BUT I'M GOING TO FAIL MY EXAMS. I MADE FUN OF GOD. NOW HE'S ANGRY.
HIDE YOUR PARENTS
DO YOU EVEN BELIEVE IN GOD?
TONIGHT
NECROTISING SWAMP
I'M DEEPLY SPIRITUAL. BUT I HAVE MY OWN RELIGIOUS IDEAS. I LIKE TO THINK OF GOD AS...A SERIES OF POINTS...OR A HOLOGRAM.
NOTHING'S GONE RIGHT LATELY...MAYBE THIS IS A QUEST...A MESSAGE FROM THE COSMOS. A *PILGRIMAGE.*
TICKETS
GIVE ME A SIGN, O LORD!
COULD *THAT* BE A SIGN?
BELIAL IS NOT OUR JAM!
MUSIC BELIEVERS NOT GREAT DECEIVERS!
STOP GLORYFYING THESE BLASPHEMERS!
I BELIEVE THAT IS *SEVERAL* SIGNS!
BOOO!
NO SATAN ROCK ON CAMPUS
TURN IT DOWN! OR OFF!

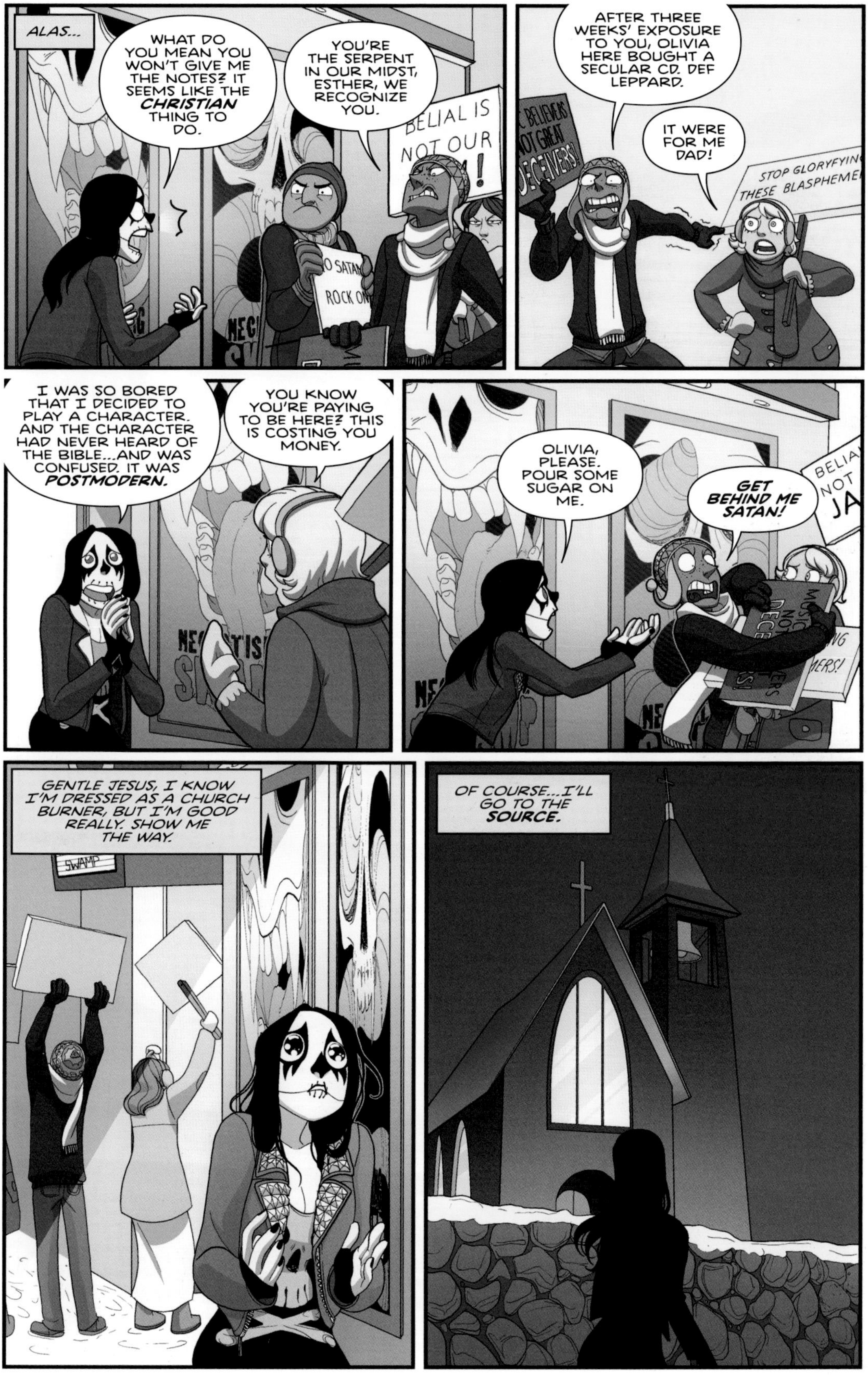

ALAS...
WHAT DO YOU MEAN YOU WON'T GIVE ME THE NOTES? IT SEEMS LIKE THE CHRISTIAN THING TO DO.
YOU'RE THE SERPENT IN OUR MIDST, ESTHER, WE RECOGNIZE YOU.
BELIAL IS NOT OUR
ROCK ON
AFTER THREE WEEKS' EXPOSURE TO YOU, OLIVIA HERE BOUGHT A SECULAR CD. DEF LEPPARD.
IT WERE FOR ME DAD!
NOT GREAT DECEIVERS!
STOP GLORYFYING THESE BLASPHEME
I WAS SO BORED THAT I DECIDED TO PLAY A CHARACTER. AND THE CHARACTER HAD NEVER HEARD OF THE BIBLE...AND WAS CONFUSED. IT WAS POSTMODERN.
YOU KNOW YOU'RE PAYING TO BE HERE? THIS IS COSTING YOU MONEY.
OLIVIA, PLEASE. POUR SOME SUGAR ON ME.
GET BEHIND ME SATAN!
GENTLE JESUS, I KNOW I'M DRESSED AS A CHURCH BURNER, BUT I'M GOOD REALLY. SHOW ME THE WAY.
SWAMP
OF COURSE...I'LL GO TO THE SOURCE.

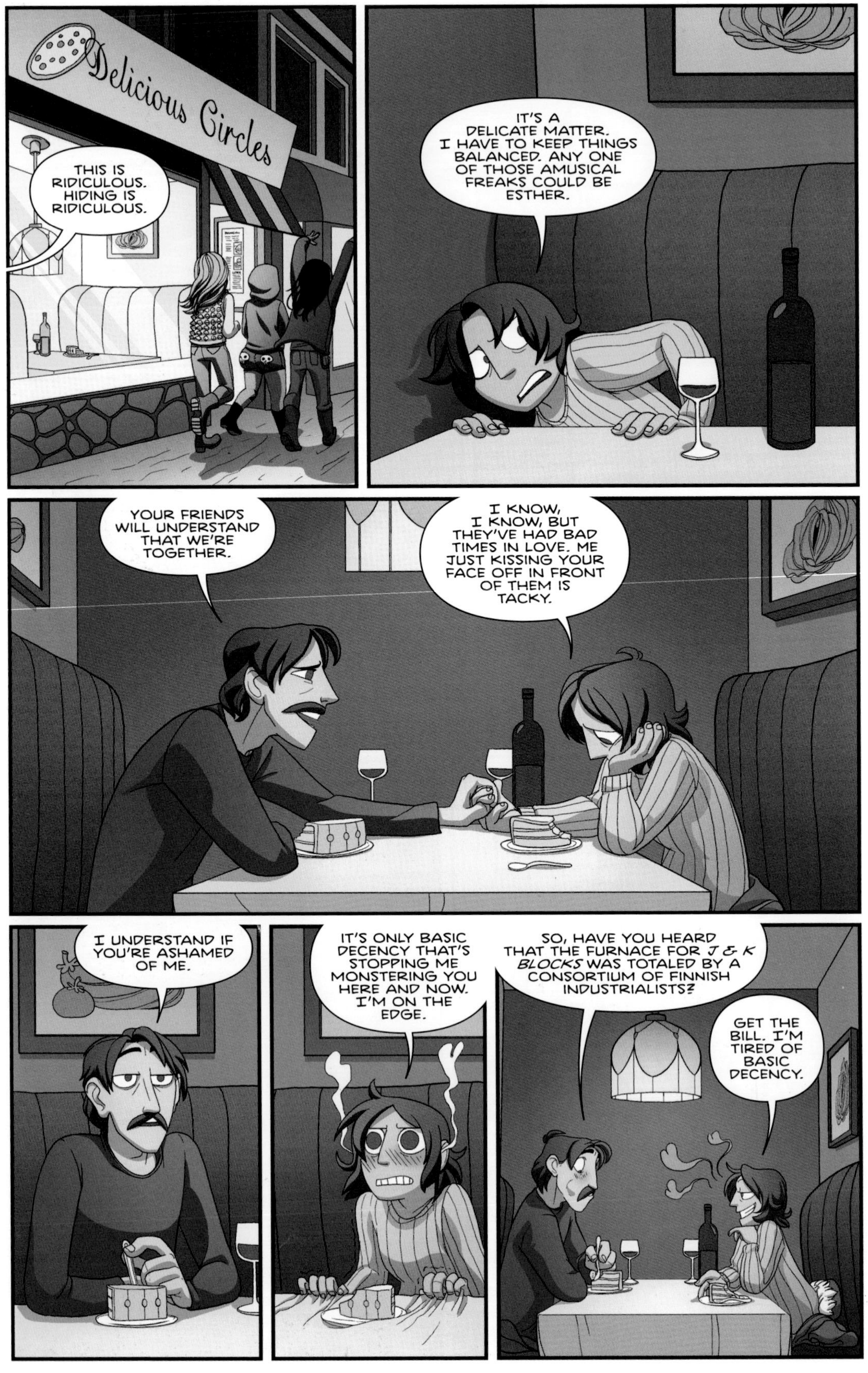
Delicious Circles
THIS IS RIDICULOUS. HIDING IS RIDICULOUS.
IT'S A DELICATE MATTER. I HAVE TO KEEP THINGS BALANCED. ANY ONE OF THOSE AMUSICAL FREAKS COULD BE ESTHER.
YOUR FRIENDS WILL UNDERSTAND THAT WE'RE TOGETHER.
I KNOW, I KNOW, BUT THEY'VE HAD BAD TIMES IN LOVE. ME JUST KISSING YOUR FACE OFF IN FRONT OF THEM IS TACKY.
I UNDERSTAND IF YOU'RE ASHAMED OF ME.
IT'S ONLY BASIC DECENCY THAT'S STOPPING ME MONSTERING YOU HERE AND NOW. I'M ON THE EDGE.
SO, HAVE YOU HEARD THAT THE FURNACE FOR *J & K BLOCKS* WAS TOTALED BY A CONSORTIUM OF FINNISH INDUSTRIALISTS?
GET THE BILL. I'M TIRED OF BASIC DECENCY.

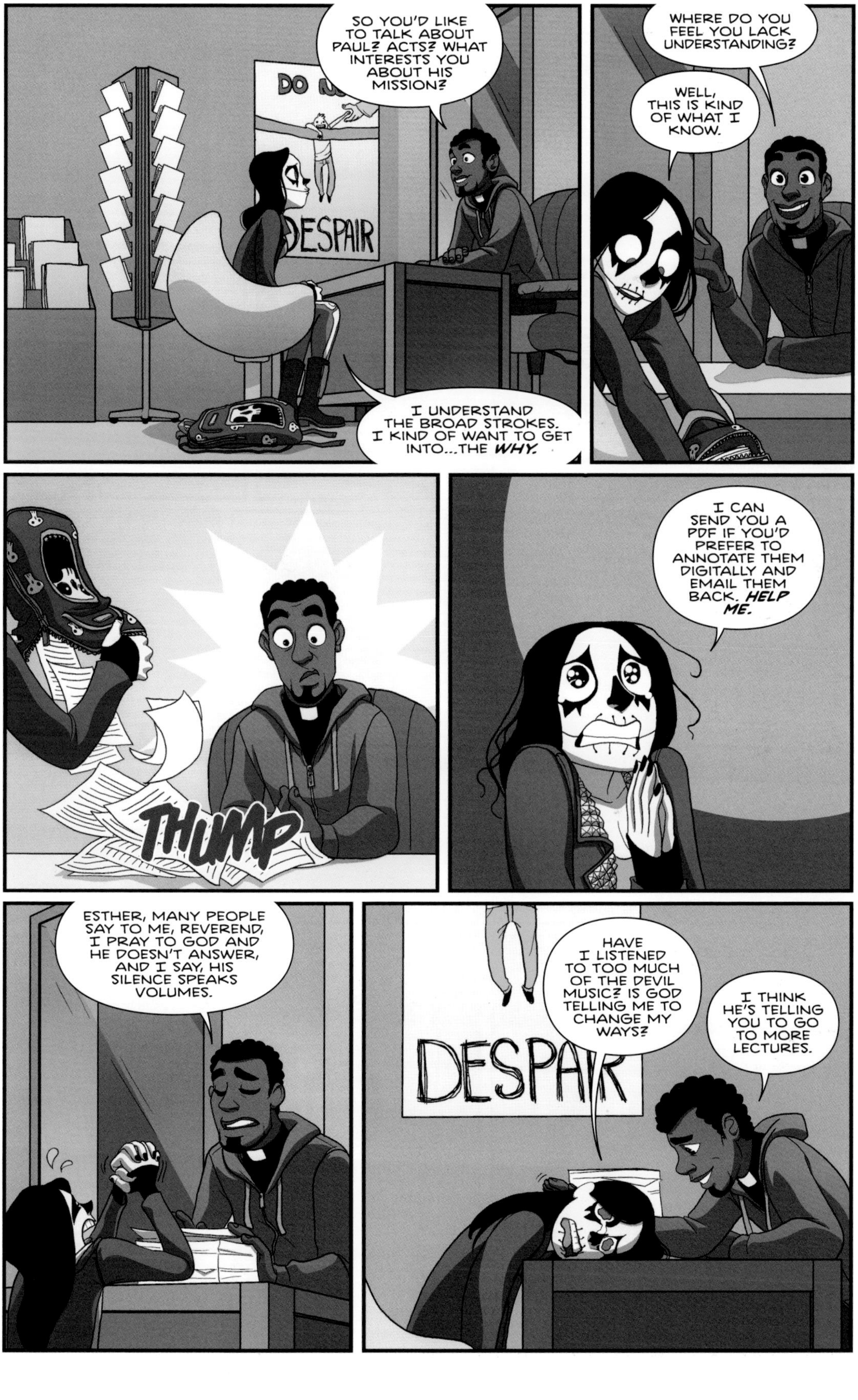
SO YOU'D LIKE TO TALK ABOUT PAUL? ACTS? WHAT INTERESTS YOU ABOUT HIS MISSION?
DO
DESPAIR
I UNDERSTAND THE BROAD STROKES. I KIND OF WANT TO GET INTO...THE WHY.
WHERE DO YOU FEEL YOU LACK UNDERSTANDING?
WELL, THIS IS KIND OF WHAT I KNOW.
THUMP
I CAN SEND YOU A PDF IF YOU'D PREFER TO ANNOTATE THEM DIGITALLY AND EMAIL THEM BACK. HELP ME.
ESTHER, MANY PEOPLE SAY TO ME, REVEREND, I PRAY TO GOD AND HE DOESN'T ANSWER, AND I SAY, HIS SILENCE SPEAKS VOLUMES.
DESPAIR
HAVE I LISTENED TO TOO MUCH OF THE DEVIL MUSIC? IS GOD TELLING ME TO CHANGE MY WAYS?
I THINK HE'S TELLING YOU TO GO TO MORE LECTURES.

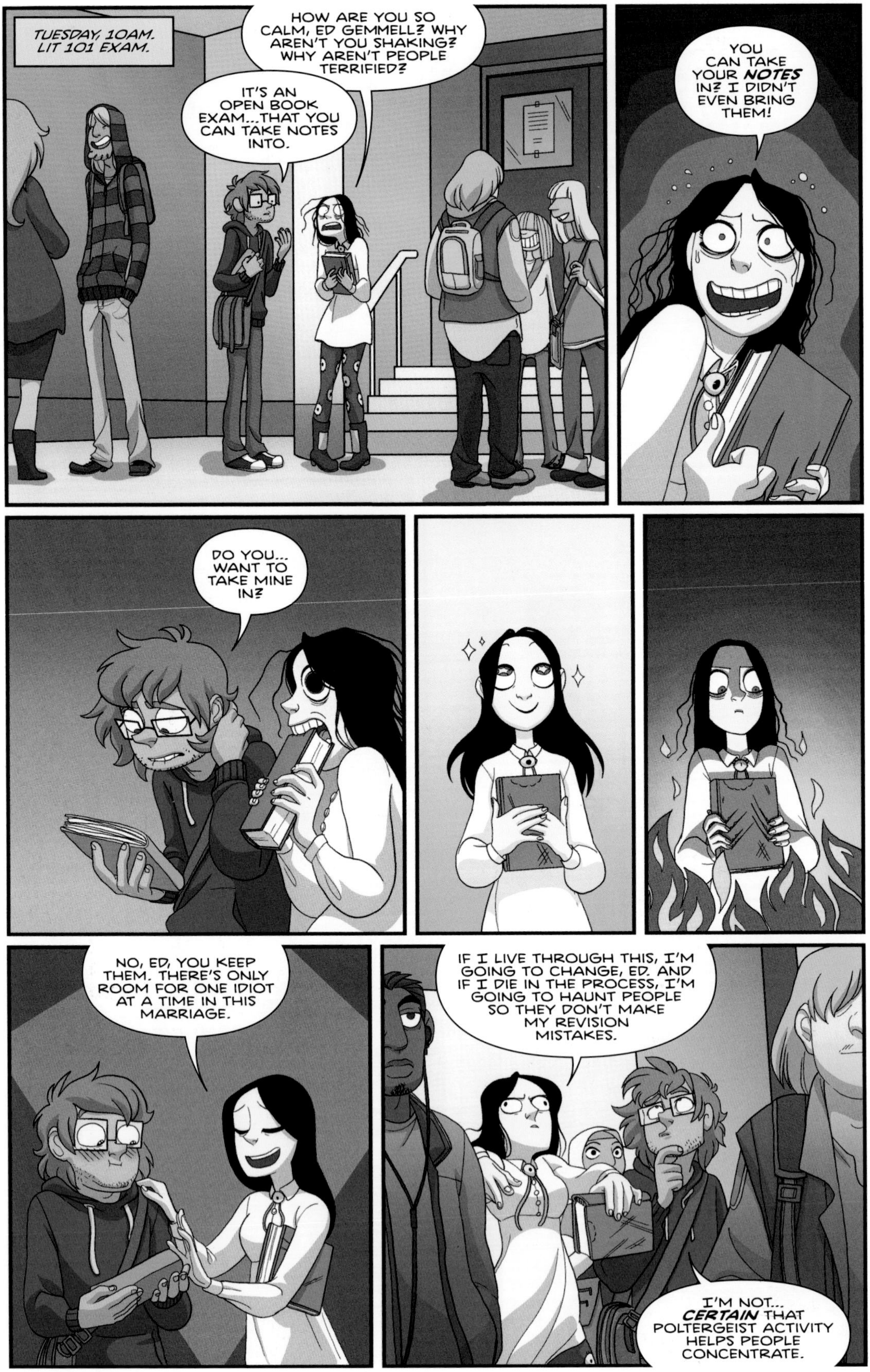
TUESDAY, 10AM. LIT 101 EXAM.
HOW ARE YOU SO CALM, ED GEMMELL? WHY AREN'T YOU SHAKING? WHY AREN'T PEOPLE TERRIFIED?
IT'S AN OPEN BOOK EXAM...THAT YOU CAN TAKE NOTES INTO.
YOU CAN TAKE YOUR NOTES IN? I DIDN'T EVEN BRING THEM!
DO YOU... WANT TO TAKE MINE IN?
NO, ED, YOU KEEP THEM. THERE'S ONLY ROOM FOR ONE IDIOT AT A TIME IN THIS MARRIAGE.
IF I LIVE THROUGH THIS, I'M GOING TO CHANGE, ED. AND IF I DIE IN THE PROCESS, I'M GOING TO HAUNT PEOPLE SO THEY DON'T MAKE MY REVISION MISTAKES.
I'M NOT... CERTAIN THAT POLTERGEIST ACTIVITY HELPS PEOPLE CONCENTRATE.

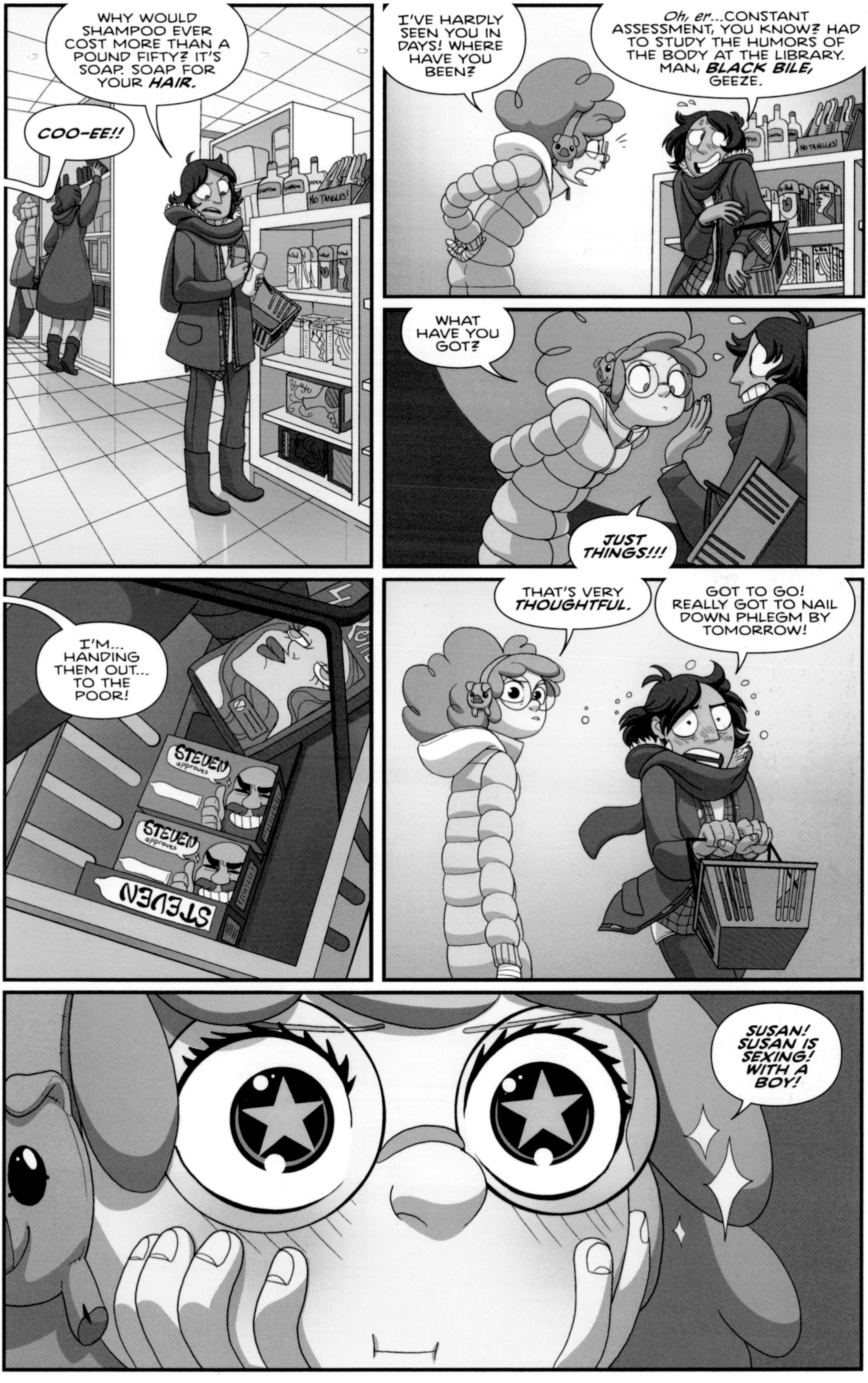
WHY WOULD SHAMPOO EVER COST MORE THAN A POUND FIFTY? IT'S SOAP. SOAP FOR YOUR HAIR.
COO-EE!!
NO TANGLES!
I'VE HARDLY SEEN YOU IN DAYS! WHERE HAVE YOU BEEN?
Oh, er... CONSTANT ASSESSMENT, YOU KNOW? HAD TO STUDY THE HUMORS OF THE BODY AT THE LIBRARY. MAN, BLACK BILE, GEEZE.
NO TANGLES!
WHAT HAVE YOU GOT?
JUST THINGS!!!
I'M... HANDING THEM OUT... TO THE POOR!
STEVEN approves
STEVEN approves
STEVEN
THAT'S VERY THOUGHTFUL.
GOT TO GO! REALLY GOT TO NAIL DOWN PHLEGM BY TOMORROW!
SUSAN! SUSAN IS SEXING! WITH A BOY!

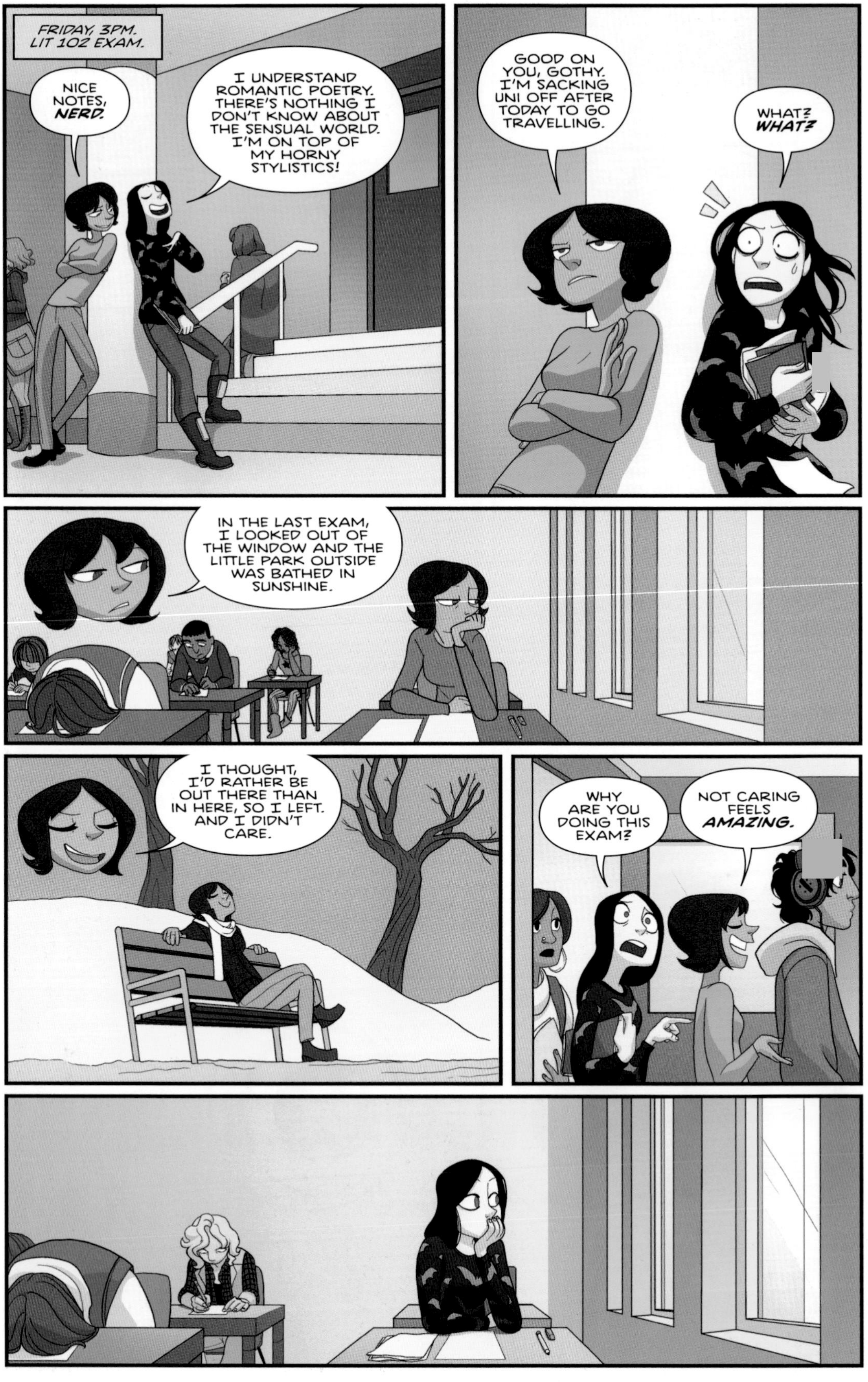
FRIDAY, 3PM. LIT 102 EXAM.
NICE NOTES, NERD.
I UNDERSTAND ROMANTIC POETRY. THERE'S NOTHING I DON'T KNOW ABOUT THE SENSUAL WORLD. I'M ON TOP OF MY HORNY STYLISTICS!
GOOD ON YOU, GOTHY. I'M SACKING UNI OFF AFTER TODAY TO GO TRAVELLING.
WHAT? WHAT?
IN THE LAST EXAM, I LOOKED OUT OF THE WINDOW AND THE LITTLE PARK OUTSIDE WAS BATHED IN SUNSHINE.
I THOUGHT, I'D RATHER BE OUT THERE THAN IN HERE, SO I LEFT. AND I DIDN'T CARE.
WHY ARE YOU DOING THIS EXAM?
NOT CARING FEELS AMAZING.

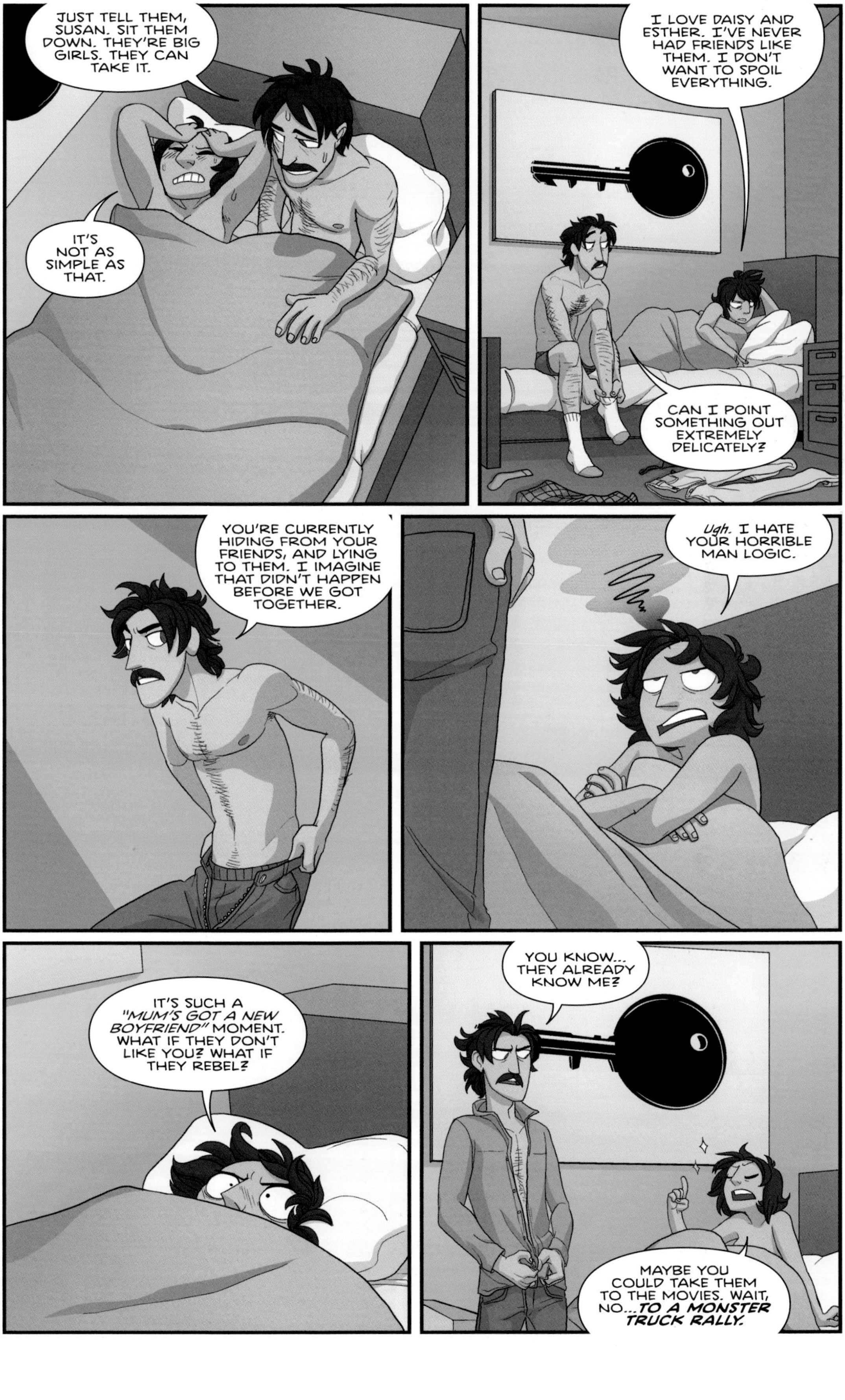
JUST TELL THEM, SUSAN. SIT THEM DOWN. THEY'RE BIG GIRLS. THEY CAN TAKE IT.
IT'S NOT AS SIMPLE AS THAT.
I LOVE DAISY AND ESTHER. I'VE NEVER HAD FRIENDS LIKE THEM. I DON'T WANT TO SPOIL EVERYTHING.
CAN I POINT SOMETHING OUT EXTREMELY DELICATELY?
YOU'RE CURRENTLY HIDING FROM YOUR FRIENDS, AND LYING TO THEM. I IMAGINE THAT DIDN'T HAPPEN BEFORE WE GOT TOGETHER.
Ugh. I HATE YOUR HORRIBLE MAN LOGIC.
IT'S SUCH A *"MUM'S GOT A NEW BOYFRIEND"* MOMENT. WHAT IF THEY DON'T LIKE YOU? WHAT IF THEY REBEL?
YOU KNOW... THEY ALREADY KNOW ME?
MAYBE YOU COULD TAKE THEM TO THE MOVIES. WAIT, NO... ***TO A MONSTER TRUCK RALLY.***

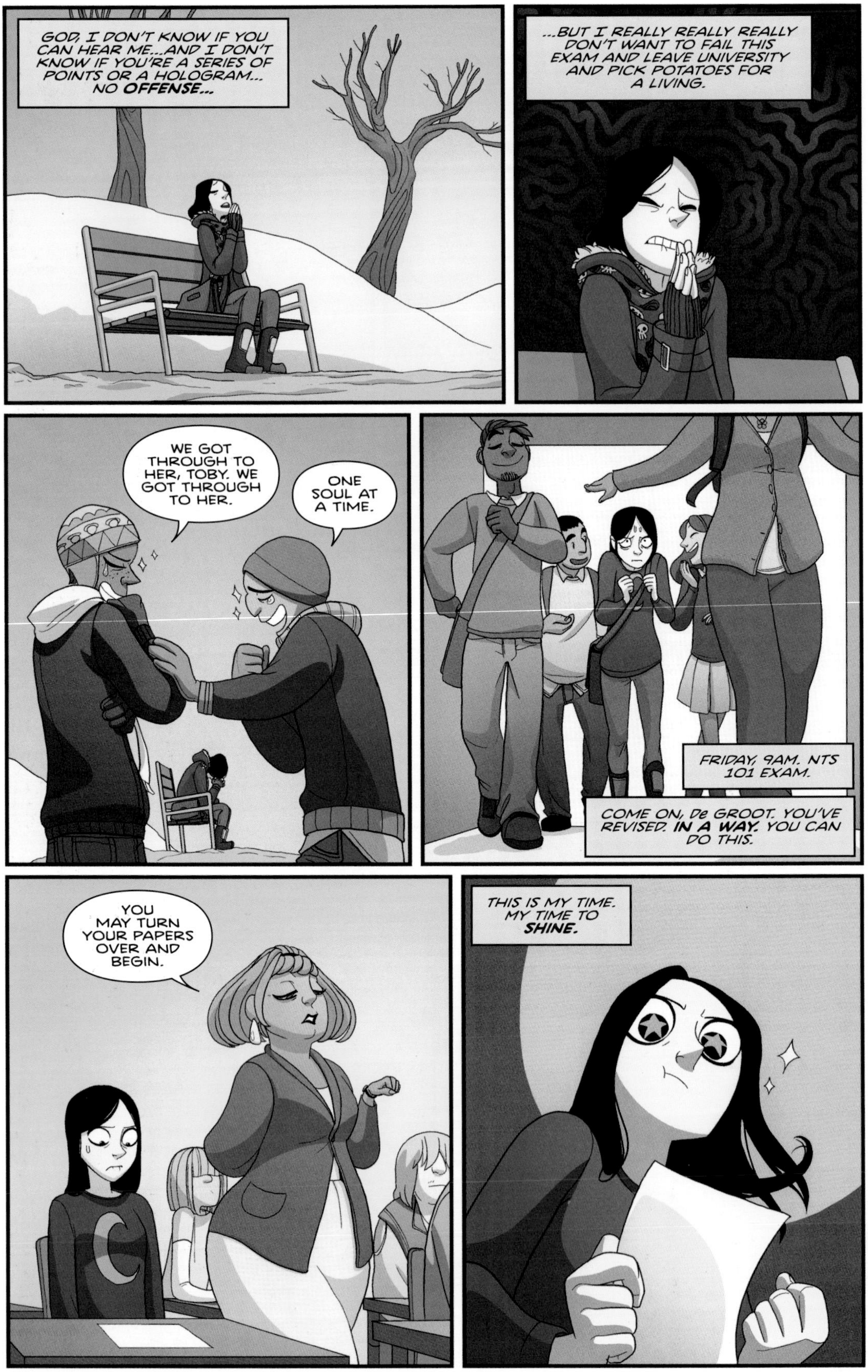
GOD, I DON'T KNOW IF YOU CAN HEAR ME...AND I DON'T KNOW IF YOU'RE A SERIES OF POINTS OR A HOLOGRAM... NO OFFENSE...
...BUT I REALLY REALLY REALLY DON'T WANT TO FAIL THIS EXAM AND LEAVE UNIVERSITY AND PICK POTATOES FOR A LIVING.
WE GOT THROUGH TO HER, TOBY. WE GOT THROUGH TO HER.
ONE SOUL AT A TIME.
FRIDAY, 9AM. NTS 101 EXAM.
COME ON, De GROOT. YOU'VE REVISED. IN A WAY. YOU CAN DO THIS.
YOU MAY TURN YOUR PAPERS OVER AND BEGIN.
THIS IS MY TIME. MY TIME TO SHINE.

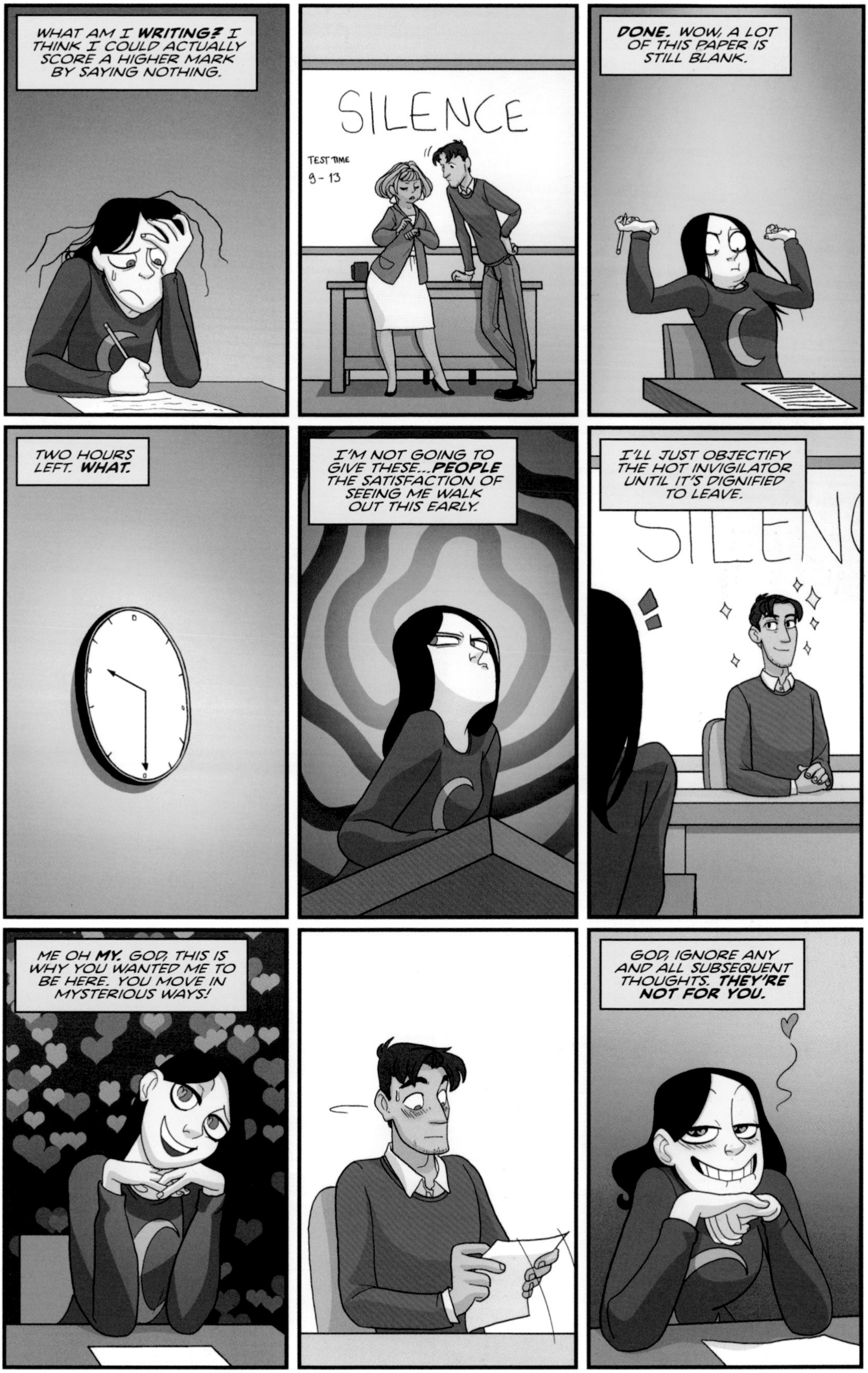
WHAT AM I **WRITING?** I THINK I COULD ACTUALLY SCORE A HIGHER MARK BY SAYING NOTHING.
SILENCE
TEST TIME 9 - 13
DONE. WOW, A LOT OF THIS PAPER IS STILL BLANK.
TWO HOURS LEFT. **WHAT.**
I'M NOT GOING TO GIVE THESE... **PEOPLE** THE SATISFACTION OF SEEING ME WALK OUT THIS EARLY.
I'LL JUST OBJECTIFY THE HOT INVIGILATOR UNTIL IT'S DIGNIFIED TO LEAVE.
ME OH **MY.** GOD, THIS IS WHY YOU WANTED ME TO BE HERE. YOU MOVE IN MYSTERIOUS WAYS!
GOD, IGNORE ANY AND ALL SUBSEQUENT THOUGHTS. **THEY'RE NOT FOR YOU.**

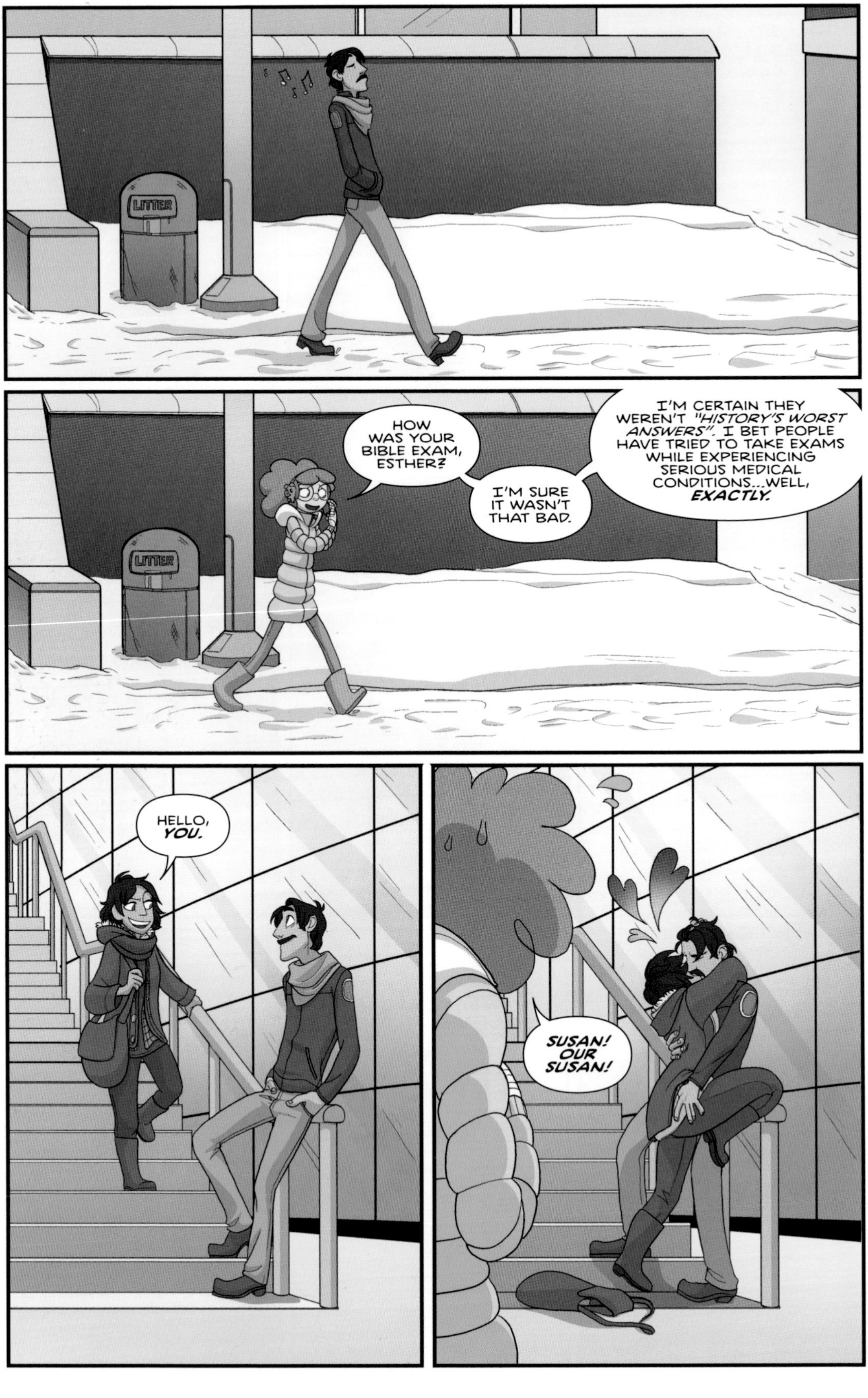
LITTER
HOW WAS YOUR BIBLE EXAM, ESTHER?
I'M SURE IT WASN'T THAT BAD.
I'M CERTAIN THEY WEREN'T "HISTORY'S WORST ANSWERS". I BET PEOPLE HAVE TRIED TO TAKE EXAMS WHILE EXPERIENCING SERIOUS MEDICAL CONDITIONS...WELL, EXACTLY.
LITTER
HELLO, YOU.
SUSAN! OUR SUSAN!

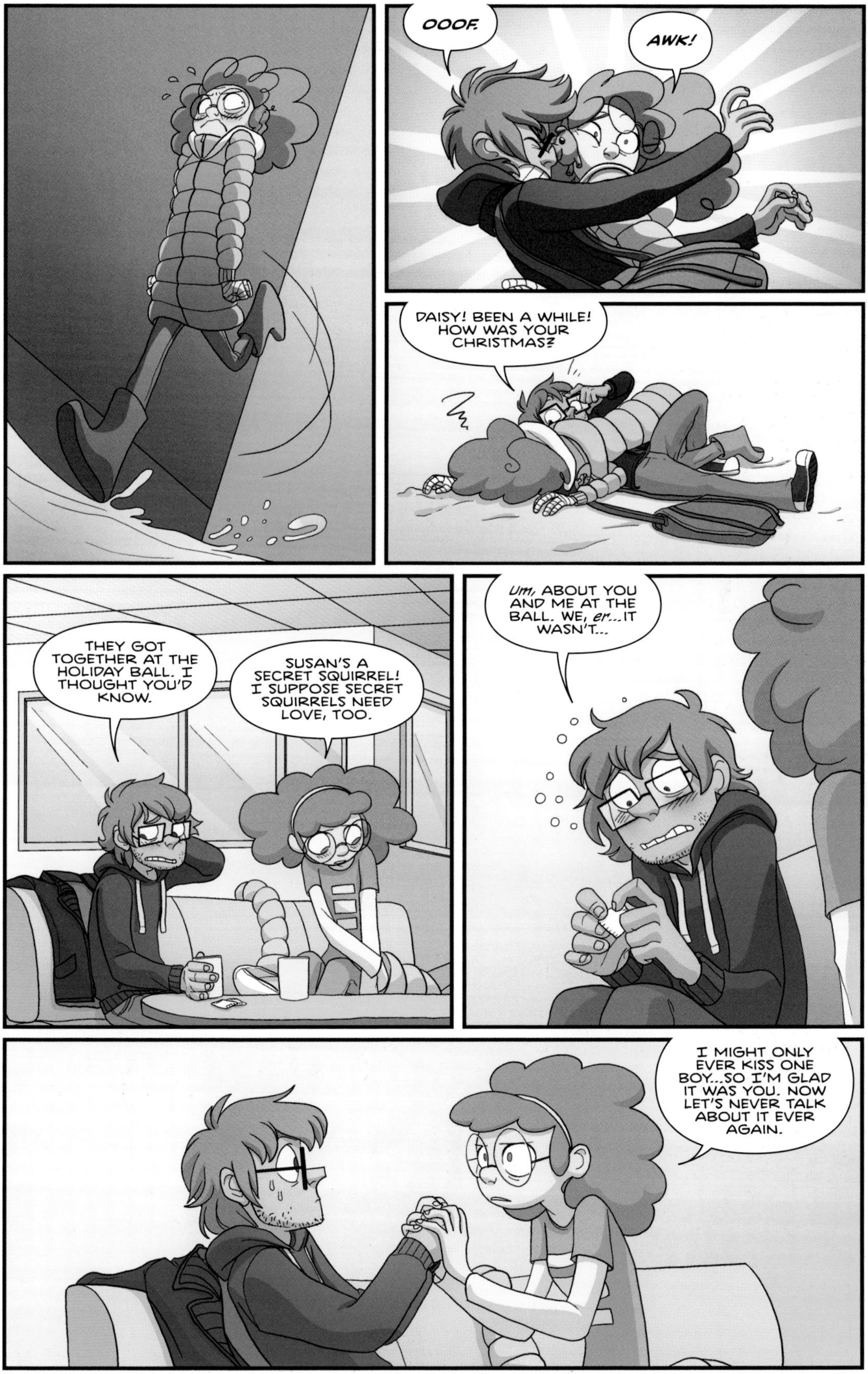
OOOF.
AWK!
DAISY! BEEN A WHILE! HOW WAS YOUR CHRISTMAS?
THEY GOT TOGETHER AT THE HOLIDAY BALL. I THOUGHT YOU'D KNOW.
SUSAN'S A SECRET SQUIRREL! I SUPPOSE SECRET SQUIRRELS NEED LOVE, TOO.
Um, ABOUT YOU AND ME AT THE BALL. WE, *er*...IT WASN'T...
I MIGHT ONLY EVER KISS ONE BOY...SO I'M GLAD IT WAS YOU. NOW LET'S NEVER TALK ABOUT IT EVER AGAIN.

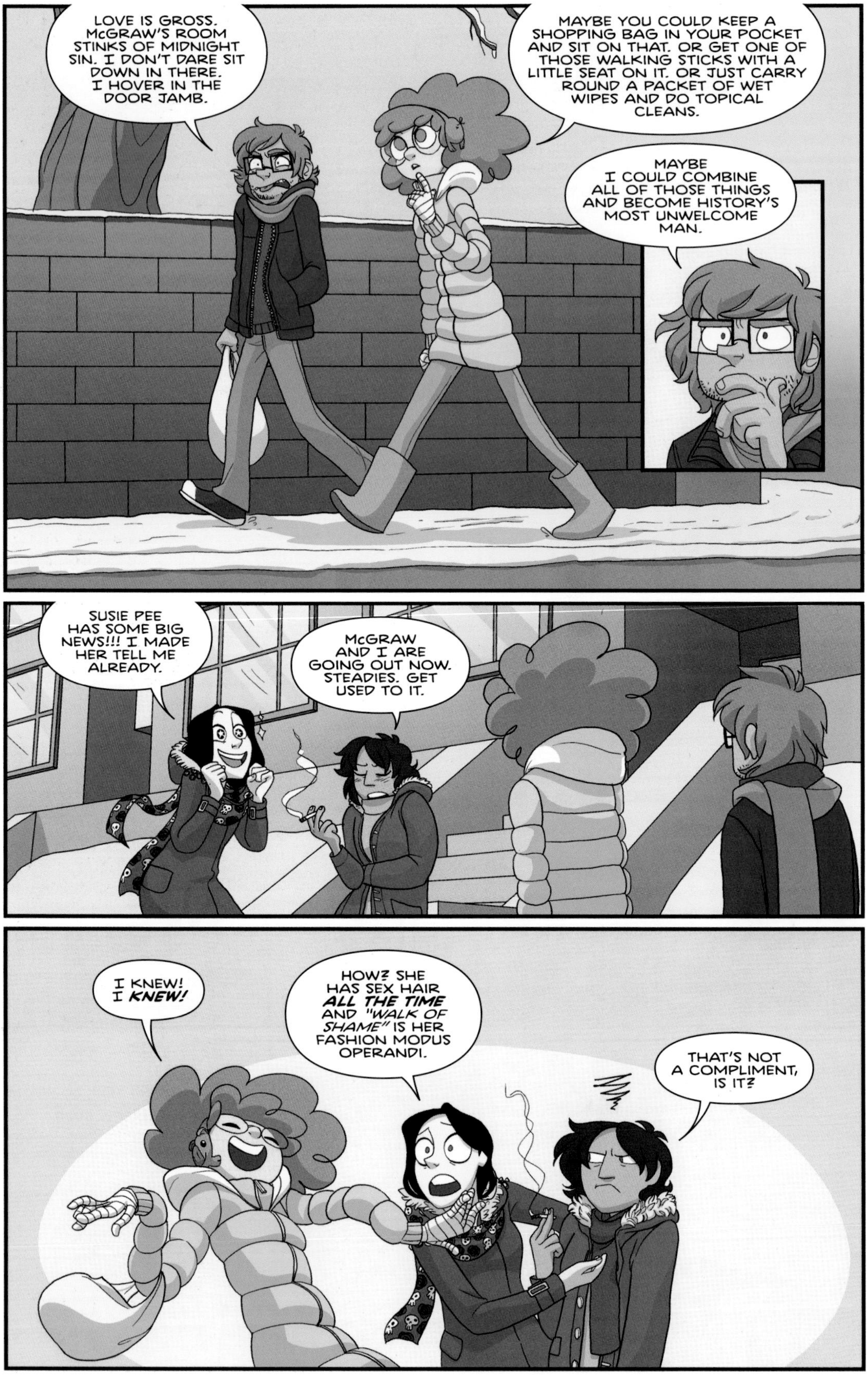
LOVE IS GROSS. McGRAW'S ROOM STINKS OF MIDNIGHT SIN. I DON'T DARE SIT DOWN IN THERE. I HOVER IN THE DOOR JAMB.
MAYBE YOU COULD KEEP A SHOPPING BAG IN YOUR POCKET AND SIT ON THAT. OR GET ONE OF THOSE WALKING STICKS WITH A LITTLE SEAT ON IT. OR JUST CARRY ROUND A PACKET OF WET WIPES AND DO TOPICAL CLEANS.
MAYBE I COULD COMBINE ALL OF THOSE THINGS AND BECOME HISTORY'S MOST UNWELCOME MAN.
SUSIE PEE HAS SOME BIG NEWS!!! I MADE HER TELL ME ALREADY.
McGRAW AND I ARE GOING OUT NOW. STEADIES. GET USED TO IT.
I KNEW! I *KNEW!*
HOW? SHE HAS SEX HAIR ***ALL THE TIME*** AND *"WALK OF SHAME"* IS HER FASHION MODUS OPERANDI.
THAT'S NOT A COMPLIMENT, IS IT?

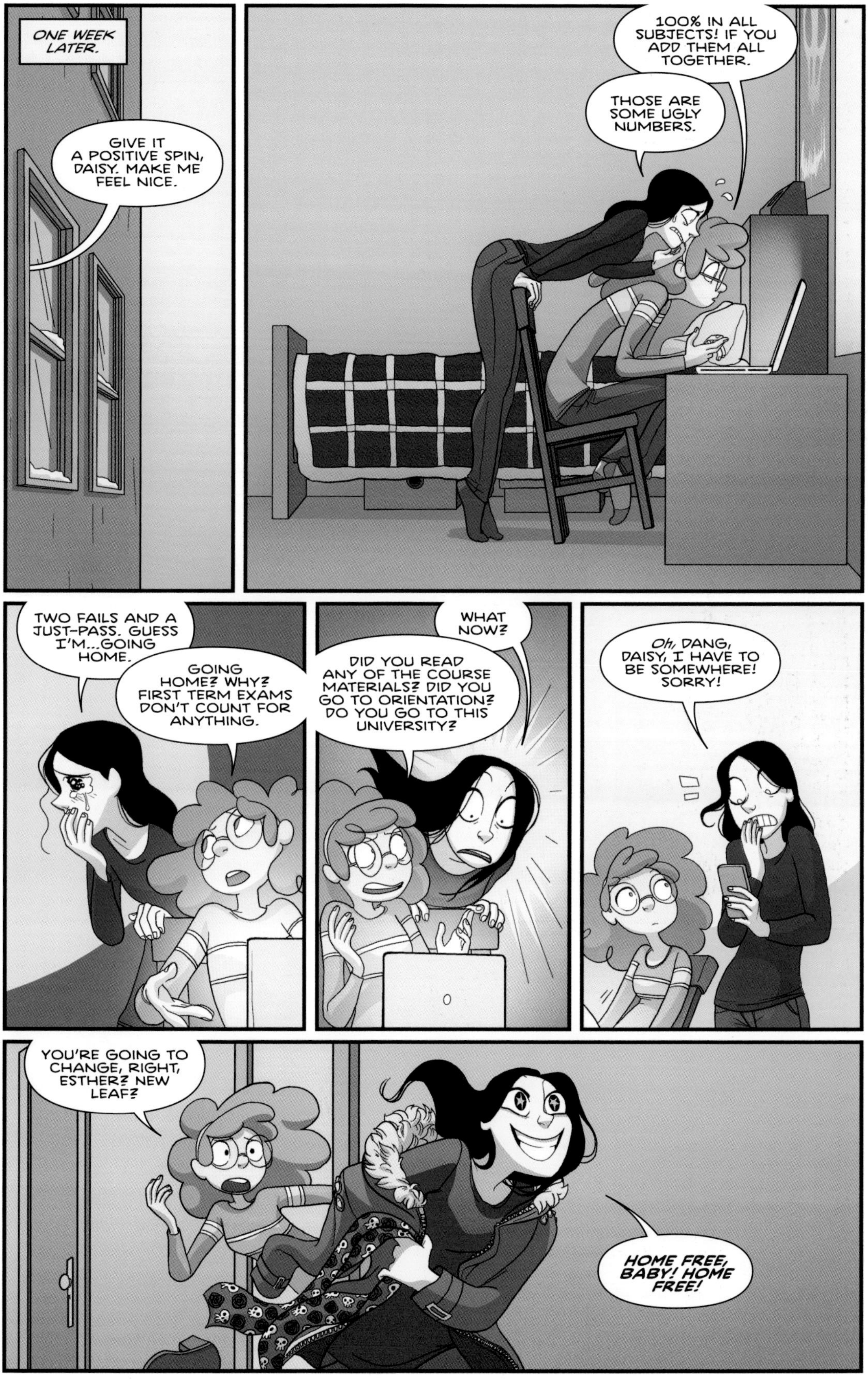
ONE WEEK LATER.
GIVE IT A POSITIVE SPIN, DAISY. MAKE ME FEEL NICE.
100% IN ALL SUBJECTS! IF YOU ADD THEM ALL TOGETHER.
THOSE ARE SOME UGLY NUMBERS.
TWO FAILS AND A JUST-PASS. GUESS I'M...GOING HOME.
GOING HOME? WHY? FIRST TERM EXAMS DON'T COUNT FOR ANYTHING.
WHAT NOW?
DID YOU READ ANY OF THE COURSE MATERIALS? DID YOU GO TO ORIENTATION? DO YOU GO TO THIS UNIVERSITY?
Oh, DANG, DAISY, I HAVE TO BE SOMEWHERE! SORRY!
YOU'RE GOING TO CHANGE, RIGHT, ESTHER? NEW LEAF?
HOME FREE, BABY! HOME FREE!

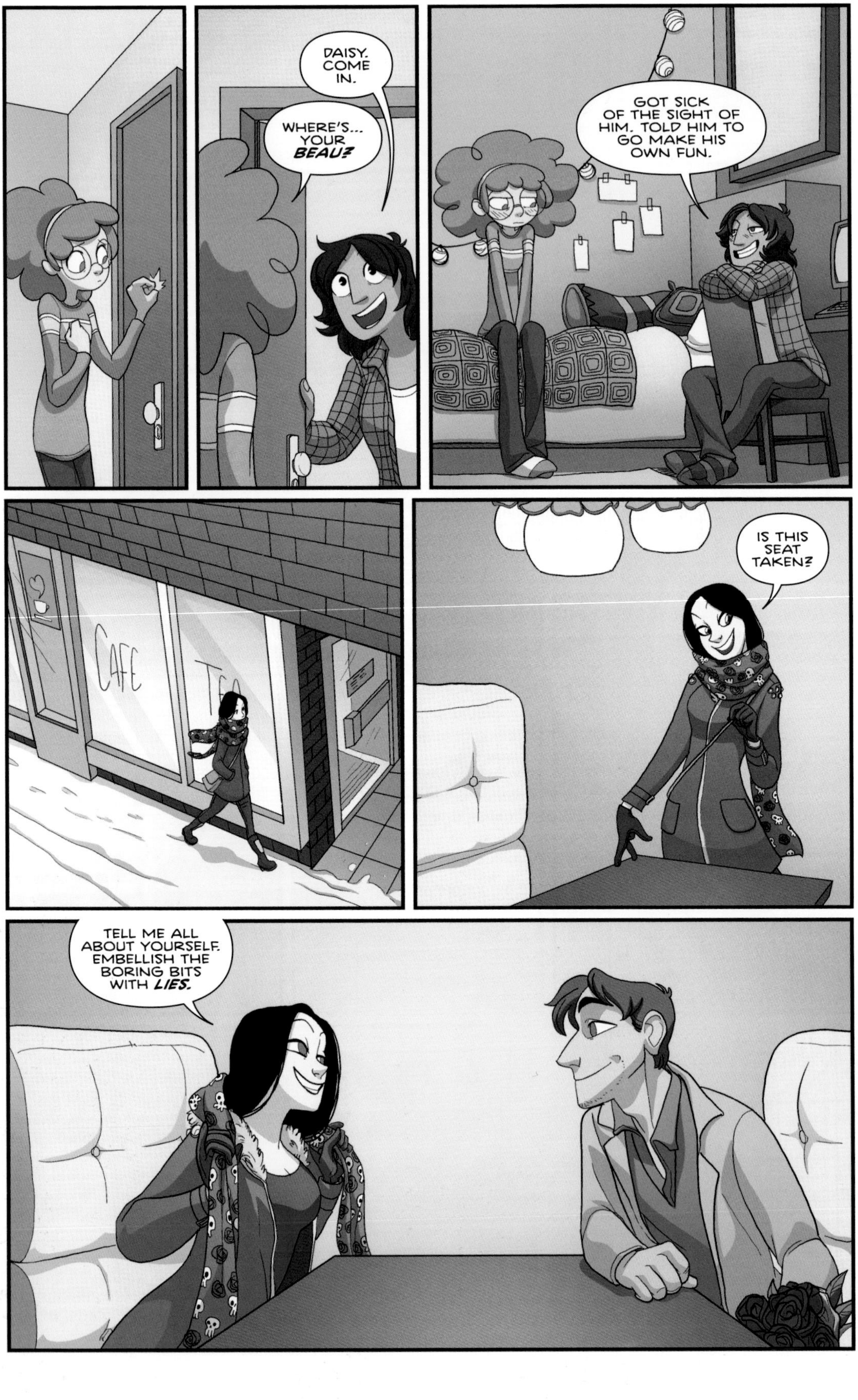
DAISY. COME IN.
WHERE'S... YOUR *BEAU?*
GOT SICK OF THE SIGHT OF HIM. TOLD HIM TO GO MAKE HIS OWN FUN.
CAFE
IS THIS SEAT TAKEN?
TELL ME ALL ABOUT YOURSELF. EMBELLISH THE BORING BITS WITH *LIES.*

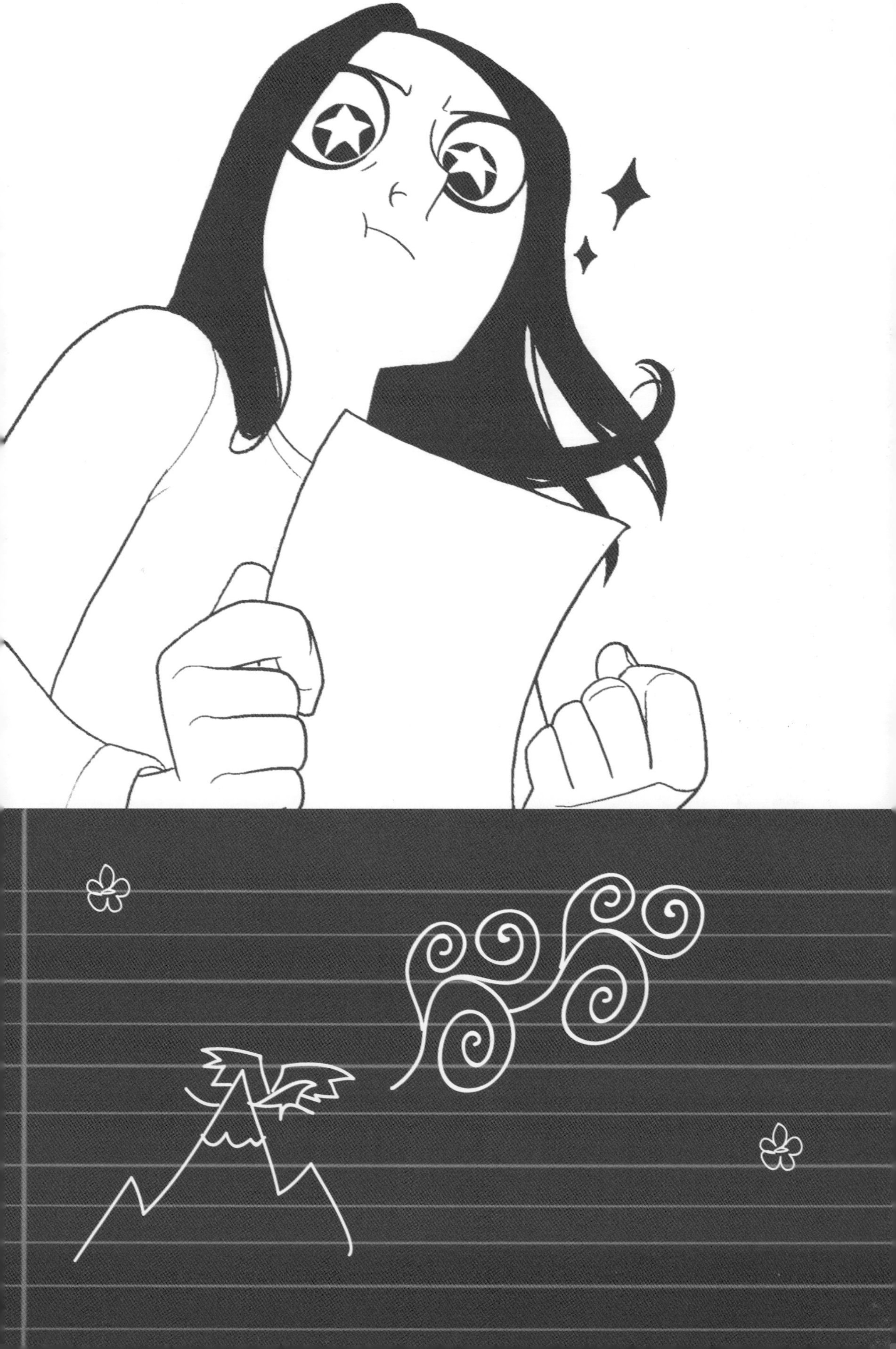

CHAPTER EIGHT

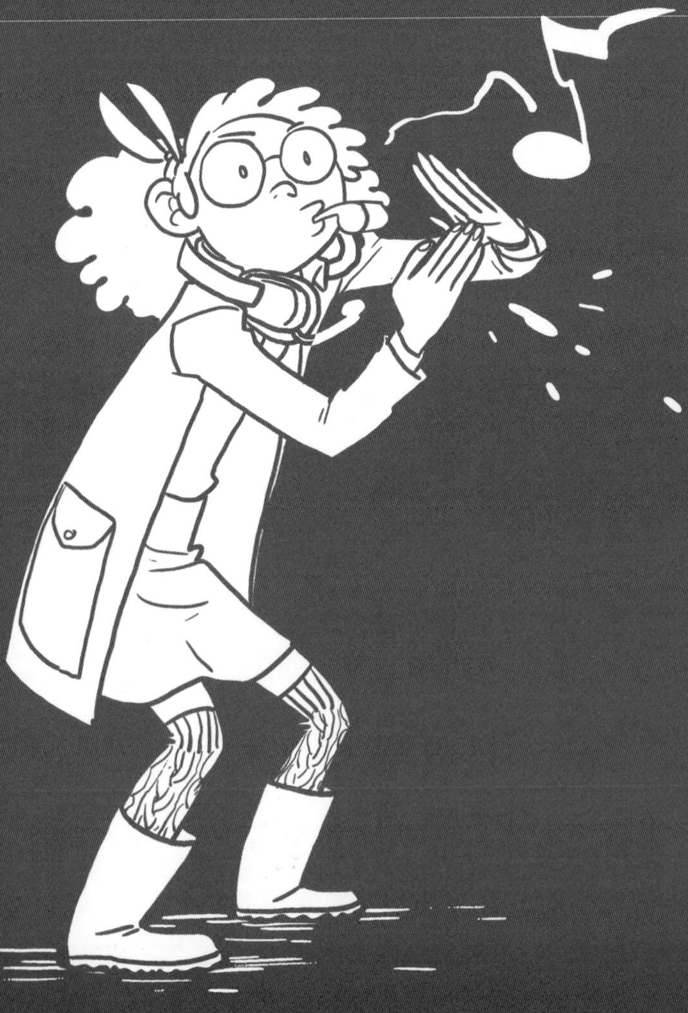

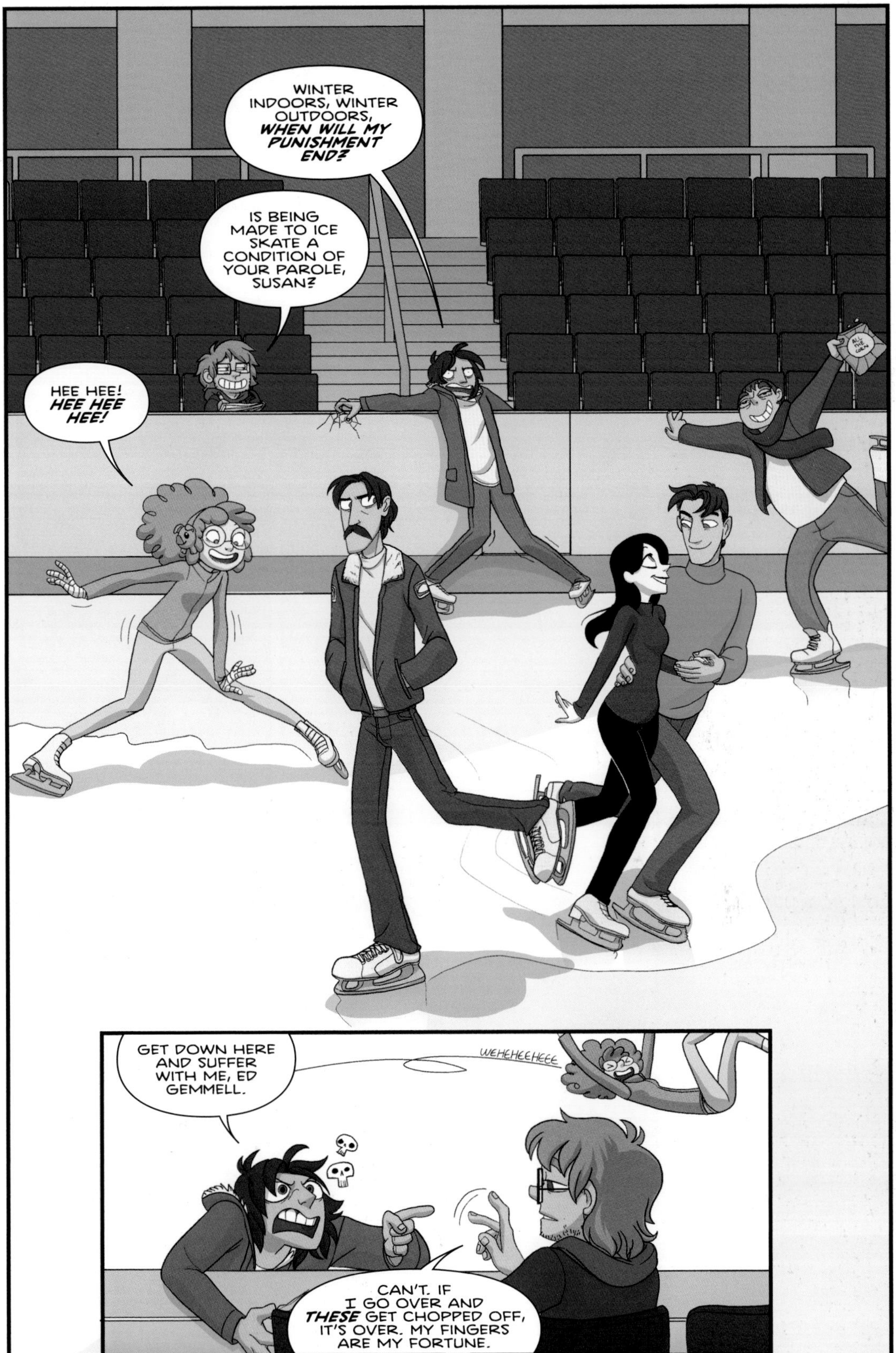
WINTER INDOORS, WINTER OUTDOORS, ***WHEN WILL MY PUNISHMENT END?***
IS BEING MADE TO ICE SKATE A CONDITION OF YOUR PAROLE, SUSAN?
HEE HEE! ***HEE HEE HEE!***
GET DOWN HERE AND SUFFER WITH ME, ED GEMMELL.
WEHEHEEHEEE
CAN'T. IF I GO OVER AND ***THESE*** GET CHOPPED OFF, IT'S OVER. MY FINGERS ARE MY FORTUNE.

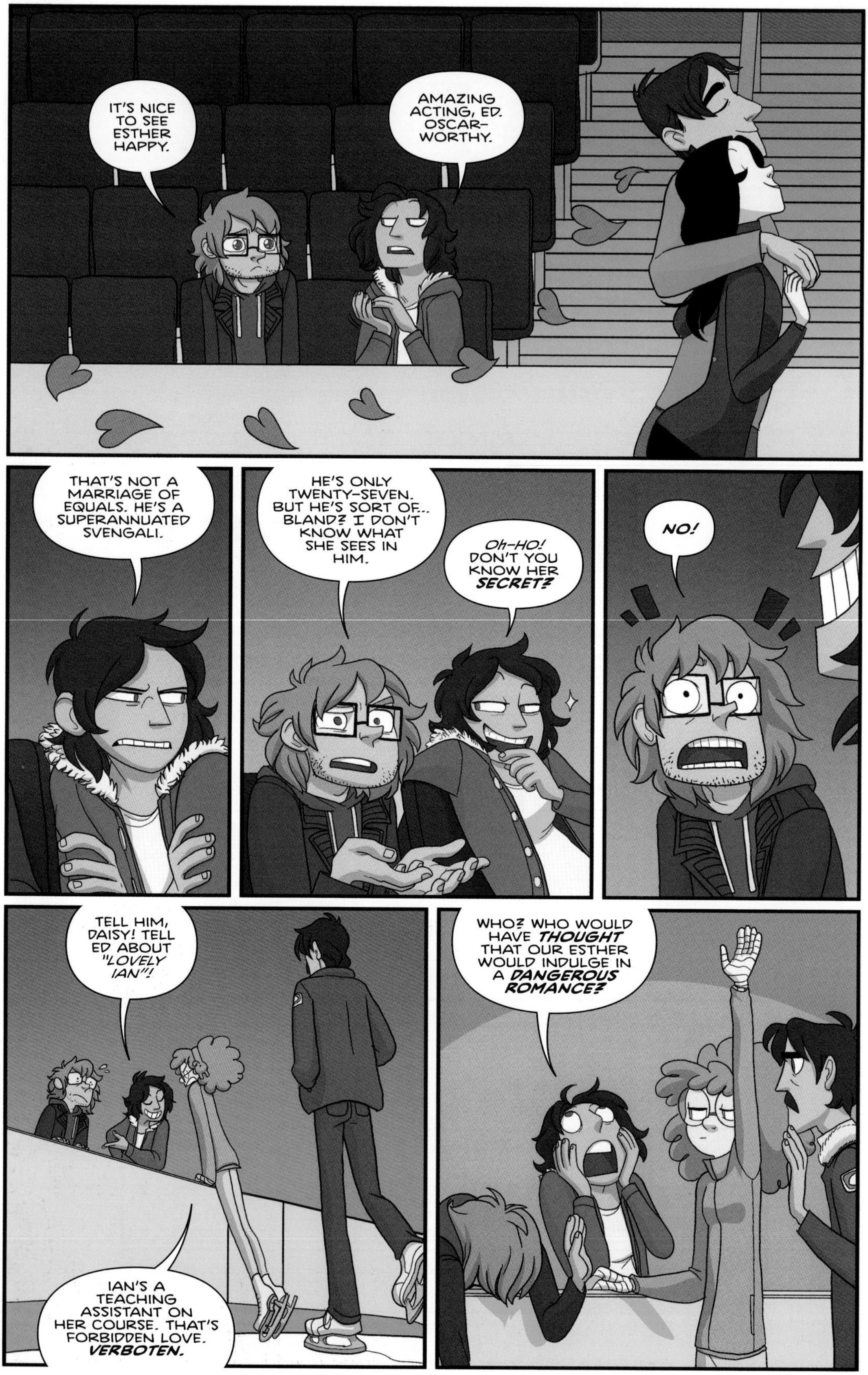
IT'S NICE TO SEE ESTHER HAPPY.
AMAZING ACTING, ED. OSCAR-WORTHY.
THAT'S NOT A MARRIAGE OF EQUALS. HE'S A SUPERANNUATED SVENGALI.
HE'S ONLY TWENTY-SEVEN. BUT HE'S SORT OF... BLAND? I DON'T KNOW WHAT SHE SEES IN HIM.
Oh-HO! DON'T YOU KNOW HER SECRET?
NO!
TELL HIM, DAISY! TELL ED ABOUT "LOVELY IAN"!
IAN'S A TEACHING ASSISTANT ON HER COURSE. THAT'S FORBIDDEN LOVE. VERBOTEN.
WHO? WHO WOULD HAVE THOUGHT THAT OUR ESTHER WOULD INDULGE IN A DANGEROUS ROMANCE?

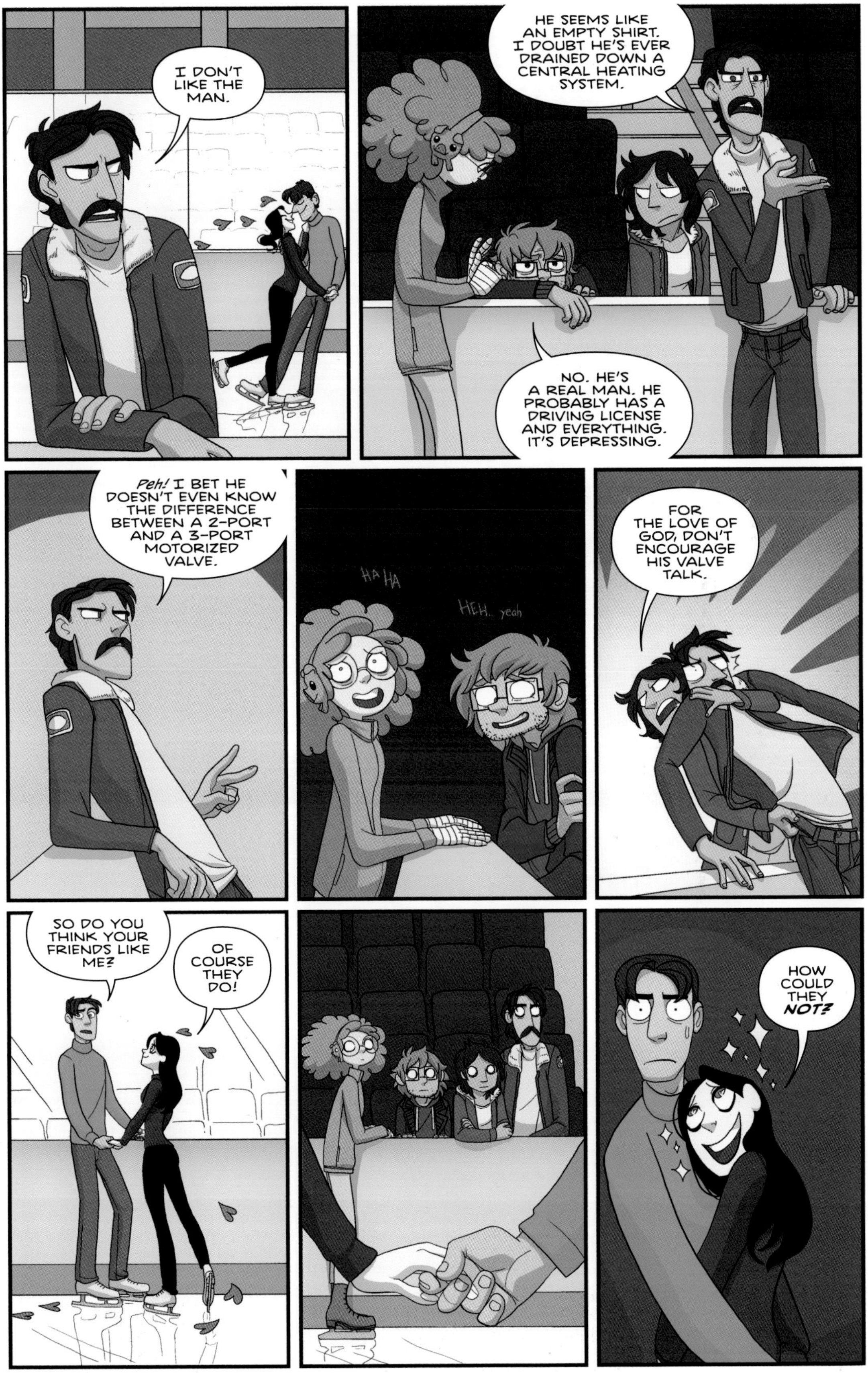
I DON'T LIKE THE MAN.
HE SEEMS LIKE AN EMPTY SHIRT. I DOUBT HE'S EVER DRAINED DOWN A CENTRAL HEATING SYSTEM.
NO. HE'S A REAL MAN. HE PROBABLY HAS A DRIVING LICENSE AND EVERYTHING. IT'S DEPRESSING.
Peh! I BET HE DOESN'T EVEN KNOW THE DIFFERENCE BETWEEN A 2-PORT AND A 3-PORT MOTORIZED VALVE.
HA HA
HEH.. yeah
FOR THE LOVE OF GOD, DON'T ENCOURAGE HIS VALVE TALK.
SO DO YOU THINK YOUR FRIENDS LIKE ME?
OF COURSE THEY DO!
HOW COULD THEY ***NOT?***

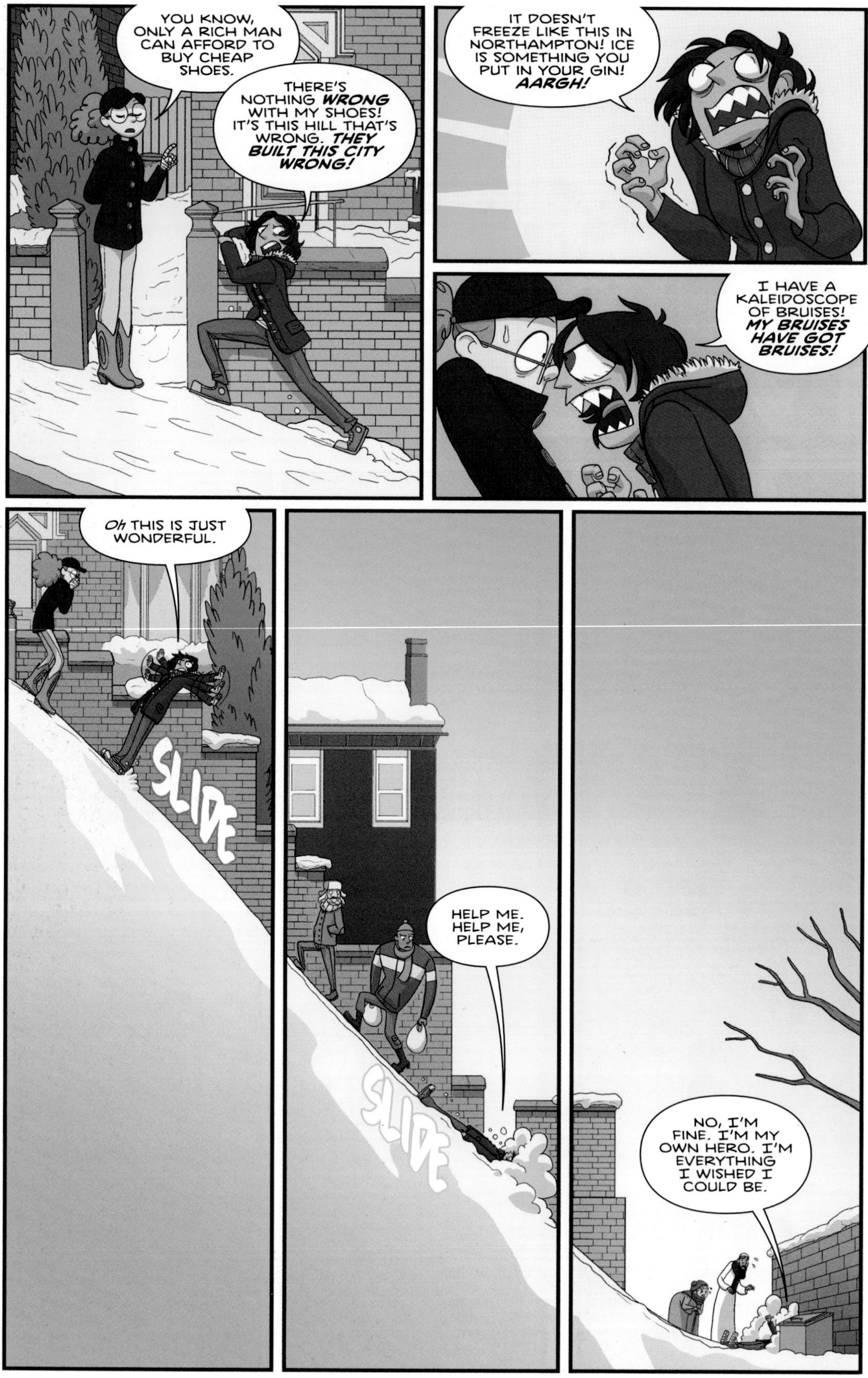
YOU KNOW, ONLY A RICH MAN CAN AFFORD TO BUY CHEAP SHOES.
THERE'S NOTHING **WRONG** WITH MY SHOES! IT'S THIS HILL THAT'S WRONG. ***THEY BUILT THIS CITY WRONG!***
IT DOESN'T FREEZE LIKE THIS IN NORTHAMPTON! ICE IS SOMETHING YOU PUT IN YOUR GIN! ***AARGH!***
I HAVE A KALEIDOSCOPE OF BRUISES! ***MY BRUISES HAVE GOT BRUISES!***
Oh THIS IS JUST WONDERFUL.
SLIDE
HELP ME. HELP ME, PLEASE.
SLIDE
NO, I'M FINE. I'M MY OWN HERO. I'M EVERYTHING I WISHED I COULD BE.

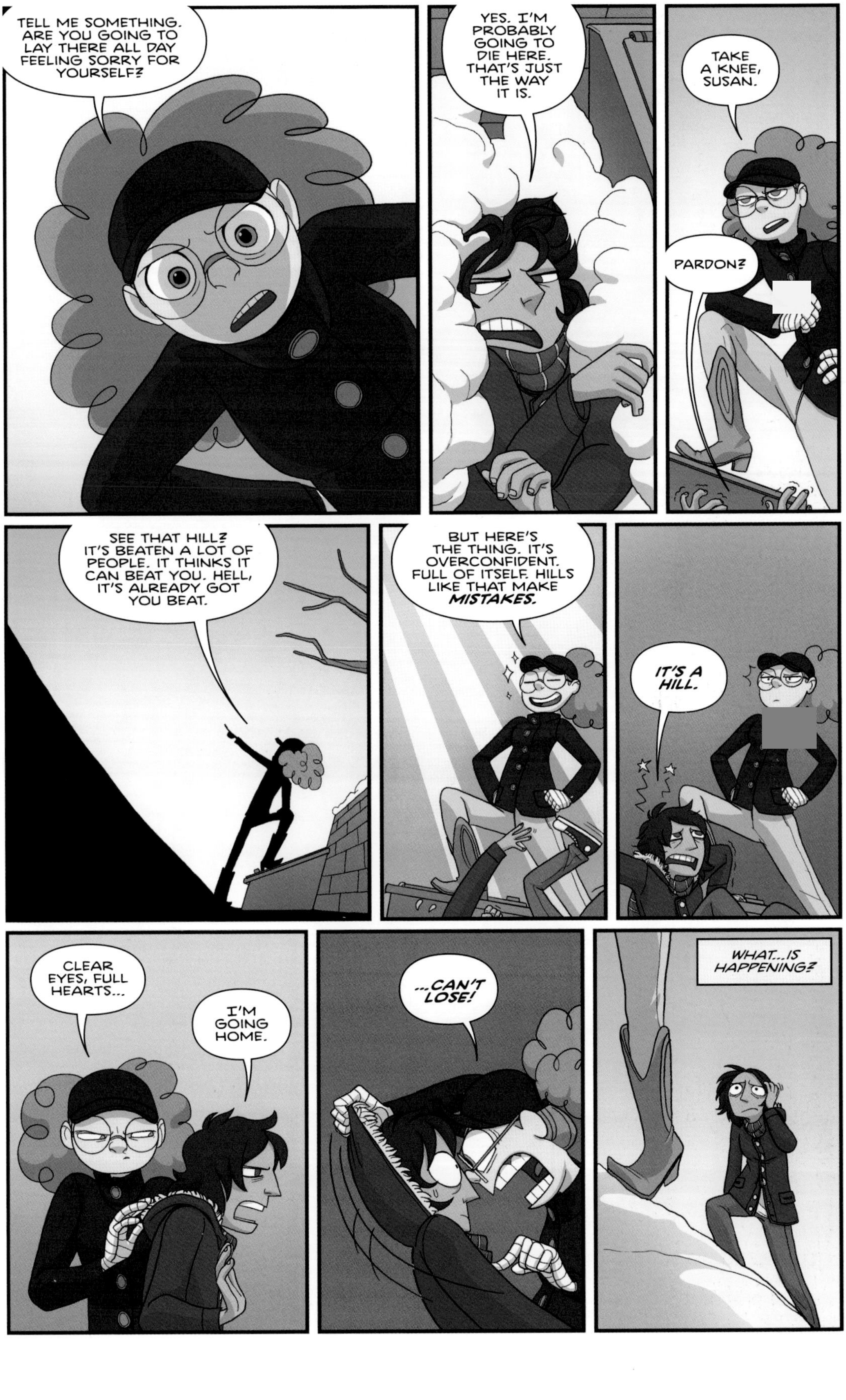
TELL ME SOMETHING. ARE YOU GOING TO LAY THERE ALL DAY FEELING SORRY FOR YOURSELF?
YES. I'M PROBABLY GOING TO DIE HERE. THAT'S JUST THE WAY IT IS.
TAKE A KNEE, SUSAN.
PARDON?
SEE THAT HILL? IT'S BEATEN A LOT OF PEOPLE. IT THINKS IT CAN BEAT YOU. HELL, IT'S ALREADY GOT YOU BEAT.
BUT HERE'S THE THING. IT'S OVERCONFIDENT. FULL OF ITSELF. HILLS LIKE THAT MAKE MISTAKES.
IT'S A HILL.
CLEAR EYES, FULL HEARTS...
I'M GOING HOME.
...CAN'T LOSE!
WHAT...IS HAPPENING?

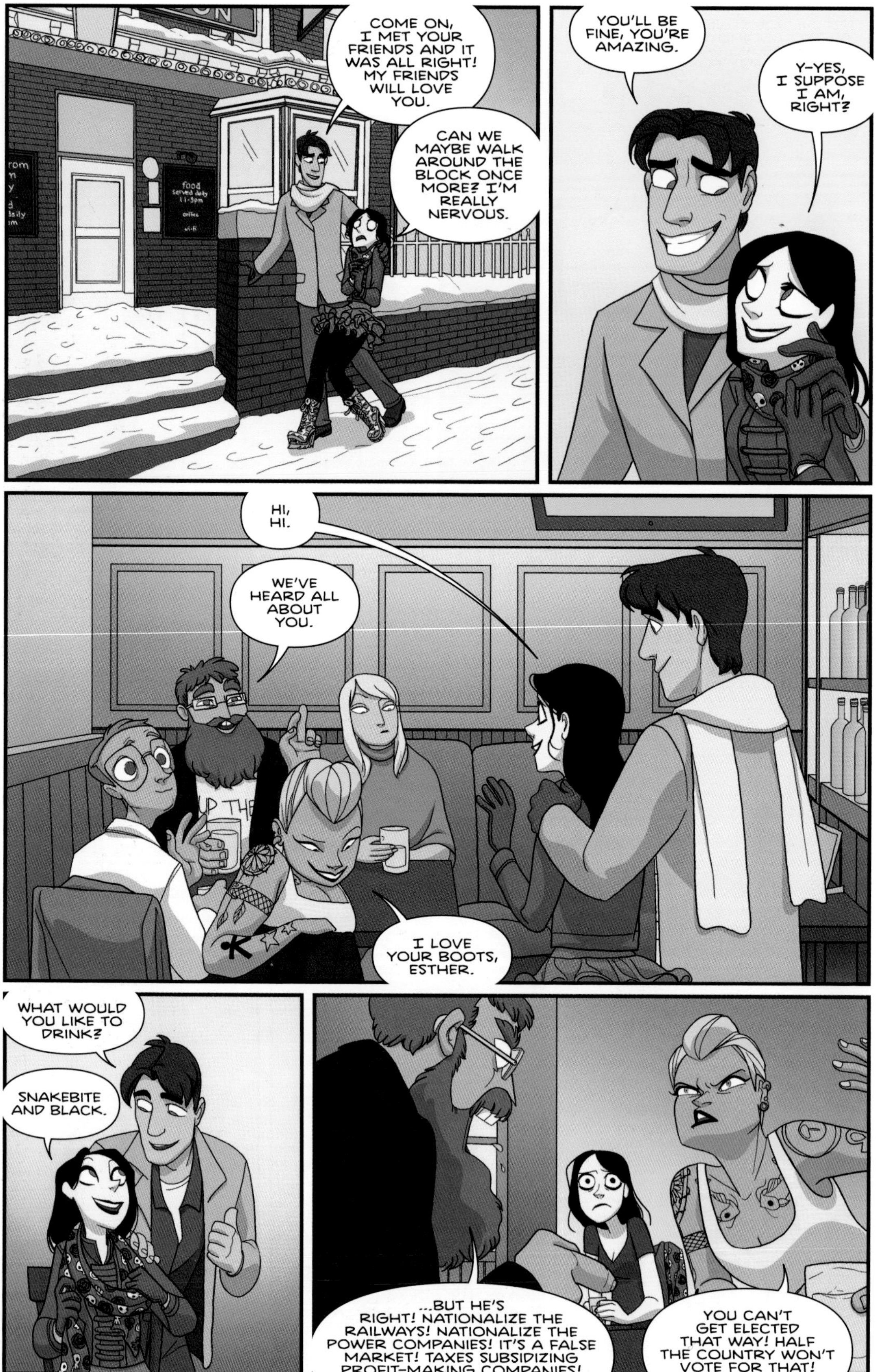
COME ON, I MET YOUR FRIENDS AND IT WAS ALL RIGHT! MY FRIENDS WILL LOVE YOU.
CAN WE MAYBE WALK AROUND THE BLOCK ONCE MORE? I'M REALLY NERVOUS.
YOU'LL BE FINE, YOU'RE AMAZING.
Y-YES, I SUPPOSE I AM, RIGHT?
HI, HI.
WE'VE HEARD ALL ABOUT YOU.
I LOVE YOUR BOOTS, ESTHER.
WHAT WOULD YOU LIKE TO DRINK?
SNAKEBITE AND BLACK.
...BUT HE'S RIGHT! NATIONALIZE THE RAILWAYS! NATIONALIZE THE POWER COMPANIES! IT'S A FALSE MARKET! TAXES SUBSIDIZING PROFIT-MAKING COMPANIES!
YOU CAN'T GET ELECTED THAT WAY! HALF THE COUNTRY WON'T VOTE FOR THAT!

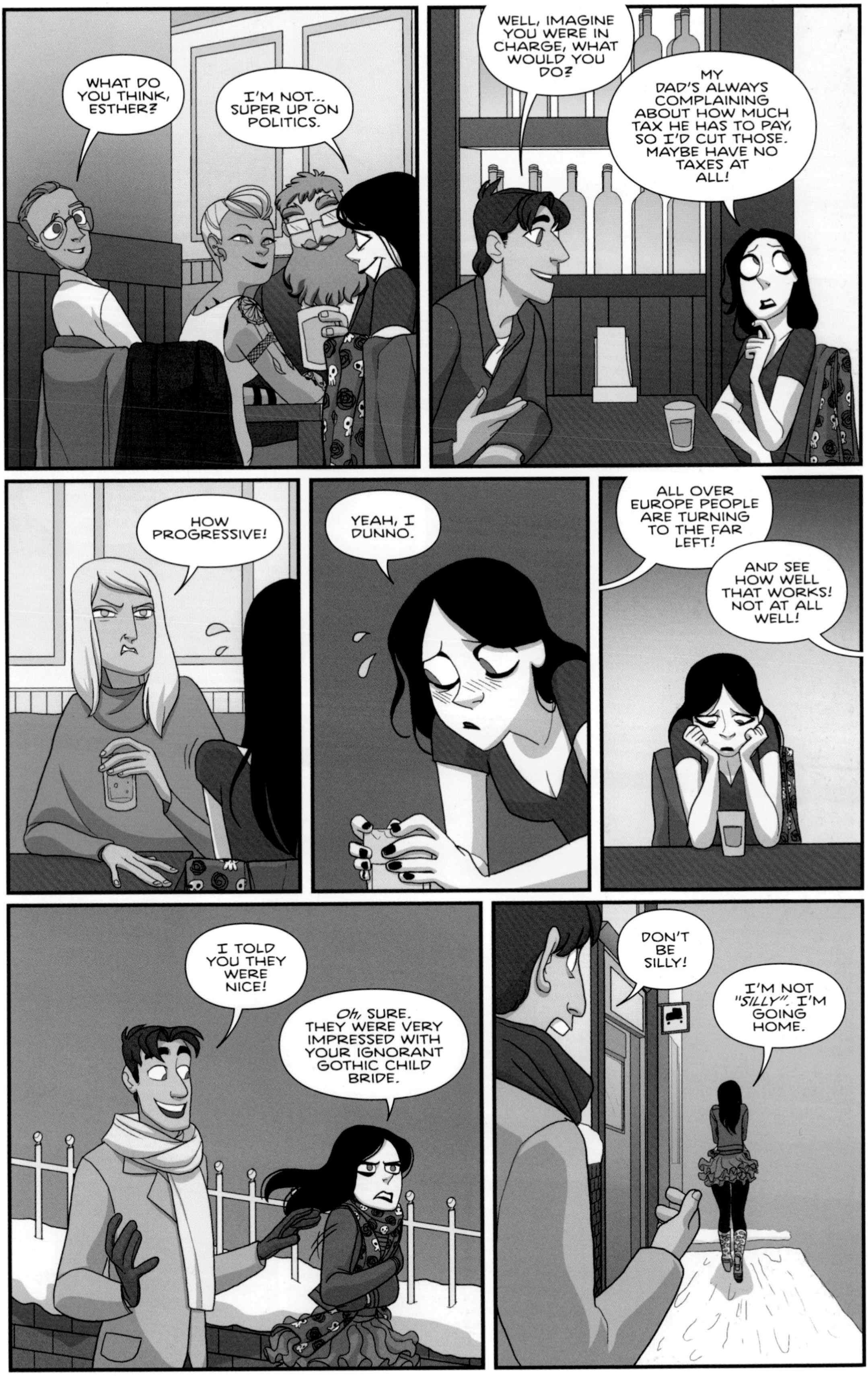
WHAT DO YOU THINK, ESTHER?
I'M NOT... SUPER UP ON POLITICS.
WELL, IMAGINE YOU WERE IN CHARGE, WHAT WOULD YOU DO?
MY DAD'S ALWAYS COMPLAINING ABOUT HOW MUCH TAX HE HAS TO PAY, SO I'D CUT THOSE. MAYBE HAVE NO TAXES AT ALL!
HOW PROGRESSIVE!
YEAH, I DUNNO.
ALL OVER EUROPE PEOPLE ARE TURNING TO THE FAR LEFT!
AND SEE HOW WELL THAT WORKS! NOT AT ALL WELL!
I TOLD YOU THEY WERE NICE!
Oh, SURE. THEY WERE VERY IMPRESSED WITH YOUR IGNORANT GOTHIC CHILD BRIDE.
DON'T BE SILLY!
I'M NOT *"SILLY"*. I'M GOING HOME.

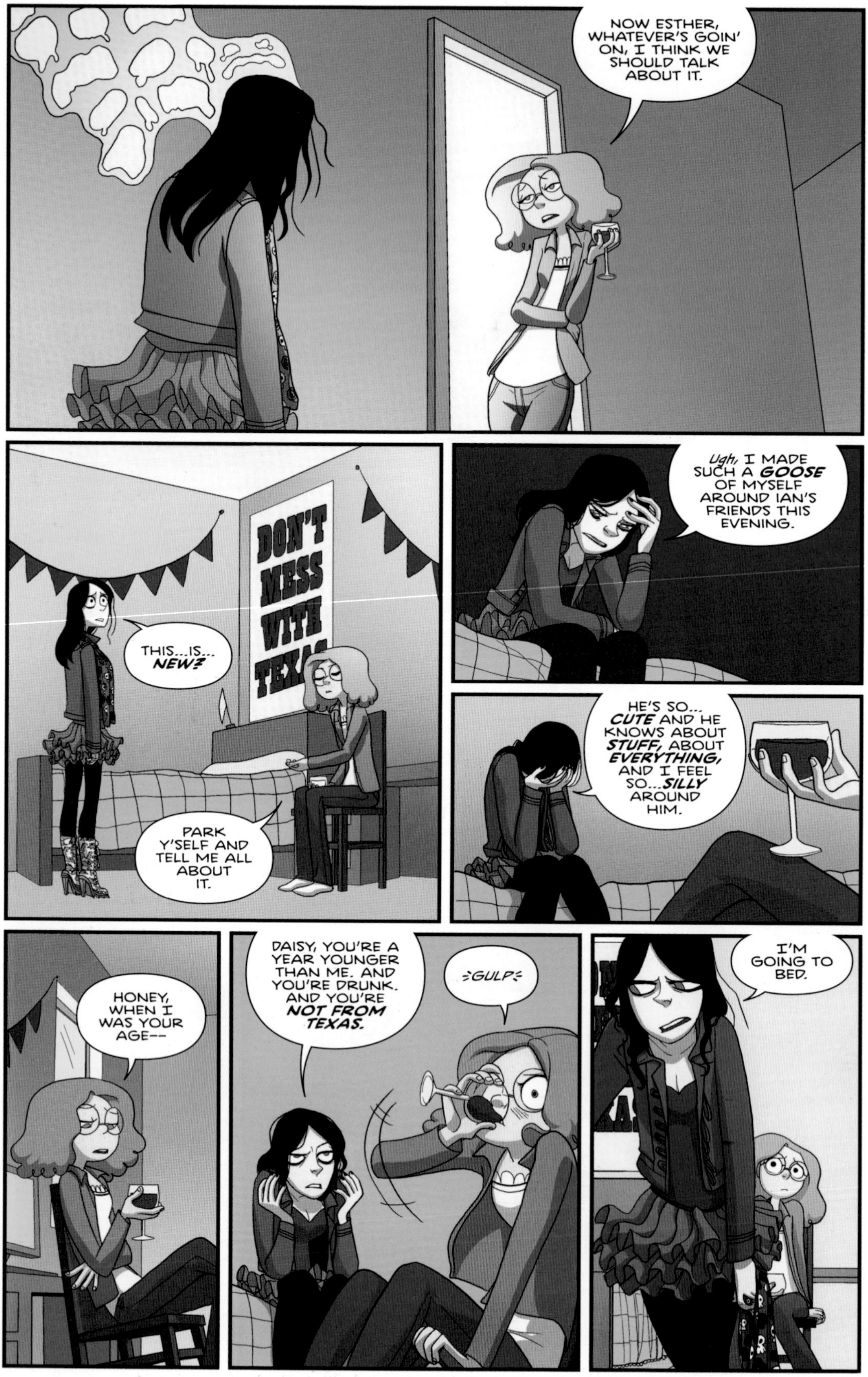
NOW ESTHER, WHATEVER'S GOIN' ON, I THINK WE SHOULD TALK ABOUT IT.
DON'T MESS WITH TEXAS
THIS...IS... NEW?
PARK Y'SELF AND TELL ME ALL ABOUT IT.
Ugh, I MADE SUCH A GOOSE OF MYSELF AROUND IAN'S FRIENDS THIS EVENING.
HE'S SO... CUTE AND HE KNOWS ABOUT STUFF, ABOUT EVERYTHING, AND I FEEL SO...SILLY AROUND HIM.
HONEY, WHEN I WAS YOUR AGE--
DAISY, YOU'RE A YEAR YOUNGER THAN ME. AND YOU'RE DRUNK. AND YOU'RE NOT FROM TEXAS.
GULP
I'M GOING TO BED.

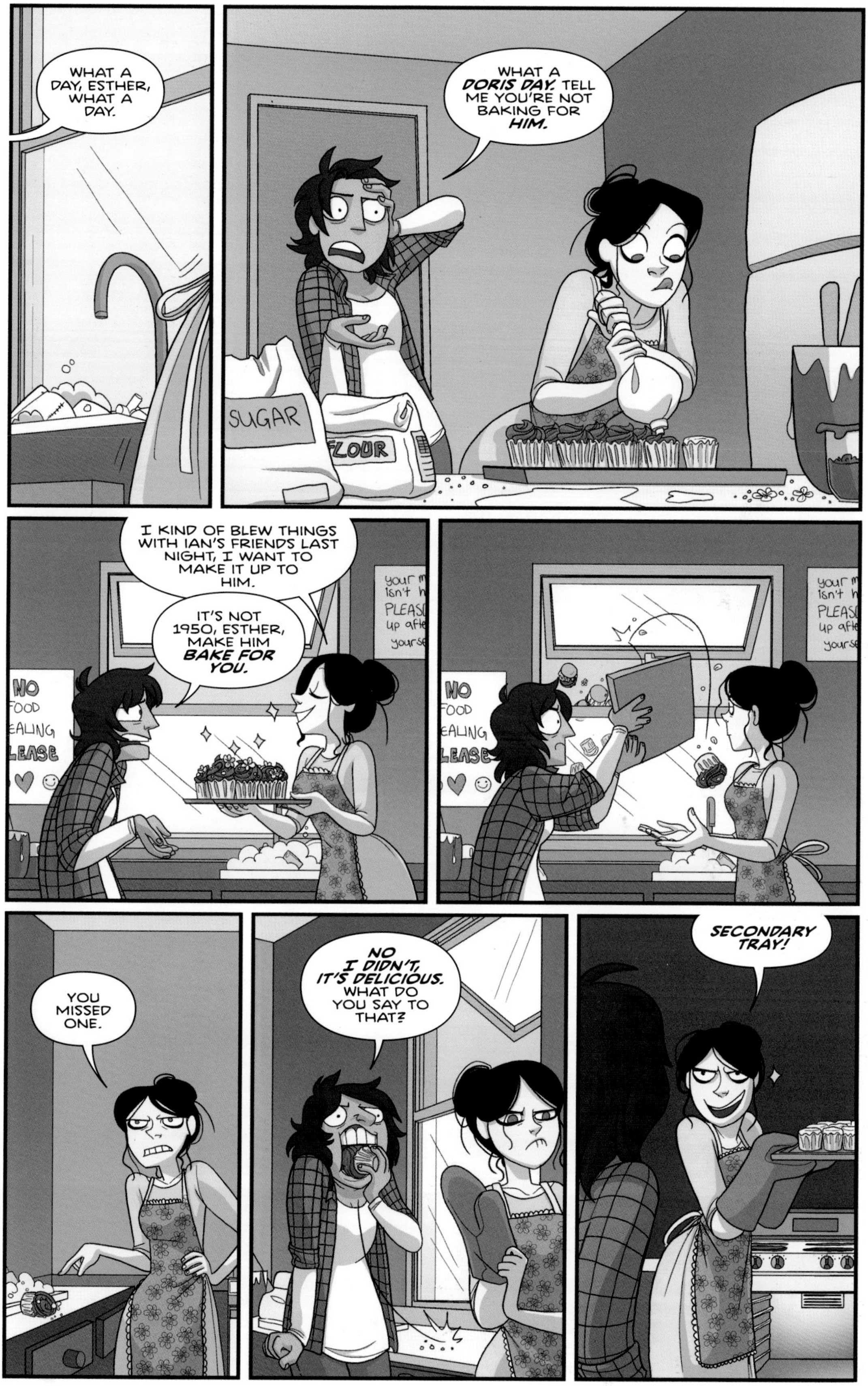
WHAT A DAY, ESTHER, WHAT A DAY.
WHAT A DORIS DAY. TELL ME YOU'RE NOT BAKING FOR HIM.
SUGAR
FLOUR
I KIND OF BLEW THINGS WITH IAN'S FRIENDS LAST NIGHT, I WANT TO MAKE IT UP TO HIM.
IT'S NOT 1950, ESTHER, MAKE HIM BAKE FOR YOU.
YOU MISSED ONE.
NO I DIDN'T, IT'S DELICIOUS. WHAT DO YOU SAY TO THAT?
SECONDARY TRAY!

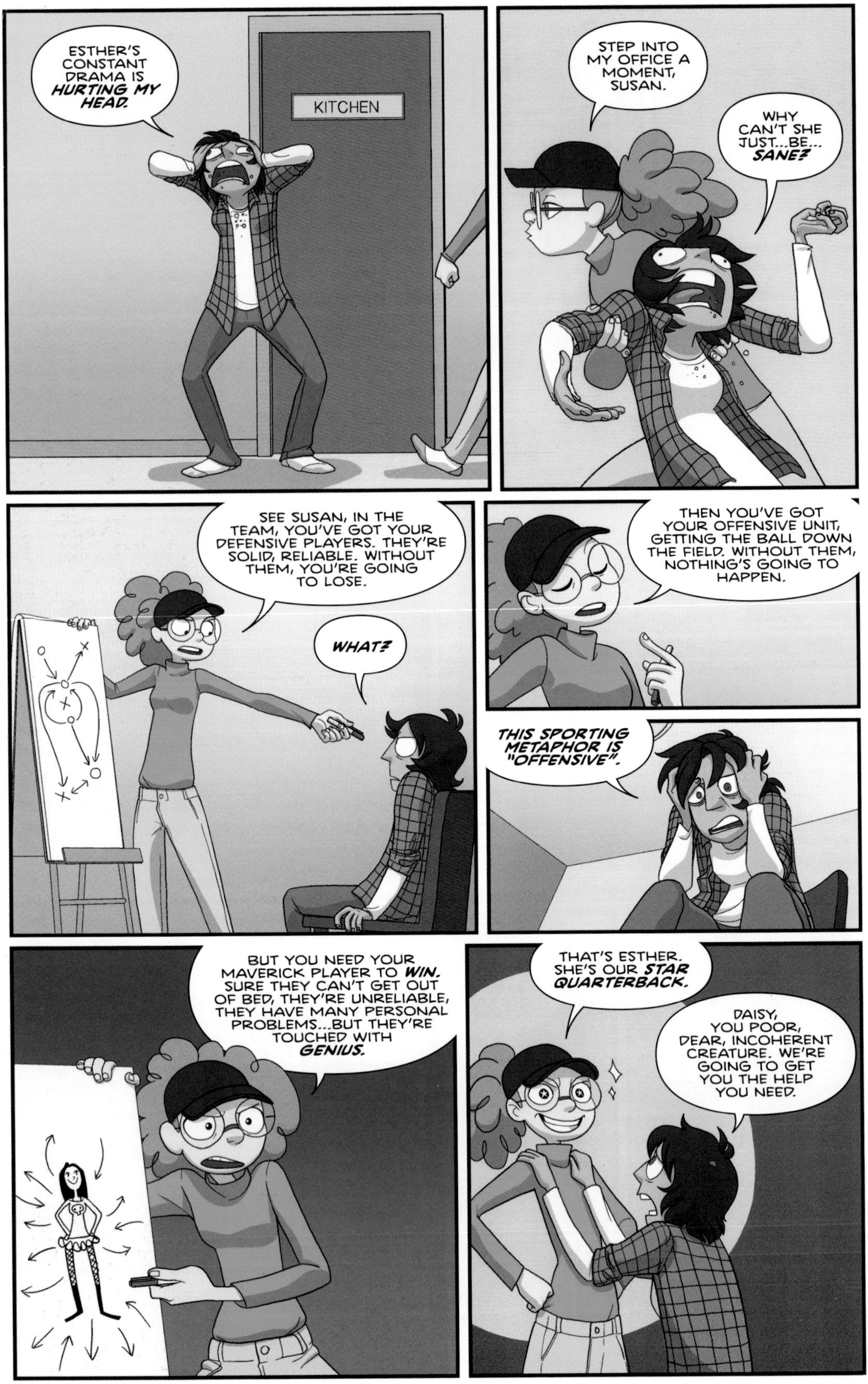
ESTHER'S CONSTANT DRAMA IS HURTING MY HEAD.
KITCHEN
STEP INTO MY OFFICE A MOMENT, SUSAN.
WHY CAN'T SHE JUST...BE... SANE?
SEE SUSAN, IN THE TEAM, YOU'VE GOT YOUR DEFENSIVE PLAYERS. THEY'RE SOLID, RELIABLE. WITHOUT THEM, YOU'RE GOING TO LOSE.
WHAT?
THEN YOU'VE GOT YOUR OFFENSIVE UNIT, GETTING THE BALL DOWN THE FIELD. WITHOUT THEM, NOTHING'S GOING TO HAPPEN.
THIS SPORTING METAPHOR IS "OFFENSIVE".
BUT YOU NEED YOUR MAVERICK PLAYER TO WIN. SURE THEY CAN'T GET OUT OF BED, THEY'RE UNRELIABLE, THEY HAVE MANY PERSONAL PROBLEMS...BUT THEY'RE TOUCHED WITH GENIUS.
THAT'S ESTHER. SHE'S OUR STAR QUARTERBACK.
DAISY, YOU POOR, DEAR, INCOHERENT CREATURE. WE'RE GOING TO GET YOU THE HELP YOU NEED.

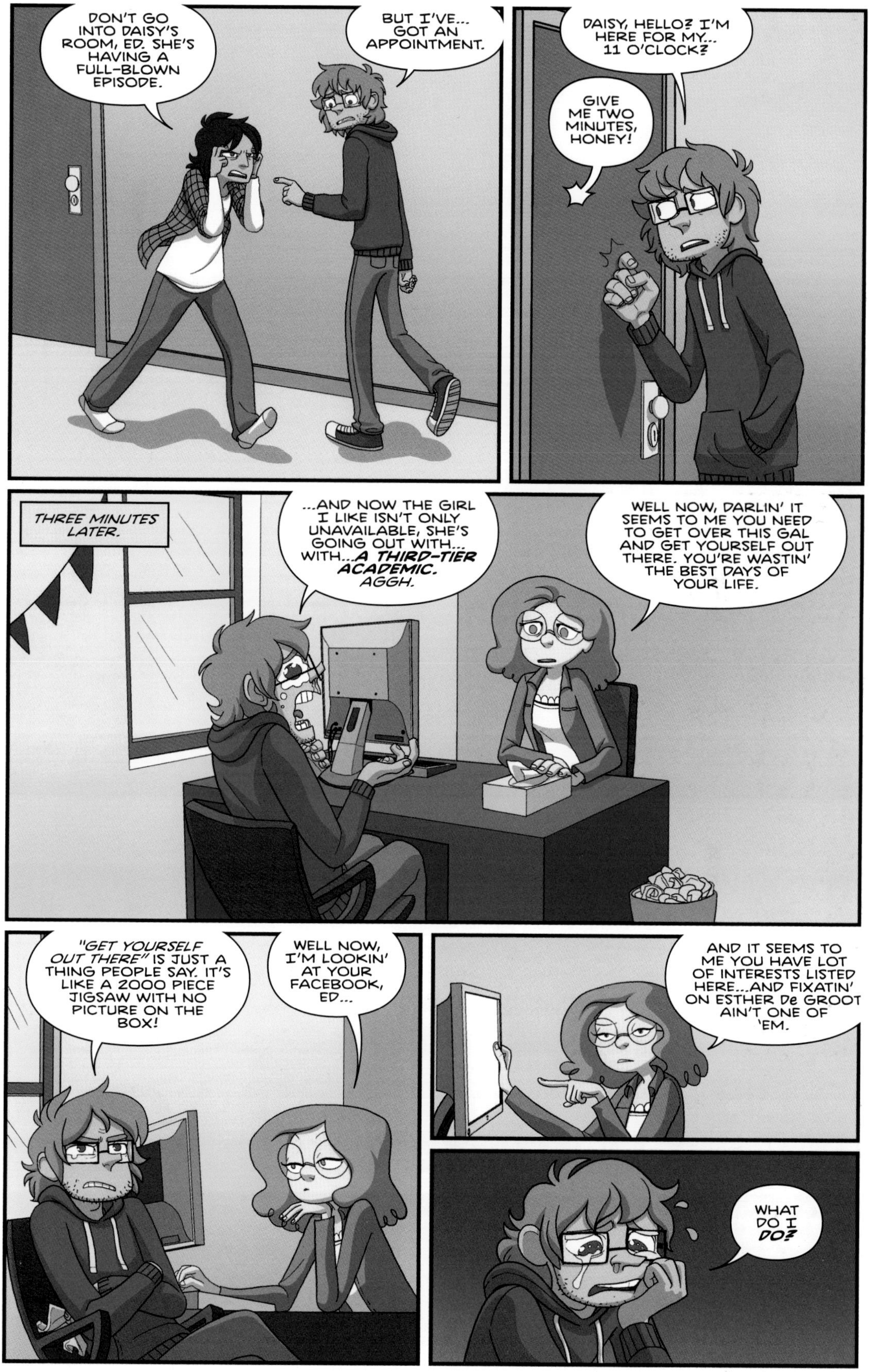
DON'T GO INTO DAISY'S ROOM, ED. SHE'S HAVING A FULL-BLOWN EPISODE.
BUT I'VE... GOT AN APPOINTMENT.
DAISY, HELLO? I'M HERE FOR MY... 11 O'CLOCK?
GIVE ME TWO MINUTES, HONEY!
THREE MINUTES LATER.
...AND NOW THE GIRL I LIKE ISN'T ONLY UNAVAILABLE, SHE'S GOING OUT WITH... WITH...A THIRD-TIER ACADEMIC. AGGH.
WELL NOW, DARLIN' IT SEEMS TO ME YOU NEED TO GET OVER THIS GAL AND GET YOURSELF OUT THERE. YOU'RE WASTIN' THE BEST DAYS OF YOUR LIFE.
"GET YOURSELF OUT THERE" IS JUST A THING PEOPLE SAY. IT'S LIKE A 2000 PIECE JIGSAW WITH NO PICTURE ON THE BOX!
WELL NOW, I'M LOOKIN' AT YOUR FACEBOOK, ED...
AND IT SEEMS TO ME YOU HAVE LOT OF INTERESTS LISTED HERE...AND FIXATIN' ON ESTHER De GROOT AIN'T ONE OF 'EM.
WHAT DO I DO?

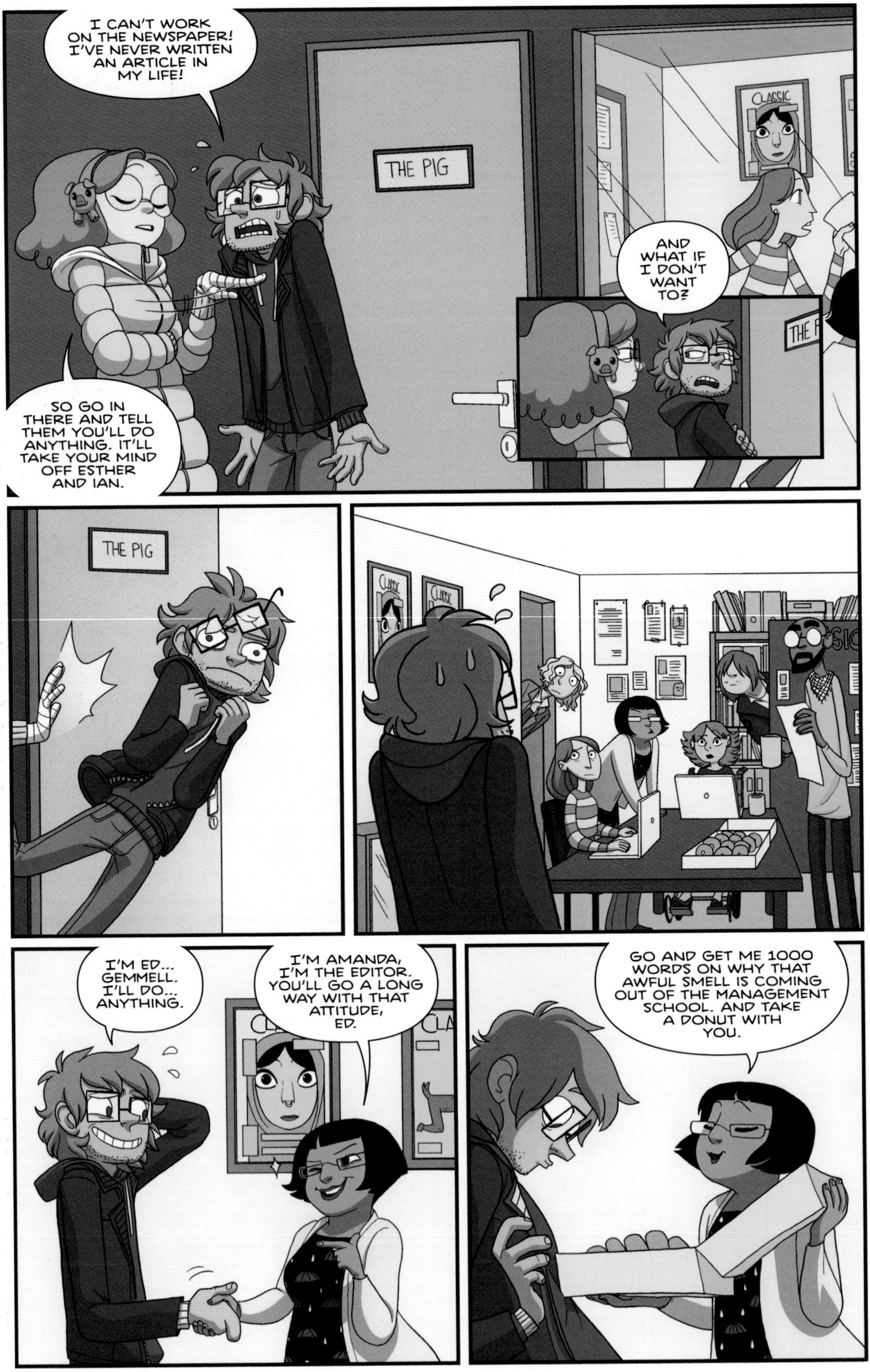
I CAN'T WORK ON THE NEWSPAPER! I'VE NEVER WRITTEN AN ARTICLE IN MY LIFE!
THE PIG
CLASSIC
SO GO IN THERE AND TELL THEM YOU'LL DO ANYTHING. IT'LL TAKE YOUR MIND OFF ESTHER AND IAN.
AND WHAT IF I DON'T WANT TO?
THE PIG
I'M ED... GEMMELL. I'LL DO... ANYTHING.
I'M AMANDA, I'M THE EDITOR. YOU'LL GO A LONG WAY WITH THAT ATTITUDE, ED.
GO AND GET ME 1000 WORDS ON WHY THAT AWFUL SMELL IS COMING OUT OF THE MANAGEMENT SCHOOL. AND TAKE A DONUT WITH YOU.

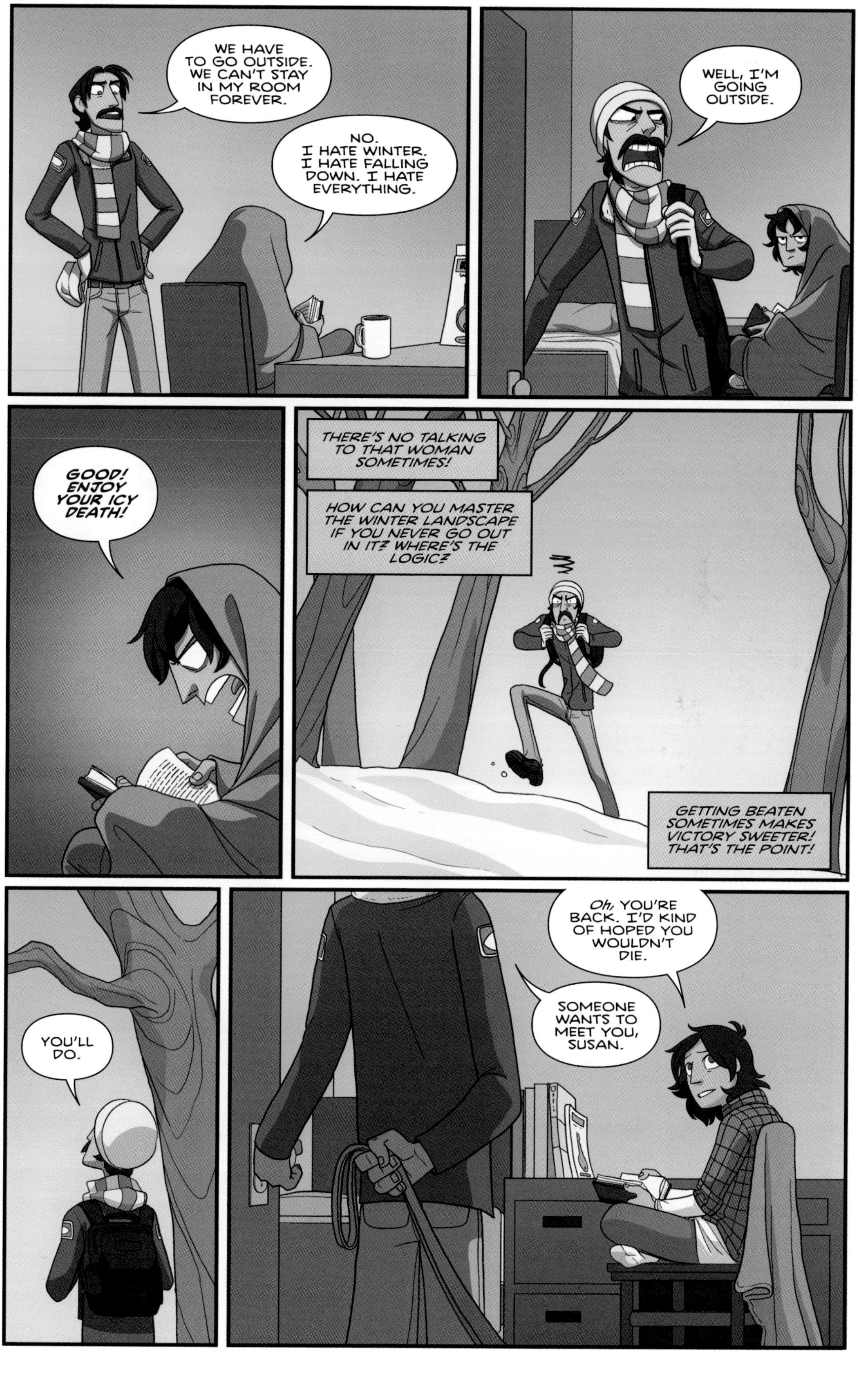
WE HAVE TO GO OUTSIDE. WE CAN'T STAY IN MY ROOM FOREVER.
NO. I HATE WINTER. I HATE FALLING DOWN. I HATE EVERYTHING.
WELL, I'M GOING OUTSIDE.
GOOD! ENJOY YOUR ICY DEATH!
THERE'S NO TALKING TO THAT WOMAN SOMETIMES!
HOW CAN YOU MASTER THE WINTER LANDSCAPE IF YOU NEVER GO OUT IN IT? WHERE'S THE LOGIC?
GETTING BEATEN SOMETIMES MAKES VICTORY SWEETER! THAT'S THE POINT!
YOU'LL DO.
Oh, YOU'RE BACK. I'D KIND OF HOPED YOU WOULDN'T DIE.
SOMEONE WANTS TO MEET YOU, SUSAN.

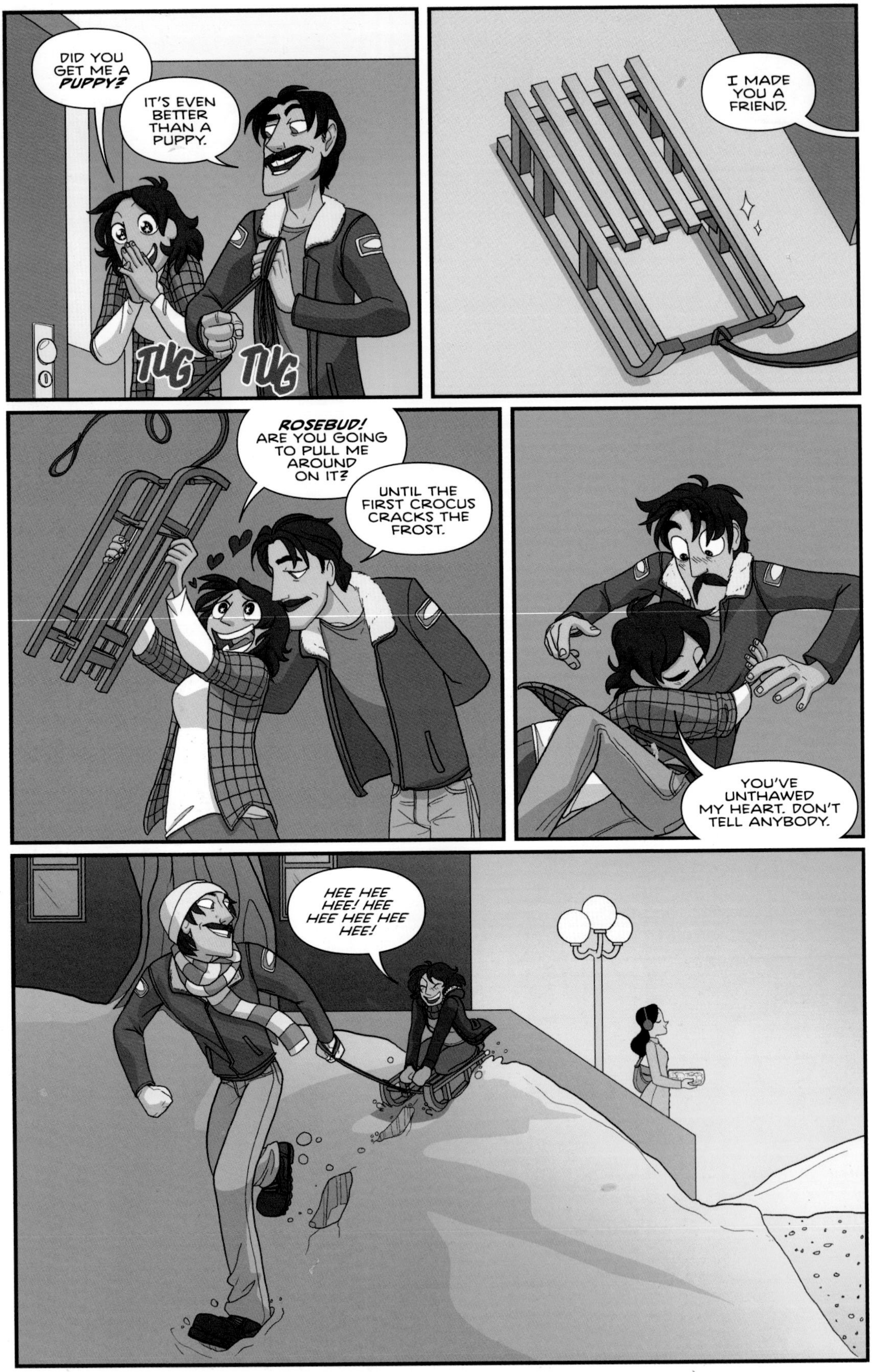
DID YOU GET ME A *PUPPY?*
IT'S EVEN BETTER THAN A PUPPY.
TUG TUG
I MADE YOU A FRIEND.
ROSEBUD! ARE YOU GOING TO PULL ME AROUND ON IT?
UNTIL THE FIRST CROCUS CRACKS THE FROST.
YOU'VE UNTHAWED MY HEART. DON'T TELL ANYBODY.
HEE HEE HEE! HEE HEE HEE HEE HEE!

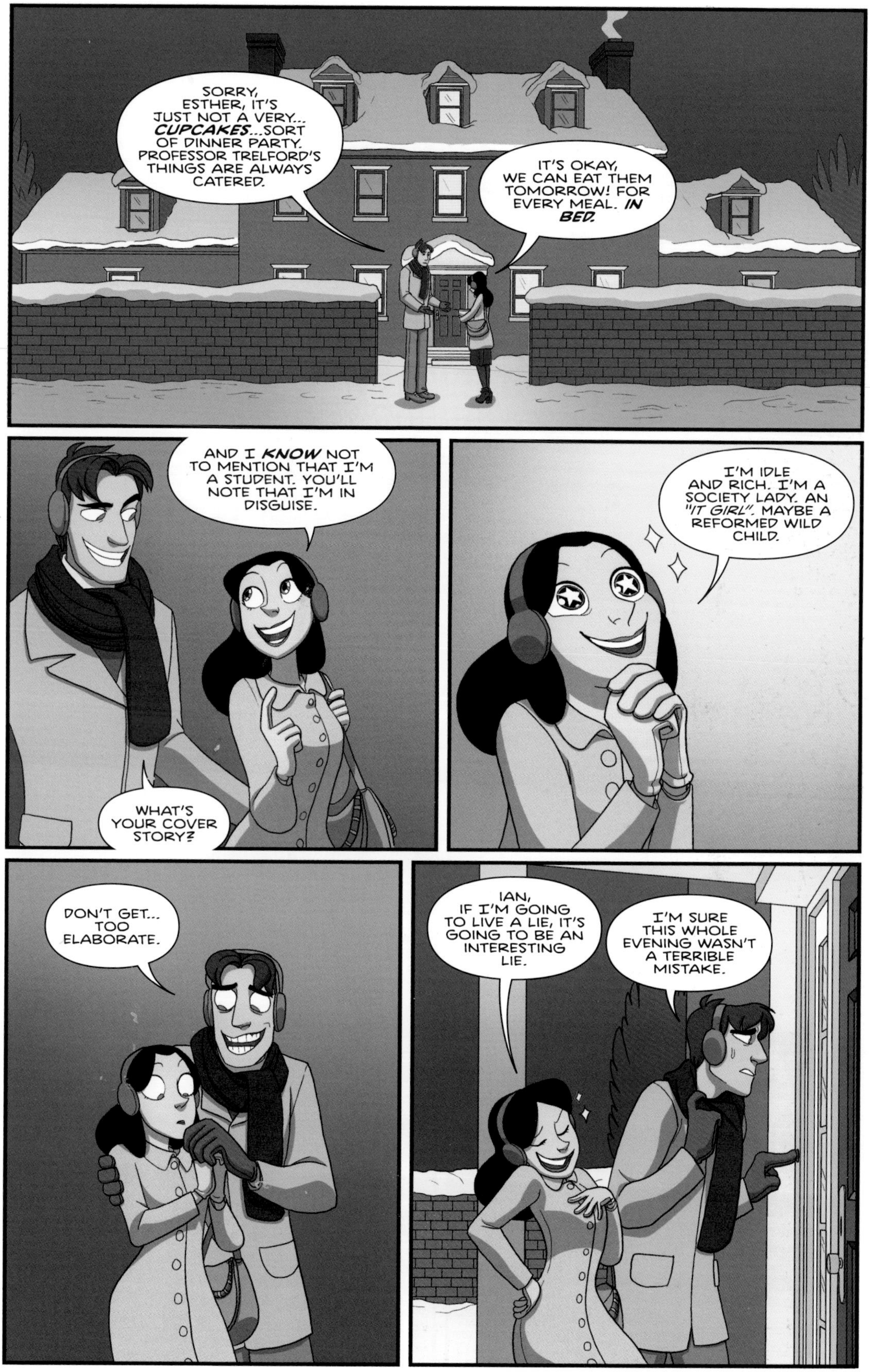
SORRY, ESTHER, IT'S JUST NOT A VERY... **CUPCAKES**...SORT OF DINNER PARTY. PROFESSOR TRELFORD'S THINGS ARE ALWAYS CATERED.
IT'S OKAY, WE CAN EAT THEM TOMORROW! FOR EVERY MEAL. ***IN BED.***
AND I ***KNOW*** NOT TO MENTION THAT I'M A STUDENT. YOU'LL NOTE THAT I'M IN DISGUISE.
WHAT'S YOUR COVER STORY?
I'M IDLE AND RICH. I'M A SOCIETY LADY. AN *"IT GIRL"*. MAYBE A REFORMED WILD CHILD.
DON'T GET... TOO ELABORATE.
IAN, IF I'M GOING TO LIVE A LIE, IT'S GOING TO BE AN INTERESTING LIE.
I'M SURE THIS WHOLE EVENING WASN'T A TERRIBLE MISTAKE.

Dinner Is Served

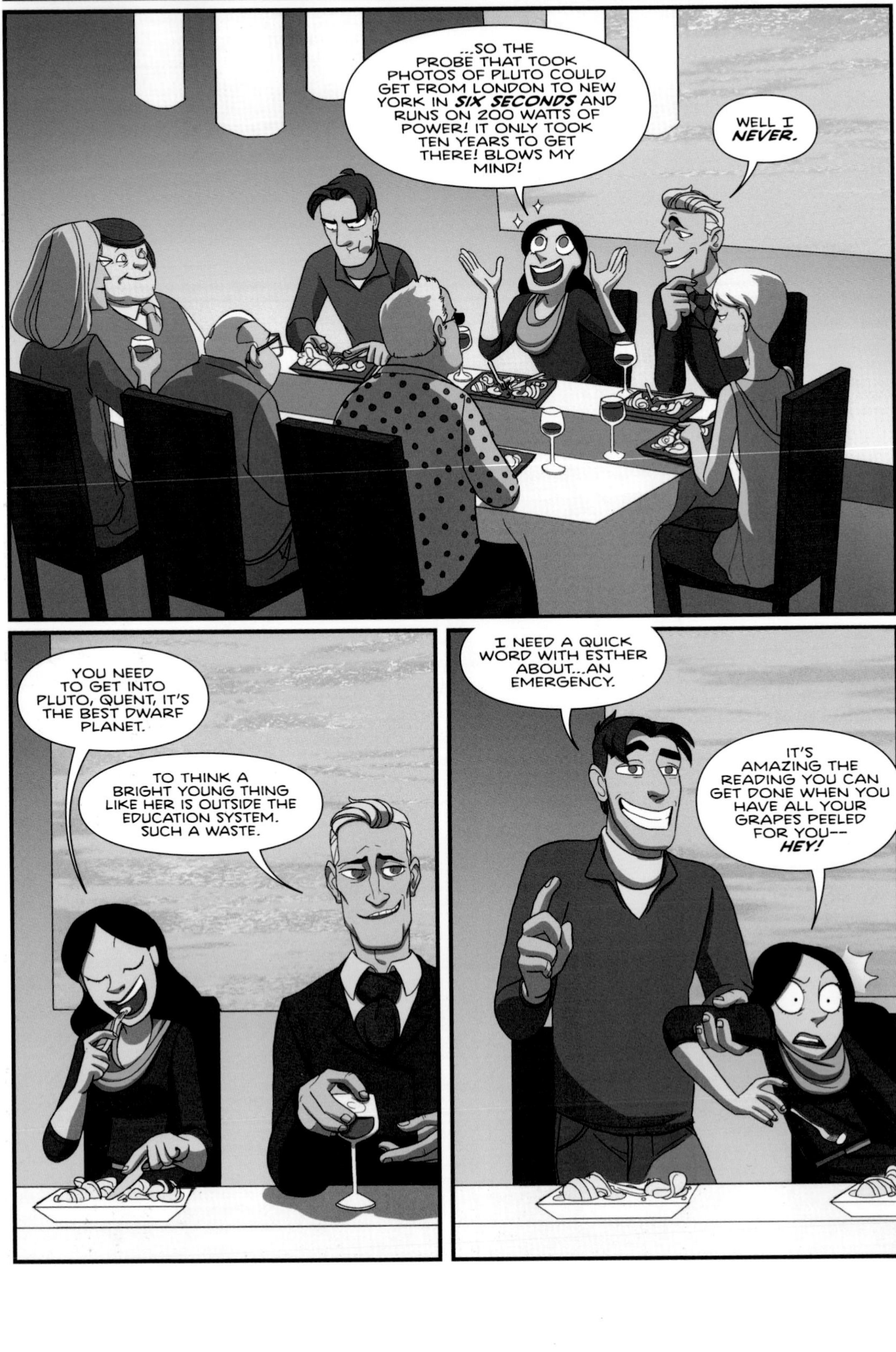
...SO THE PROBE THAT TOOK PHOTOS OF PLUTO COULD GET FROM LONDON TO NEW YORK IN SIX SECONDS AND RUNS ON 200 WATTS OF POWER! IT ONLY TOOK TEN YEARS TO GET THERE! BLOWS MY MIND!
WELL I NEVER.
YOU NEED TO GET INTO PLUTO, QUENT, IT'S THE BEST DWARF PLANET.
TO THINK A BRIGHT YOUNG THING LIKE HER IS OUTSIDE THE EDUCATION SYSTEM. SUCH A WASTE.
I NEED A QUICK WORD WITH ESTHER ABOUT...AN EMERGENCY.
IT'S AMAZING THE READING YOU CAN GET DONE WHEN YOU HAVE ALL YOUR GRAPES PEELED FOR YOU-- HEY!

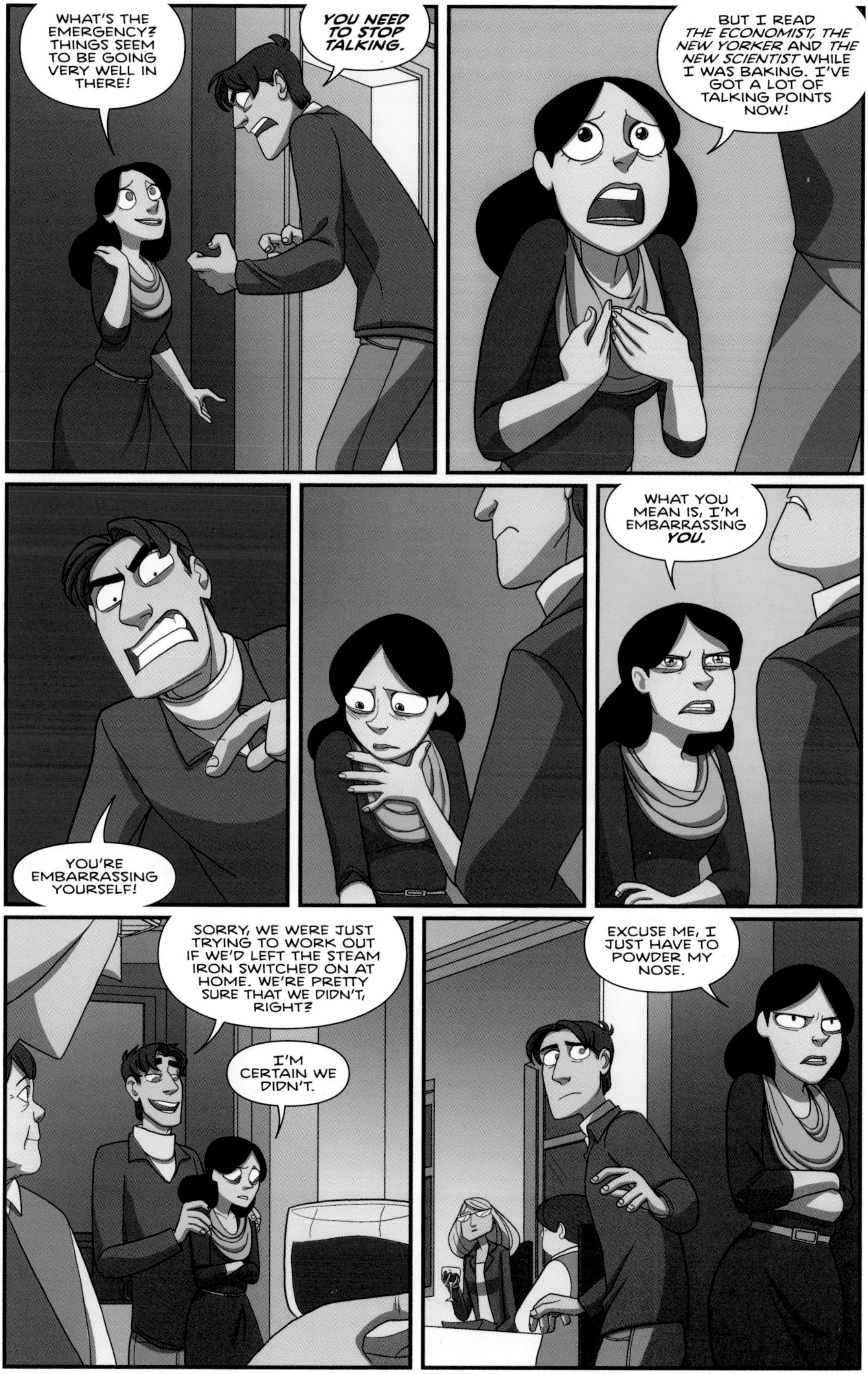
WHAT'S THE EMERGENCY? THINGS SEEM TO BE GOING VERY WELL IN THERE!
YOU NEED TO STOP TALKING.
BUT I READ THE ECONOMIST, THE NEW YORKER AND THE NEW SCIENTIST WHILE I WAS BAKING. I'VE GOT A LOT OF TALKING POINTS NOW!
YOU'RE EMBARRASSING YOURSELF!
WHAT YOU MEAN IS, I'M EMBARRASSING YOU.
SORRY, WE WERE JUST TRYING TO WORK OUT IF WE'D LEFT THE STEAM IRON SWITCHED ON AT HOME. WE'RE PRETTY SURE THAT WE DIDN'T, RIGHT?
I'M CERTAIN WE DIDN'T.
EXCUSE ME, I JUST HAVE TO POWDER MY NOSE.

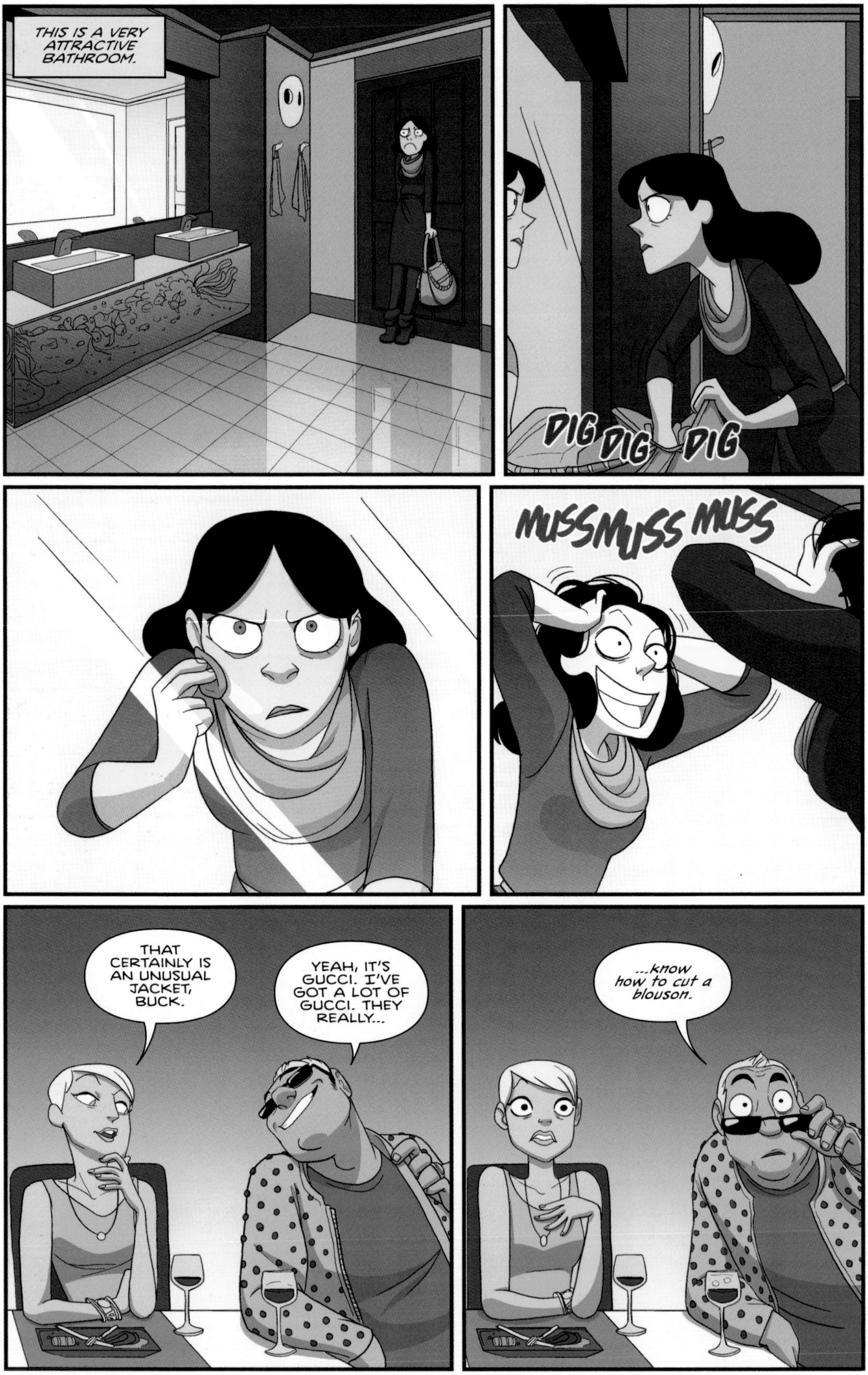
THIS IS A VERY ATTRACTIVE BATHROOM.
DIG DIG DIG
MUSS MUSS MUSS
THAT CERTAINLY IS AN UNUSUAL JACKET, BUCK.
YEAH, IT'S GUCCI. I'VE GOT A LOT OF GUCCI. THEY REALLY...
...know how to cut a blouson.

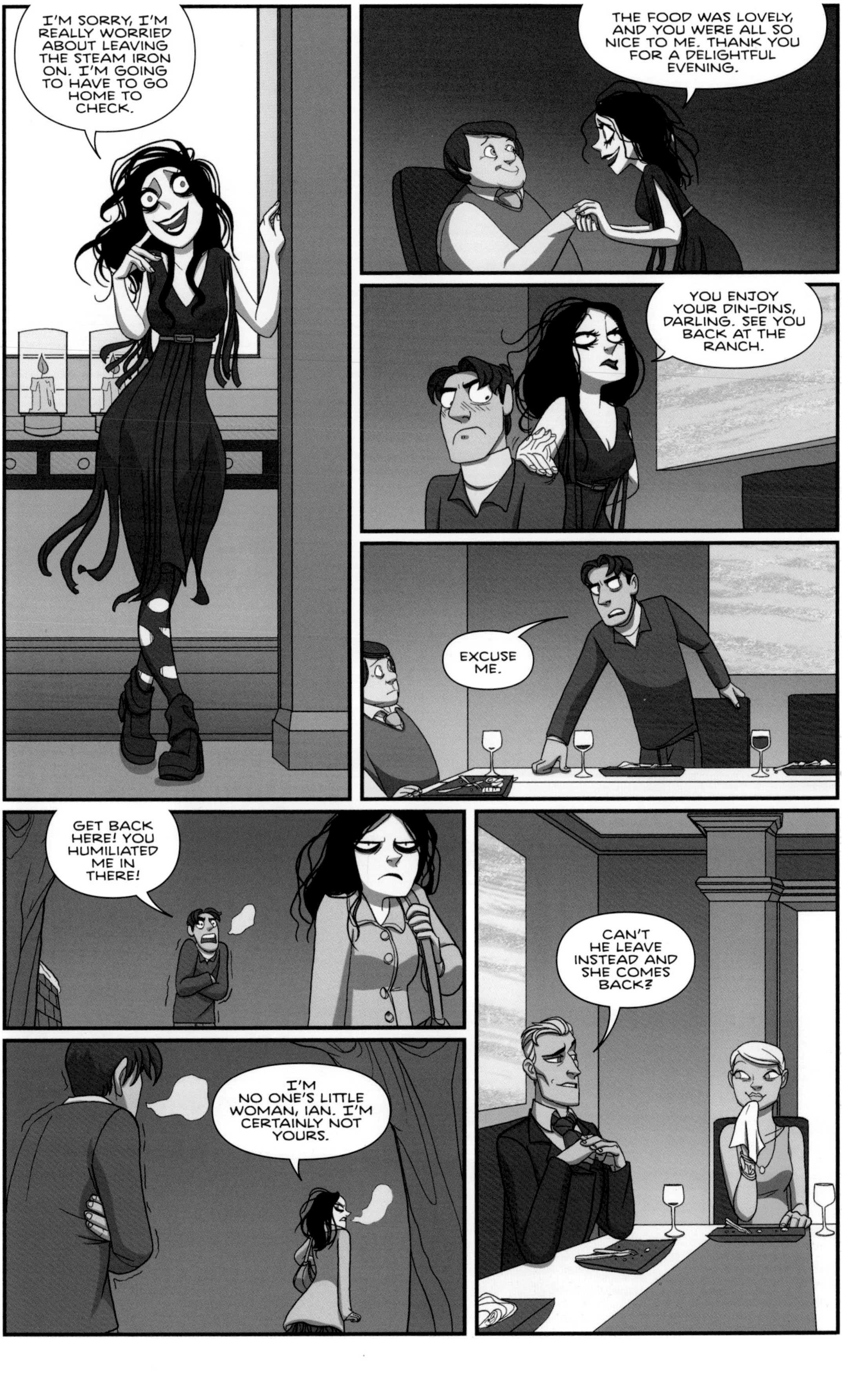
I'M SORRY, I'M REALLY WORRIED ABOUT LEAVING THE STEAM IRON ON. I'M GOING TO HAVE TO GO HOME TO CHECK.
THE FOOD WAS LOVELY, AND YOU WERE ALL SO NICE TO ME. THANK YOU FOR A DELIGHTFUL EVENING.
YOU ENJOY YOUR DIN-DINS, DARLING. SEE YOU BACK AT THE RANCH.
EXCUSE ME.
GET BACK HERE! YOU HUMILIATED ME IN THERE!
I'M NO ONE'S LITTLE WOMAN, IAN. I'M CERTAINLY NOT YOURS.
CAN'T HE LEAVE INSTEAD AND SHE COMES BACK?

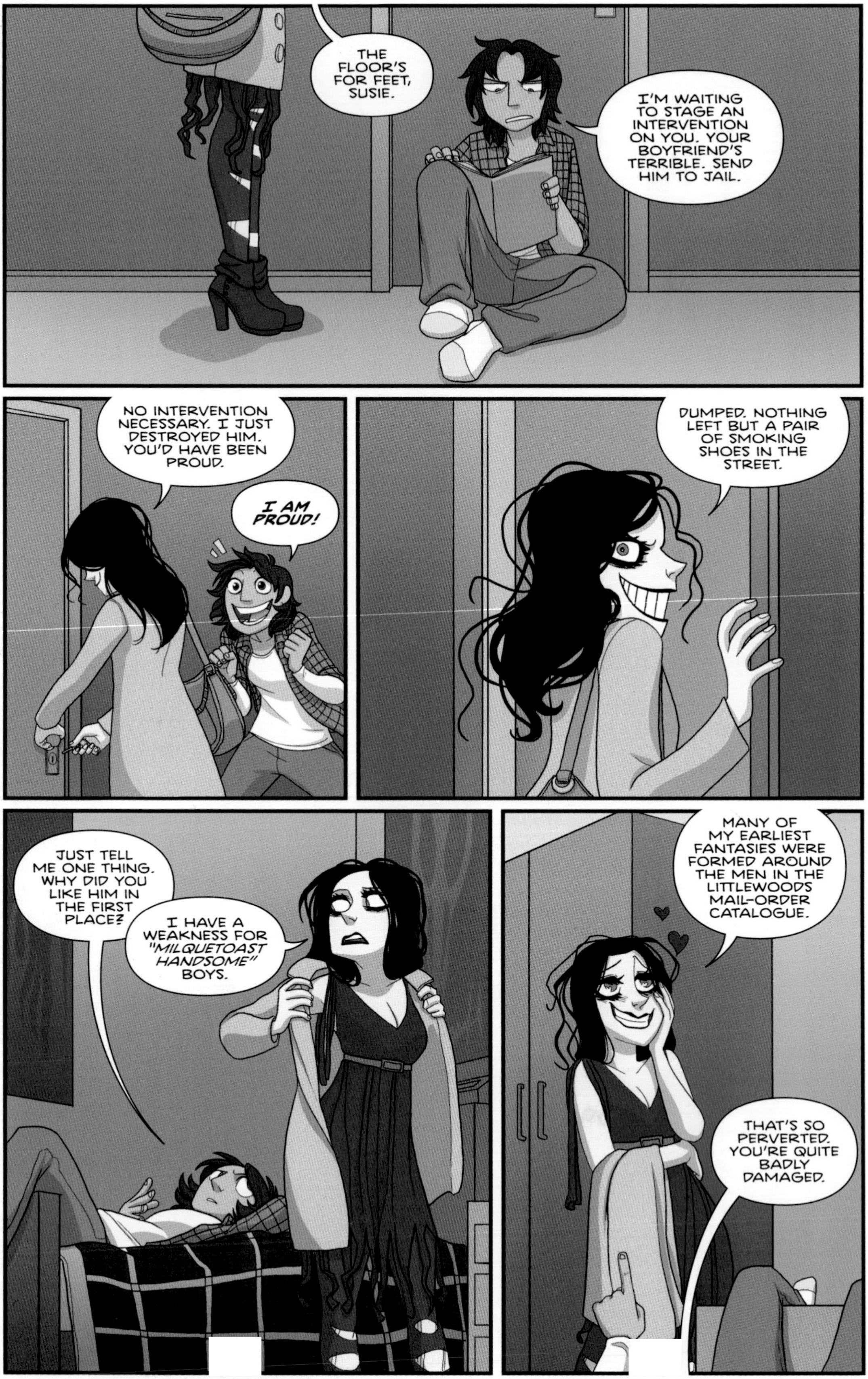
THE FLOOR'S FOR FEET, SUSIE.
I'M WAITING TO STAGE AN INTERVENTION ON YOU. YOUR BOYFRIEND'S TERRIBLE. SEND HIM TO JAIL.
NO INTERVENTION NECESSARY. I JUST DESTROYED HIM. YOU'D HAVE BEEN PROUD.
I AM PROUD!
DUMPED. NOTHING LEFT BUT A PAIR OF SMOKING SHOES IN THE STREET.
JUST TELL ME ONE THING. WHY DID YOU LIKE HIM IN THE FIRST PLACE?
I HAVE A WEAKNESS FOR "MILQUETOAST HANDSOME" BOYS.
MANY OF MY EARLIEST FANTASIES WERE FORMED AROUND THE MEN IN THE LITTLEWOODS MAIL-ORDER CATALOGUE.
THAT'S SO PERVERTED. YOU'RE QUITE BADLY DAMAGED.

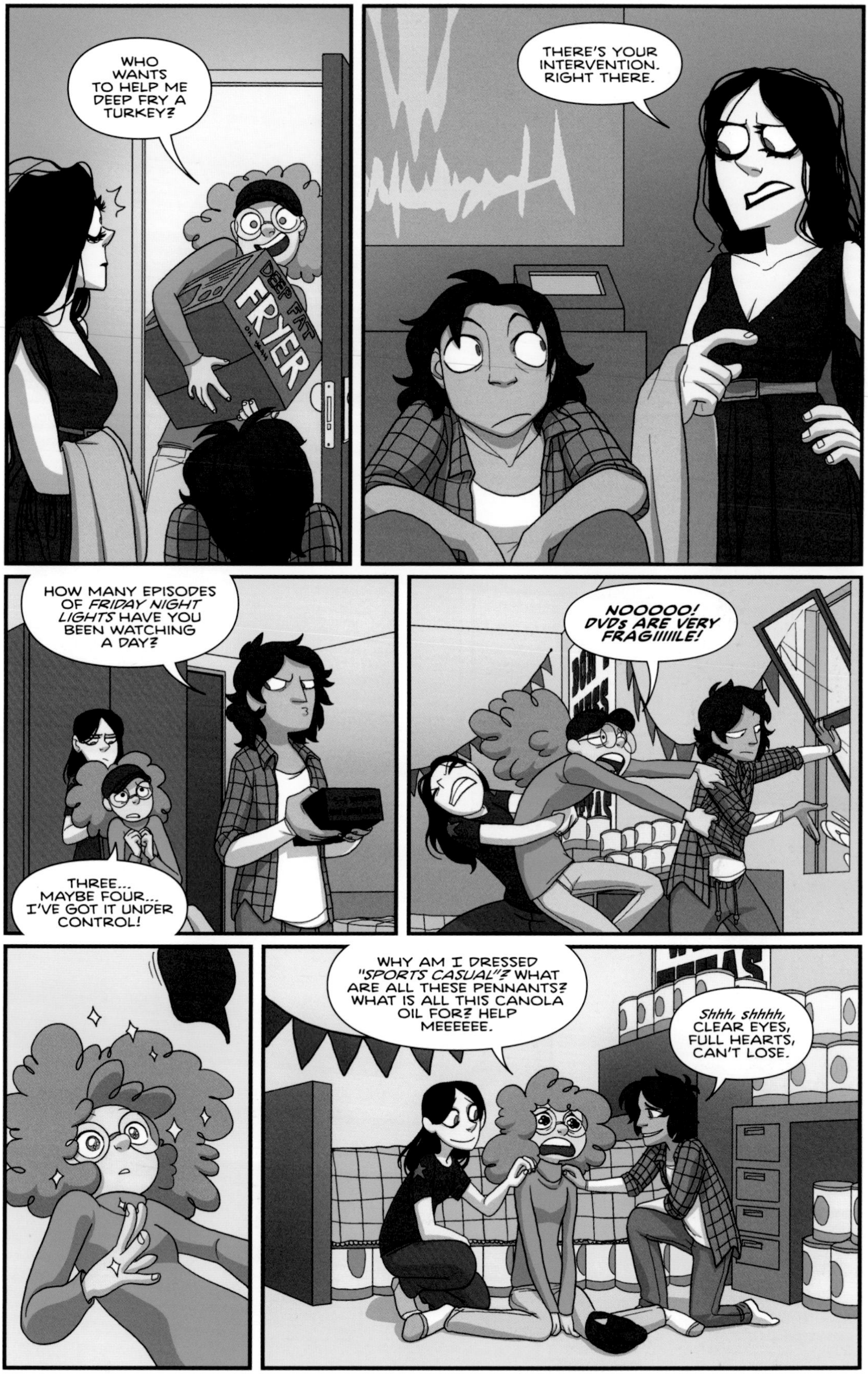
WHO WANTS TO HELP ME DEEP FRY A TURKEY?
DEEP FAT FRYER
THERE'S YOUR INTERVENTION. RIGHT THERE.
HOW MANY EPISODES OF *FRIDAY NIGHT LIGHTS* HAVE YOU BEEN WATCHING A DAY?
THREE... MAYBE FOUR... I'VE GOT IT UNDER CONTROL!
NOOOOO! DVDs ARE VERY FRAGIIIIILE!
WHY AM I DRESSED *"SPORTS CASUAL"?* WHAT ARE ALL THESE PENNANTS? WHAT IS ALL THIS CANOLA OIL FOR? HELP MEEEEEE.
Shhh, shhhh, CLEAR EYES, FULL HEARTS, CAN'T LOSE.

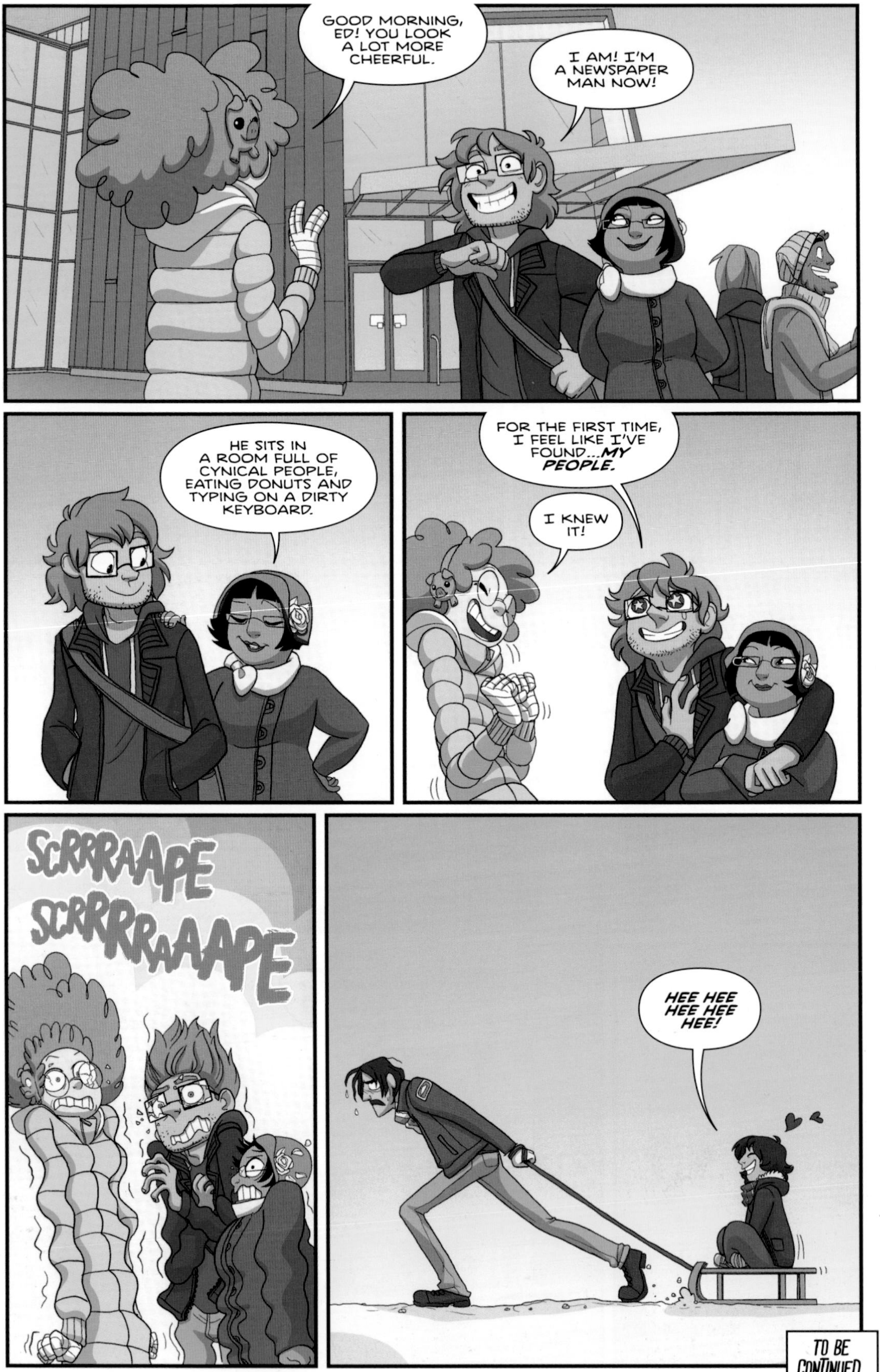
GOOD MORNING, ED! YOU LOOK A LOT MORE CHEERFUL.
I AM! I'M A NEWSPAPER MAN NOW!
HE SITS IN A ROOM FULL OF CYNICAL PEOPLE, EATING DONUTS AND TYPING ON A DIRTY KEYBOARD.
FOR THE FIRST TIME, I FEEL LIKE I'VE FOUND... *MY PEOPLE.*
I KNEW IT!
SCRRRAAPE
SCRRRRAAAPE
HEE HEE HEE HEE HEE!
TO BE CONTINUED...

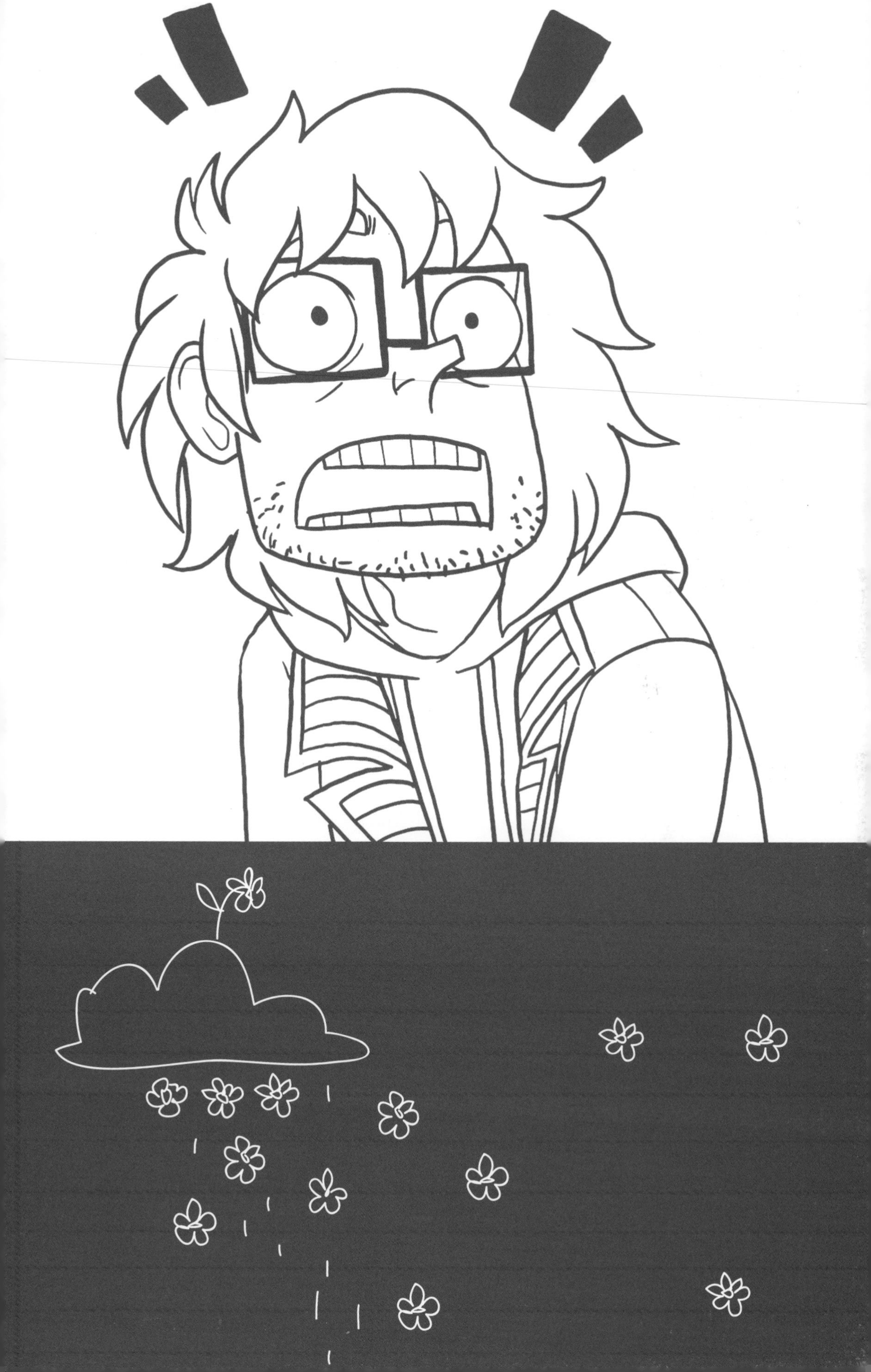

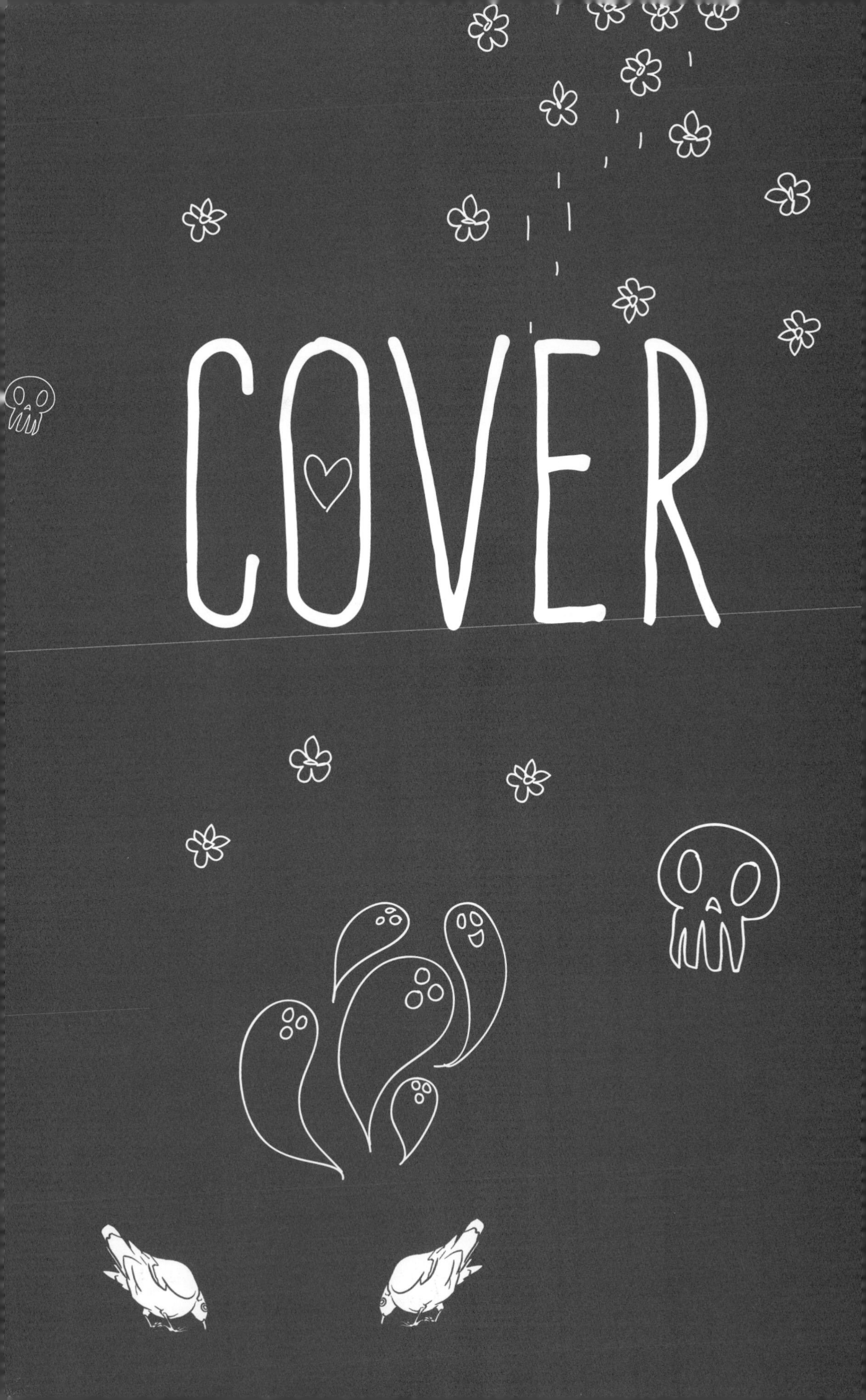
COVER

GALLERY

ISSUE #5 COVER
LISSA TREIMAN

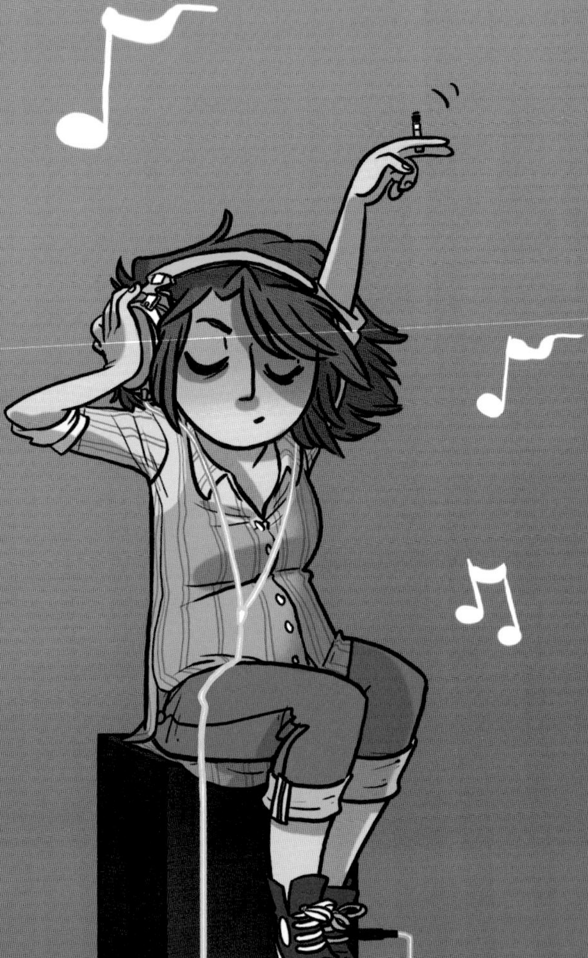
LT
15

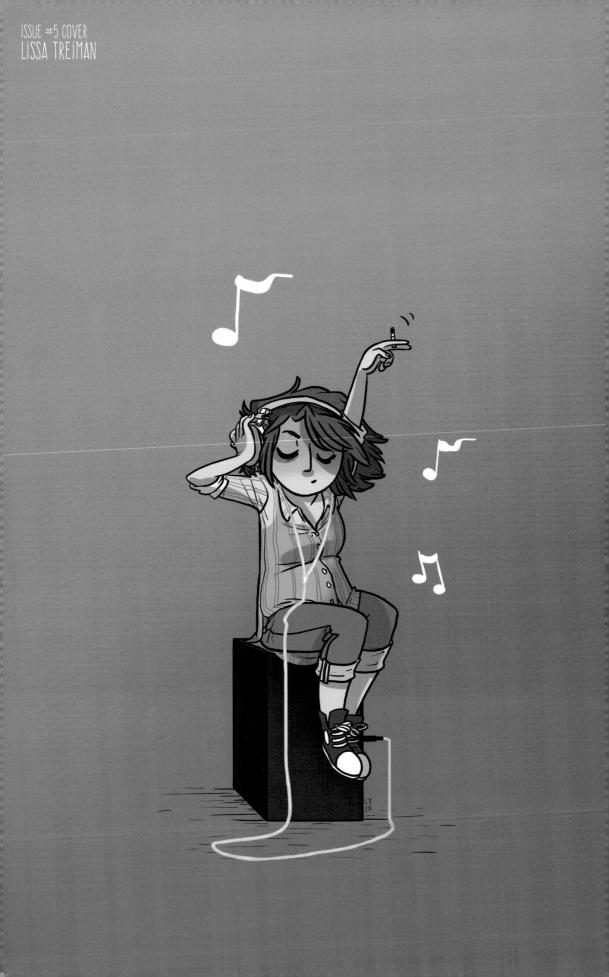

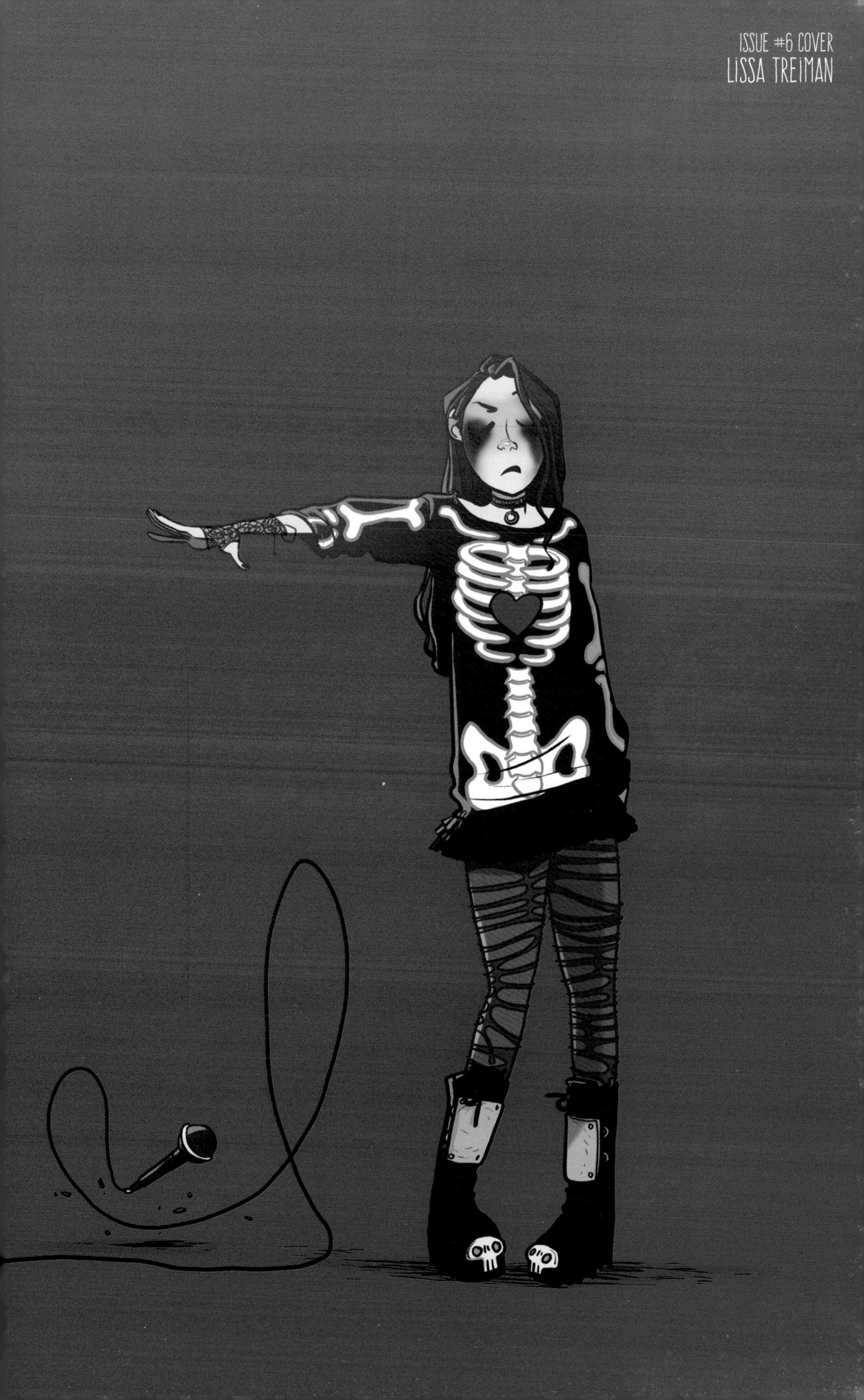

ISSUE #6 COVER
LISSA TREIMAN

ISSUE #7 COVER
LISSA TREIMAN

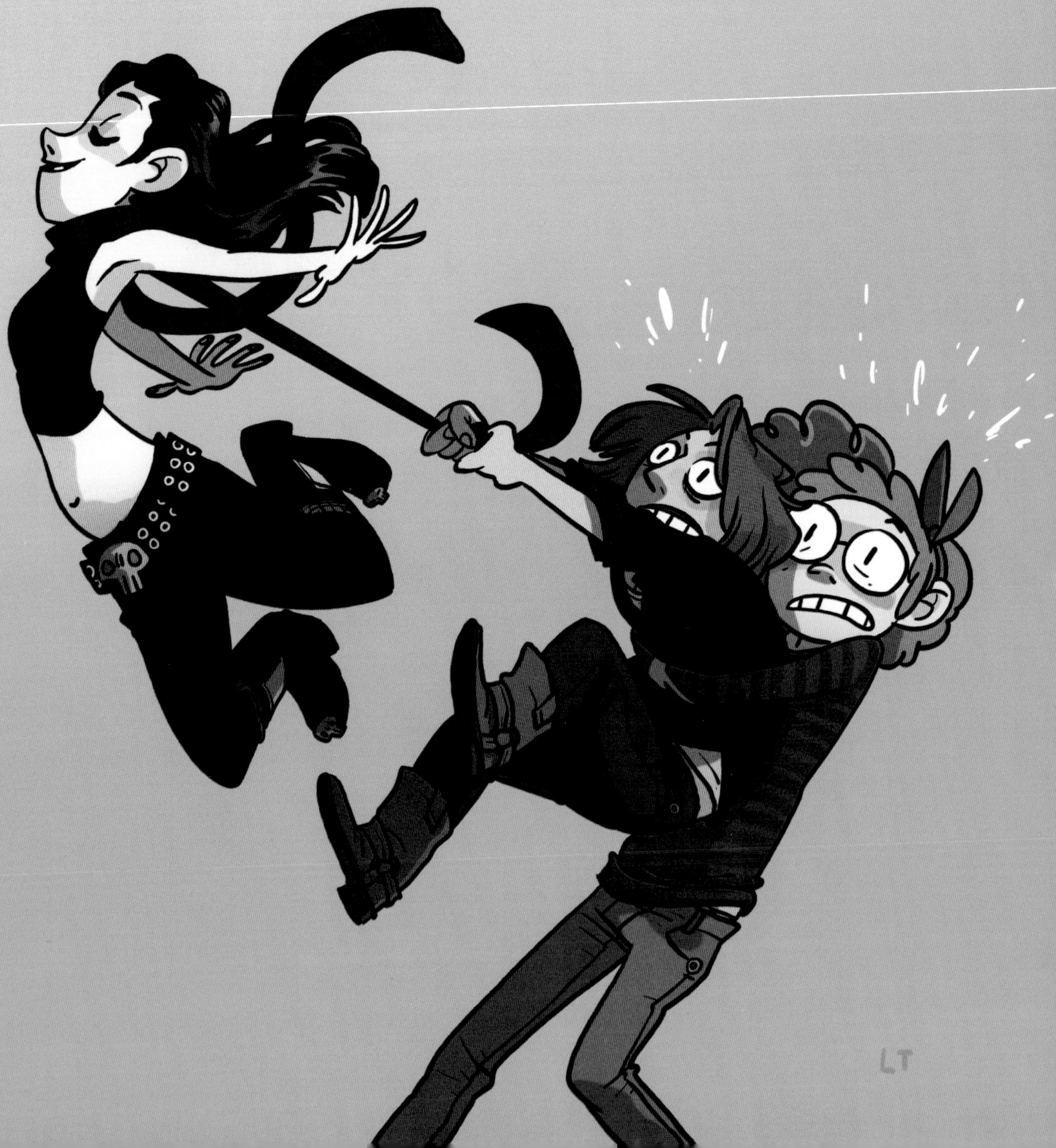
LT

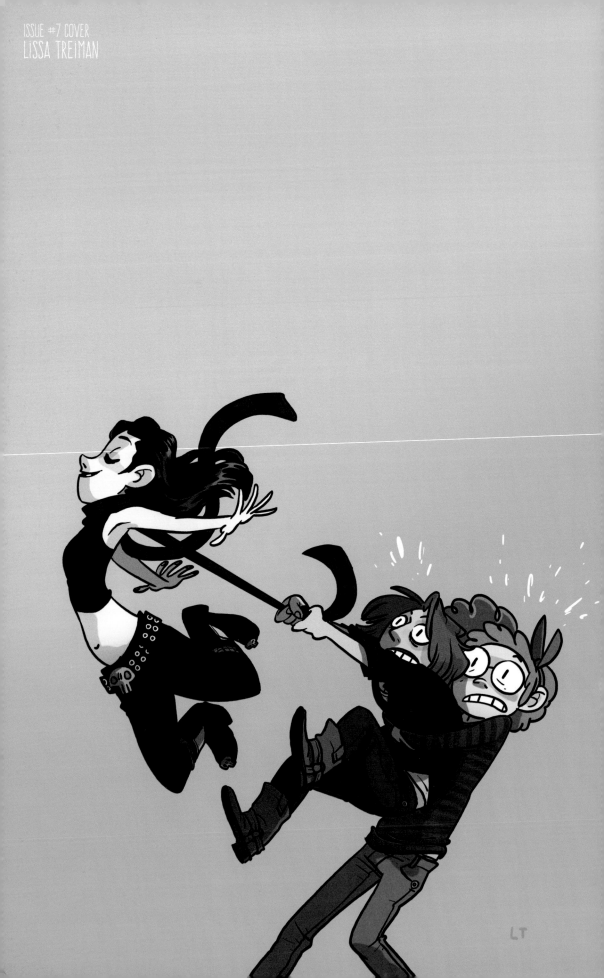

ISSUE #8 COVER
LISSA TREIMAN

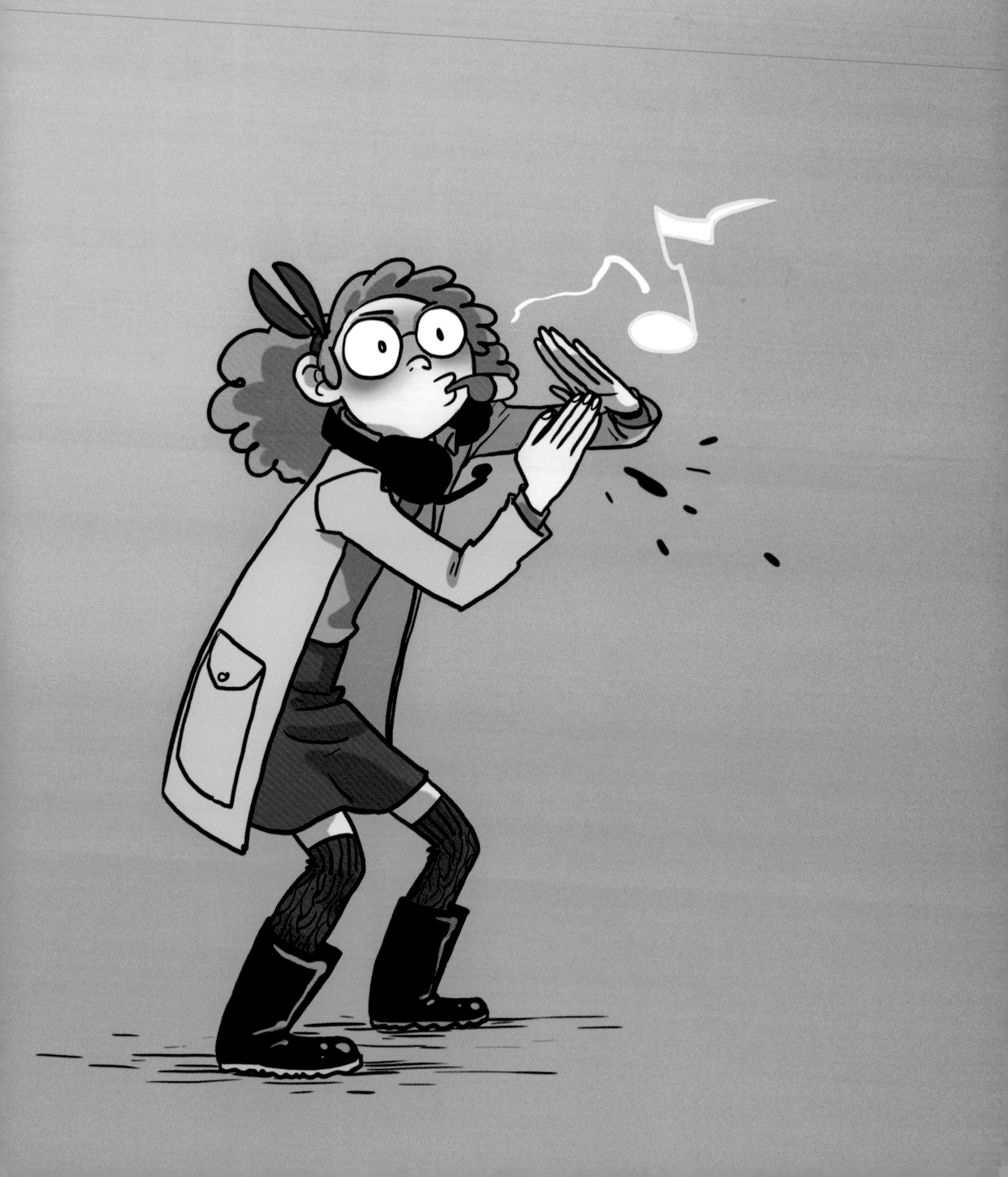

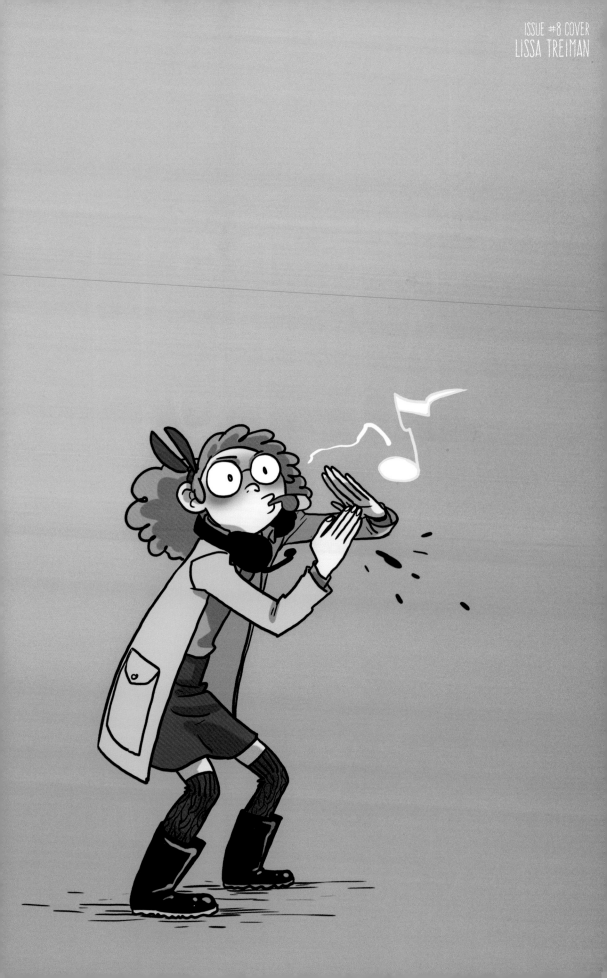

SKETCH

GALLERY

SKETCHES BY LISSA TREIMAN

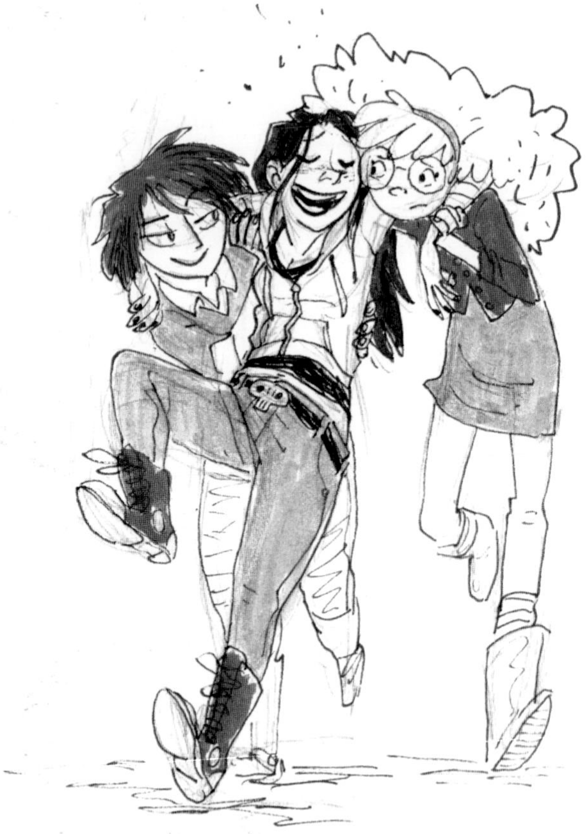

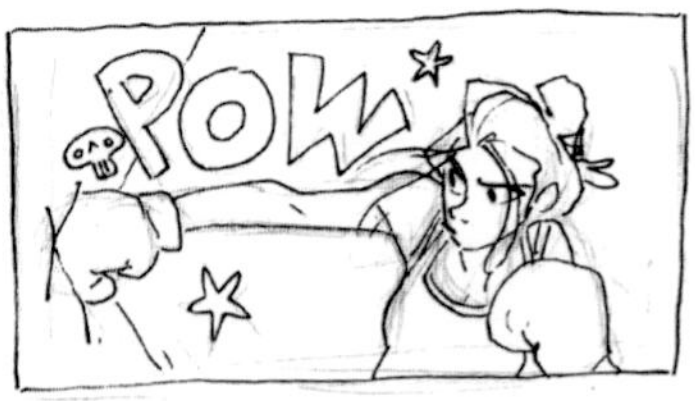
POW

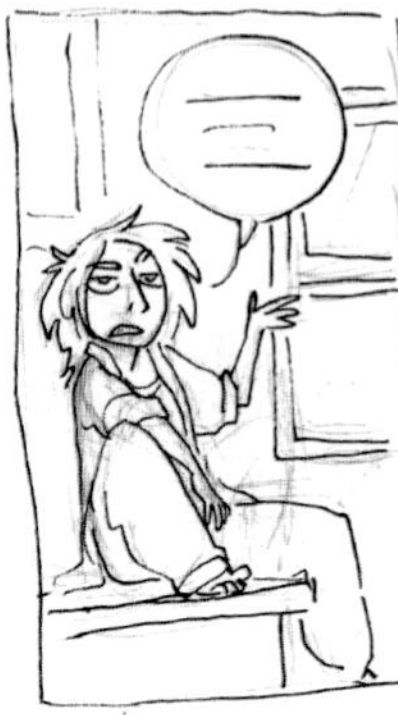

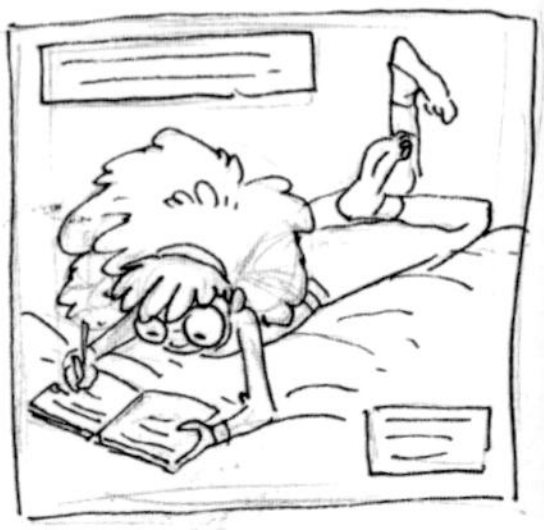

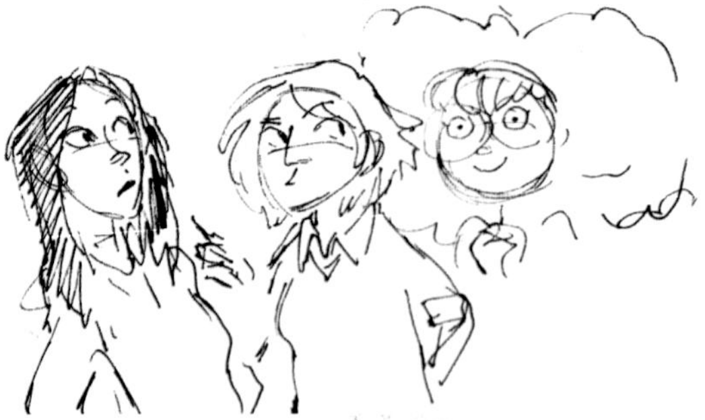

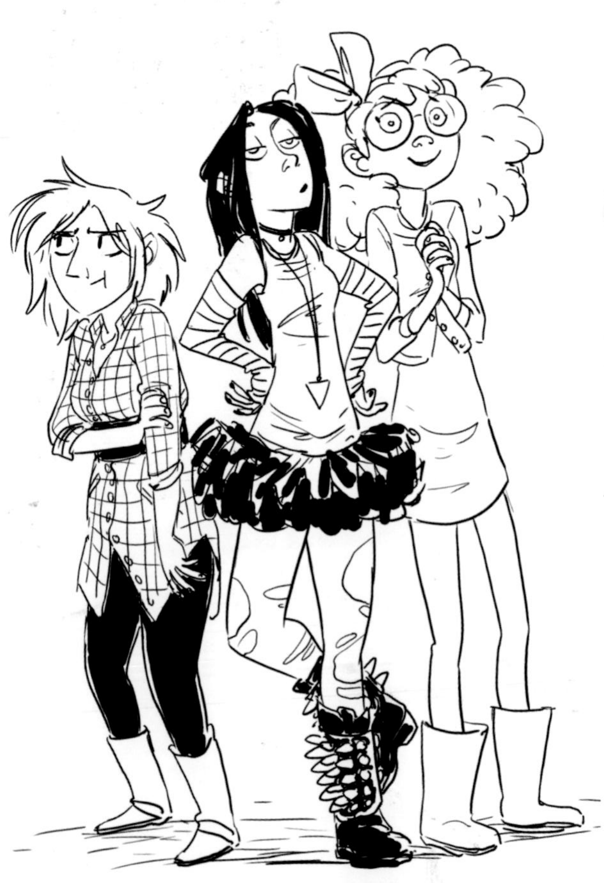

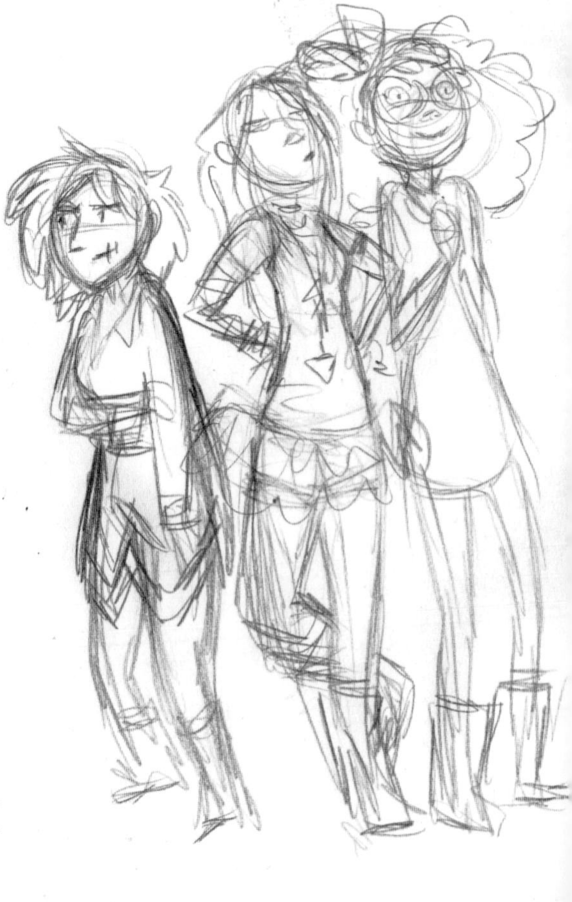

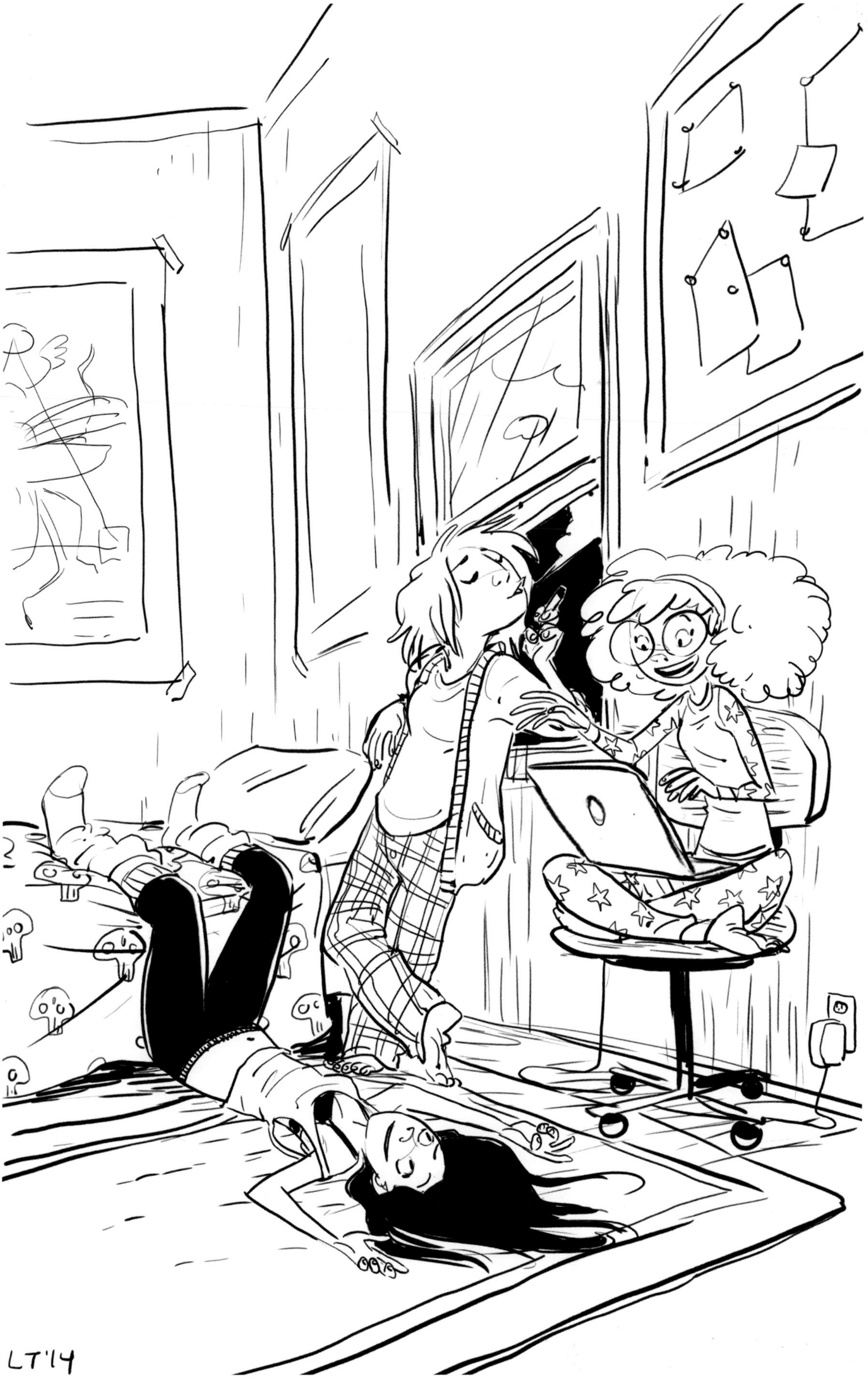
LT'14

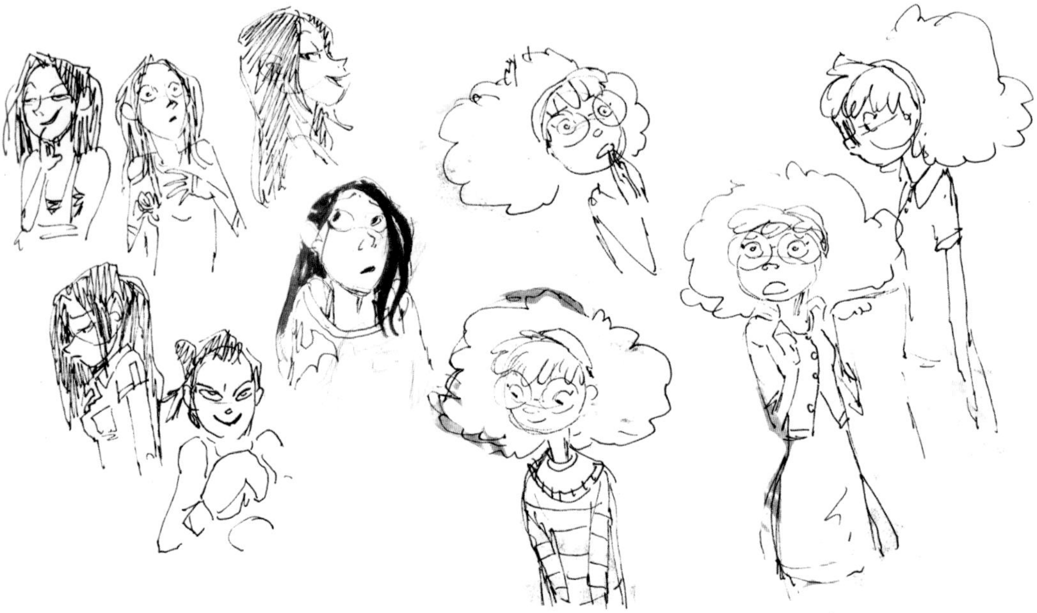

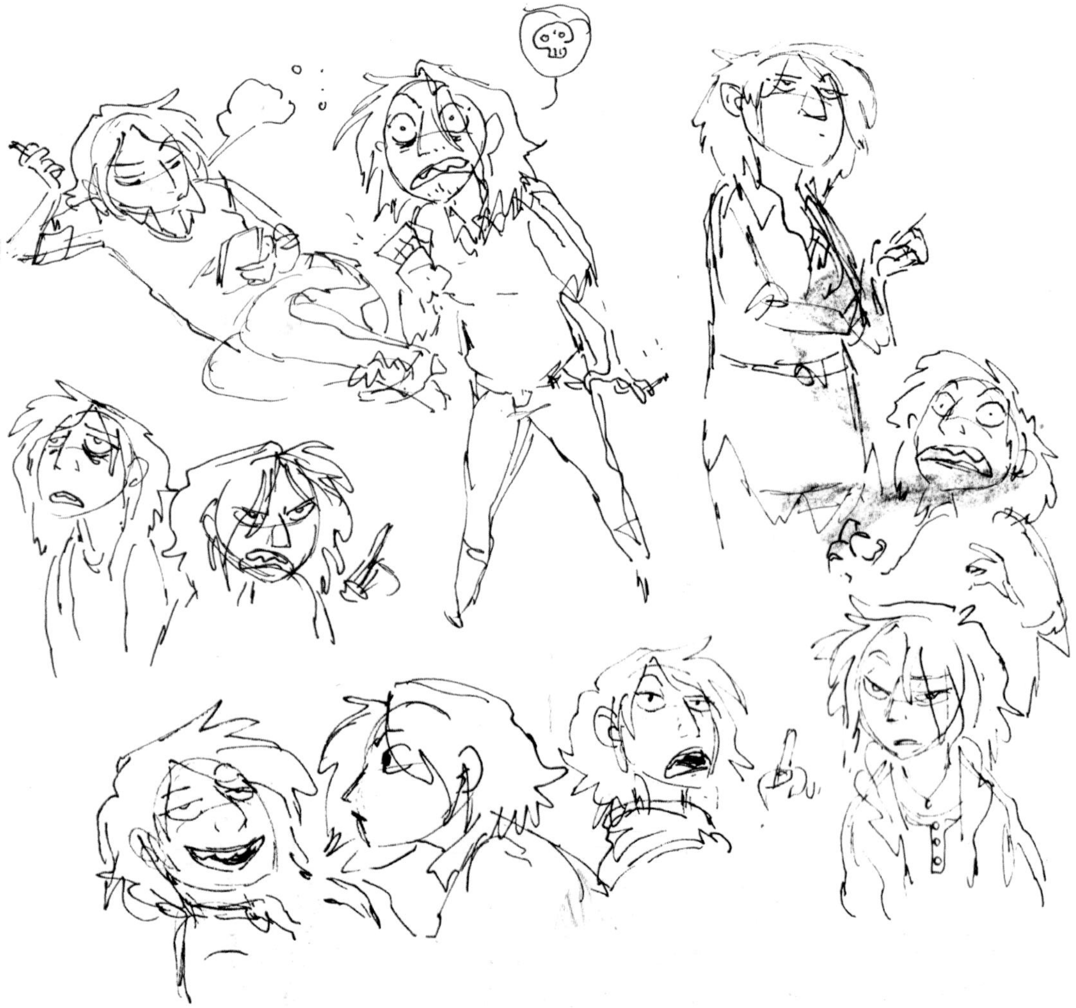

SKETCHES BY MAX SARIN

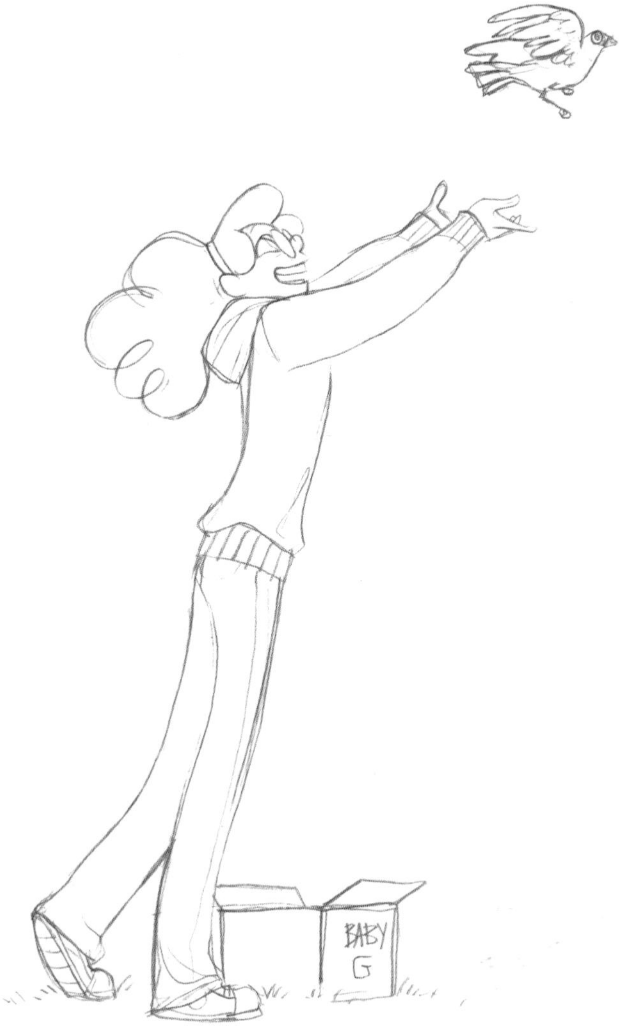
BABY
G

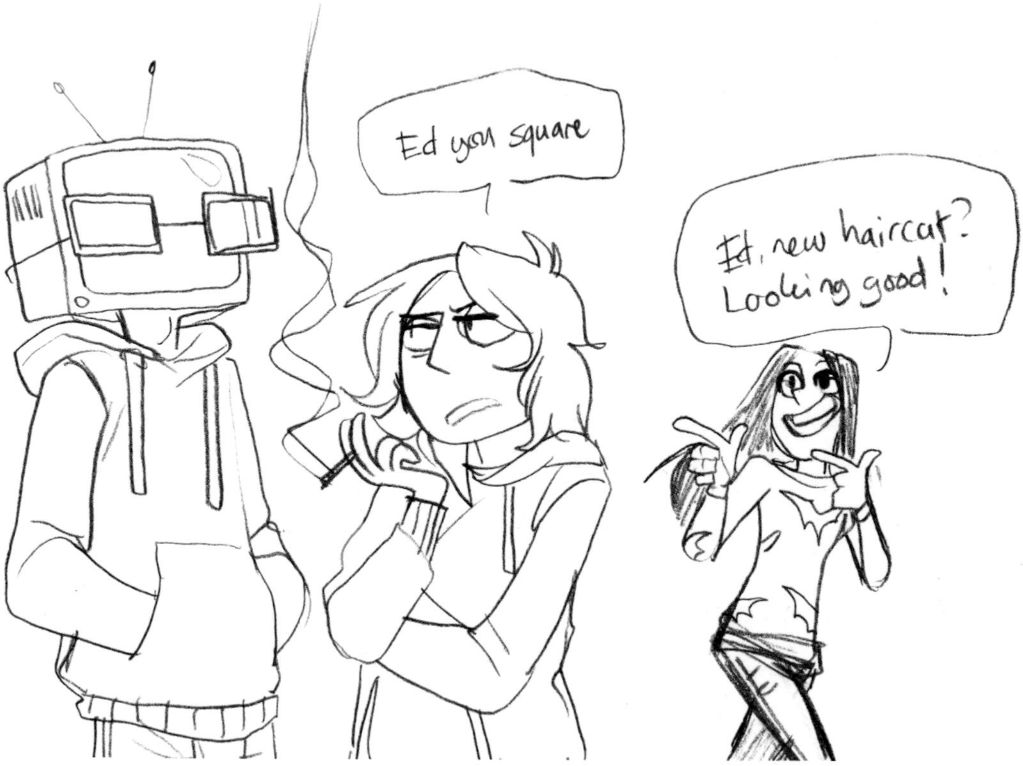
Ed you square
Ed, new haircut? Looking good!

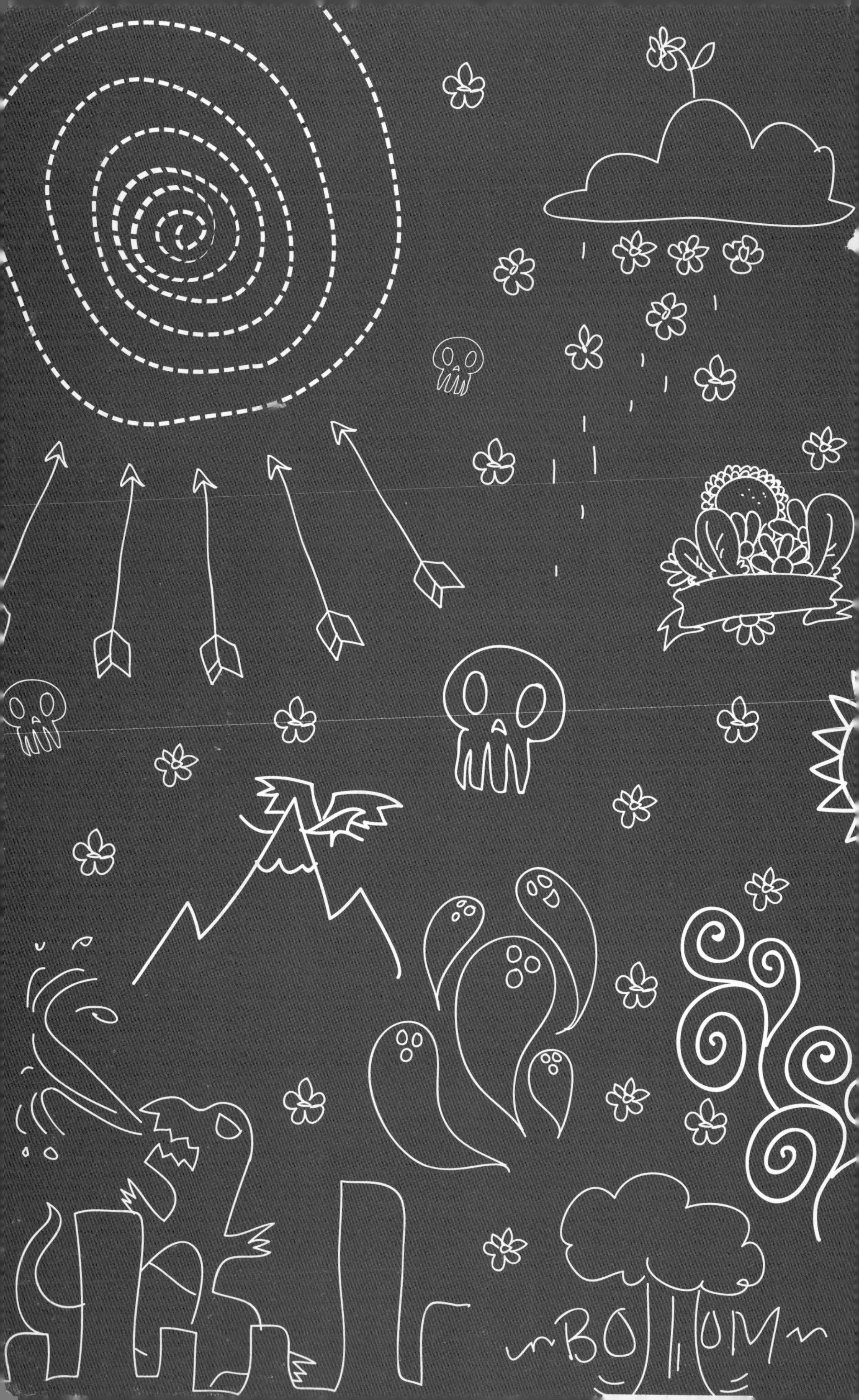

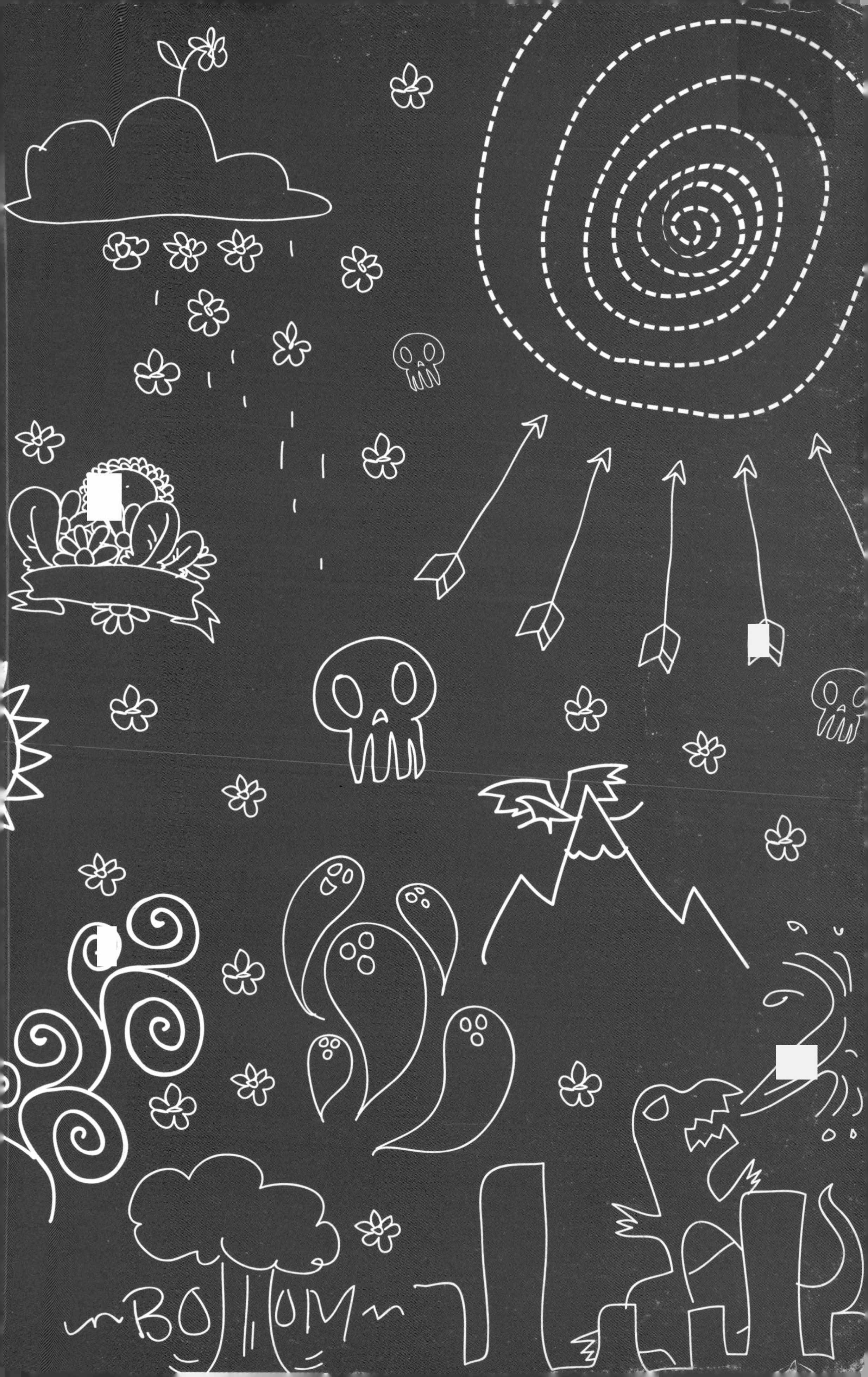

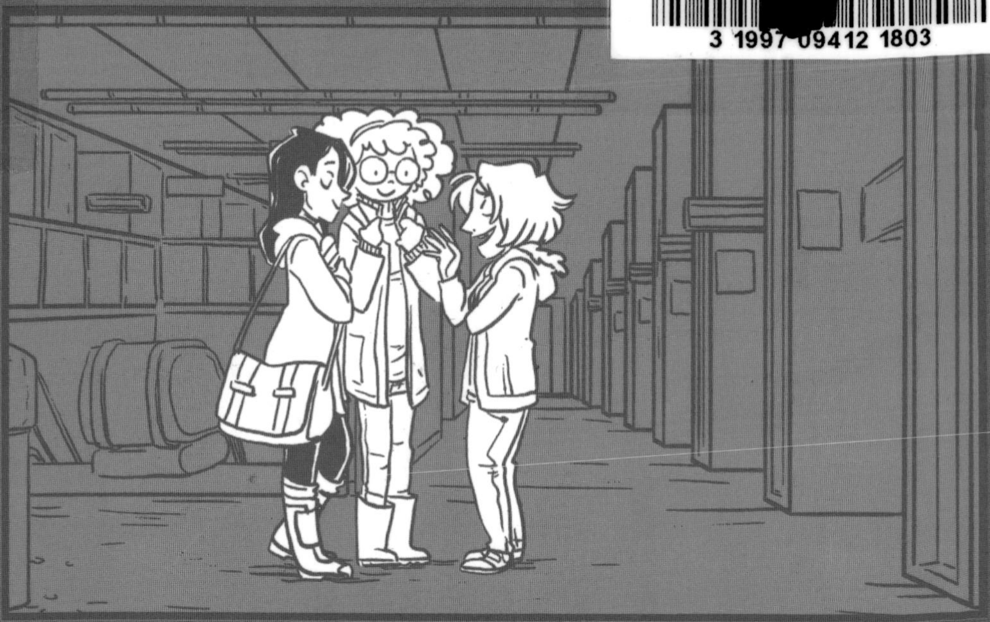

CONTINUING THEIR FIRST SEMESTER AT UNIVERSITY, FAST FRIENDS SUSAN, ESTHER, AND DAISY WANT TO FIND THEIR FOOTING IN LIFE. BUT IN THE FACE OF HAND-WRINGING BOYS, HOLIDAY BALLS, HOMETOWN RIVALS, AND THE WILLFUL, UNWANTED INTRUSION OF "ACADEMIA," THEY MAY BE LUCKY JUST TO MAKE IT TO SPRING ALIVE.

GIANT DAYS, THE COMEDIC SLICE-OF-LIFE SERIES FROM CREATOR JOHN ALLISON (*BAD MACHINERY, SCARY GO ROUND*), DISNEY ARTIST LISSA TREIMAN, AND NEW FAN-FAVORITE ARTIST MAX SARIN HAS GRADUATED TO A SECOND VOLUME, COLLECTING ISSUES 5-8 OF THE CRITICALLY ACCLAIMED SERIES.

"THERE'S A SECRET INGREDIENT IN JOHN ALLISON'S WORK, AND IT'S THAT SPECIAL, FUZZY FOUR LETTER WORD: LOVE..."

—*COMICOSITY*

"GIANT DAYS HAS ALWAYS HAD ME GRINNING FROM START TO FINISH..."

—*COMIC BASTARDS*

"THE WORLD THAT ALLISON AND TREIMAN HAVE CREATED HERE IS REAL. THE RELATIONSHIP WEBS WEAVING IN AND OUT OF GIANT DAYS FEEL TANGIBLE, THEIR CONNECTIONS BELIEVABLE AND ENDEARING. THIS IS A CONTEMPORARY AND FORWARD-THINKING COMIC BOOK, FOR ANYONE WHO ENJOYS THE VIBE THAT STEWART, CLOONAN, TARR AND FLETCHER BRING TO THEIR FLEDGLING BATGIRL-VERSE..."

—*NEWSARAMA*

$14.99 US • $18.99 CA • £10.50 UK

www.boom-studios.com